When I got to language arts, everyone was looking at Kendra Hilferty. Kendra was new this year, and ever since she'd moved here, there'd been rumors, crazy ones, about her. People speculated she was a spy, hired by the school board to expose weak teaching practices. That she had grown up in a commune. Or a convent. Or a circus. That she'd had to leave her previous school because she'd threatened another girl, and then the girl disappeared. Of course, no one bothered to ask Kendra if the rumors were true. It was more fun to gossip. Besides, people were afraid of her.

BEWITCHING

BEWITCHING

ALEX FLINN

SCHOLASTIC INC.

ISBN 978-0-545-60830-5

12 11 10 9 8 7 6 5 4 3 2 1 13 14 15 16 17 18/0

Printed in the U.S.A. 40

First Scholastic printing, September 2013

To George Nicholson

If you read fairy tales, and who doesn't, you might believe there are witches all over the place—witches baking children into gingerbread, making princesses sleep hundreds of years, even turning normal teenage boys into hideous beasts to teach them a lesson. But, actually, there are only a few of us. The reason it doesn't seem like that is because we're pretty long-lived. We live hundreds of years, as long as we don't find ourselves fueling a bonfire.

Which leads us to another quality of witches: We move around a lot. It's easy for us to get into trouble, and sometimes, we need to beat a hasty retreat (in the dead of night or on the business end of a pitchfork) to another town or another country. So that explains the existence of many tales from different times and places, many of which involve the same witch.

In quite a few cases, that witch was me. My name is Kendra, and I'm a witch.

Here's my story—well, some of it. It involves romance, drama, even death.

It started in England, many years ago; 1666 to be exact. When I was a teenager, the first time.

Girl to Woman to Witch: England, 1666

When Mr. Howe called from the street to ask if I had any dead for him to bury, I told him I did. The chore did not tax me, not physically, though I was but four and ten and small for my age. Little Lizzie, my youngest sister, weighed barely more than a sack of flour even before the plague ravaged her body and our village. After months of hardship, she weighed even less. I hated to give her over to the gravedigger, but what choice did I have? I had no parents left. I had next to no one.

"Are ye alone now, Kendra?" Mr. Howe asked me.

I shook my head. "No. There is still Charlie. And Charlie will be well."

He seemed doubtful but only said, "I am sorry."

I nodded and did not wait for him to take her. I could not. I was accustomed to death now, accustomed enough to know not to dwell upon it. It was the only way to survive.

The first to leave had been Sadie, my older sister. How we had wept and regretted, not merely because Sadie was kind and good, but also because she was only a month from marriage to Henry, the dairyman's son, who would have kept our large family supplied with sorely needed milk. Young Henry had not even come to Sadie's funeral. Too scared was he of catching the dread disease himself. He caught it anyway, though, and was gone in two months' time, too long to blame Sadie. People in our town were all looking for someone to blame for what happened.

The reverend had told us to have the funerals out of doors, that we should not spread the disease, but it had not helped. The reverend also told us to stay in the village, so as not to spread the plague abroad, but those with means had left nonetheless. Those with means did as they wished. The reverend lived still, but his wife was gone.

Next was my youngest brother, John, a mere babe and barely known to us. Still, we said a few words over him. Babies dying was sad business, but not unusual.

By the time Mother died, there was no funeral, no time for prayers for the dead, only prayers for the living—that they might stay that way.

They did not. The month past had been a whirl of vomiting, fever, complaints of painful limbs and swelling blisters on arms and legs, cracked lips begging for water and death, so much death. One by one, all who I loved were ripped from this earth as I stopped being a child and became a woman, a sad one. By the end of it, Father and another brother and sister were lost to me, their bodies dragged out between checking to see if the hen had laid and tending the cow.

Two days ago should have been a particular blow, for it was James whose body Mr. Howe took from me, James, my twin, whose shadow I had been even before we were born. But I had no thought for James or any of them. Had I thought of anything besides how to get food, had I thought of why I, alone, was given the dubious gift of health, I would have lain down beside those once-loved bodies and succumbed myself. Yet the good Lord, if good he was, did not see fit to have me die. He saw fit to have me find scant milk from the cow and no eggs from the chicken and to care for my sick brother—my now only brother—Charlie, age eight, in the luxury of a house that had once held nine but now needed room for only two.

Human beings, I had learned, could become used to anything.

This morning, when I went out to collect our one egg, I found, instead, that the hen had died. Then, all the losses I had suffered came down to this one loss. I sat in the sparse hay, buried my head in my hands, and sobbed.

And then, I plucked that stupid chicken and cut and boiled it for, at least, if Charlie was going to die too, he could die with a good, hot chicken soup in his belly.

But Charlie was too sick to eat, and as I turned away from him, I knew I must try Lucinda.

Lucinda Baker was our town's healer, a woman who knew how to use herbs to cure illness. Once, she had been my friend, but when the plague struck us, Mother had warned me away from her. There were those, Mother told me, who said Lucinda was a witch and that witches were the ones who had started this plague. She worried that, were I too much in Lucinda's company, suspicion might fall on me by association, particularly because I had always been thought strange due to the odd bright green color of my eyes and a moody nature that differed from the other village girls. Perhaps Mother knew that Lucinda had begun to instruct me in the use of herbs. Lucinda told me that she saw the gift in me and believed I could someday be a healer like her.

Were healer and witch one and the same? Perhaps. It mattered not now. If a witch was what my brother Charlie required, then a witch was what I needed. There was no mother to caution me otherwise. There was no one but me now, and I would risk all to save Charlie, even being seen in the company of a known witch.

Thus, I made my sad way through the town, a town which had once been a bustling village of over three hundred, now so empty and silent that I could hear the wind in the trees, even at midday. I passed one, maybe two others, trudging as wearily as I did, but there was no talk, no laughter, no wagon wheels, nothing to drown out the wind.

My step quickened as I came to Lucinda's house, and for the first time in weeks, something other than despair gripped my heart. Hope held my hand and tugged me closer. Lucinda could help Charlie. I was sure of it. I only wished I had come sooner.

The cottage, made of brown bricks, neatly laid, was strangely silent. Only one black crow perched on the eaves, staring down at me. I approached the doorstep with a fawn's cautious steps and gave an almost silent knock.

Nothing.

I knocked again. Still nothing but the crow's caw.

"Who is that?" A voice from the street shook me in my shoes. I turned and thought for a moment I saw a ghost.

But no, it was Mrs. Jameson, mother to Anne and Alice, two uppity girls who had teased me about the ugliness of my flaxen hair. Still, I felt close to weeping at the sight of a familiar face.

"Mrs. Jameson! It is Kendra Hilferty!"

"Kendra!"

I ran down the stone pathway to embrace her. But when I reached the street, Mrs. Jameson's arms were closed. "Kendra, what are you doing here?"

I faltered. "I was . . . visiting . . . Lucinda."

"Visiting?" The expression on Mrs. Jameson's face was strange.

I thought it best to change the subject. "How are dear Anne and Alice?"

Her face crumpled like papers in flame, and I knew.

"Gone," she said, "all gone."

"All?" I was sorry now to have thought them snobbish girls. "Mr. Jameson too?"

She nodded. "Of my family, only I have been fated, nay cursed, to survive."

"I am the same," I said. "My brother Charlie, he is the only one who lives yet, and I may find him gone when I return." It was the first I had thought it, and I glanced back toward the house. Had death become so routine for me? Was I turned to a monster?

Then, she did take me in her arms, and we held each other and wept and wept as if weeping were the cure for our troubles.

Finally, I said, "I beg your leave, Mrs. Jameson. I was searching for Lucinda, that she might have some herbs for Charlie."

She looked at the house, and her eyes seemed to burn. "Lucinda Baker was a witch who brought the plague upon all of us!" she spat.

Was that what was being said? "'Twas George Viccars who brought the plague from London on a bolt of fabric. Besides, Lucinda is my friend."

"If she is your friend, you may be a witch as well, and should be hanged as one."

"How can you say such a thing to me? My family is as dead as yours. I only want—"

"Oh, Kendra." Her face broke, and she began to sob again. "I know what you want. Would that you could have it, but it is too late. Lucinda is gone."

The crow on the eaves cawed and turned its black head away.

"Some say she left in the night to avoid those who threatened to try her by water. Others say she came to a different end."

I glanced in the window, which was black and empty. Lucinda was gone and, with her, every last impossible hope. I wanted to fall to the ground and weep, but I had not time for that. Instead, I said, "Perhaps there is something left in her garden for Charlie."

Mrs. Jameson nodded. "I am sorry for your losses, Kendra."

"And I for yours. Perhaps . . ." I stopped. I had been about to say that perhaps she could come and live with us, that we might not each be alone. Yet I knew I would not be staying in the village. I must leave the site of all this tragedy and go far away. "Perhaps I will see you again."

She nodded again and moved on.

I ran to Lucinda's garden and gathered what I could of the different herbs. I tried to remember the uses for each. Yarrow, to heal wounds and reduce fever, dandelion for boils, horsetail for strength. I piled all into my apron. In the back of the garden was an herb I did not recognize, yellow and pointy as a cat's claw. The crow swooped down upon it, as if pointing it out. I did not know its use, but something told me it was the most valuable of all. I took a bunch.

The crow cawed as I shuffled away home.

Charlie lived still, and slept. I watched as a shiver wracked his frail body. Without stopping to check for fever, I went to the well, then the stove. I spent my morning brewing teas and making salves, and the afternoon forcing them on him.

By nightfall, he had improved not at all. Lucinda's herbs had failed me, and Charlie's chills had worsened. The boils on his neck seemed redder. Abandoning medicine, I took his hands and began to pray, pray as hard as I could, even knowing that it would not be enough. God, it seemed, had not time for us, certainly not time for me. Who would blame him, for there were so many sick, not only here but in all England, maybe all the world? As I prayed, the telltale odor of rotten meat met my nostrils, and I knew it would not be long before Charlie too was dead, before I was alone, all alone in the world.

And then, along with my tears, my prayers became more fervent, more desperate, only the words changed to something beyond my comprehension. I leaned forward, holding Charlie's hand, and felt my own fingers vibrate with a strange energy that combined with the words and flowed from me to Charlie, from Charlie back to me, until the room spun and filled with a strange, sparkling light. I was light-headed from hunger and despair, arms throbbing with the effort of saving him, bizarre ancient words coursing from my lips. I did not know what was happening. I only knew that something was, something stronger than prayer, something stronger than grief had hold over me.

Finally, I collapsed from exhaustion.

I woke to the morning sun's first rays and to Charlie's voice.

"Kendra? Kendra? I am tired of always lying around."

I started. "What?"

"I am tired of lying in bed. I want to go outside and play with Tommy and James."

He was alive! Alive, and wanting to run and play. I rushed to put my hand to his forehead. His fever was gone and the boils on his neck were gone, gone as if they had never existed. I lifted the covers and examined the rest of him. All gone. He was well!

"Stop it, Kendra. What are you doing?" He squirmed away from my touch. "Where is Mother? She will let me go out."

"Shh. Mother is very sick, in her bed over there." I gestured at the pile of empty blankets and hoped he would not look too closely. Charlie was alive!

Now, what should I do? I decided there would be time enough for the grim task of telling Charlie of our parents' demise. I said, "If you can be quiet all day today, I will bring you some chicken soup and tell you a story and tomorrow, yes, tomorrow, we will go outside."

He nodded and said, "I am hungry."

Warm the soup. I must warm the soup. But I stood too quickly.

I stumbled, and the room spun purple around me. I thought of Mrs. Jameson's words: *You may be a witch as well.*

Three thoughts whirled past me, over and over:

Charlie was cured. I had cured him.

It had been a spell I had cast.

I was a witch.

Once, about a year before, I had been on the way to town, bringing eggs to sell for Mother, when I heard footsteps behind me. Then, a voice.

"Hey, there. You, Kendra."

I turned. It was William Butterworth, an older boy, six and ten perhaps, who thought himself important, for his father was a merchant who did business in London, while my father was only a farmer. I did not care for him. Yet, he was running to meet me.

"Can I walk you to town?" he asked from behind me.

"Thank you. But I am in quite a hurry. I have no time for talk." It was true. I had taken a shortcut through the woods to save time. I thought it strange that he followed me.

"I can hurry." He was a big boy with a piggy little nose, and already he was panting to catch up with me.

I walked faster, as fast as I could without the eggs jumping from their basket, but finally, he ran and was before me, blocking my path.

"Gotcha."

"Indeed." I stopped walking. "What do you want from me?"

Now that he had cornered me, he seemed at a loss for words. "Nothing . . . I mean, I see you at church, you're . . . I wondered if, maybe we could take a walk together sometime?"

"We are walking now," I said, trying to step around him, to continue on the path.

He moved left, to impede my progress. "No, but . . . of a Sunday, maybe. I could walk you home from church, or come to your house?"

He liked me, thought me pretty, perhaps. It was a compliment. I should have said yes, or made some polite excuse, such as Mother believing me too young. But I was unaccustomed to being a girl boys liked, so instead I said, "I do not think so."

"Why not?" he asked, and when he did, his piggy face twisted into an expression that scared me.

"I have to go." I tried, again, to walk around him, but, again, he blocked my path, and I was forced into the trees.

"Think you're too good for me then?" His voice was a low growl.

"I said nothing of the sort. Please let me go by." I started to run. The eggs jostled against one another, and one fell, but I did not care. I had to get away.

He grabbed my skirt, then my arm. I dropped the basket, all the eggs crashing to the ground. He pulled me toward him. With one hand, he forced my arm behind my back. I screamed in pain, but there was no one to hear. "Turn me down, will ye?" With his free hand, he pawed at my bodice. His tongue protruded from his mouth. He twisted my arm harder until I thought it would break. The pain was unbearable. I concentrated hard on pulling my arm away. My vision blurred, then went all colors and then black.

And then, next thing I knew, he was on the ground, doubled over, clutching at his stomach in apparent agony and screaming foul words. I stared at him in amazement but did not offer to help him. I was free, though I did not see how. In fact, my arm did not even hurt.

The basket of eggs had fallen a few feet from where he lay. I scooped it up and ran as fast as I could through the woods to town.

I went to the shop even though I no longer had wares to sell. Mother would have my hide for breaking the eggs. And yet, when I reached the threshold, I notice that they had not dripped through the basket to my skirts. I opened the cover.

Every single egg was intact, as if they had never been dropped. Even the first egg, the one I had seen smashed, was back in place.

Had I imagined it, William in the woods?

Impossible. And when I saw him the next week at church, he avoided my eyes.

I told no one about the incident. There had been other signs, like my talent with herbs or the way some animals, particularly crows, seemed to follow me, or the fact that, indeed, bad things seemed to happen to those who tormented me, but none were this blatant.

Until now.

"Where are we going?" Charlie demanded as we left our house before dawn the next morning. I had plied him with soup and stories all day long, not daring to leave his side lest he rise and learn the truth, that our entire family was gone, or lest he become sick again. But, as the day wore on, he became stronger and louder and more demanding. My wispy hopes became solid things. After nightfall, I began my work.

I had decided I must leave town. Mrs. Jameson knew Charlie was sick. If he was suddenly cured, she would tell others and then, there would be suspicion. In our town, there were some, like Mr. Howe, who, like me, never sickened with the plague, and there were those who died, but none who had gotten it and survived. That alone would be looked upon as strange, an act of witchcraft in a town looking for someone to blame for their woes. But if William remembered how I had defended myself against him, that would make it worse.

It occurred to me that if I could cure Charlie, I might be able to cure others. I doubted, however, that I could do it before they drowned me for witchcraft.

"The truth of it," I lied to Charlie now, "is that the others are very sick still. We have little food left and must walk to the next village to find more."

I took with me a jug of milk and the last of the chicken, then tied

Bossie outside with a note that read "Please take care of this cow. You may have the milk" and hoped that the village would forgive me. I took, also, the last of the wheat.

"Once we leave town, sprinkle this on the ground. Then we can follow the trail to find our way back."

Charlie nodded. I knew we were not coming back. We would find another village, a new life.

We headed past the boundary stone and out of town. I hurried Charlie toward the hills, the better not to be seen by anyone passing by. We would not be able to enter any other town if the people there knew we were from the plague village, as it had come to be called. I encouraged Charlie to run.

We stopped only for a lunch of chicken when the sun was highest in the sky. Hours later, my stomach growled again. There was no village in sight. There was nothing, no food, no one to help us. We would survive the plague only to die of hunger.

"Let us lie down, Charlie. We will search more tomorrow."

"But I am hungry."

"I know. I am hungry too, but there is nothing to be done for it. We will gather berries in the morning."

"Berries? I thought we were going to a village. What about Mother and the others?"

"Tomorrow will tell. The good Lord will provide."

His very hunger must have persuaded him to stop arguing, for he lay down beside me. I sat longer until the sun faded in the sky. I wondered if I might use magic to conjure food. I tried to remember the mystical words I had said the day before, to make the magic come once again. Doubt overcame me, and finally, I too fell asleep.

The dawn's light pried open my eyes, and I looked for Charlie. He slumbered still. I allowed myself the luxury of worry. What would we do? Where would be go? I had been so certain of my powers, and yet,

I must not be a very good witch if I could not even conjure a bit of food. We would starve. It was over.

I looked to my other side. Did my eyes deceive me?

I shut, then opened them again.

They did not deceive me. It was a house—a darling little house of brown with white on the eaves and a sort of fence around it. Perhaps we were saved after all.

I crept across the craggy ground. As I approached closer, I noticed something strange about the little house. It did not appear to be made of wood or brick and certainly not of stone. Instead, it was made of something smooth and golden brown, with trim of every color. Closer still, the most delicious smell met my nostrils. Was I delirious? Was I so near death from starvation that I had lost all sense? Still, smell brings memory, and this scent held a memory so sweet, so dear, a memory of a long-ago trip to Shropshire with my father.

A sob caught in my throat. Father!

He had called it gingerbread and said it was made with a spice from the Far East and had strange, medicinal uses.

I inhaled. Was someone baking gingerbread in that house? With not a glance back at my sleeping brother, I ran to the cottage, searching for a window. Maybe I would be turned away. Still, I had to try. The alternative was starvation.

I snuck closer. The smell grew stronger, drawing me toward it like a mother's arms. I found my window. Dared I look in?

As I rested my hand on the house, I noticed something very strange. The smooth, brown wall was soft. What strange material was this? And, when I pressed it, my thumb sank inside. I sniffed. Gingerbread. Could the whole house be made of gingerbread?

Impossible. The smell was overpowering because I was so hungry, not only for food but for memory, my parents, my past. I inhaled deeply and remembered walking through the marketplace, a slab of gingerbread in one fist, Father's hand in the other. I pressed my thumb deeper, and again, the wall gave way.

Impossible! And yet, it had to be gingerbread. Either that or I was sinking into an enjoyable delirium. I hunched down, searching for an inconspicuous spot to nibble. Perhaps this was the magic I had tried to make. What else could it be? But if I could heal the dying and make food, what more could I do? The possibilities were endless! Endless!

And yet, I could not bring back my family.

No, but I could save the one left.

I grasped a windowsill and twisted. Bits crumpled in my hand. I chomped into it.

It was! It was gingerbread. I took another bite, then another. I was like an animal, ravenous, incapable of satisfaction.

"Hey!"

I jumped. Could it be the house's owner?

"Kendra, what is that you have?"

It was only Charlie. I crowed. "Sweet boy! The house is made of biscuits!"

I handed him a piece. He seized, then bit it. I watched as the grin bespread his face.

"We are saved!" I cried. Then, I grabbed him, and we did a dance around in circles, round and round, up and down, like the children we used to be, the children we maybe were again at this moment. When it was over, we fell back, eating ravenously, until our faces felt likely to break from the effort of it. We were saved!

By some tacit agreement, we both decided to eat from inconspicuous parts of the house, so as not to break it too badly. Still, we each had to try a bit of the frosting eaves, the candy trim, and of course, the low-sloping gingerbread roof.

"Gotcha!" It was a woman's voice.

I was roped, trapped in some sort of spider web. Someone or something was pulling me away from the lovely house, even as my jaws kept chewing, chewing automatically.

"Teach you to eat someone else's house! And now, the other!"

Before I could even twist to see who was speaking, I heard Charlie scream. She'd got him too. I struggled to free myself from the web of threads that seemed to multiply even as I assured Charlie, "I will save you."

"There is no saving him," the voice said. "Yourself either. You stole from me, you greedy children. I will take you both and bake you into gingerbread for my fence."

Too late, I got a close look at the fence that encircled the house. The strange-looking pickets were not pickets at all. Rather, there were faces at every post. They were gingerbread children—baked children!

Trying to shut out Charlie's shrieks, I twisted further, as far as I could, and made out a woman, a beautiful woman with flaming hair. Though Charlie and I both struggled, she seemed to use no effort to hold us. Rather, she was laughing.

"New gingerbread for my little fence." Her eyes sparkled green as ivy, a glowing, inhuman green that seemed all too familiar. I knew what she was.

"You're a witch!"

"Perhaps I am, but protecting what is mine doesn't make me one." She pulled us closer. Charlie was crying, but I tried to keep calm.

"I know . . . it is only . . ." I stopped. I had been about to tell her I was a witch too, but I sensed that, perhaps, it was best to keep something hidden, particularly because I was still unsure of my skills or if I had them at all. Perhaps Charlie's survival had been mere luck. "My brother has been very sick. He could be contagious."

"A likely story. I will not let you go."

"See for yourself. See how skinny he is."

The woman—or witch—shook her head. "I will not catch any disease. However, you are right that he is too skinny to make a proper addition to my fence. You both are."

I glanced around at the tortured gingerbread children. "If you release us, I promise we will run far away, and you will never see us again. We apologize for eating your house."

If she let us go, we would run, our bellies full of food, as far away as we could, perhaps to the lonely moors near Yorkshire or even Shropshire, anywhere but here.

The witch appeared to think, and as she did, her eyes grew more intensely green. Then, they flashed scarlet.

Suddenly we were someplace else.

The scent of gingerbread was, if possible, stronger. My hands were bound, as were my legs. In fact, the only parts I could move were my eyes. They sought Charlie.

He was tied, hand to leg, like a calf for branding. I tugged at my own bonds. They would not give. If anything, they tightened. I tugged again. Pain seared up my arm.

Charlie said his first words since we were caught. "Kendra, what will you do?"

It all seemed to collapse in on me then, and I wanted to scream at him that it wasn't my fault. I had rescued him from the plague. I had changed everything about myself.

"Don't worry," I whispered. "I will get us out."

"Ah, there you are, lovelies, ready for the fattening."

"Let us go!" In spite of myself, I pulled at the threads. When I did, they clenched around me so that my arms felt cold, as if they had no circulation.

"Let you go?" The witch laughed. "But you are so hungry, and it is so far to the next village. If I let you go, you will starve. No, no,

I would be a poor hostess were I to let you go unfed. This will be better."

From the air, she produced two spoons of gleaming metal, the likes of which I had never seen before. She waved her hand, and the spoons filled with something gray and soupy. They began to move toward Charlie and me.

"Open up, dear children. Have your porridge!"

My mouth began, involuntarily, to open. "Hey!"

Too late. It was filled with oatmeal that tasted exactly like Mother's, just the right bit of sweetness. I wanted to cry. If I were baked into gingerbread, would I join Mother and Father in heaven? Or would we stay on earth as cookies? There were those who said that witches had no souls. Had I sold mine to save Charlie? Or was I a witch whether or not I engaged in witchcraft? Had I been doomed from the start?

I could think of it no longer. All I could do was chew and swallow, chew and swallow as mouthful after mouthful of porridge slid down my throat.

"Stop! Stop!" Charlie was gurgling as the spoon approached him over and over.

I tried to shut my lips. It worked for a moment but then, some stronger magic forced them apart. The witch nodded, satisfied, and left.

The spoons continued force-feeding us, barely allowing time to swallow one bite full before presenting the next. I tried again to shut my mouth. This time, in my mind, I brought myself back to the day I had made Charlie well. I had been praying. But then, my prayers had turned into something else, turned to words coursing from deep in my belly, words in an ancient language I did not understand. Yet, I did, and that understanding had caused the magic to flow from me.

Perhaps it was merely a matter of concentration.

With all my might, I stared at Charlie, stared at the only one I had left in a world where even a hen could not survive. His mouth struggled against the spoon's intrusion, and his eyes pled with his older sister to stop it. Soon, I could not bear to look, nor could I look at my own spoon. Instead, I rolled my eyes far back inside my head the way I used to when I was a little girl and wanted to irritate Mother. I took myself back to our house, that once-dear place. I willed the witch part of me to the surface.

She came. I felt the room spin around. I opened my lips wide despite the wretched spoon, and I felt words course out of me, around my head, and spiraling through the room like a magician's scarves. That was how they appeared to my mind's eye, words of scarlet, emerald, and gold, words swirling out of me and around the room, and somehow, I knew what they meant even though I did not. I was calling upon ancient spirits to do my bidding, to move earth and make thunder, and suddenly I realized I was no longer being force-fed. I heard the spoon clatter to the floor. Then another one, Charlie's.

"Wha . . . what happened?" he asked.

I looked forward, shaking my head. "I do not quite know."

"Did you make it happen?"

"Of course not, silly." I made myself laugh. It would be better for him not to know.

"You did it," Charlie insisted. "You talked to the spoon, and it stopped. How did you—"

"I did not."

"You did. Stop saying that. Can you untie us too?"

I shook my head again. Then, my whole body was quivering, not only with hunger and fear but with the enormity of what I had done. Charlie's cure could have been a coincidence. This was no coincidence. I had summoned magic, and magic had come. I was a witch.

But was this what witches did? Trapped children? Baked them into gingerbread? If it was, I did not want to be one. The sweet smell of gingerbread invaded my nostrils and sickened me. I knew that, should I survive, I would never eat it, never use magic. Saving Charlie was enough. But did I have a choice? I was unsure.

Perhaps witches could use their powers only for good, to help those in need or to punish wrongdoers. That was the sort of witch I wanted to be. I vowed that, if Charlie and I survived, this would be the sort of witch I *would* be.

Yet, all I had ever heard of witches told me they were evil, daughters of Satan, devil's harlots. I did not want to be like that.

"Can you untie us now?"

I did not want to be evil. I did want to free Charlie. What choice had I?

None. I held my head as stiff as I could and whispered, "Yes, yes, dear. But tonight, when she cannot hear us. In fact, we should be quiet now, just in case."

"I want to go home!" His voice quavered, as if he was trying not to cry.

"I know, I know." I went cold in my heart, remembering the ruined place that had been home. "Soon. But be a good boy for now. We will escape tonight."

"Kendra!" He nodded at the abandoned spoons and bowls. I would need to clean those up somehow, before the witch saw.

"I know. Let us play a game, the game where we see who can go longest without speaking. You always win that one."

He never did, but I could try.

With one look around, he said, "All right. Go."

We were silent, very silent, but my thoughts would not lie down as easily. My eyes darted around the room, searching for a possible escape. The only windows were the spun sugar ones we'd seen from outside the house, but they were near the ceiling. Yet, the walls were still made of biscuits. We could tunnel through.

Trouble was, the room was empty but for the bowls and spoons. The witch had given us little means of escape. Perhaps the spoons might be useful for digging, could I but conceal one. I concentrated on the bowls, wondering whether I might be able to cast a spell without words if I waited long enough. I did not recall saying anything the time I escaped from William. I would try. I listened for footsteps. There were none. With no danger imminent, the cocoon of webs felt almost safe, like a blanket, or my mother's arms.

Mother.

Would she be angry to know I was a witch or grateful I had saved Charlie?

She would be frightened, as was I.

I grew used to the scent of gingerbread. I watched the light change and gave Charlie my eye every time he ventured to speak. I had to concentrate.

I stared at the bowl and felt, rather than thought, the meaningless words I had said before. I blocked out Charlie's whimpers and only stared. After many moments, my vision blurred, then blackened. The room seemed to tip on its side, and I closed my eyes to prevent the sick feeling. But that was worse, for the room seemed to spin. When I opened my eyes, the bowl was empty, and I felt the spoon, stuck into my hand.

I had done it. I could do it. I must only wait until it was dark.

Seconds later, the witch entered the room.

"Ah, you have finished, pretties. Did you enjoy your porridge?"

"Let us go, you witch!" I tried to shush Charlie, then thought better of it. Were we too complacent in our imprisonment, the witch might suspect my escape plan.

"Please let us go," I said. "Our parents are looking for us. They will find us so."

"Your parents are dead. You've come from the plague village

yonder. Almost everyone there is gone."

Charlie let out a cry, and I met his eyes, begging him to be still.

"Nay, Mum." I could not let her know our family was dead. "We are not from Eyam, but from Shropshire. We—our whole family—are on our way to London on holiday. We stopped to sleep, but my brother and I woke early and wandered off. Our parents will be searching for us."

"I doubt it."

"If they find your house, they will alert others. The law will not look kindly upon . . ." I pictured the baked children's faces and blanched. ". . . what you have done."

"The law will not find out, nor will your parents, who are dead as doornails. Stay, my lovelies. I will be back soon." She stooped to get the bowls. "What is this? Where is the spoon?" Her eyes searched mine.

I clenched the bowl of the spoon in my fist. "How can I know? I am tied up."

She giggled. "Indeed, you are. Ah well." She took up both bowls and one spoon. "It matters not. I will return shortly."

I heard her departing footsteps. When they faded into the distance, Charlie said, "Is it true what she said, Kendra? Are Mother and Father gone?"

I could not stand this. I could not stand one more thing. I tried to make my voice sweet, rather than scalding, and said, "Of course not, Charlie. Did you not see Mother in her bed?"

"I must know the truth, Kendra. I am a big boy and can bear it."

But I could not. "Let us put our minds to the situation at hand, and then we will worry about getting home to Mother."

"And Father?"

"And Father." My voice almost broke when I said the word, but I held it steady. "Now, please be silent. I must hear what she is doing."

But I heard nothing, and many hours passed. Charlie, apparently satisfied, as children will be, with lies that favor the way they wish the world was, slumped over and fell asleep. Finally, the room grew dark, then light again as the moon rose. My arms, bound together, ached as if I had been at the washboard for days. I had heard of men being pulled apart, drawn and quartered. Was this how it felt? I yearned to use magic to remove my bindings, but I dared not. The witch had said she would return. I must wait.

Then, I heard a voice. "Hello?"

Through the dim, I looked for Charlie. He slept still. The voice was my imagining.

"Hello? Can you hear me?"

It *was* a voice, a girl's voice from outside. Someone was here! We were saved!

"Who's there?" I whispered.

"Miranda. I am one of the . . . the gingerbread girls."

"You can speak?"

"Aye, and hear and see and everything but run away. 'Twill be the same for you, if you do not escape."

"I wish to escape. I was merely waiting for the witch to leave before I tried."

"Wait no longer. She is gone now, to consort with her fiendish sisterhood. I saw her leave. If you wait, it will be too late."

"You are sure?" Beside me, Charlie stirred in his sleep.

"Yes. Get to it," said the tiny voice. "You have little time."

My heart thundered like horse's hooves on the empty road. I had to concentrate. Concentrate! I blocked out Charlie, Miranda, blocked out my aching, throbbing arms, everything. I sat, face turned skyward, and tried to summon the magic.

It was easier this time. In seconds, I could feel the bindings unravel. I stretched my arms. I stood. Now, Charlie. Outside, I heard the small, strident voice of the gingerbread girl. I ignored her, carried away by my own voice, my magic. I stretched my arms toward Charlie.

"What is this!"

I stared, fingers outspread. The room was bathed in light, not moonlight nor candlelight. Rather, the room simply glowed.

I turned. The glow came from the witch. Outside the window, I now heard Miranda's cries. Too late. "Stop, stop! She is back!"

"How did you do it?" the witch demanded. "How did you escape my bonds?"

I did what any child in trouble would do. I lied. "I wiggled out. Anyone would to keep from being baked."

"Anyone wouldn't, couldn't." The witch surveyed the fallen webs. "My knots are magical ones. If you untied them, you must be a witch yourself."

Despite my fear, I made myself face her. I had to decide. Tell the truth? Or argue? Was it good to be a witch? Perhaps she would let me go if she thought I was one of her kind. What was it Miranda had said, her sisterhood? But then again, she might see me as a threat.

I had no choice. She knew.

"'Tis true. I untied the knots, not by wiggling, but by magic. I am a witch." I looked down, trying to decide what to say next. To admit my inexperience was risky. Yet, to pretend to powers I did not possess might be more so. Still, it would be better for her to think me powerful. "I untied myself, and now, I will untie my brother."

She cackled. "Unlikely."

"Very likely."

I began, as before, to concentrate on the mystical words, on what I now knew was a spell. I willed the ropes to unbind Charlie as they had me. Yet, something was different, as if a powerful force bore down upon me. When one moment my concentration wavered, the witch's greater powers overcame me. I was tired, so tired from weeks of struggling against death, disease, hunger, and grief. I had had enough. I wanted only to lie down, to stop fighting, but if I stopped fighting now, it would all be for naught. Charlie would die. I might die, or as good as die—be all alone in the world.

I pushed back. It was passion that had given me power, the passion that came from danger. My passion was my power and my power was my passion, and I shoved with all my might, my mind, my heart, until I could feel the blood coursing through my body, my head, about to flow out my mouth and onto the floor. I willed myself to untie Charlie. I could not see, could not hear anything but blood. Yet, it must work. It must! I had to save my brother.

Then, just as I was about to collapse on the floor, weak and helpless, I felt a grip upon me loosen. That and something else. I felt Charlie's hand in mine.

Power and passion wrapped around me like a mother's arm. Though I was inexperienced, I knew now that I could summon the power. I had conquered death itself, had I not? Suddenly I had wings if I needed them, wings of darkness like a giant bird, had fire and water and all the powers of light and darkness at my disposal. If only I could use them in private and not have to fight against this other witch. But I did. Our spirits fought invisibly, and I felt Charlie's hand slip from mine. I grabbed it, grabbed it fast. I pulled.

"Enough!" the witch screamed. I thought she meant to trick me, make me relax my grip on Charlie, that she might own us both. Instead, she relaxed her own. I felt the power fly from the room. Charlie's grip upon my hand tightened. I opened my eyes and looked up at her. In the dim light, her eyes glowed fearsomely, and her lips seemed red with blood.

"So it is true," she said, "the girl does have powers."

"She does." I straightened my shoulders. "Yes, she does, and she does not intend to let you kill her, or her brother. I have worked too hard to save us. Now, will you let us go?"

"Yes, let us go!" Charlie screamed.

The witch pointed a long, red-clawed finger at him, and he immediately fell asleep. She turned her attention to me. "I cannot have children getting out and about, telling tales of me and my little picket fence. No, I am afraid that, once captive, you must stay here forever."

"Stay? Forever? But I have no intention of dying."

"I have no intention of killing you. Witches cannot be killed by ordinary means anyway."

Ordinary means? "There was a witch in . . . our old town. They say she died by water."

"If she did, then she was no witch. Witches do not drown. Those who do are merely unfortunates. Our kind are stronger."

It chilled me to hear her say "our kind" and know she meant herself and me. I did not wish to have kinship with the likes of her.

"No." She drew a long finger across her forehead. "There is only one way to kill our kind."

"Which is?" Even as I said it, I knew the answer. I mouthed the word as she spoke.

"Fire. The only way to sacrifice a true sister of darkness is by fire."

I tucked this knowledge away in case I lived long enough to use it. "Indeed? And do you not intend to kill me in your oven, as you have the others? I hope not, for you see, I will not give up easily. I may be young, but I am strong. I have power born of passion."

"Passion. An odd way to phrase it. 'Deed, you are an odd girl. But I have no intention of baking you. You alone of all my children would give me something else I want."

"And what is that?"

"A family." In that instant, her eyes softened to the green of new shoots, rather the color of my own eyes, which disturbed me. She seemed to be not a monster, but a woman, a woman like many I knew in our village, like Mrs. Jameson and Mother. "A witch's life is a lonely one. We live forever unless killed."

"We do?"

She wagged her finger at me. "Did you not wonder why you, of all your family, were spared from the plague?"

I started to protest again, that we had no plague, but with her hand she stopped me. "Waste not your breath with lies, pretty girl. I know the truth. I recognize the scars on your brother's body, the haunted look in your eyes. I have lived through many a plague, buried husband and children. I have seen that expression in my own eyes. A witch's existence is lonely. To be immortal is to belong to no one, no time. I have met few of my kind, fewer still I would call friend. Those who are not witches do not wish to consort with us, lest they be hanged by association. Besides, they die. But a girl such as yourself could be the daughter I lost, better than a daughter. Together, we could live forever."

Inwardly, I blanched. I did not want to be this woman's—this monster's—daughter. Yet part of me felt strange sympathy for the witch too. I knew loss. Perhaps I had not yet lost Charlie, but if what the witch said was true, if I were to live forever, I would lose everyone over and over. Be alone. Could hundreds of years alone drive one to madness? To child baking? *Judge not and ye shall not be judged.* That was a verse the reverend often repeated at church, though few heeded it. Perhaps I should not judge the witch too harshly until I had lived her life. Or perhaps this was merely an excuse because, as I gazed into her eyes, I realized she could be of use to me. I had never been a stupid girl. Rather, my mother often pronounced me too smart for my own good, too smart to find a husband. I was also smart enough to know opportunity when I saw it. The witch was bad, possibly deranged, but she was older, wiser. She knew how to cast spells not merely from passion, not merely when danger bade her to, but from intent. She wished to be my mother. Though the thought revolted me, I knew what mothers did. They taught their daughters. If she thought I respected her, she would teach me. I pushed back the thought of my own dear mother. It was worthless to think of such things. Mother was gone. My powers had come too late to save her. Besides, Mother would not wish me to die, to let Charlie die. I was sure of it. Equally, I was certain that, if I refused the witch's request, she would kill Charlie. I did not know, did not care either, what she would do to me.

And once I learned all I could, once I had gained her trust, I could escape.

"And what would it entail, to be your daughter?"

"Entail?"

"What would I have to do, and what would you do for me? And for Charlie?"

The witch drew in a breath. "I had not thought that far."

"Then think."

"It has been a great while since I had a daughter." She stopped and stared ahead, eyes growing misty. "I lost the last of mine these two hundred years."

"But when you had daughters, what did you teach them?"

"Ordinary things, baking and . . ." My neck snapped toward the wall through which I had heard Miranda's voice. "Not that sort of baking. I wasn't about that then. Regular baking, bread and cakes and, yes, gingerbread. It was rather a favorite of my dear Adelaide's and, of course, she helped with the sewing. Not mending. I used magic for such dull work, but fine sewing, quilts and samplers. We discussed her future, the husband she would find, the babes she would carry. Of course, none of that came true. She too died of plague." She shook her head.

"Ah, I see. So you want companionship. If I were to provide it, you would give me advice and guidance . . . like a mother?"

It was all I could do to force the word *mother* from my lips, but it had its desired effect.

The witch's blood red lips formed a smile. "Of course, my dear. I wish to be your mother in every sense. If you were my daughter, I would teach you to be a better witch. This is what I want, and what you want also." She reached to arrange a hair that had fallen across my face. "I want you to love me."

I tolerated her touch. I had to. "And my brother?"

She hesitated long enough for me to know that he was not to have been part of the bargain. Finally she said, "I will take care of him too. Like my own son."

I smiled. "Then I will do as you wish."

And this was how I became, in fact if not in heart, the daughter of a witch. I did not forget my real mother, but I was so busy learning many new and useful things that the pain of losing her, of losing all of them, lessened. I had lost my family, lost my home. Yet, I had gained something else, something few women of that time ever possessed.

I gained power.

And I learned how to use it. Each morning, instead of making breakfast or milking the cow, the witch would teach me a new trick to make short work of it, so that the cows milked themselves or the butter self-churned. Then, in the time we saved, we studied more serious spell work. I learned to make magic, not merely through passion but by design, not merely by chance repetition of magical words but by movement of my mind. I gained power over objects to make them dance about the room. I made plants grow and animals obey my command. The only power I was unsure of possessing was over people. There were no people upon whom to test power, other than Charlie, and I did not want to do that to him.

Charlie was a bit of a problem. At first, while he was still recovering, he was content to sleep many hours a day, giving the witch ample time to school me in her—my—craft. As he recovered, though, he wished to run and play like other boys, not to be cooped up in a cottage (even one made of gingerbread) with two women. The witch used magic to hold him, magic to keep him from leaving the house. She could use no such magic on me now, for I knew how to break this simple spell. She knew me well enough to know I would never leave without Charlie. Still, Charlie sulked and sometimes ran and played and broke things. Sometimes, the witch used spells to buy his sleep, but the price was steep. As every mother (or sister) of a new babe knows, a child kept sleeping too long by day will repay this by waking at night.

This annoyed the witch greatly because, by night, she wished to tell me the exploits of her centuries of life, of her work in the court of Henry VIII ("Had he but asked for my help, he could have had a son"), and her dalliance with someone named Vlad somewhere called Wallachia ("a cruel one, he—liked to impale people on sticks"). "Being a witch can be a curse, Kendra," she told me, "but never forget, it is a blessing as well. Women, we are powerless, often at the mercy of a father or husband. When I lost mine, I might have been forced to take in laundry or . . . worse. But because of witchcraft, I survived and survived well."

"Kendra." Charlie pulled at my skirt.

"What does that boy want?" the witch snapped.

"Not now, Charlie."

"But Kendra, look. Look what I found."

"What is it, Charlie?"

He opened his hand and held out a black and green beetle.

"Ugh," the witch said. "I will turn you into a beetle if you do not watch out."

"He is but a child," I said.

Yet, I sensed the witch becoming more and more perturbed.

Due to the witch's trust of me, or her blackmail, I was permitted to venture outside on occasion, to gather magical herbs and flowers. It was on one such trip that I strolled past the corner of the house and heard a small voice.

"You! Girl!"

I started. I had heard no voice other than the witch's and Charlie's for weeks now.

"Please, please, Miss! You are in grave danger. Or rather, your brother is."

Now I recognized the voice of the gingerbread girl, Miranda.

I turned to face her. She was a child, close in size to my sister Sarah, who had been but ten. Her ringlets must once have been golden. Now, they were of white frosting. Unlike the other gingerbread children, whose faces were frozen, she could move and speak.

"Danger? Why?"

"The witch! This morning, before you woke, she was outside, gathering wood."

"Wood? She has no need of wood."

"Exactly. She has no need, for she makes her meals and warms her home by magic. She needs wood for one purpose only. The oven! Where she makes the gingerbread."

"But why?"

"I know not. Perhaps it is special witch-wood, the better for baking children. All I know is, one morning she went out, gathering wood. That very afternoon, I was in the oven."

I shuddered. Powers, when used to cure the sick or even lighten the workload, were wonderful things. To use them otherwise was disgusting. But could I have one without the other?

I would have to find out. But first, I had to make sure the witch didn't bake my brother!

I reached for Miranda's gingerbread hand, again thinking of dear little Sarah. Had I refused to lend her my hair ribbons? Spoken a harsh word? I was sorry.

"Thank you, little friend. Thank you for telling me. May I ask . . . ?" I hesitated, not wanting to heap insult upon injury.

"Ask me anything. It is lonely never to be asked anything anymore."

Lonely. That word again. Could it be that the world was merely a collection of lonely existences? If so, perhaps mine would not be any worse.

To Miranda, I said, "How is it that you can speak and move, and the others cannot?"

Her brow furrowed so much I worried it would crack. "I believe I was undercooked. 'Tis hard to believe, for the cooking was so painful that, when the witch came to check to see if I was done, I determined to be quite still. In that way, I was released from the oven half-baked. 'Course I cannot do much."

"I am sorry."

"No. 'Tis better this way. I was able to warn you. I wish someone had warned me."

"How did you get here?" I glanced around, the better to make sure the witch was not coming, not listening. But no. She was resting. Charlie had kept her up all night, singing and banging pots, and then she had gone out early.

"I ran away," Miranda said. "My father was cruel. He beat me and worse, so one night, I ran. I had grand dreams. I would go to London and meet the king! But, by the first night, I was powerful hungry. The next morning, I saw this house."

So like my own story.

"I meant to take a few bites only and leave. I was not raised to steal. But the gingerbread was so good, and my stomach growled so. So I took more. Then more. And then, the witch was upon me. She trapped me in a room and, next thing I knew, was gathering wood to bake me."

"I see. And where did she do this?"

Miranda winced. I could see that the memory still pained her.

"Please," I said, "I must know."

"Of course. I am sorry. It is just that I can practically feel the flames, licking my arms."

Involuntarily, I clenched my own arms. "But I have seen no such oven in her cottage."

"No, Miss. 'Tis not there, but over yonder in the woods." Miranda pointed to a spot beyond the house.

The woods! I was seized with an idea. To take Charlie to the oven, the witch would have to release him from the spell. Then, we could escape. It was a small hope, but it was the only hope we had.

"Thank you, Miranda." I squeezed her hand as hard as possible.

"Please, Miss, do escape, and if you do . . ." She squinted. "Perhaps you can tell someone about us. I feared my father, 'tis true, but I wish my mother knew what had become of me."

I touched her frosting hair. "If we escape—when we escape—I will tell them."

When I returned to the house, I did my best to act natural, and also to keep Charlie quiet. I required time to think.

That night, I prepared a special potion that put Charlie to sleep, then approached the witch, offering to read to her from her book of Irish mythology, which was her favorite. It had been my practice to read each night until she was quite tired, but on this night, I stopped midway through, saying, "Madam, you have been very good to me, teaching me the ways of witches."

She reached to caress my hair. "It is no less than any mother would do."

"It is wonderful."

"Do you love me as much as you once loved your real mother?"

I hesitated. I remembered mother, making my dresses, adjusting my hair ribbons, and teaching me not to lie. Still, I suspected she would permit an exception in this one case. "Of course I love you."

"Call me mother then."

"M . . ." The word stuck in my throat like spoiled meat from a long-dead cow. I coughed it out. "Mother! But one thing you have not told me about is the gingerbread ornaments which adorn this house. How came they do be here? And why?"

The witch screwed up her face, trying to decide whether to tell me. "The why is simple. I was lonely and wanted company. That is why I built my house of gingerbread. Soon enough, children did come, the brats of travelers, nibbling upon my walls. I wanted merely to play with them, to hold them, as I could not hold my own. Yet, the children would not agree to this. If you can believe it, they wished to escape my loving embrace despite the promise of gingerbread."

"They wanted their own parents."

"Exactly! Oh, perhaps you will say 'tis understandable, but what was I to do—bear more children only to see them perish, see them age and die while I lived on for centuries? Besides, once the children escaped, they would alert their parents, who then found the authorities. Soon, the townspeople were upon me with a hangman's noose or, if I were unlucky, with torches."

"This happened?"

"Aye. More than once. My first gingerbread houses were in Germany. When I was chased out of that country, I built the next here. But this time, I knew better."

I nodded. I saw what she had done.

"Now, when I caught a child, I baked it into gingerbread, the better to keep it here. I may not have my own Adelaide or Karl, but I have Maggie and Henry, Oliver and Em, all around the house. They are mine forever."

I shivered. The air had grown suddenly cold. I remembered the reverend saying that colder weather would lessen the plague. Too late for us.

"But they're dead," I said.

"Not dead. Frozen. Safe. Safe from the world, my own darlings."

She smiled, and I knew I must not argue, must not—as Mother said—talk back to my elders. Good advice, as mothers often gave. It would not do to let the witch know that I was disgusted by her doings. I must pretend to agree with her.

So I clapped my hands and smiled like the sort of insipid girl I hated. "How wonderful! I suppose if you went away on holiday, you might bring them with you for companionship."

"Aye. Though I have not often been on holiday. I am an old woman, in mind if not in body. I prefer to stay here, with these, my children."

She glanced toward the window at the cookie children. I could see one, a boy smaller than Charlie. His hair stuck up on his head, and I thought how he must have struggled when stuffed inside the oven. Yet now, his face seemed placid, accepting of his fate. His frosted lips even turned up in a smile.

"They seem so happy," I said.

"Oh, they are. In this way, they too can live forever."

I tried again. "Will you teach me to do it?"

The witch's brow curled under. "Why would you wish that, my dear?"

I reached to touch her shoulder. "Because, M-Mother, since you have taken me in, I have felt very close to you. Like all daughters, I wish to be exactly like you. But perhaps . . ." I stepped away. "I presume too much. You may not feel the same toward me. Forgive me."

The witch took my wrist in her fingers. "No, no, I adore you as my own and would teach you all I know. It is only that I have no children to bake."

"Truly?" My eyes met hers now. They were still as shockingly green as the first day I saw her.

"'Deed. Of course, when I first captured you, I did intend—and I say this with every apology—did intend to add you to my picket fence. It would not have worked because, since you are a witch, the flames—even magical flames which keep other children alive—would have killed you."

I nodded.

"However, now, I would no sooner bake you than I would sear my own flesh. So you see, my dear Kendra, I have no dough for my gingerbread."

"Ah." I remembered what Miranda had said about the wood. Could she have been wrong? I needed to test it. "Of course. I know you would not harm, er, bake me, but I thought perhaps . . . my brother."

"Your brother? You would not be angry?"

I screwed up my mouth as if in thought. "I would miss him . . . at first, I suppose. But he can be a trial. Besides, he would not live forever anyway. Indeed, were it not for magic, he would be dead already."

The witch's chin twitched. "'Tis true enough. I will admit I had thought of baking him. Boys yell and run about so. But I thought you would be angry."

The witch's fingers felt like worms, crawling, ready to chew my eyes out. I glanced away. It was true what Miranda had said!

I collected myself. "I have learned much from you, Mother. I will do what you think best. You have lived so much longer than I. Besides, if Charlie is baked, we could have him as part of our family forever. Otherwise, he will only grow old and die. Right?"

I dared not move. Yet I wanted her hand off me. It was a relief when she finally released her grip.

"Oh, Kendra! I had hoped you might see it that way. Yet I know children are sentimental. I can tell you all now. I had prepared the oven, and this morning, I gathered the wood. I was only waiting for an opportune moment to take him. I had planned to tell you he had run away, but now, I will not have to resort to such trickery. I am so happy!"

"I am too."

"We can do it tonight," she said.

"Tonight?"

"Why not? The oven is prepared."

"Why . . . yes. That is true." The sleeping potion I had given Charlie would prevent his escaping if we went tonight. I had to think of a reason to delay. "It's just that he sleeps. I gave him a sleeping potion. I was tired of the noise."

"That is quite all right. It is easier if he sleeps."

"Yes, but . . ." What to say? "I suppose you were right before, about sentiment. I am not so sentimental as to wish my brother alive at the expense of valuable training. But . . ."

"What?" Her disgusting worm-hand once again sought my hair. "I wish you to be happy, Kendra. I wish us to be happy together."

"I only want to see Charlie once more, awake. I know it will not matter in a hundred years. Still, I have a childish wish to say good-bye."

She blinked, then again. "And yet, you wish to bake him. You wish to see it happen? Perhaps it would be better if I accomplished it without you."

"No, no! I wish to learn. It is a childish desire, but please indulge me . . . Mother?" I made my eyes wide, pleading.

It worked. The witch stroked my hair. I tried not to shudder. I must not react.

"Of course, my dear. I forget that you are still a child, for you are so wise. Let us to bed, Kendra, and when morning dawns, I will tell you my last secrets, teach you as only a mother can."

"Thank you, Mother."

I went to bed at Charlie's side, but I did not sleep. What if she had lied to me? Or changed her mind? This could easily happen if she thought I was reluctant.

The matter of escape consumed me also. I knew I would likely have to kill the witch in order to free us. It should have been a trifle. I had now little fear of death, after all I had seen. But death was one thing, murder quite another. Killing the witch was justifiable, but would that make a difference when I was forced to impel her into flames? She was a human being after all.

Or was she?

She was. If she was not, I was not either, for we were the same. She was human, but she was evil. She meant to harm Charlie. I had to stop her.

As the dawn broke, I squeezed Charlie's hand. He stirred in his sleep.

"Dear brother," I whispered, "there is something I must tell you. Listen carefully, for I cannot repeat it or speak too loudly. Nod if you understand."

Charlie nodded but made no sound. I had cast a spell upon him to bring about his silence. I could take no chances.

"Good." I tiptoed to the door, cracked it open, and looked out. The witch was not to be found. I returned to Charlie and whispered, "The witch intends to cook you today."

Charlie turned a bit white but still said nothing. I continued quickly. "Of course, I will not allow this to happen. I will protect you as I have so far."

Now Charlie's expression indicated I had not done a very good job so far.

"She will take us out to the woods. You may get an opportunity to run, but remember, she is powerful. If you fail, there will be no second chance. You must wait until I distract her."

He nodded. I heard a noise, the creak of a door. The witch was awake. I gave Charlie one last look, then laid back and pretended to sleep beside him. I was so weary. Yet my pulse pounded, and I hoped this would serve to keep me alert.

The door opened, and the witch came in. "Wake up, dearies. You are in for a treat."

"We want no treats from you, Madam," I said. "Our last treat got us trapped here."

The witch winked at me. She was dressed in what must have been her finest, a green satin gown with a purple feathered hat. "Ah, you will like this treat then, for you will be untrapped. Free. It is a fine morning. We will have a walk in the woods. Get up."

I did not want to go. Thoughts of all that could go wrong flew around me like so many blackbirds. I wished that I could stay right there. Or, better yet, since I was already wishing the impossible, I wished I could turn back the strangling hands of time, not a day, not a week, but two years, to before our capture, before all the death, before the wretched plague. Had we only known! I wished to be a girl of twelve, concerned only with my weaving and whether I was being given more than my fair share of chores.

But I was a witch, not a genie. My life, once lived, could not unlive itself.

I stood. "That does sound fun. Come, Charlie." I tugged at his arm, and slowly, he rose.

The path we walked was covered in pine needles, but clear of grass and weeds. The witch had walked this way often; once, at least, for each child-picket in her fence. I squeezed Charlie's hand. Several times he tried to break away, but I tightened my grip. Not yet. I only hoped I was correct in anticipating a better opportunity. Pine trees marched on all sides of us, like threatening guards. Finally, we reached a clearing. I knew it by the smell of gingerbread. Gingerbread and something else. Seared flesh. I thought of little Miranda and the others. Would that there were a spell to quell my emotions, silence my thoughts. There was none, only my own talent for artifice. "So this it is?" I asked the witch, smiling.

"Indeed, it is, love."

I turned to Charlie. "This is where she makes the gingerbread."

The oven, made of black iron, was the size of our lean-to at home. The door had a lock upon it. Charlie's eyes widened, but he said nothing.

"Perhaps you should stand over there, Charlie." I pointed to a spot far away.

"No!" The witch grabbed his arm and pulled him back. "I need him beside me."

"Of course." I laughed. "How silly of me."

"A bit too silly."

"I apologize." I made my face pretty. "Will you teach me how to do it, Mother?"

"Of course." The witch gestured toward the oven. "Perhaps you and your dear brother could crawl inside and light it."

I raised an eyebrow. "Me and Charlie? Light the oven?" In a tree high above, a crow sang its homely song. I looked up. When I finally found it, I noticed its feathers were not solid black, as I had been used to thinking, but rather reflected purple and green. As I watched, its song changed from its usual caw to a different tune, one Mother had sung:

Dear love, call in the light;
Or else, you'll burn me quite!

Burn! Was I delirious? Or was this bird warning me away? I needed no such warning, but perhaps the bird was suggesting a strategy by reminding me of Mother.

Or perhaps it was Mother?

"Indeed," I said to the witch. "I wish to help, but I cannot light the oven."

"Cannot? Of course you can." The witch grabbed my elbow. "You are a big girl and must be able to accomplish such work."

I shook my head. "I cannot. My sister Sadie always did it. I never learned."

"You will learn now." The witch pulled me toward the oven. Charlie followed along. I could not let go of him, else the witch would surely throw him inside alone.

Above, the bird sang:

My bonny lass, she smileth;
When she my heart beguileth.

Beguile.

"Please." The tears in my eyes were real. "Please, Mother, I am afraid of the fire. I was burned once as a girl. You are so much wiser. I know you can show me how to do it."

"Silly girl!" The witch reached for the oven door. "Any fool could do it."

"Then I am less than a fool, for I cannot. Please, show me. We shall be together many years, forever. If you show me now, I will do it many times henceforth."

The witch sighed but said, "You need only take a stick, make fire as I have shown you, then light the wood inside." She plucked a branch from the tree. "Crawl in, and do it."

Now, the crow flew down from its perch. It circled around, singing the refrain:

Fa la la la la la la la la

It dove at the witch's head.

"Oh! Horrible creature!" With the hand that didn't clutch my wrist, the witch battled the crow. This gave me an idea. I let go of Charlie's wrist and nodded at him to run.

Yet he did not move. Why did he not? The witch was engrossed in fighting off the swooping, singing bird. He could escape.

He waited for me, I realized.

The oven door was fully open now, and I said to the witch, "Perhaps if you made the fire, I could light the oven."

"Oh, of all . . ." Yet she obliged, waving the stick in the air. It burst into flame. As she did this, the bird swooped again, causing her to duck and stumble. "Oh!"

Only then did Charlie move out from behind me. With both hands freed, he shoved the distracted witch through the oven door. The flame inside had not lit, but as she was propelled into the oven, her skirt caught, glorious red and orange. She shrieked, "I'm on fire! I'm on fire! Kendra, help me!"

I stood, frozen, until Charlie stomped on my foot. Then I flew toward the oven door. The witch turned back, clawing at me, but it was too late. Her hands, even her face, were melting before my eyes like butter. I slammed the door and threw my back against it. Charlie locked it. All the while, the witch's screams echoed through the silent wood. Black smoke belched from the sides of the oven door.

I stood there a long time, feeling the heat on my back, until the witch's shrieks waned, and I knew she was dead. I touched my eyes then, and found I was crying. Then I was wracked with sobs. I did not speak, nor did Charlie. Finally, there was silence but for the cawing of the crow above. I glanced up. It flew down and perched upon my shoulder, singing:

When she her sweet eye turneth;
Oh, how my heart it burneth!
Fa la la la la la la la!

I was shaking, but I stroked its head. "Yes. Yes. You are a good bird."

I remembered the crow at Lucinda's house, the day I'd saved Charlie. Probably just a coincidence.

I turned to Charlie. "Why did you not run?"

He gestured toward his mouth, and I realized he still could not speak. Quickly, I uttered the words to the counterspell. He said, "Had I run, the witch would have cooked you."

"Not true. 'Twas I who persuaded her to light the fire."

"But 'twas I who stuffed her into the oven."

I sighed. "I suppose. But, Charlie, if ever again I tell you to run, you must run." I had a premonition, as I had stood with my back to the oven, of the difficulties that lay ahead for a witch like me. "Promise, Charlie."

"I will protect you."

"No. You will protect yourself first. Promise."

Finally, reluctantly, he agreed.

With nowhere else to go, we trudged back to the witch's house. When we arrived, the sun was high in the sky, the better to see the change that had occurred.

"Where is the picket fence?" Charlie asked.

A smile spread across my face as I now fully believed that the witch was dead and gone. "The children, they are free. They are free!"

"Girl?" A small voice came from behind the house.

I knew that voice. "Miranda?" I ran to her. She was a sweet little thing, with red-gold curls and freckles.

"You . . . you killed her?"

"Charlie and I did. And now you can go home, to your mother."

"All the others have left already, but I, I wanted to thank you."

I embraced her. "You will be safe?"

"I think so."

"Then you should leave." I broke off a bit of gingerbread from the windowsill. "Here. For your trip."

And then, she left.

Charlie and I, with nowhere else to go, entered the gingerbread house. We were free! We were alive. The house was on fine, farmable land, and I knew that we would leave behind our dismal past, build a real house, and live happily for many years to come.

Epilogue

Or a few days, in any case. For, you see, one of the escaped children ran straight to the next village with his tale of a gingerbread house and the witch who resided there. Of course, the constable would not believe such a wild story . . . until it was corroborated by a second, a third, a tenth child. Perhaps little Miranda tried to tell them what had truly happened, but her voice was too small, and too late.

They showed up in a pack, with nooses. I knew there would be no trial, least of all a fair one. I only thanked Providence they had not brought torches.

"Run!" I told Charlie. "Do not look back, and if anyone asks, tell them only that you escaped an evil witch who would have baked you into gingerbread. Do not mention your sister. They will not believe you. Or they will think you a wizard too."

This time, he listened. At least, I think he did, for he left. They came moments later.

They hanged me. It hurt, but I did not die. The next morning, as the sun rose, I felt a crow, pecking, pecking at the rope around my neck.

And that was how I came to leave England. The bird turned out to be my friend, Lucinda. She advised me to travel. I did, first to Scotland (where I met the witches who had inspired Shakespeare's *Macbeth*), later to Spain and Italy, Greece, and eventually France, where I lived many years. Lucinda showed me how I too might change to a bird to escape, a useful skill.

I never saw Charlie again.

That's another thing about witches.

We are often lonely.

And so, to alleviate my loneliness and to honor the vow I made in the gingerbread house, I've made it my life's work to help people. There are many who do so, using their own special talents for reading, baking, or envelope stuffing. I try to use my own talent for witchcraft. Unfortunately, as you might have noticed in this story of the gingerbread children, using my talent sometimes backfires. Actually, my failures kind of outnumber my successes. Over the years, I've been banished from more countries than most people ever see. For this reason, I have learned to choose my victims—er, people I help—carefully.

It's hard for me to make friends. People don't, I am surprised to say, usually like me, and those who do tend to grow old and die. I haven't had a real friend in many years.

I can change my looks at will. I've used magic to stay young and pretty, the way other people use Botox, and I've found it easiest to stay in school as much as possible. I don't need school, of course. I can make the necessities of life from thin air, and after all these years, the curriculum is a bit dull. (Can you imagine taking Algebra Two more than once?) This is particularly true of history, as I've lived it. It irks me how often the books get it wrong, and reading Shakespeare is dull when one has seen it performed in the great theaters of Europe (though, for reasons I will perhaps explain later, I was unable to see the great Sarah Bernhardt when she was in France). Even the people are, for the most part, boring. The school queen who thinks she's one of a kind would be surprised to learn she is one of a million, and bullies have plagued every generation. But teenagers make good companions. Absorbed as they are in their own worries, they tend not to notice me much.

And, occasionally, I find, if not a friend, a deserving (or not so deserving) soul who needs my magical assistance. Or correction.

Like now. There is a girl named Emma. She lives in Miami, and I've had my eye on her for quite a while. She's had some problems involving a member of her family, her stepsister. I'd like to help her out, but first, I have to decide if she's worth the risk.

Her story? Well, here it is.

Part One
Lisette and Emma

1

My mother, in her sweet way, always reminded me that Daddy wasn't my real father. "Be on your best behavior, Emma," she'd said since I was old enough to remember. "He could ditch us anytime." Sooo comforting. I don't know why she said those things. Maybe she was jealous. True, Daddy and I looked nothing alike. He was tall and slim, blond and hazel-eyed, while I was short and clumsy with frizzy hair the color of rats. Yet on days like this one, as we sat across from each other at Swenson's Ice Cream, it seemed impossible that I wasn't Daddy's and Daddy wasn't mine. We had been together since I was three, after all; ten years since he and Mother had married. If I'd known my other father, the father that *had* left, I didn't remember him. This was the only dad I had.

It had been his idea to spend the day together, "Daddy-Emma

time," without even Mother. I'd found out just the night before. He'd come home from work and told me he'd gotten tickets to the national tour of *Wicked.* It had been sold out except for nosebleed top balcony seats. At least, that's what Mother had said when I'd begged to go. But Daddy told me one of his clients had given him second-row seats and he was taking me as a special surprise.

I'd breathed a secret sigh of relief. He and Mother had been arguing all week behind closed doors, alternately whispering and yelling, the sound muffled by television shows I knew neither of them watched. I'd sat in the family room, worrying in front of endless *Full House* reruns. Maybe Mother was right and they were getting a divorce. Maybe I'd end up like Kathleen, this girl in my class who'd had to be a flower girl in her own mother's wedding. Maybe I'd lose Daddy. Occasionally, I'd hear my own name. Mother would say something like, "What about Emma?" and Daddy would reply, "What about Emma? I'm thinking of Emma." Thursday night, Daddy had said, "I won't discuss this anymore, Andrea!" and the house had gone silent.

But now, I understood. The whispered conversations had been about this. Mother was obviously angry because she'd wanted to go to the play herself, but Daddy was taking me. Me!

Our seats had been so close I could see the actors spit when they sang, and the play had been perfect, perfect for me because the ugly girl, the weird girl, the girl no one understood was the heroine. I identified with Elphaba, the outcast, except for the part about magic powers. Perfect, also, because Daddy had taken me, which meant he got it. He understood me as my mother never could.

After the matinee, we went for dinner, and even though I'd ordered an adult cheeseburger instead of the kids' meal Mother would have pressured me to get in the name of "portion control," Daddy let me get a Gold Rush Sundae too. "Not much of a meal without ice cream," he'd said, and I agreed. I tried to eat slowly, like a lady, and also to make the day last longer. Plus, I had on a new dress, BCBG, and I didn't want to stain it. Dad said, "What do you want to do now?"

"Now?" A bit of fudge dribbled onto my lip, and I caught it quick with my napkin. Mother would have said it was piggish, but Daddy didn't wince.

"Sure. I told your mom we'd be late. Gameworks, maybe?"

Most people I knew would rather go there than anywhere, but the sounds of *Wicked* still filled my head, and I didn't want to drown it out with pulsing game music. So I said, "Oh, I don't know. Maybe the bookstore instead?" I loved going to the big bookstore, selecting a pile of novels, then spending an hour or more examining them over tea. "Would you be bored?"

Daddy grinned. "No, I can read. They prob'ly even have some of them there magazines with pitures in."

"I didn't mean that." The kids at school all thought I was a nerd too.

"I know you didn't, Pumpkin." He glanced to the side. "Hey, don't look now, but you've got yourself an admirer."

"Yeah, right."

"Right. Nine o'clock. Redhead's been looking at you since dessert arrived."

"Guys don't look at me."

"See for yourself."

I shook my head. Parents lived in some happy place where everyone my age dated or had guys in love with them when, in truth, only popular girls like Courtney and Midori did. I looked around. To one side was a crowd of stick-thin girls in Greek letter shirts, pigging out on Earthquake Sundaes. But when I got to Daddy's "nine o'clock," I was surprised to see he was right. Someone *was* looking at me. It was Warner Glassman, a boy from school, a smart boy who'd won a playwriting contest. As soon as I saw him, I wondered if my face was clean, if I had whipped cream on my lips. It wasn't like I could lick them now, though, not in front of Warner. I'd look like a perv. I fumbled with my napkin. Warner looked away.

"He's a boy from school, Daddy. He's looking at me because he knows me, that's all. He's probably trying to figure out where he's seen me before."

Daddy took a sip of his coffee. "You are a beautiful girl, Emma."

"Mother says I'd be pretty—pretty, not beautiful—if I lost ten pounds and did something about my hair."

"Mothers are too picky. You look great. Boys are going to be swarming."

"Right." Still, I straightened my shoulders and resolved to eat extra neatly until Warner and his family left. Maybe, if they passed close enough, I'd say hi. I took a minuscule bite of ice cream and glanced at Warner again. He *was* looking. This was the coolest day ever!

I knew I wasn't ugly or fat either, just plain, like the heroines in books I loved, like *Jane Eyre* or *Little Women*. Of course, those girls usually ended up getting the guy.

"There's something I have to tell you, Emma," Daddy said.

"Sure." I took another nibble, trying not to look at Warner. Still, I could sort of see him out of the corner of my right eye.

". . . and her name is Lisette," Dad was saying.

"What?"

"I said her name is Lisette."

"Whose name? Start at the beginning." I slurped up the ice cream that had melted to soup on my spoon. "I'm sorry."

"It's okay. I said I wasn't sure if you remembered that, before I married your mom, I had another wife, and we had a daughter named Lisette."

Remembered? I was three. But, yes, I knew he'd had a wife before Mother, in some foggy part of my mind. The daughter was news, though. I'd have remembered a daughter. "Where?" I choked out.

"She's been living in Lantana with her mom."

Lantana. Lantana wasn't far. We passed it all the time when we drove up to visit my aunt. My aunt was two hours away, and Lantana was closer. How weird was it, that I'd never met her? Had my father had a secret life all these years, like one of those guys on talk shows who turns out to have two families? What else was there, what else I didn't know?

". . . here on Friday," Dad was saying.

"Wait? What, again?"

"She's coming here on Friday."

"Coming? To visit?" No wonder Mother had been freaking out. She wasn't big on things that weren't all about her.

"No. To live. Aren't you listening, Emma? Her mother passed away, and Lisette is coming here. You should get along great. She's exactly your age."

The chocolate ice cream fell from my open mouth and onto the front of the BCGB dress. I glanced down at the huge splotch, then at Dad, then at Warner.

Of course, everyone was looking right at me.

2

The first time I saw my stepsister, Lisette, she was crying. A battered white economy car with patches of rust so big it looked like a calico cat pulled into our driveway. The door opened and it disgorged its contents: a girl who was, as Daddy had said, my own age but taller; a carry-on, which I later found out held all her clothes; and a black plastic garbage bag, which I later learned held everything else. All her stuff in one suitcase and one garbage bag? We gave more than that to the Salvation Army. We threw more than that away.

It was Friday afternoon. I was in the tree house Daddy had built me when I was five, reading *Vanity Fair* (not the magazine, the novel by Thackeray, which Daddy had bought me after I got my jaw undropped from our talk), waiting for Lisette, but not waiting. Mother said I was too old for tree houses, that it ruined her landscaping. It was Daddy who said we could keep it and was always too busy to take it down when Mother complained. I liked to go there to read. And hide.

I was doing both that day, plus spying on Lisette. Mother was out, even though she'd told Daddy she'd be home. She'd wanted me to go too, but I said I had homework. I wanted to see Lisette. Since my conversation with Daddy, I'd been wondering what Lisette would look like. Would she be pretty? Prettier than me? Taller? Thinner? I hoped she'd be plain too, so we could be friends. Would she look like my father? Would he like her better? Would she think I was a geek? Would we be like sisters?

I peeked out from between the branches. Lisette tugged the black bag across the bright green lawn. Whoever had driven her didn't offer to help. The engine started and the car was gone before Lisette was even halfway to the door.

Her head was down, so I couldn't see her face. What I could see was her hair, gold-blond like Princess Aurora's at the Disney character breakfasts we went to on vacation and spiraling to her waist. My fingers stole to my own frizz. She wore a black dress a size too small and black sneakers that were too large, but even in that, I could see that she was skinny, skinny and graceful, like a ballerina. She stopped to check a hole in the bag, which had something sticking out of it, a bit of sapphire-colored fabric. Her hand reached to stuff it back in but, instead, lingered on it, and that was when she began to sob.

Something black soared into my peripheral vision. I turned my head and saw it was a turkey buzzard. Two of them, actually, diving and bouncing at some dead thing in the street.

I should have welcomed Lisette, or at least introduced myself. That would be the normal thing to do. But I wanted to put off the time in my life when I became Lisette's stepsister.

As long as I didn't meet Lisette, everything could be the same. Everything could be possible. My father would still like me best, even though Lisette was his real daughter. I could still imagine that Lisette and I would be best friends. As long as I stayed in the tree house, there was still the possibility that Lisette might love me. But as soon as I approached her, that would all end. She'd take one look at me, with my curly hair and freckles, and realize I wasn't worth knowing, just like girls at school did.

I ducked my head lower and went back to reading about Amelia Sedley and Becky Sharp, BFFs even though Becky was evil, and about Dobbin, the grocer's son, who was in love with the wimpy, goody-goody Amelia and stood by her for years, even when she married his unworthy friend George. I had a secret crush on Dobbin and pictured him looking like Warner Glassman. The book was eight hundred pages long, and it was the second time I'd read it since Sunday.

Which I knew Lisette would think was completely weird.

Everyone did. Most of the kids at school, even in the smart classes, which I was in, didn't read books that weren't assigned, certainly not classics. Sometimes, I'd try to act like them, force myself to slip a *Seventeen* or an *Elle* into my binder or spend the time before class texting. But always, by lunchtime, I'd be at the media center, begging for my Brontë or Austen fix. It was pathetic.

I pressed my face hard against the slippery slats of the tree house floor, looking down at her crying.

Mother and Daddy's arguing had continued all week, and I'd read and read to drown out the yelling, but it didn't always work.

"There must be someplace else," Mother had said.

"We've been through this. There are no relatives on Nicole's side."

"On your side, then. Maybe she could move in with your mother."

"Give me a break. My mother's eighty."

"There are other alternatives besides relatives."

"Don't go there, Andrea. I'm not putting my own daughter in foster care for your convenience."

"Not convenience, safety. Who knows what sort of upbringing this girl has had. She could be into drugs or . . . worse. But maybe you don't care about Emma."

"Of course I care about Emma. I've always taken care of your daughter."

Your daughter. My father's words were like a shard of ice through my heart.

"Besides, I'm sure Nicole's done a fine job raising her. She was always a sensible woman."

"Unlike me, I suppose."

"Who said anything about . . . never mind. I know you'll see reason in this. The girl is coming to live with us, and that's final."

And with that, a door slammed.

I'd known better than to ask Mother any questions, but the day before, she'd come into my room without knocking and sat on my bed. Taking me by the shoulders, she'd said, "Don't worry, Emma. This is just temporary. Your father loves you. We won't let anything change that."

Which is when I started worrying that it would.

Now, I stared down at Lisette. I still couldn't see her face. She'd pulled the piece of fabric from her bag. It turned out to be a shawl, which she sniffed deeply before draping it around her stooped shoulders. She knotted the broken bag, then pulled it the rest of the way toward the doorstep. Guilt tugged at me, urged me out. I knew I should go down the ladder. I didn't. In my lap, my hands were working. I pulled out a page of *Vanity Fair*, then a second. Only when my hands were so full of the crumpled, ripped pages that I couldn't hold any more did I stop. What was I doing?

Lisette rang the doorbell. No one answered. She rang a few more times, then she sat down on the garbage bag and cried some more, great, racking sobs that shook her shoulders. We sat that way for a long time, me in the tree house, Lisette sobbing by the door.

It struck me for the first time that my father was a jerk. A real jerk who'd left his wife and daughter and had never seen her again, just like my own father had. Lisette and I were the same.

Finally, the air was quiet. This was my chance, my one chance. I had to sneak down when she wasn't looking.

The tree house creaked as I made my way down the ladder. Instead of walking toward the porch, I went in the opposite direction, toward the street.

Just as I reached it, she looked up. She stared at me full in the face and smiled through her tears.

In that moment, I knew I hated her.

Lisette was the most beautiful girl I had ever seen, more beautiful than Courtney or any of the popular girls at school, more beautiful than my dolls. She looked like a grown-up, like one of those people on *Inside Edition*. Her eyes were the same color as the sparkling, royal blue shawl, and her lips were large and a shade of red my mouth only got if I drank a red Slurpee. I knew the girls at school would soon make her their queen, and that made me hate her even more.

"Are you Emma?" she said, and I could only nod, frozen.

"Oh, God! I'm so glad!" She rose to walk closer to me. Her eyes fell on my book. I should have left it in the tree house.

But Lisette's eyes grew even wider. "Wow, you're reading that?" When I nodded again, she said, "You must be really smart."

I went through a big-time internal debate about whether to nod again or deny it. Finally, I said my first words ever to my new stepsister.

"Well, I'm bad at math."

"Really? Math's my favorite. I'm bad at English. Maybe we can help each other out." Then, she opened her arms and said, "Oh, Emma, I know we're going to be just like real sisters."

And, in that moment, I really wanted to believe her. A sister had to love you, right?

3

I brought Lisette up to my room. I debated doing this because, actually, it was two rooms, a suite with a bathroom between. At first, Daddy had suggested I give up one to Lisette, but Mother had vetoed that. "Bad enough she has to share her life with some stranger without having to share a bathroom."

Finally, they decided that Lisette would take the spare bedroom, which was downstairs near the laundry room. Mother called it the guest room, even though we never had guests.

It had seemed like a good idea, but as I helped Lisette drag her garbage bag from the doorway, I thought it might have been fun to share with her. I remembered slumber parties I used to have with Courtney, when we'd put up tents and eaten Mike and Ikes. That was before she got cool in sixth grade and dumped me. I was almost about to offer to share my room with Lisette, ignoring the fact that Mother would completely freak if I did (though maybe that wouldn't be a bad thing) when we reached the door of Lisette's room. She gasped.

"Is this . . . do we share this room?"

The room had one bed that took up half the space. I said, "No, this is your room."

She dropped her suitcase and took first one, then a second step in. "It's beautiful. I've never had a room of my own."

"But you're an only child."

She nodded. "But Mom . . ." She stopped, eyes flitting to her feet, then back. "We had a one-bedroom, so we shared. Then, at the end, she was so sick I took the sofa bed in the living room. This is so pretty, though. You're lucky to live here, Emma."

I couldn't meet her eyes. I was lucky because my mother had stolen her father and all his money too. But, apparently, Lisette was too nice to notice. Now, she threw herself onto the bed, her face sinking into the pillows, which were old ones Mother had removed from other beds.

I waited a moment before saying, "Can I help you put your things away?"

It didn't take long. Her clothes took up less than half the tiny closet plus a single drawer. She had no books, no dolls, certainly nothing expensive like a laptop, only a few stuffed animals, notebooks from school, and a framed photo of a fragile-looking blond woman, her mother. This, she put by the bed. There were no other photos of friends, no yearbooks either. I took more to sleepaway camp.

When we finished, I offered to show her around. At every door, her eyes widened. "Wow. My mother always said my father was rich, but I didn't think it would be like this."

Her words made me feel like I hadn't brushed my teeth in a

week. We weren't rich. Our house was average for the neighborhood, and I went to public school. It wasn't like we were the Kardashians. Still, I saw her taking in the flat screen TV, the pool, the Jacuzzi. I remembered her comment about sharing a room with her mom. Only poor people did that. Hadn't my father paid child support?

When we reached my room, I didn't want to go in. But Lisette said, "So this is yours?" and I had to admit it was. I saw the room the way it would look to Lisette, crowded with what now struck me as excess—expensive stuff, my own TV, which I barely even watched, American Girl dolls I'd outgrown, with houses of furniture, a rack for all my earrings. I'd even left the closet door open so she could see it was stuffed within an inch of its life with clothes.

She did notice. "Wow, it's like a mall in there."

"Yeah." I tried to push the door closed, but it rebelled, swinging back. "I need to clean it out. There's a bunch of stuff that doesn't even fit." I pushed again, then spied a pair of True Religion jeans Mother had brought home last month. Size: Tiny. Status: Never worn.

"Hey, you want these?" I pointed at them. "My mom got them too small. It was supposed to motivate me to lose weight, but . . ." I gestured at my size-seven hips. "Guess it didn't work."

Lisette looked at the jeans like they were booby-trapped. "Are you sure?"

"Positive. They'll never fit."

"Wow, thanks." She took them from me. "But you don't need to lose weight. You just have more of an athletic build."

Except I tripped over my own feet, even when I was standing still.

She held up the jeans and examined the stitching. "You sure you don't want to return these? Or sell them on eBay?"

"I have tons of stuff that doesn't fit me, if you want it." I held out a Hollister button-down that had been too tight in the bust last time I wore it. "Like this?"

She grinned. "Wow, thanks. I always hear about sisters sharing stuff."

After that, I kept finding more clothes, clothes that were still new and things that had fit me before but wouldn't now. I pushed back the envy I felt, knowing it would all look a thousand times better on my beautiful new sister than it ever had on me. Lisette had nothing. This was the least I could do. Besides, I wanted her to like me. It was obvious I'd misjudged her, based solely upon her looks. Didn't I hate when people did that with me?

"Try this on." I held out a Guess dress. "It'll look so cute with your hair."

But Lisette shook her head. "Later. I'll put together an outfit for dinner. Does our father come home for dinner?"

Our father. "He should be here around six."

"Cool. Hey, do you have any nail polish? We could do each other's toes."

This type of stuff was catnip to me. Actual girlfriend stuff, bonding over noxious chemicals. Before you could say "slumber party montage," I had out my pedicure stuff my aunt had given me for Christmas. I spread out twelve bottles of polish on my Animal Planet Panda Exploration bedspread, hoping Lisette wouldn't notice how babyish and lame it was. "Which one?"

She studied them, like an artist choosing a tone. "Oh, I don't know. We should match, don't you think?"

"Absolutely. I mean, sure." I didn't want to commit to a color. I'd let her pick.

"Come on."

"Okay." I selected some bottles from the group. "I narrowed it down to three. You pick one. That's what my friends and I do when we can't agree."

I left out the fact that I hadn't been hanging out with those friends in middle school. Might as well let Lisette think I had real friends, not just people I sat with at lunch and never saw on weekends.

Lisette chose the royal blue polish *and* the one with silver sparkles. "Okay?"

"It's like you read my mind."

"I try."

We sat with our feet dipped into the little blow-up footbath that came with the pedicure set. She said, "So, tell me about my father."

I shrugged and curled my toes under. I felt like, maybe, he wasn't who I'd thought he was, but I said, "What do you want to know?"

"Anything. Everything. My mother totes wouldn't tell me anything about him. I've never even seen a picture—she cut him out of all my baby pictures. In one, there was just a left hand. I used to look at that hand and wonder if I'd recognize it if I saw it again."

As she spoke, my eyes fell on a photo, me and Dad at my fifth-grade graduation. Mom had taken the picture, and Dad's hand was draped over my shoulder. I looked away before Lisette could follow my eyes.

"Well," I said, "he's really into gardening. We have a butterfly garden out back." Did that sound lame? "Once, last year, we had twenty monarch cocoons, and they all hatched the same day."

"Wow, wish I'd seen that."

I hoped I hadn't sounded like I was bragging. "Maybe it will happen again. The monarchs lay eggs on a plant called milkweed. Sometimes, we catch them and put them in a butterfly house so they build their cocoons there."

Lisette wiggled her toes in the warm water. I tried to think of something else to tell her, something that didn't sound like Daddy and I were attached at the hip.

"Oh, and he has a sailboat. I'm not that into sailing, though. I get seasick, and the sun's bad for my pale skin. I hate my skin."

"Your skin's fine. You could squeeze those little blackheads, but other than that."

"The magazines say not to squeeze them."

"Well, yeah, but are you going to walk around with a hundred blackheads? You just have to get them the second you walk out of the shower."

I nodded, amazed at how stupid I'd been. Lisette had perfect skin, so obviously, she knew. This is why people needed friends.

"Ready for polish!" Lisette tapped my foot. "Stop curling your toes."

"My feet are so ugly."

"They're okay. Having a second toe longer than the first is supposed to be a sign of leadership."

"Your feet are tiny." I remembered this book I read about foot binding in China, where the girl with the tiniest foot got the richest husband. And then, there was Cinderella. In older versions, the stepsisters cut off their toes and heels to try and trick the prince into marrying them. I looked at my big toes, and I knew which one of us would be the stepsister in the story.

"I hate my feet," Lisette said. "I do ballet, and I couldn't get pointe shoes until last year. My teacher said my foot was underdeveloped. Then, just when I finally got them, I had to quit."

"Why did . . . ?" My voice trailed off. Of course she'd had to quit because of her sick mother. "That's so cool that you do ballet. Maybe you can do it here."

She shrugged. "I guess. I miss my old studio, though. I miss . . ." She looked away. "I miss everything."

She glanced at the photo of me and Dad, so I knew she'd seen it. After a minute, she picked up the clear nail polish. "Okay, then!"

An hour later, we had identical matching fingers and toes, and Lisette had finished grilling me about Dad. That's when Mother came home. She walked in without knocking and took in the scene: me and Lisette as buddies. "Don't you have homework?"

"I did it in class."

She looked only at me, not acknowledging Lisette. "Wasn't there a project in Ms. Dillon's class?"

"Not until next Friday, and I'm half done."

Why did she have to be so helicopter? I knew my mother had been a lawyer before she'd married Daddy. They'd met at work, actually. And sometimes, I felt like she really needed to get a job again, so she could stop obsessing about me all the time. I always did my homework with no nagging from her.

But Mother said, "I hate how you wait until the last minute. You might have other homework during the week. Do it now."

"Can't I even wait for my nails to dry?"

"Don't talk back."

"I wasn't."

She gave me that look, where it looks like her brain's going to come shooting out her eyes, and I shut up. Only then did she finally look at Lisette. "Emma showed you your room?"

"Yes, ma'am."

"Then I suggest you go get unpacked. Dinner will be at six."

"Thank you, ma'am."

Mother stared at Lisette until she left, not taking any of the clothes with her. When she was gone, Mother went to the door, looked out, shut it, then sat on my bed.

"I'm warning you, Emma. Don't get too chummy with that girl."

"Chummy? We were just—"

"Talking? Painting each other's toenails?"

"So?"

"I know her type, Emma. Did you hear her just now—'yes, ma'am, thank you, ma'am.' What thirteen-year-old talks like that?"

"So you don't like her because she's polite?"

"She's trying to get something."

"Oh my God. That's just crazy."

"No it's not. No it's not. She wants information out of you, something she can use against you with your father, *her* father. Did you tell her anything, anything private?"

I remembered how I'd said I didn't like sailing, but I said, "Of course not. This is deranged."

"I assume you like living in this house, Emma? Having nice things?"

"Can I just do my homework now?"

"She's his flesh and blood, Emma."

"Daddy loves me."

She sighed. "Just watch out, Emma." She stood and walked toward the closet. "And change your outfit. That one looks all sweaty. And do your project."

I did work on my project, at least until I heard the shower start up in her bedroom. Then, I gathered the pile of clothes and also some books I thought Lisette might like, not nerdy classics, but the kind even the popular girls read, books about faeries. Maybe Lisette would be like a faerie visitor who would change my life in mysterious ways.

Okay, that sounded dumb, even to me.

I snuck downstairs and knocked on Lisette's door. "You forgot these," I said when she answered the door, red-eyed.

She gestured that I should come in. "Your mom hates me."

"She's just . . ." Just what? Selfish? What could I say that wouldn't make her sound awful? Nothing. "She doesn't like change."

"I was trying to be so perfect, but she didn't even give me a chance."

I remembered Mother's comment about Lisette saying "ma'am." Trying to be perfect would explain that.

"Maybe don't try so hard. She'll like you better once she gets to know the real you." I knew she wouldn't.

"I hope so." Lisette's eyes darted to the garbage bag still on the floor. "God, I miss my mom."

I held out the armload of clothing and books. "I brought you some outfits. And some books too. I thought maybe if we read the same things, we could discuss them, and that would help you in English."

"Cool!" She took them from me. "The books look awesome! You're so generous."

"No big deal. I already read them."

"Still." She threw her arms around me. "Oh, Emma, I'm so glad you're here at least."

I hugged her back, listening for the shower to go off upstairs. I could not believe this cool girl was going to be my sister.

4

It was five-thirty when I heard the garage door open and, through the window, saw Daddy's car pull in. I ran downstairs to greet him. I wanted to be there when he met Lisette.

But, when I got there, she was already wrapped in his arms.

"Oh, baby," he said, "it's been so long. Too long."

Lisette was crying. Again. "I always wanted—"

"I know. I'm sorry. I'm sorry it had to be like this, but at least we're together now."

I started to back away. It had been dumb of me, thinking I could horn in on their moment, their reunion. As I stepped back, I stumbled into the sunken living room and plunged headfirst into the sofa, my knee hitting the edge of the glass coffee table. I squeezed my teeth together to keep from shrieking. Lisette saw it all. She looked down.

Finally, my father let go of her. "Let me take a look at you. Man, you've grown."

That was when I saw what she was wearing. My jeans, the ones I'd given her, and one of my shirts. The jeans fit all wrong, huge in the waist and hips but way too short, and the Hollister shirt had a big yellow stain on it. Now I remembered spilling Coke on it. The expensive clothes looked like they'd come from the Salvation Army.

"But we need to get you some new clothes," Dad said.

"Oh." Lisette gestured down at her outfit. "Emma gave me these. Wasn't that sweet of her, to let me have her old clothes she doesn't want anymore?" She whirled around, modeling the mess of an outfit. As she did, the pants dropped down, and she had to pull them up. She must have been a size zero. "They're fine. I just need a belt, maybe. I have one though. You don't have to buy me anything."

"Nah, I'll take you shopping. Those things don't even fit."

That was when he spotted me. "Hey, Em. Can you tell your mom to wait dinner? I'm going to take Lisette shopping."

"You don't have to do that," she protested again.

"I've missed ten years of Christmases and birthdays. Now's my chance to make them up." He hugged her again. I limped out of the room.

During dinner, Mother glowered at me. Daddy had called to tell us to go ahead and eat without them. He and Lisette were going to Swenson's.

After dinner, I went to my room and waited. Had Mother been right about Lisette, that she was trying to steal Daddy from me? It almost seemed that way. I hadn't noticed the spot on the shirt, but now I wondered if Lisette had purposely chosen the worst thing I'd given her, just to make herself look more pathetic. Couldn't she have worn her own pants if mine hadn't fit? Did she just want to make me look bad?

I didn't go downstairs when Lisette came home, but a few minutes later, there was a knock on the door. Lisette was there, holding a shoebox. She held it out.

"I noticed you didn't have any cute sandals to show off your pedicure. I got Dad to buy you some."

I opened the box. It even smelled expensive. Inside were the cutest strappy sandals exactly the color of the blue polish we'd used.

"You're about a size eight, right?" Lisette said.

I nodded. "Yes." I was three or four inches shorter but had much bigger feet.

"I thought so. I got the same ones, see?" She held up her foot. "We can wear them to school Monday if you want."

I did want. "That's so sweet of you to think of me."

"Of course I did. You've been so nice. How's your knee, by the way? It looked like you really banged it."

"It's fine."

"Good. Dad said, if you wanted, he could drop us at the mall tomorrow night, to see a movie or something."

My doubts about Lisette dissipated. She definitely wanted to be friends. I guess I couldn't blame her for going out with Daddy. She couldn't go to school in stuff that didn't fit. And the other thing, wearing the shirt with the spot on it, must have been an accident, just like my giving her the shirt had been.

"So you can go?" Lisette said.

I could just picture the girls at school, especially Courtney, seeing me at the Falls with my cool new sister.

"Yeah, I'd like that."

"Try them on." She wiggled her blue toes.

So I did. The shoes fit perfectly, and from the ankles down, we could have been twins.

5

Monday, Daddy went late to work so he could drive us to school and register Lisette.

"I'm so excited!" Lisette squeezed my hand.

I squeezed back. I was too. The more I got to know Lisette, the more I knew my—and my mother's—fears were unfounded.

I hadn't been sure at first. When I'd awakened Saturday, Lisette and my dad had already left the house.

"They were gone when I woke up," Mother said with a nod. "Left a note saying they went sailing."

I spent the day reading. Lisette and Daddy returned that afternoon, sunburned and laughing. I met them downstairs.

"Hey," Lisette said. I noticed she was holding Daddy's hand.

"Did you have fun?" I tried to keep the hurt from my voice.

"Hi, darling." Daddy kissed my forehead. "You were sawing wood when we left."

"I wish you'd woken me."

"I know you're not much into sailing," Daddy said. "Lisette said so."

Something she could use against me.

"Yeah," Lisette agreed. "Now you don't have to go anymore."

"I was thinking I'd like to try again." Which wasn't true. A week ago, I'd have been thrilled at the chance never to go sailing. "Maybe now that I'm older, I'll like it better."

"I'm sorry, Pumpkin," Daddy said. "I didn't know."

He really had looked sorry, so I said, "It's okay. I just wanted to do something together, all of us." My voice sounded whiny, even to my own ears. "Maybe tomorrow we can do the butterfly garden."

Daddy rubbed his arms. "I don't know. Your old dad's not as young as he used to be. Maybe next weekend."

"Sure." I wanted to stomp my feet and whine that he wasn't doing anything with me, just Lisette, but I knew that would be a bad idea. Lisette's mother had just died. I'd look like a brat.

"Are we still on for tonight?" Lisette's newly pink cheeks accented her bright blue eyes and the highlights in her hair.

"Sure. I thought you'd forgotten."

"Never. We're sisters now, right?"

I nodded. "Sisters."

That night, walking around the Falls with Lisette in her new clothes, I felt like I was with a movie star, like I *was* a movie star. Everyone stared at us, and I was special by association. I kept searching the crowds, looking for Warner Glassman. It was stupid. He wasn't there, of course. He was probably sitting at home, reading a book, which is what I'd have been doing but for Lisette. I did see Midori, though, Courtney's best friend. I hoped she saw me.

Now, as we got out of Daddy's car, I said, "Can I go to the office when you sign up Lisette?"

"It may be a long process," Daddy said. "You shouldn't miss class."

Daddy touched Lisette's waist to lead her into the building, but Lisette pointed at a poinciana tree. "Let's meet there after school, so we can compare notes."

"Great." I'd been looking forward to walking through the hall with Lisette. At least she'd wait for me after school.

When I got to language arts, everyone was looking at Kendra Hilferty. Kendra was new this year, and ever since she'd moved here, there'd been rumors, crazy ones, about her. People speculated she was a spy, hired by the school board to expose weak teaching practices. That she had grown up in a commune. Or a convent. Or a circus, where she was principal contortionist. That her mother had been a famous dancer, and Kendra herself was the illegitimate daughter of the president of France. That she'd had to leave her previous school because she'd threatened another girl, and then the girl disappeared. Of course, no one bothered to ask Kendra if the rumors were true. It was more fun to gossip. Besides, people were afraid of her.

Today, she wore her usual black, a lace dress that looked like it was from a thrift shop. I noticed it only came to her knees. That was another rumor, one I happened to know was true—that the school had asked that she stop wearing floor-length skirts that could conceal a weapon. I knew that because, the day it happened, I was in the office calling Mother about a stomachache when Kendra exited the guidance counselor's office. "You've just made dress code history," she had said. "You've got a hundred girls in microminis, and you're asking me to wear a *shorter* skirt."

Kendra spent a lot of time in the guidance counselor's office, another rumor that was true. Whenever Kendra was in class, stuff happened, stuff like the fire sprinklers going off or the earthworms we were dissecting in science class heading en masse for the parking lot. Or once, the tennis balls the teacher put on chair legs to make them quieter all got loose at the same time and started bouncing around the room. No one could ever pin this stuff on Kendra. It just happened when she was there.

I didn't have anything against her, but I had her in three of my classes, and she sat next to me in all of them. That meant when people stared at her, they stared at me too.

Right now, she was balancing a pencil by its point on her fingertip, staring with great concentration. I couldn't figure out how she did it, but I guessed she'd been at it awhile.

I realized Kendra probably sat next to me not because we were such great buds but because I was the one who always had an empty seat beside me. Maybe now that Lisette was here, that would change. I hoped to have her in at least one class.

"Hi," I said to Kendra, because it was the polite thing to do.

"Hi, Emma." The pencil clattered to the floor. Ms. Dillon told us to be quiet because the Pledge was starting.

During the moment of silence, there was a knock on the door. Everyone looked up from their talking and texting to see who was there. Then, they stared.

It was Lisette. She found my face, as if she'd known I'd be there, and smiled before turning to Ms. Dillon. "I'm Lisette Cooper. They said I'm in your class."

"Welcome, welcome, Lisette. We were about to discuss *Of Mice and Men*. There's an empty seat in back."

I twisted to look. Of course. The empty seat was right next to my former BFF, Courtney, who sat with her new posse, Midori and Tayloe. Lisette walked toward them but, as she passed, she dropped a sheet of paper on my desk.

A note? I checked it out. It was her schedule. Five of our six classes were the same, the only difference being German Two, fourth period. Lisette was in Spanish One. I glanced back at her. Had she asked to have the same schedule? To be with me 24/7? She smiled and gave me a thumbs-up.

"Okay, then," Ms. Dillon was saying. "What can you tell me about the character of George Milton? Yes, Courtney?"

"I think maybe he was named for John Milton, the author of *Paradise Lost*, and that symbolizes his quest for utopia, just as Adam and Eve fell from grace when they were banished from the Garden of Eden."

Fell from grace? Quest for utopia? Who talked like that? Certainly not Courtney. She'd obviously gotten this stuff from the internet or maybe Cliff's Notes. I doubted she'd even read the book. Back when we were friends, I told her the answers to every single Accelerated Reader test I'd ever taken, so she'd get enough points for class. Teachers never questioned the fact that we'd read the exact same books every quarter. If they had, we'd have said we were best friends, that we did everything together.

That had changed in sixth grade. The month before we'd started middle school, my family went on vacation to North Carolina, in the mountains where there was sucky cell phone reception. I texted Courtney every chance I got, but she didn't always text back. When we returned, I called her. And again. After about the fifth try, I got a text from her saying she was busy, but she'd see me the first day of school.

But when I got there, she was ensconced in a group of girls who hadn't gone to our elementary school, prettier girls, cooler girls, girls who looked like they'd been born with the best cell phones attached to their hands, born to hang out in a clump, girls whose parents had no rules. "Hey, Courtney," I'd said.

"Hey," she replied before turning back to the others, giggling.

I sat next to her at lunch because that's what I'd done every single day since kindergarten. Even when we hadn't been in the same class, I'd always snuck over to her table, or she to mine.

"Sorry," she said. "This seat's saved for Midori."

"Okay." I started for the seat across from her.

"And Tayloe's sitting there."

The seat diagonal from Courtney was empty, so I took that one. When Midori and Tayloe showed up, Courtney didn't introduce us. They all ignored me.

I never figured out what I'd done to lose Courtney's friendship. As days passed, I tried to talk to her, but she acted like she didn't know why I was bothering her, and her new friends started picking on me. Then, Courtney herself had. At home, Mother kept asking me why I didn't ask Courtney to sleep over anymore. When I said she didn't like me anymore, she offered to call Courtney's mother. Like that would help.

The whole thing was like a divorce. When we divided everything up, Courtney got my dignity, and I got the heartache. I didn't understand. Popularity was like a kind of science, but unlike my school subjects, I couldn't learn it.

Now, Ms. Dillon said, "That's exactly right, Courtney. Anyone else? What was George like? Emma?"

"Um . . ." I squirmed and looked at my chipped nail polish. Ms. Dillon always called on me because she knew I'd have the answer she wanted. I hated it, though. I knew that the other kids, that Lisette, would think I was a suck-up. I considered giving the wrong answer, or even saying I hadn't read the book. How much did middle-school grades really matter, after all? But somehow, I just couldn't do it.

"He was lonely. That's what the book was about, the lonely lives of migrant workers. George hung out with Lennie, and he acted like he had to, but really, he was a loner. He didn't fit in with anyone else."

Why did I say that? Stupid! Sure enough, behind me I heard a giggle. "She should know about that," someone—maybe Midori—whispered.

The comment stung like a jellyfish in calm water. I'd learned not to let their barbs hurt me, but now Lisette was there. Lisette, who maybe hadn't noticed that I was the geek of the universe. Why did they have to ruin it for me with her?

I wanted to look back at her, to see if she'd heard. No. I had to keep talking.

"George is really responsible, though," I told Ms. Dillon. "He takes responsibility for Lennie. In the end, he even takes responsibility for—"

"Uh-uh," Ms. Dillon interrupted. "No spoilers! I want everyone to finish, and they're not all as voracious readers as you."

More giggles from behind me, and Courtney said, "She has nothing else to do."

Sigh! I'd better shut up now. I glanced back at Lisette, to see if she was disgusted by the fact that I'd finished the book. She smiled. Beside her, Courtney widened her eyes, like what was I looking at. I didn't care. As long as I had Lisette, I'd be happy. I pictured us being like Jo and Beth in *Little Women* or Elinor and Marianne in *Sense and Sensibility*, real sisters, confidantes.

Midori made a face. "What a suck-up," she whispered. "Ow!" she shrieked.

"What's the matter, Midori?" Ms. Dillon's voice was a sigh.

"I don't know. Just—ow!—I'm getting these weird shooting pains." She clutched her abdomen. "Ouch!" She squeezed her eyes shut, like she was trying not to cry.

"Cramps," Ms. Dillon said, and a few people giggled. At Midori. "Go to the nurse, then. Courtney, why don't you take her?"

Midori limped out, still holding her stomach. Courtney followed her.

After class, Lisette stood by my desk, waiting for me to put my books away. She said, "Isn't it cool? I asked if we could have all our classes together, so they made them all the same, except Spanish."

"Wow. They're not usually that nice about scheduling." I was amazed she'd even asked.

She shrugged. "I guess because of what happened." She glanced away. "I told Dad to ask, and he agreed it would be good to have a familiar face."

I wondered if she'd just asked to impress my father. No, that was stupid. Why couldn't I just believe that Lisette liked me, that she wanted a sister, like I did?

We walked to second period together and actually got to sit together in third. When we split up for our language arts classes, Lisette said, "See you at lunch."

But when I got to the cafeteria, Lisette was walking in with Courtney.

6

Our cafeteria looked the way I'm guessing most school cafeterias do, white and black spotted floors dulled by years of spilled chocolate milk and dirty sneakers. Louvered windows that let in barely enough light to see your food . . . probably a good thing. Skinny girls sat by the salad bar. Those with weak stomachs were near the door. I walked down the rows of tables, my soles sticking to the floor. Usually, I sat toward the middle, where I could be most invisible, with some girls from my fourth period whose names I probably wouldn't remember in a year.

The one weird feature of our cafeteria was, it had a single table with four chairs attached to it. Probably it was for the teachers, until the teachers realized they didn't have good enough health insurance to risk the cafeteria's version of empanadas. Courtney, Tayloe, and Midori, as the most "popular" eighth-grade girls, sat there. The fourth chair was always empty. Once, some clueless sixth graders had parked there. The first day, Courtney and Company had allowed it. The second, the sixth graders had stood to reveal red food coloring all over the butts of their Abercrombie jeans. No one could prove anything, but the next day, they sat on the benches.

I watched Lisette head, with Courtney, to the fourth seat.

Okay, so that was how it was going to be.

I glanced around, trying to find Erin, the quiet girl from my fourth-period class. I usually sat with her, but I'd left her in the dust to make sure I caught Lisette.

But wait! From across the room, Lisette was waving.

"Hey, Emma! Em, come over here!"

Courtney grabbed her elbow, and I saw her gesture at the table, pointing to each seat, showing Lisette there was no room.

Lisette started to walk away.

Courtney glanced around, as if trying to decide if she was hallucinating, or if she'd been transported to some alt universe where people preferred to sit with me. It was a difficult concept, even for me, and Courtney had never been bright. Courtney's size-one rear hovered over her chosen seat. She stood, then half sat again, like a competitive toddler playing musical chairs.

Finally, she strode, a little too fast to be completely dignified, after Lisette. People were noticing now, probably wondering if there was going to be some kind of mean girl takedown with Courtney shrieking, "No one turns their back on me, beeyoch!" Lisette had almost reached me when Courtney touched her shoulder.

"Wait!" Courtney gestured to one of the rectangular tables. "We can all fit here."

Lisette glanced at the seats, then at me. "Oh. Okay, if you're sure."

"Of course." Courney grinned, or bared her teeth. "Em and I are old friends. We've literally known each other since birth. Right, Emma?"

"I guess." It was raining, and I glanced at the window to see if rain was falling up.

"So we can all sit here," Courtney said. "Together."

While we were standing around, two girls started to take Courtney's chosen seats.

"We're here," she informed them.

"I thought you sat there." One of the girls pointed to the little table.

"Does it look like we're there? Duh. People are so stupid." She sat and gestured for Lisette and me to spread out. "Leave room for Tayloe and Midori."

The table for four sat empty. No one dared sit at it. I bet it would be empty all year.

Midori and Tayloe showed up then, Midori obviously feeling better. They glanced at the table but didn't dare comment. Courtney leaned toward Lisette. "Sooooo, how do you know Emma?"

"She's my stepsister."

"Stepsister?" Courtney looked at me. "Did your parents get divorced, that I don't know about?"

"They were always divorced," Lisette said. "My dad married Emma's mom when Emma and I were three, but I've been living up in Palm Beach with my mother."

"That's so weird," Courtney said. "I always thought he was your real dad."

He was!

"So, Palm Beach." Midori did a bit of hair-ography with her dark hair. "Do you play polo and hang with Tiger Woods?"

Dad had told me Lisette was from Lantana, which was in Palm Beach County, but not rich Palm Beach, where the millionaires lived. But Lisette didn't correct Midori. People didn't. "Well, not polo, but the shops on Worth Avenue are totes to die for." She did some hairography of her own, fluffing her blond curls back.

And that's when I noticed them. Shell-shaped earrings with aquamarines on top. They were beautiful.

And they were mine. Daddy had bought them on a cruise we'd taken for my birthday last year. Aquamarine was my birthstone.

"Wow, great earrings," I said. "I have a pair just like them."

Lisette reached her hand for her ear, as if trying to remember what earrings she had on. "Truly? They were my mother's. Her birthday's in March. How weird that you'd have the same ones." She grinned. "It must be fate, to show that we're truly meant to be sisters."

Courtney rolled her eyes, and I exhaled. It sounded like something from a novel, like the locket in *Oliver Twist.* Of course there was an explanation. Lisette wouldn't steal my earrings and wear them right in front of me. Still, I'd go find mine when I got home. We could even wear them together.

"How cute," Courtney said. "You always said you wanted a sister, Em." She went back to Lisette. "So what's your schedj for the rest of the day?"

And neither she, nor her friends, talked to me the rest of lunch.

When the warning bell rang, I started gathering my stuff. I didn't want this. I was over Courtney. I didn't want to be back in her web.

Courtney said, "We're walking to Starbucks after school. There's this hot barista Tayloe's lusting for."

"Not lusting," Tayloe protested.

"Ahem. You don't even like coffee."

"Okay, he is cute."

"You should come, Lisette," Courtney said, "and bring Emma."

I knew I'd go.

I didn't get to sit by Lisette in chorus. Even though we were both sopranos, Miss Hakes put her in back because she was taller. I sat by—who else?—Kendra. Miss Hakes announced that, next Monday, she'd have auditions for a solo. Kendra nudged me. "You should try out."

"Oh." I turned to see if she was kidding. "Really?"

"You have a beautiful voice."

I wanted to return the compliment, but it seemed like Kendra usually just mouthed the words. I'd actually been planning on trying for the solo. I'd been practicing at home for weeks. I'd even gotten Mother to pay for some voice lessons with Miss Hakes. I thought I had a good voice, but no one had ever told me I did.

"Thanks," I said.

"Show of hands if you're trying out," Miss Hakes said.

"Put up your hand," Kendra urged.

I did. Three other hands went up, but two were seventh graders. I saw Lisette nod her approval at me.

Since everyone cool went to Starbucks after school, I never went. Now I was there with the most popular girls in the class, and Courtney was regaling Lisette with the details of our friendship, leaving out the fact that it had ended two years earlier. "Do you remember, Em, how we met because we wore the same outfit the first day of kindergarten?" she'd say. Or, "Do you remember when we took the limo to Kendall Ice Arena for your birthday in fifth grade?"

I did remember. It was Courtney who hadn't seemed to. But I didn't say anything. I wanted Lisette to think I had friends. Courtney wouldn't give me away. Obviously, she wanted to hang with Lisette, and I was part of the deal. The other two girls had never really known me.

"What do you think of *la bruja gorda*?" Courtney asked Lisette.

"That's what we call the Spanish teacher," Lisette explained.

We? She'd been there a day.

"Fat witch," Midori translated.

"She speaks zero Spanish," Tayloe chimed in. "I asked her a

word once, and she looked it up, real sneaky, in this dictionary under her desk."

"And she's so fat," Courtney said, "that I heard last year, she had a baby, and she didn't even realize she was pregnant."

The four of them started giggling, and I felt like Lisette was the one who'd known them since kindergarten. I searched for something to say, something funny and evil.

"Some people call my German teacher The Nazi," I said.

Everyone stared at me.

"Because he's really hard," I added.

They kept staring. Then, Midori said, "That's not funny, Emma. My grandmother was killed in a concentration camp."

I felt my face start to burn and my vision blur. "Omigod, Midori. I didn't know." I was so stupid. I wasn't even the one who called Herr Webb that, just heard other people say it.

Tayloe laughed. "She's messing with you, Emma. She's not even Jewish." She rolled her eyes. "And I've met both your grandmothers."

"Good one, Midori." Courtney raised her latte in a toast.

I stared at my frappuccino, not daring to look at Lisette, who said nothing.

"I was kidding, Emma."

"You never could take a joke, Emma. The girl literally has no sense of humor."

I wanted to protest. I *could* take a joke, just not a joke about people's families being gassed to death. Why did I even want to hang with people who thought that was funny? I said none of it, though. If I said something, I might start to cry, and then it would be worse. I sipped my frappuccino.

Midori turned to Lisette. "You should hang with us Saturday. We're going to Adventura Mall."

"Sure," Lisette said. "Emma too? I mean, if you want to go,

Emma." Her earrings sparkled in the fluorescent light.

Midori frowned. "Um, I'd say yes, but my mom's taking us, and her BMW only fits five." She smiled at me that fake way girls do to show how much they enjoy destroying your soul. "Sorry, Em."

Lisette said, "Oh, well, maybe we could go another time."

"You can go," I said. "I don't care."

"Of course not. We're sisters." She looked out the side of her eyes at Midori, and I could see it was a challenge. "Unless someone's mom has a minivan, maybe?"

Midori glanced at Courtney.

Courtney said, "Um, doesn't your mom have a big SUV, Emma?"

My mother did have a Suburban. She'd gotten it to drive around the loads of friends I didn't have, but now, it mostly towed Dad's boat. At this point, I didn't really want to go to the mall with them. They obviously didn't want me. But if I said no, I'd look like a brat.

"I guess," I said, "if my dad isn't using it for his boat."

"I'll tell him I want to go out Sunday," Lisette said.

"Then it's settled," Courtney said.

Just then, I saw Kendra Hilferty walking outside. "Oh, look, it's Kendra," I said, then regretted it.

Midori made a disgusted noise. "Oh, I hope she doesn't come in here."

"She's a friend of yours?" Lisette said.

I shook my head. "Not really. She just sits next to me in language arts. And chorus."

Courtney made a face. "Poor you. She's weird."

"And what's with the outfits?" Midori pointed, obvious enough that Kendra could see. "Look what she's wearing now. Halloween isn't for two weeks, dear."

"Weirdo," Courtney agreed. "That hair!"

Suddenly Courtney's latte dumped over. The weird thing was, it actually seemed to jump up, then down, without anyone touching it. "Oh!" She looked at me, but since I was nowhere near it, she turned to Tayloe. "Spaz."

"I didn't touch it." But she went to get napkins.

I looked out the window. Kendra was gone.

When I got home, I went to tell Mother she was driving us to Adventura Saturday. I expected her to swallow her tongue with joy. Instead, she said, "You're going with Courtney?"

"I guess she really likes Lisette."

"I suppose that's to be expected, with all those expensive clothes your father bought her."

"I have expensive clothes," I pointed out. "They don't seem to help."

"You have greater depth, Emma. Not everyone can appreciate quality. Sometimes intelligence is off-putting."

It was close to a compliment. But then she added, "And, of course, Lisette takes care of her hair and skin."

I was sorry I'd brought it up. "Lisette's nice," I said.

"I'm sure she is. She's happy, getting everything she wants."

This didn't seem totally fair, considering Lisette's mother had just died. Still, I decided to drop it. I knew I'd never change her mind. "I have homework."

"If you want, I could get you one of those Brazilian keratin treatments," she said.

"Yeah, Mom, that's exactly what I want." I left the room.

I didn't remember to check my jewelry box for the earrings until just before dinner. Of course they were there. I put them on, planning on showing Daddy the coincidence that we both had them. But when Lisette came to dinner, she wasn't wearing them anymore.

After dinner, Monday through Thursday, Dad and I had a tradition. No matter how much homework I had, we always stopped to watch

Jeopardy at seven-thirty. But when I went to sit down that night, Lisette was on one side of Daddy, the end table on the other.

"Oh." I stopped.

"Plenty of room for everyone." Daddy pointed at the loveseat. At least I was pretty sure I'd be smarter at the game than Lisette. I usually knew answers even Daddy didn't get. I sat up straight, ready to show off.

The first question was about birds. "This is the largest living species of bird."

Knew it.

"What is an ostrich?" Lisette shouted before I got the chance.

"This bird is the only one that can fly backwards."

"Hummingbird!" Lisette screamed before I could. I resisted the urge to complain that she hadn't phrased it as a question.

Lisette also knew the name for a group of ravens (a murder) and which bird turned its head upside down to eat (the flamingo). I was abnormally stupid about the other categories too. When they broke for commercials, I sat there, not having opened my mouth once. Daddy said, "You sure know a lot about birds."

Lisette tilted her head to one side. "Oh, well, Mom was really into ornithology."

"That's right," Daddy said, like he'd just remembered. "We used to go bird-watching when you were a baby."

Lisette nodded. "I know. Mom used to take me to this place where they'd dress you up as a scarecrow, and the birds would land right on you."

"You remember that?" Daddy said. In the background, there was this stupid car insurance commercial with an animated pig. Lisette stared at Daddy.

"Yeah," she said. "Did you go there?"

"I was the one who took you there first. You were so little. It was right before . . ." He stopped. "Those were good times."

"Oh my God." Lisette shook her head like she was trying to conjure up the memory. "I can't believe you were there. I really remember you now. I can see you. You had on a blue polo, and it had a bird on it too. Right? Did you have a shirt like that?"

I knew he did. It was his college shirt. I wondered if he'd been wearing it in one of the photos with his face cut out. The TV had switched to a commercial about a bear using toilet paper.

"The University of Kansas jayhawk," Dad said. "How'd you remember that?"

"I didn't know I did. I thought I'd forgotten everything."

"Oh, look," I said. "It's starting again."

Mercifully, they stopped talking about their wonderful past together. On TV, Alex asked the next question, the thousand-dollar question in the bird category.

"This bird destroys eggs in other nests and replaces them with her own."

"What is the cuckoo?" Lisette and Daddy both said at the same moment.

"You know, I have a lot of homework," I said, and excused myself. Neither of them protested, even though I always watched *Jeopardy* with Daddy, no matter what. I didn't like it. But I didn't like what I was feeling either. I knew I shouldn't feel competitive with Lisette. It sounded petty, like something Mother would do, and Lisette had been so nice. Yet, I kept thinking that Mother was right. Lisette was my father's real daughter, and I wasn't. What if he loved her better, and I lost the one person who'd liked me just as I was?

7

All that week, I walked to school with Lisette, ate lunch with Lisette, walked home with Lisette. Being Lisette's sister was like being in a spotlight, the center of attention. That was something I'd never wanted, but now that I was there, I found out something about spotlights. They're really warm. For the last two years, I'd been telling myself I was a loner, happy to hang out at the library with the March girls or Harry and Hermione as friends. I'd lied to myself. With Lisette, I was suddenly part of the real world. Like, one day at lunch, the school turned on the Electric Slide over the P.A. system, and everyone got up and danced around. Normally, I'd have buried my nose in the latest dystopian novel and reflected upon the evil of all human beings, everywhere. But that day, I'd forgotten to bring a book to school at all (First. Time. Ever.).

When everyone started dancing, Lisette tugged on my arm. "Come on!"

I tried to wave her off. "I can't dance."

"It's the Electric Slide. Little kids do it. It's so lame it's cool."

"Really, I can't. Little kids ridicule me when I dance."

Courtney and Midori were tugging Lisette's arms, and I figured she'd go then. Instead, she said, "You know, Emma, sometimes you need to get out from under yourself."

With that, she grabbed my arm and whisked me into the sliding, writhing, boogie-woogie-ing mob of teendom, then kept holding my hand, whispering the steps in my ear.

Finally, it all clicked into place, and I had it. Me!

That's when Lisette moved away, and I found myself dancing beside a boy. And not just any boy—Warner Glassman!

I moved left, with everyone else.

Warner moved right and crashed into me.

"I'm sorry!" I said.

"My glasses! I lost my glasses!"

Just as he said it, I felt my foot come down on something.

Oh, no!

I was on the floor, surrounded by sliding legs, trying not to get stepped on. Warner was with me. I reached, groped for the glasses, praying I hadn't shattered them. I handed them to him.

"I'm so sorry," I said.

He took them and pushed them onto his nose, which was long, longer than it should be, but still cute.

"They're fine." He looked at me through them. "I can't believe I tried dancing again. I'm such a geek. I attempted to learn for my bar mitzvah last year, and I couldn't."

I shrugged. "You know, I couldn't either, but a friend of mine said, 'Sometimes, you need to get out from under yourself.'" I reached for his hand, like Lisette had with mine. "Let me help you."

Then we were dancing along with the others, and Warner was actually following me.

Too soon, the music ended, and it was time to go to class. I figured that was the end of that, but as he turned away, he said, "Hey, I'm Warner, by the way."

"Emma."

"Nice dancing with you, Emma." A long pause. "Uh . . . maybe . . ."

"Maybe?"

He looked down. "Maybe I'll see you around."

I walked to class, Lisette teasing me about having a boyfriend. For the first time, it seemed sort of possible.

Every day that week, Lisette and I sat in my room and did homework. I read through her essays and short stories, correcting her spelling and grammar. She said she'd help me with math sometimes, but so far, she hadn't. Thursday night, Dad looked in on us. "It's been so quiet in here, I thought something was wrong. It's so nice, you girls getting along."

"Of course we get along," Lisette said. "We're sisters. I was just helping Emma with her math."

She hadn't been, but I let it slide.

"I'm having so much trouble learning the music in here," Lisette said the next day after chorus.

"You know, I have it on my iPod. Maybe you could listen to it."

"Really? That would be so cool. You're so sweet."

"Of course you can borrow it." You just couldn't *not* be nice to Lisette.

That afternoon, Thursday, I had to study for a German test, so Lisette and I didn't do homework together. But when I finished, I went to my nightstand drawer to get her my iPod. It wasn't there.

I went down to her room. She was sitting on the bed, texting.

"Hey, you didn't take my iPod to listen to that song, did you?"

Lisette adjusted her position on the pillows. "Of course not."

"I just, you know, couldn't find it." Now I felt like I needed to explain that I wasn't accusing her of stealing or anything. I just wanted to let her know why I didn't have the iPod, even though I promised it to her. That was all. "So I thought maybe, since I said you could borrow it, you might just have taken it. I mean, gotten it."

She looked up now, staring at me with her cool blue eyes. "I said no."

I nodded. "Okay, I guess I must have left it lying around somewhere." I looked down, but I could still feel her staring at me. I wanted to change the subject, make everything okay. "So, do you want to do the algebra assignment?"

"Finished it."

"Language arts?"

"Finished that too."

Language arts had been twenty-seven sentences with the vocabulary words. No way could she have finished all of them. Not without time traveling.

"Look, I'm busy," she said.

"You're texting."

"I'm texting my friends from home."

I nodded, still not wanting to leave. Why had she turned on me so quickly? "So, we'll do it later?"

"I already told you I was finished."

Finally, I had to leave.

Back in my room, I went through every drawer, every closet, rummaged under the bed. The iPod was nowhere to be found.

8

Friday night, I went to the mall with "the girls," and Saturday to a different mall. Saturday night, they all came over to watch movies, while Mother hovered over us, offering popcorn and fresh-squeezed lemonade.

It was fun being part of the group, but I could barely understand a word they said. I hoped Mother couldn't understand at all.

"Wagwan, Midori," Courtney said, looking at her phone. "I see you friended Jacy Davis. She's a total skank."

"I did it for the lulz," Midori said. "Did you see the stuff she posts? Last week, she took selfies of her getting blazed at Crispin's party."

"I know!" Courtney said. "And she's literally hooked up with a thousand guys."

Mother, who had been handing out Rice Krispies squares, now tried to look invisible. She'd seen every episode of Dr. Phil and read

Dear Abby daily. Plus, she'd been forwarded a million cautionary emails by her friends, outlining the evils of posting photos on the internet, much less getting high. *Please don't let her say anything.* I tried to telepath to her: *Don't speak. After all, you want me to be friends with these girls.*

She must have heard me, because she kept her mouth shut.

The weird thing was, after two solid days with Courtney and Company, I was starting to . . . I don't know, long to go upstairs and read a book. Yes, I'd been friends with Courtney in the past, but now I realized we'd grown apart. We were nothing alike. In fact, she was kind of annoying. It was Lisette I wanted to be with now. I admitted to myself that I'd had this fantasy that she wouldn't need any friends besides me. Then we'd read by the fireplace while toasting s'mores every Saturday night until it was time to be college roommates, then marry identical twins. Okay, probably not.

So when Midori said, "We should make this a sleepover party," I said, "Oh, no."

"No?" Midori obviously wasn't used to the word.

I looked at Lisette. "We have plans tomorrow morning, early. Right, Lisette?"

"Oh, yeah. Yeah, right?"

"Remember? Dad's boat? We told him we'd go." Dad had already turned in, but Lisette had said she was up for it.

"Oh, yeah." She nodded. "Some other time then."

They left a little while later. Before I went to bed, I asked Lisette, "What time are we going?"

"Oh, I told Dad since we were going to be up late, maybe nine."

It was after one, but I said, "Great. I'll set my alarm for eight."

The next morning, my alarm didn't ring. When I woke up at eight-thirty, Lisette was already gone. I didn't have to ask to know where she was—out with Daddy on his sailboat.

Why? Had she misunderstood that I'd wanted to go? Or had Daddy not wanted me? It must have been some kind of misunderstanding. They couldn't have just ditched me.

I tried to tell myself I hadn't really wanted to go. It was true. I'd much rather spend the day at home with a good book than fighting sails and frying my skin. I just didn't want Lisette to go, didn't want to be left out.

But that was selfish, right? I'd had Dad my whole life. Lisette was just getting to know him.

When Mother came down an hour later, I was eating a muffin and reading. She said, "I thought you were going with them."

I shrugged. "I don't really like sailing." It wasn't a lie.

"You should have gone. Don't let her worm her way into your spot."

"She's not doing that." I turned a page of my book, even though I wasn't finished with it.

"Emma, pay attention. That's just what she's doing. She's a pretty girl, and she knows how to get what she wants, whether it's clothes or your father."

"That's not fair." She made me sound so pathetic, so helpless, like there was no way my father could possibly care about me, as a person.

"Watch out for her, Emma."

I looked at the book, but said, "You make it sound like she's some evil viper or something."

"I don't know how she was raised."

"You're the one who stole Dad from her mother, not the other way around."

As soon as I said it, I regretted it. What was I thinking? Me, who'd rather get kicked a hundred times than tell someone to take their foot off my chair, who ate PB&J every day for three years rather than tell my mother I didn't like it. I was making soap opera revelations now? Mom stood frozen, and I tried to shove the words back. "Look, I'm sorry."

"Clearly, that's what you think of me."

"It's not."

She turned to leave. "Clear the dishes when you've finished."

I knew I should go after her, say I hadn't meant it, that I wouldn't go over to the dark side with Lisette. But I had meant it. Mother was the villain in the story. Lisette was the victim. I'd never thought about it before, never had to. Now I had, and once thought about, I couldn't unthink it. Unless I was in a car accident and got brain damage, which might be easier than thinking all the time, but which would come with its own set of problems.

Yet part of me knew that Lisette had ditched me on purpose. Mother was right. I just didn't want to admit it, to Mother or myself.

I sat in my room all day, reading and avoiding Mother. Lisette came home with Daddy, blue eyes shining through the sunburn I knew would turn to tan, and knocked on my door.

"I tried to wake you up this morning," she said before I asked. "But you just yelled at me to go away."

"Really? I don't remember that. I thought I set my alarm."

"Huh. It's so weird when that kind of thing happens. One time, my mom went to let our cat out in the middle of the night and got locked out. She pounded on the door until I let her in, she said, but the next morning, I didn't remember it. Even though I got up and everything."

"That's weird."

"Anyway, maybe that's what happened."

I nodded. "Probably." It sounded possible. I had been up really late. I usually went to bed around ten-thirty.

"Anyway, we missed you."

I wanted to change the subject, so I asked her if she wanted to listen to this song I liked (my iPod had miraculously reappeared under my bed, even though I'd looked there five times). She did. When Mother called us to dinner, I had Lisette tell her I wasn't feeling well. I couldn't face her.

I wasn't surprised when there was a knock on my door, an hour later. I unlocked it, dreading seeing Mom. I started back toward my bed and my copy of *Sense and Sensibility*, which I was rereading for the fifth time.

"Feeling better?"

I turned, startled to hear Dad's voice. "What?" Had he come to talk about my argument with Mother? Of course not. She'd never tell him what I'd said. "Oh, yeah. Better." I picked up my book, which I'd dropped.

"Good book?"

"Sure." He didn't care. He wasn't a big reader, except the newspaper. It was just one of those things parents do, asking you a question, just so you'll have to talk.

"Haven't seen much of you lately," he said.

Maybe if you hadn't ditched me this morning. But I didn't say it. I was back to being the quiet one, the nonconfrontational one. I'd had my outburst for the decade. I said, "I want to go sailing next time."

He nodded and didn't say anything about Lisette trying to wake me. I wondered if it was true. Instead, he said, "How've you and Lizzie been getting along?"

"Lizzie?" The question surprised me. Dad wasn't usually the one who looked for trouble when there was none apparent. He left that to my mother. "Great. Fine. She's super-nice."

"Would you tell me if there was a problem?"

No. "Of course. But there isn't one." My book closed, losing my place. Did he think there was a problem? Like, did he suspect Lisette had blown me off on purpose?

"Because Lizzie was telling me she's worried you're jealous of her."

"Jealous? Why would I be jealous?" *Just because she's skinny, blond, perfect, and my old friends love her even enough to deal with me?* "She's really nice."

"She said you accused her of stealing your earrings."

"What?" I started, and the book bounced off the bed. "No, I didn't. I didn't say that. That's not true. She just had the same earrings as me, the shell ones you bought on our trip, and I said . . ." I tried to remember what I said. Dad was nodding, the way adults do when they're pretending to believe you, but they really don't. "I just said we should wear them together sometimes, because we had the same ones. That's all."

He kept nodding.

"Don't you believe me?" I reached for the book on the floor, even though I knew I looked stupid, fumbling for it and wouldn't be able to find my page, mostly because I didn't want him to see my face, how red it was.

"Of course I believe you. Just remember, this is a hard time for Lisette. Her mother has passed away. She's in a new place, all new people. Just try to be friendly."

"I have been friendly. I've been nothing but nice to her, even when . . ."

"Even when what?"

"Nothing. I never said she stole my earrings."

"I'm sure you didn't."

"She must have misunderstood."

"That's probably it." He touched my head.

I chose a random place in the book and started reading. "I have homework."

"We okay?" he asked.

"Of course."

Finally, he left. I stared at the book until the letters moved and swirled to look like they were written in Russian or Arabic. Only after Dad left did it occur to me that he hadn't said the things parents usually say to their old kid when there's a new kid around, stuff like how they loved the old kid just as much, how they knew it was hard for the old kid—for *me*—to adjust.

No, Dad hadn't been concerned about my feelings at all. He'd only cared about Lisette.

Another thought occurred to me. I'd never thought Lisette had taken my earrings.

Now, I was positive she had.

I turned back to the beginning of the book and started reading.

Another hour passed, an hour in which the characters in the book stood stock-still, accomplishing nothing because I was too busy playing and replaying the conversation in my head. Unfair. So. Unfair. Someone says something about you, and just because they said it first—because you were trying to be *nice* and not complain, you're in the position of denying it. You have—as those lawyers on TV would say—the burden of proof. And, if the person who says it is perfect and sweet-looking and blond and—let's face it—Dad's *real* daughter, it's a pretty heavy burden.

My stomach growled, a long, skinny growl that spiraled from my belly to just below my heart, but I couldn't go downstairs and get something to eat, couldn't face Mother, now that I knew she was right. I knew I'd be up at midnight, making a sandwich. I wanted my mother, but I couldn't go.

Someone knocked on the door.

I glanced at the clock, considering whether I could ignore it, whether I could pretend to be asleep.

Eight-thirty. Probably no one would buy it.

Another knock. Then, a voice. "Emma?"

Lisette!

"Emma, let me in!"

I sighed and said, "It's open." I couldn't be rude to her, not now that she was all about reporting me to Dad.

"I brought you a sandwich." She held it out to me.

I looked. Ham and cheese on marble rye, mustard, not mayo,

tomato, but no lettuce, cut in triangles exactly the way I'd have made it myself. Was she spying on me?

I wanted to refuse it, but I was hungry.

"Thanks." I took it.

"Your mom wasn't too happy at dinner. Did you have an argument?"

She paused, like she was waiting for me to contribute something, to tell her what we'd argued about, which wasn't going to happen. I couldn't rat out Mother. I took a bite of sandwich and chewed it a really long time. Lisette said nothing, watching me eat. It reminded me of staring contests Courtney and I used to have when we were kids, to see who'd blink first.

I blinked. "Why'd you tell Dad I was jealous of you?"

She looked stunned. "He wasn't supposed to repeat that."

"He's a parent. That's what they do."

"I guess I'm not used to that."

"Besides, whether he was supposed to repeat it or not, you said it. I never said you took my earrings."

"It felt like you did."

"I just said I had the same ones, not that you stole them. You just said that to make me look bad in front of Dad."

The ceiling fan overhead repeated my words, *look bad, look bad, look bad.*

And that's when Lisette burst into tears.

Oh, she was good.

"I'm sorry." The word came out as a huge gasp, and she buried her head in her hands. "I'm so sorry, Emma."

I stared at her. Was I supposed to put my arms around her or something?

"I wanted you to like me," she sobbed.

"And you thought lying about me would help?"

"I wasn't . . . I just . . . I wanted us to be like best friends, like sisters. And when you said that, I just thought . . ." Her next words were lost in sobs that even made her toes shake.

"What?"

"My mother's dead, Emma. For years, she didn't go to the doctor, said we didn't have the money for it, and by the time she went . . . it was too late. She's dead. In a box in the ground. Do you know what that's like, Emma? Do you?"

In that instant, I pictured my own mother, lying cold and still, unreachable. My grandmother had died when I was nine. Mother and Dad had debated and debated whether I should go to the funeral and finally took me because my cousins would be there. But when I saw Memaw, her hair poufed up in a way it never had been, her skin unnaturally pink, I'd started screaming. For weeks after, I had nightmares about Memaw's ghostly face, jumping out at me like a horror movie. If I closed my eyes, I could still picture it, and the worst thing was, I couldn't remember how she'd looked alive.

I grabbed Lisette's hand. "God, Lisette, I'm so sorry."

"She's gone. I have nothing and no one except some father I've never seen before, a father who didn't want me."

I put my arms around her. "That's not true. Of course he wanted you."

But I knew she had it right. He'd ditched her, her and her mother. He hadn't even mentioned them all those years, like they didn't exist. If her mother hadn't died, he'd probably never have seen her. Poor Lisette!

"He didn't! He doesn't. He wanted you and your mother. And you . . . don't you see, Emma. You're all I have."

I held her as her body shook with sobs. "*I* am?"

"You're my sister, but I was worried you didn't want me here either."

"I do want you. I want to be your sister. I never thought you'd taken my earrings."

Instinctively, my hand wandered up to my ears, the earrings. I had them on. I pulled away to look at Lisette, hoping she had hers on too. It would prove, to both of us, that she hadn't taken them, that she was telling the truth.

But she had no earrings at all, which proved nothing.

I said, "We're sisters, Lisette. I . . . I love you."

9

The next day, in chorus, Kendra was sitting, listening to music, sort of dancing. When I sat down, she said, "Listen to this."

I took the earbuds, mostly to be polite. Immediately, a shrilling violin assaulted my ears, then a wild dance of horns and bells, bells and horns. I pulled the earpieces out. "What is that?" Usually, she was more into Sheryl Crow.

"*Symphonie Fantastique* by Berlioz." She said this casually, as if it was a perfectly normal thing for an eighth grader to be listening to at school.

"Nice." I glanced around, looking for Lisette. The violins danced like moshers in the space between the earbuds and my eardrum.

"It's very romantic," Kendra said.

"Sounds it." I laughed.

"Really, it was. Hector Berlioz, the composer, fell in love with this actress named Harriet Smithson when he saw her in a play. He sent her love notes, but she thought he sounded like a wack job. She wouldn't meet him. Also he didn't speak English, and she didn't speak French. But Hector became so obsessed with Harriet that he wrote this symphony for her."

I smiled. *Hector* and *Harriet*, like she knew them. Only Kendra.

"Harriet came to the concert," she continued, "and they finally met. Soon, they fell in love and were married."

"And did they invite you to the wedding?" I joked.

"No." Kendra shook her head, then said sadly, "No, I never got to meet him."

Ooookay. Kendra often did that, talking about historical figures as if they were real people. Last week, in American history, she told a long story about General Lafayette that even our teacher had never heard. It occurred to me that it would be fun to hang out with Kendra. She was interesting, and I could be myself around her. But I knew I couldn't be friends with her and Lisette's group too.

"It is really romantic." The violins hit a still-higher note, so high I pulled the earbuds away. "This music is sort of creepy, though."

"Oh, that's because this is the part where Hector dreamed he had murdered Harriet. Then he died, and a coven of witches was dancing on his grave."

Before I could think of an appropriate response, Miss Hakes said, "We're going to start auditions for the solo in *Laudate Dominum*." She kept talking. I couldn't really concentrate. I slipped Kendra's iPod back to her.

"You're trying out?" she whispered.

"I guess so."

"You'll definitely get it."

We started warm-ups. I hadn't eaten lunch, so as not to mess up my throat. I felt a little light-headed now, but I was going to get this.

I'd been in choir since fourth grade and never had a solo. But now I was a big-deal eighth grader. Also, I'd been practicing constantly. Saturday, Lisette had walked into my room and commented how great I sounded. I checked out the competition. Two girls trying out were seventh graders, and Celia Ramirez, who went off-pitch on high notes. I had it.

When it was time for tryouts, Miss Hakes chose one of the seventh graders first. She had a nice voice. I could afford to be charitable because I knew Miss Hakes wouldn't give such a big solo to a seventh grader. She believed in paying your dues.

When it was my turn, I stepped up and tried not to look at any individual faces. A few girls reached into their purses, texting. Good. If they weren't paying attention, they weren't waiting for me to mess up. I met Lisette's eyes. She smiled and nodded like a good sister. The music started. I took three deep breaths, then began.

Laudate Dominum omnes gentes
Laudate eum omnes populi

I did everything right. I remembered to breathe. I remembered to over pronounce my consonants, like Miss Hakes had said, and when I hit the high note on "*manet*" (which Miss Hakes said meant "endures"), I noticed even some of the texters looked up and nodded. I remembered to crescendo and decrescendo at the conclusion.

And there was applause. Not just, I told myself, polite claps, but a little more, like they really did think I was good. I looked up at Lisette, but she stared at her hands. Kendra, however, gave me a thumbs-up, and when I sat, she said, "You go, girl."

"Anyone else?" Miss Hakes said.

I knew there was no one. There had been four hands. We'd all gone, and I was the best. I got a giddy, smiley feeling all the way up from the pit of my stomach, like I got when I knew I aced a test. I had done it. I was going to get this.

"Oh, okay, one more," Miss Hakes was saying.

I followed Miss Hakes's eyes to the seat behind me, where Lisette was standing.

Lisette? She'd been here, like, a week. She couldn't even *know* the solo!

Except from listening to it on *my* iPod, I realized, and hearing me practice.

Relax. She probably can't sing.

Who was I kidding? She was perfect at everything, even ornithology.

Now, she stood in front of the room, calm and serene, as I hadn't been. The music started. Then, her voice.

After I'd finished, I'd been sure I'd sung as well as any eighth-grade girl could.

Lisette sang as well as those people on TV who are supposed to be teenagers but are really twenty-five-year-old Broadway stars. The song was a prayer, and Lisette's voice floated to the heavens. If she breathed, I couldn't hear it. If she thought about what she was doing, it didn't show. Her expression was angelic, and when she finished, no one applauded. They were too mesmerized.

Then the room erupted with clapping.

"That was . . . ," Miss Hakes stammered. "That was incredible."

"I totally understand if you don't want to give it to someone new," Lisette was saying. "It's only fair for people to pay their dues. I had solos at my old school, so I know how it is."

But Lisette and I and everyone else knew she was going to get that solo. I knew it, and I hated her, hated her for having more talent, for being more beautiful, and mostly, for not staying in Lantana where she belonged. And I hated her for making me hate her too.

As Lisette returned to her seat, she grabbed my hand. "I hope you get it," she whispered.

I squeezed her hand back, hard.

* * *

So, of course, the next day Miss Hakes announced that Lisette had the solo. I was the understudy.

Everyone clapped when Miss Hakes announced it, except Kendra, who said, "Man, that stinks. I thought you had it."

I shrugged. "Lisette's just better." I knew it was true. I glanced back. Lisette wasn't even smiling. In fact, her blue eyes glistened with tears. What was up with that?

After class, I tried to avoid her, but she ran after me. "Emma, wait!"

I stopped. Couldn't she just let me go? "What?"

"Nothing just . . . we usually walk to class together."

Was she so clueless she had no idea I was upset with her? "Sure." I adjusted my backpack. "Congratulations on the solo."

"Oh, thanks. I wish we could both have gotten it."

"No big deal. The better singer won."

"That's sweet of you." We were almost out the door of our class when she put her hand on my shoulder to stop me. "I had a solo in chorus at my old school, but my mom couldn't come to the concert. She was doing chemo then, and she was always sick and throwing up, but she told me to go anyway."

Her voice broke, and her eyes were tearing up again. This must have been what she was thinking of in class.

"Emma," she said, "do you believe that people who are . . . gone can look down on us? Like, do you think my mom's watching me now?"

I didn't know what to say. Finally, I nodded. I felt terrible for wanting the solo now.

"I hope so." She was crying harder. "The first thing I wanted to do, when I got the solo, was text my mom and tell her about it. I do that, sometimes, text her old number. Do you think they have cell phones in heaven?"

Oh, God. People were trying to shove past us all around, looking at us like we were nuts, but I put my arms around Lisette. "It's okay. I'm sure she knows about it."

Which only made her cry harder.

"And you're not mad at me, are you, for getting the solo you wanted?"

"Of course not." I patted her hair. "How could I be mad at you? We're sisters."

10

In school, Lisette was really fitting in. It amazed me that I'd been here for three years and yet I didn't know as many people as Lisette had met in a week. I could say people gravitated to her because she was so pretty. It was more than that, though. Lisette really tried to get to know everyone. If someone was cynical (and I wasn't, despite having been raised by my mother), they could say she went in like someone in an online role-playing game where the object is world domination. First, she went for the easy targets, the adoring sixth graders, elves in her army. Maybe I was one of them. They were always offering her gum or an extra pencil or just staring. Next were the boys, her unicorns and cyclopses. They were all in love with her, and when Lisette mentioned in language arts class Tuesday that she was planning on attending the Key Club meeting at lunch that day, the club had such an unexpected swell in membership that they'd had to move to the auditorium.

Finally, she won over the dragons and gorgons, the eighth-grade popular girls, the ones who'd see her as competition. If she wasn't French-braiding Jacqueline Ortiz's hair before school, she was teaching Jordyn Pryor how to make friendship bracelets after. She always complimented people's new outfits. Everyone adored her, but I was the only one who was her sister.

The cool thing about Lisette's popularity was, it made me fit in too. I liked it. Like, I was going to the school's annual hoedown. I'd never gone before, mostly because I'd had no one to go with.

It was almost Halloween, and fall was in the air. Well, as much as it could be, considering we were in Miami, and it was eighty degrees out. Still, the scent of Bath and Body Works' caramel apple room spray filled the bathrooms at school, and on the morning announcements, they talked about the hoedown, which had games, hayrides, a pumpkin patch, and even a way to throw your friends in jail.

"Should we wear costumes?" I asked Lisette when she finished high-fiving a girl who'd gotten an A on a math quiz. "Like Western wear? I could get my mom to take us to Party City."

Lisette shook her head. "Tayloe says only little kids do that. Just wear something cute, like the sundress we bought last week."

But the next day, when I went out to Tayloe's mom's car, she, Courtney, and Midori were all wearing matching denim minis, plaid skirts, and boots. "Lisette will be out in a sec."

"Oh, whoops!" Tayloe said. "Didn't you get the memo?"

I stared at her. "Memo?"

"It's an expression, Emma. There wasn't an actual memo." This was Courtney, talking real slow, like I was stupid. Maybe I was. "But we discussed it at dance yesterday, that we'd all wear minis and boots."

I nodded. Lisette had tried to talk me into signing up for hip-hop class with them, but I'd taken a year of dance when I was little, and at the end of that year, Miss Janie had explained to Mother that I might want to find another outlet for my talents. "Everyone is good at something. With Emma, it just isn't dance," she'd said.

Now, I looked at Courtney. "But Lisette told me you weren't . . ." I stopped. Lisette was finally ready, and as she stepped out the door, I took in her outfit. Denim skirt, True Religion. Plaid skirt and boots, exactly like the others. "You told me no costumes," I said.

"Oh, we changed our minds later and decided to wear denim after all." She climbed across me to the seat behind. "I told you."

"You didn't."

"Sure I did. Last night. Maybe you had your earbuds in and didn't hear me."

I shrugged. "I'll just go change then."

Tayloe's mom tapped on her watch. "Honey, I have to drive Linc to his game. I really can't wait anymore."

"It's okay," Tayloe said. "I'm sure a lot of people won't have Western stuff on."

I sat back down. What else could I do?

Of course, when we got there, every single person had on a Western costume, from the parent volunteers, in designer boots and jewelry from trips out West, to little kids in cowgirl outfits and sheriffs' badges. I was the only one there not at least wearing jeans.

I thought about calling Mother, asking her to bring me something. I considered what girls like Courtney or Lisette would do in this situation. They'd act like it didn't matter. Or like it was intentional and they wanted to stand out.

So that's what I did. I started toward the games.

I saw Kendra, who was wearing a cowgirl outfit that looked about a hundred years old, with a leather skirt, fringe, and even a holster, though that was empty, and a huge ten-gallon hat.

"Hey, you look just like Annie Oakley," I said.

"That's what I was going for. Did you know she started shooting when she was six?" She scowled. "But they made me check my pistols at the door. You can get in trouble for bringing even a water pistol to school." She pointed at the empty holsters.

"Crazy, right?" I said.

"Emma, are you coming?" Courtney said.

"You're with them?" Kendra asked.

"Um, yeah. They're friends of my sister's."

Kendra nodded.

"Come on, Emma," Courtney called.

"See you. I really love the outfit."

I went to join the others, walking toward the games. They were little kids' games, like a fishing game where you caught cowboy hats instead of fish.

"She is sooo weird," Courtney said when I joined them.

"Shh." I noticed Kendra was still behind us, though she'd paused to adjust her hat. "She'll hear you."

"So?" Courtney cast a glance backwards. "She's obviously begging for attention, so I'll give it to her."

I wanted to say that Kendra was always nice and they shouldn't just judge people by how they were dressed. I wanted to. But I was already dressed all wrong and, unlike Kendra, I didn't like drawing attention to myself. I nodded and shut up.

"Step right up!" the guy behind the baseball toss game said. "Get the ball in the horse's mouth and win a prize!"

I recognized his voice and, looking under his cowboy hat, his face. Warner. He had on a blue plaid shirt that matched his eyes, and he looked cute. "Wanna try, li'l missy?" He tipped his hat. Our eyes met, and he smiled. "Hey, it's Dancing Emma. You going to play?"

"Oh, I'm not good at sports." Dad had tried for years to teach me to throw, and my balls always ended up yards short of the target.

"I'll try." Courtney handed Warner her ticket and stepped back, backing right into Kendra. "Do you mind, freak?"

Kendra's eyes widened, and I could have sworn I actually saw them flash green, like a cat in headlights. "I'll give you all the space you want. It won't help."

"Good." Courtney held out her hand to accept a softball. "Watch an expert, people!"

I knew she was, in fact, an expert. Courtney had played softball for years, until she decided it was tomboyish and that she preferred shopping. When she threw the first ball, the old Courtney coordination came right back. It soared toward the target, then suddenly swerved wide left, almost hitting Warner. He leaped out of the way.

"Whoa, pardner. That's quite a curveball."

"Fail!" Kendra yelled.

"Sorry." Courtney glared at Kendra. "My hand slipped."

But the second ball did exactly the same thing. Warner ducked. "Last one," he said. "I hope."

"Ha, ha, you're sooo funny. I wasn't concentrating. Now, everyone quiet." Courtney looked back at Kendra again. "Do you have to stand there?"

"It's a free country. I'm waiting my turn."

"Fine. Just be quiet."

This time, Courtney took a long time positioning herself, then stared at the target. I could tell she was really mad about missing the first two. Courtney had never been a good loser. She whispered, "Eye on the ball. Follow through." Then, she let it go.

The ball soared through the air as if magnetized to its target. It would definitely go in. Then suddenly it looped upward, bounced off the back of the booth, and then directly into Courtney's nose.

"Oh!" She clutched it. Then she started screaming at Warner.

"How did you do that? This game's fixed."

Warner had been stepping forward, probably to see if she was okay. He backed off. "Are you kidding? It's a kids' game. Why would it be fixed?"

"I don't know. So the PTA won't have to give out lame-o prizes."

"I know how you could settle it," Kendra said. "If someone else threw, and they got it in, it would show it wasn't fixed."

"No one could." Courtney turned to me. "Can you stop gawking and get me some ice?"

"How about you, Emma?" Kendra said. "Why don't you try?"

"Oh, I can't throw." I wasn't particularly excited about displaying my extreme lack of coordination in front of Warner.

"It's not hard," Warner said. "You get three tries. Hey, I tried dancing."

"Yes, Emma," Courtney—who knew how bad I threw—agreed. "You should try. If you miss too, it will prove it's rigged."

I knew my missing would prove nothing, but I shrugged. "Sure." I stepped up to the game and accepted three softballs. Mr. Hunter, the assistant principal, moseyed by in a sheriff's costume. He had a packet of "warrants" people could purchase for a dollar, to put their friends in jail. He tipped his hat.

"Just throw it lightly." Warner stepped around the table so he was standing beside me. He took my arm and demonstrated. His grip was firm, and his hands were warm. His chest pressed against mine as he swung my arm, and I could feel his heartbeat. "Good. That's the secret."

"No coaching," Courtney said.

"Courtney, years of lessons couldn't help me." I lined up behind the counter and aimed. I wasn't even really trying, but to my surprise, the ball flew right into the hole.

"Very good!" Warner patted my shoulder.

Behind Courtney, Tayloe was clapping. Courtney glared at her, and she stopped. "Lucky shot!" She held her nose. "Try again."

I threw the ball, this time without aiming or anything. Again, it went right in.

"Two for two," Warner said. "You should try out for softball. One more and you win the big prize."

I knew that was the kiss of death. Any time I expected to win, I messed up. So I threw the third ball, expecting an epic fail.

It went in.

"Look at you, Emma!" Warner crowed. "Do you want the teddy bear or the Snoopy?"

"Um . . ." I couldn't believe it. "I guess Snoopy. It's Halloween, right? Great Pumpkin and all."

Warner pulled one from a box under the table. "Here you go, Emma."

I loved the way he said my name. God, that was so hokey. I took the dog from him. He held on to it an instant longer than necessary, and our fingers touched.

"Come on." Courtney yanked my arm so hard I almost dropped Snoopy.

"One sec," I told her. I held up Snoopy to Warner. "Thanks. It's so cute."

He smiled. I noticed when he smiled, he had a dimple on the right side but not the left, and it had freckles in it. "Well deserved. Hey, listen, I told my mom I'd work until eight, but after that, um . . ." He looked down at the box of Snoopys.

"Emma!" Courtney said.

"Would you, um, would you want to go on the hayride with me?"

I hugged Snoopy tight. "Really? I mean, yeah, I'd love . . . like that."

I looked around to see if Courtney was mad, but all four of them had disappeared. Only Kendra stood behind me still, grinning.

"Great." Warner looked at Kendra, like he'd just realized she was there. "So meet me here at eight?"

I nodded. I knew I should go find Lisette and the others, but part of me just wanted to stay there with Warner and Kendra. It was less stressful, hanging with the nerds because I was one too.

Then, Tayloe came back. "Are you coming, Emma?"

"I guess I should go," I told Warner.

I tried to keep myself from skipping. Midori, Lisette, and Courtney were all at the fishing game. When I got there, Courtney pointed at Snoopy. "You should give him to me. After all, I'm the one who got injured."

I hugged Snoopy closer. I knew I should probably give him to her, just to shut her up, but I didn't want to. It was like Warner had given it to me. I remembered how it had been, back when we'd been friends, how Courtney had always called the shots. I looked at Lisette for help.

"You should give it to her," Lisette agreed.

"Maybe I can win you another one," I said.

"Let's not pretend that was anything but beginner's luck," Courtney said. "I know you can't throw. I literally tried to teach you a thousand times. Besides, I'm not going back to that geek."

"Did you see his neck?" Lisette said. "He looks like one of those pencils, the kind with a head for an eraser."

"Yes!" Courtney shrieked. She looked at me, still hugging Snoopy. "Oh, forget it. It's a dumb prize anyway. What do you guys want to do?"

"I told my mom I'd buy a pumpkin," Tayloe said.

"Great idea." I was glad to change the subject. I turned to Lisette. "Dad and I always carve one together. We could buy one and bring it home. Last year, I even bought this special book with jack-o'-lantern designs that cast a shadow on the wall in back of it."

"I've seen those," Tayloe said. "They're cool. Let's go."

We headed toward the pumpkin patch. I snuck a glance back at Warner over the top of Snoopy's head. He was watching me. I smiled and glanced at my watch. Half an hour until our date. Was that what it was? I felt energy surge through my body. Okay, so he was a little geeky, but in a cute way, and I was geeky too.

The pumpkin patch was crowded with people our age, plus families with little kids running around. I remembered when I was younger, we'd come here to choose our pumpkins, Dad and I debating the merits of each one, tall and skinny versus short and round. I glanced back at Lisette. She was talking to Mr. Hunter, but then she ran over to me.

"Find anything?" she asked.

"Hmm." I pointed to one. "This one does have a good face." The design I had in mind was a tree, so I wanted a tall pumpkin.

"How about this one?" Lisette held up a short, fat one.

I pretended to examine it. "Bad stem."

"Stem?" Lisette said.

"Daddy says it has to have a good stem, to pick it up by. He's really picky about pumpkins."

"Oh." Lisette scowled and pointed to another round pumpkin. "How about this one?"

"Maybe. It will be so much fun to do this together."

"Hey, guys," Midori said. "Let's take a picture of us with the scarecrows."

"Good idea." Courtney gestured Lisette and me toward the display of scarecrows and hay bales. "Come on."

They all got out their cell phones. I didn't like having my picture taken, so I said, "I'll take it. You guys pose."

"No, Emma," Lisette said. "I'll have someone snap it. You pose with us. Put your purse down there."

Flattered that they wanted me so much, I joined them. I tried to stand behind Tayloe, to hide. Lisette recruited a seventh-grade boy and handed him our phones. We crowded into the display.

"Say pumpkin pie!" the boy said.

"Pumpkin pie!" we all chorused.

Just as he finished taking the picture with the fifth phone, mine, Mr. Hunter approached us. "Is one of you young things Emma Bailey?"

"Um, that's me."

He held out a sheet of paper. "Well, little lady, I'm afraid I've got a warrant for yer arrest."

"What?"

"Yep, we don't tolerate horse thievin' around here. I'll have to escort you to the hoosegow."

I looked at my friends to see who'd done it. Lisette.

"It's just hoedown jail, silly," Midori said.

"We'll bail you out, Emma," Lisette said. "Sometime."

I tried to laugh—this was fun, right?—and followed Sheriff Hunter. I checked my watch. Fifteen minutes still until my meeting with Warner. It would be fine. I waved to Lisette. "Send me a cake with a file in it!"

"None of that insubordination, ma'am," Mr. Hunter said.

When I got to the "jail," which was really the PE shelter, I noticed it was mostly the most popular kids who were there. I wondered who'd arrested me. The deal was, you paid a dollar to arrest someone, then someone had to pay another dollar to bail them out. The money went to the Eighth-Grade Dance Committee.

"What are you in for?" a girl I'd seen around but didn't know asked.

"I'm not sure."

"It's on your warrant." She pointed to the paper Mr. Hunter had given me.

"Oh." I checked. "Horse thievery. How about you?"

"Impersonating a sheriff. I had on one of those little badges. My boyfriend's bailing me out. He's the one who got me arrested in the first place."

I wondered if maybe Warner had had me arrested. But, if he had, he wouldn't be here until after eight, when his shift ended. I checked my watch again. Seven fifty-five. Maybe I should call and tell him where I was.

Except, duh, I didn't have his number.

I decided to call Lisette, to see if she'd bail me out.

I reached for my purse. That's when I realized I didn't have my purse or my phone. I'd put them down for pictures. All I had was Snoopy. I hugged him.

If I'd had my purse, I could have paid a dollar and bailed myself out. As it was, I had to wait for Courtney or Lisette and hope they hadn't gotten distracted by cute guys.

Where were they?

Eight o'clock came and went. Eight-oh-five. Everyone else was getting bailed out. Would Warner think I was purposely blowing him off? Of course he would. I approached the high school guy who was in charge of the jail. "Can I go?"

"You got the bail money?"

"No. I left my purse. But my friends aren't coming, and I've been here a long time."

He shrugged. "I don't know. I'm just volunteering 'cause my mom's on the PTA. Hey, Mom!" he yelled to a woman in a gold vest. "Can she leave if no one's bailed her out?"

"It's for the PTA, honey," the woman said to me.

That's when I lost it. "Is this even legal? Can they hold me when I've done nothing wrong? I've been here . . ." I checked my watch. ". . . twenty-five minutes. I'm missing the whole hoedown. This is extortion!" I remembered the word from one of Dad's cases. "Or false imprisonment!"

"It's all for fun, honey," the mom said. "Can't you take a joke?"

"No! I'm not having fun." I was crying now. "I was supposed to meet someone, and . . . forget it. I'm leaving. You can't stop me." I shoved past the boy.

"You can't do that."

"Watch me." I yelled to the kids behind me. "Who's up for a jail break?"

No one followed. Actually, they were all staring like I was nuts. Maybe I was.

That's when Lisette showed up. She held my purse on one arm, a short, fat pumpkin in the other. "Oh, Emma, there you are. Sorry we took so long. We had to pay for the pumpkins."

"Pay for the pumpkins?" I shrieked. "And you just ditched me here?" I grabbed my purse and ran out, toward the game area.

But when I got there, of course, Warner was gone. I approached the woman at the game, hoping it was his mother, that she'd know where he was, but she said, "He left a while ago."

I had to find him. I walked over to where the hay wagon was giving rides, but he wasn't there either. It was close to eight-thirty now.

I looked around for the next half hour. No luck. He must have gone home.

"Hey, you okay?"

I turned around. Kendra. "Fine." I hoped we wouldn't talk that long.

"Ditch the mean girls?"

I laughed. "Lisette's not mean."

She raised an eyebrow. "Really?"

"She's my stepsister."

"And that's why she tried out for your solo, to be all sisterly?"

Um, yeah. She'd noticed that. Kendra, I was starting to realize, noticed everything.

"It's hard for her," I said. "Her mother died."

Kendra nodded and looked away a second. Then, a second longer. I tried to figure out what she was staring at, but there was nothing there except a blond little boy in a red and brown cowboy outfit. "Kendra?"

"Sorry. I was thinking. It's hard when you lose someone. I've had it happen. It changes your world, everything, but it doesn't change who you are. People who are heroes are still heroes. They may get more heroic. People who are the opposite—well, watch out."

"That's what my mother says."

"Mothers can be right about things."

"Emma!" Lisette was running toward me like I was some long-lost relative. "There you are. Come on! We're going on the hayride."

"Great." I turned to Kendra. "I have to go."

"Think about what I said."

I followed Lisette. I was hoping maybe, by some miracle, Warner would be on the hayride. He wasn't.

When I got home, I put away the jewelry I was wearing and checked the box for my aquamarine earrings.

Of course, they were gone.

11

Monday morning, I searched for Warner in the hall. I didn't see him. But why would I? We had no classes together. I saw him rarely. Still, I took different routes, long, circuitous ones to each class, searching for him. I planned on telling Lisette I was going to my locker, that that was why I couldn't walk with her, but she didn't ask. In fact, she hung back in each class, checking homework assignments or searching for her purse, so I didn't have to explain.

I never found Warner.

He couldn't think I'd blown him off, though. I mean, I wasn't the type of person who blew people off.

Unless, of course, he'd seen me with Midori and Courtney and thought I was a snob by association.

At lunch, I looked for Lisette in our usual spot. She wasn't there. Neither were Courtney, Midori, or Tayloe. What was with this day?

I sat down. The table vibrated with the thrum of hundreds of feet.

A moment later, through it all, I heard a giggle nearby. I turned. It was Lisette.

The smell of watery cafeteria taco meat met my nose, making me feel like I was about to puke. Since Lisette's arrival at school, the table for four, the table Courtney and her friends had commandeered for the past two years of middle school, had sat empty. Even though they weren't sitting there, apparently no one else had dared. I'd imagined it being handed down in some special ceremony at the end of the school year. Possibly, there'd be a plaque or something, the way parents commemorated their athletic children on the tile wall outside the school. But, so far, it had been empty.

Until today. Now, Courtney, Lisette, and Midori moved back to the table. They sat down. One empty seat remained, and I started to walk over.

Just then, Tayloe walked through the door. Midori started yelling, "Tay-tay!" really loudly and pointing at the chair.

All living creatures are born with an instinct for self-preservation. It is this instinct that inspires small animals to burrow, butterflies to masquerade as dead leaves, or birds to take flight at the snap of a branch. It inspires us to flee what is dangerous.

I didn't follow that instinct. Heart racing, I walked to their table, reaching it just before Tayloe did. "Hey, guys." I slid my books onto the empty spot.

"That's Tayloe's seat." It was Lisette.

Tayloe had reached the table now. She saw the situation, took a step back. "Hi."

"Sit here, Tayloe," Courtney said. "We saved it just for you."

Tayloe gestured toward me. "Maybe we could . . ."

"No!" Midori snapped. "It's your chair. We're all in agreement, right?" She glanced at Lisette.

Lisette nodded. "Absolutely."

Courtney smirked. "Sorry, Em. No room."

God, it was sixth grade all over again. I said, "Fine. Whatever," and turned away. I scanned the room. The girls from fourth period, the ones I'd sat with before Lisette came, were clear on the other side of the cafeteria. No way was I making it that far. I stumbled back to the seat I'd had before and sat. Kendra was on the other side. She didn't say hi or anything, nor did I. I choked down my lunch in silence, then lay my head down on the table, the way we used to do in first grade, listening to the noises inside it. It sounded like the ocean. What did it mean? What did it mean? Had I done something to them? To Lisette? No. Lisette, Lisette was a dream come true, sort of. I glanced back at her. Her face blurred and looked like the Picasso paintings we'd seen at the Museum of Modern Art, where the features were all different sizes and in the wrong places. Where Lisette's left eye was supposed to be, there was an ear, an ear with an aquamarine earring.

I looked away, down at the mica cafeteria table, where someone had written *Miss Hill is a pill.*

"Are you okay?" a voice, Kendra's, asked. At least, that's what I think she said. She sounded like she was underwater.

I knew I was going to throw up. I stood and lunged to the door, out of the cafeteria, practically knocking someone over on the way to the bathroom. Only when I got there did I realize who that someone was. Warner. I didn't care. I didn't care. About anything. I rammed into the girls' room door, flew through the crowd of girls reapplying eyeliner, to the stall. I didn't have time to close the door before I started retching.

"Nice!" someone yelled.

"Are you high?" said another.

"Or pregnant?"

When I was done, I closed the door and sat inside the stall, satinsidethestall, SATINSIDETHESTALL until everyone left and the room was silent. I was late to chorus and drifted through my next two classes like a ghost.

After school, Lisette had dance, so I walked home alone. I got into bed and lay there, not reading, not sleeping, nothing. When Mother called me for dinner, I said I was sick. I *was* sick. The next day, for the first time in nine years, I went to school without my homework done. After school, I repeated everything from the day before.

Finally, at eight, I decided I was hungry. I hadn't eaten since I'd puked up lunch the day before. I went to the kitchen. I stopped.

Lisette and Daddy were sitting at the kitchen table. They were carving a jack-o'-lantern

Daddy saw me first. "Emma, are you feeling better?"

"Um, yeah. Yeah, I am." I walked over to the pumpkin-gut-strewn table and examined the pumpkin. It was the design I'd wanted to do, from my special book (which lay beside them), a tree with a full moon behind it. There was a cat carved on the back, so the jack-o'-lantern would cast a shadow on the wall behind it once lit. "What are you doing?"

"Pumpkin, Pumpkin." Dad laughed. "Lisette found this great book of designs."

"Really?" I glanced at her.

She smiled. The odor of slightly rotting pumpkin met my nostrils, but maybe it was my imagination. "I've always wanted to make a really special jack-o'-lantern. Mom and I could never afford luxuries like that." She got a sort of faraway look in her eyes, like she always did when she talked about her mother.

"I'm sorry." Dad patted her shoulder.

"And since you haven't been feeling well, I told Daddy we should do it together, as sort of a get-well surprise for you."

I realized anything I could say was going to sound catty and selfish and childlike. Mother was right. Lisette was Daddy's real daughter, and he wanted to do things with her, only her. Or she'd fooled him just like she'd fooled me. Whichever it was, I was the loser. I said, "It's beautiful."

Lisette nodded, her aquamarine earrings glinting in the fluorescent light. "Let's take it out where it's dark."

We found a candle and a lighter and called Mother down to see too. I wasn't sure if Mother knew I hadn't helped, but I didn't say anything, just smiled like I meant it and admired the jack-o'-lantern, which cast a cat-shaped shadow on the wall.

Hours later, after midnight, I rose. I hadn't slept at all. I snuck downstairs. There was one door, the door to the pool bathroom, that wasn't connected to our alarm. The wiring was broken, so it didn't beep when opened. I snuck out that door and walked through the dark yard to the front.

They'd blown out the candle to save the pumpkin for Halloween. Still, I could see it in the moonlight. I seized it in both hands and carried it out to the street. Then, in the dim glow from the streetlights, I lifted the pumpkin over my head and dashed it down with all my might.

It shattered, smashed into a thousand pieces, and I knew that the next morning, when cars came down the road, it would be orange, then brown pulpy muck.

I didn't know why that made me feel better, but it did. I stomped on the pieces in a wild dance, my shadow reminding me of the coven of witches dancing in Kendra's wild symphony. Like those witches, I was dancing on a grave, but it was my own. There was no Emma, no sweet, trusting, gullible Emma who just wanted to paint Lisette's toenails and pretend to be sisters. That Emma was dead. She was dead, and a new one was born. And that new one knew how to dance, and she danced in the shadowy moonlight, and it felt good to be bad for once, really bad and get away with it, good to be someone else.

Finally, breathless and sweating, I snuck back in the same way I'd gone out.

When I reached my bedroom, the light was off. Funny, I was sure I'd left it on.

I flipped the switch.

"Hello, Emma." Lisette sat by the window. She held out her cell phone, the new one Daddy had bought her. Without being told, I knew she'd had it trained on the street below, that she'd taken my picture. Still, I approached the window and looked down. Sure enough, in the circle of bright street light, I could see the litter of smashed pumpkin shards.

In case I didn't get it, she showed me the screen.

It was me, clearly me, a short girl in lime green pajamas, curly brown hair disheveled, holding a jack-o'-lantern over her head. With her finger, Lisette scrolled to the second photo, the same girl, dancing in the smashed pieces.

I wanted to grab the phone away from her, to destroy it. I held back. If I took it, she'd scream. Then they'd run in, and there'd be immediate retaliation.

Instead, I said, "What do you want?"

She gestured around the room. "This."

"What?"

"I want this, the life I should have had, the life I would have had if you hadn't stolen it."

"I didn't steal anything. I was three years old."

She shrugged. "Your mother stole it for you, then. It's the same thing. I want it back."

I didn't understand. "You have everything. You're here now, with my father—your father. You have the house, the nice clothes, everything. What did I take from you?"

"I don't have everything."

"What don't you have? You even took my earrings."

The second after I said it, I knew.

"My mother. She'd be alive if not for you and your mother. For years, we didn't have insurance, couldn't afford doctors. She didn't go. When she finally did, it was too late. She was already terminal. There was nothing she could do. I had to watch her die."

"But that's not my fault. Couldn't we just—"

"Just what? Be friends? Do you think I'm a sucker, Emma, this sweet little girl who just wants to be your bud? I'm not. Why would anyone want to be friends with a loser like you?"

She'd voiced what I'd always been thinking. "What are you going to do?"

"Nothing, as long as you behave. Give me what I want, and I'll let you and your mother keep living in my house. But if you give me a hard time . . ." She waved the cell phone. "Well, let's just say if one of us has to win, it will be me. I can make it so it's just me and my dad, the way it should be."

"So what do you want?" I couldn't believe this. I remembered bringing her up to my room, barely more than two weeks ago, to try on clothes and giggle. How could things have changed so much?

"My room's not exciting me too much. Seems like you should give up yours. Other than that, just keep out of my way. You're not going sailing with us, Emma, or watching *Jeopardy* or carving pumpkins. You're going to be the ungrateful little brat you always were and leave me alone with my father. Got it?"

I said nothing, staring out at the pumpkin-strewn street. Finally, I nodded.

KENDRA SPEAKS (YOU DIDN'T FORGET ME, DID YOU?)

Okay, so now Emma has (finally!) figured out that Lisette's sort of, um, evil. Hands up if you saw it coming. Everyone's hand up? Just as I thought, everyone but Emma. Yes, she's a sweet girl but a tad too trusting. She should listen to her mother, but I sort of understand why she didn't. Stepmothers get a bum rap, just like witches.

I mean, yes, Andrea's a little cranky. Some might even say mean. But when you're right, you're right, and Andrea was right about Lisette. Lisette was trying to steal her husband, who happened to be Emma's father too. And what could Emma do about it? Nothing without help.

But help has its issues. I've learned the hard way that no good deed goes unpunished. I learned it in England, and I really learned it in France.

Ah, France . . .

If Emma thought her mother was difficult, she should have met Queen Marie. Emma's problems were nothing compared to those of poor Louis, Marie's son. I had to help him. What choice did I have? But it wasn't a happy ending, at least for me. Sometimes, I'm just a sucker.

I spent many years in France, lounging at Parisian cafes, admiring art, and generally living *la vie en rose.* I saw Notre Dame Cathedral (which had no hunchback to speak of) and sometimes visited Voltaire at his chateau. I could have been happy there and was for some time. But I was not there for the French Revolution, and I never danced at the Moulin Rouge. I never met Toulouse-Lautrec (or my dear Hector Berlioz) or had my portrait painted by Boucher. This story of Louis tells why—and you will see why I hesitate in deciding whether to help Emma.

It was 1744. . . .

The Story of a Lonely Prince with a Helicopter Mother
Paris, 1744

Sometimes, it was difficult to be a prince. Oh, most people do not see it. They tend to concentrate on the superficial aspects of the profession, such as living in a palace or having fancy carriages. Indeed, my home, the Palace (or Chateau, which makes it sound smaller) of Versailles, was the envy of all, with seven hundred rooms, grandiose gardens, and sixty-seven staircases. Also, a prince need not seek employment as a chimney sweep or a boot black.

Indeed, few would dispute that these were recommendations for princedom. But there were pitfalls as well. One's mother, for example. Mine was Queen Marie, and it was probably not her fault that she was a bit overprotective of me, since she had two children die, one baby born dead, and my sister, Marie-Thérèse-Félicité, was chronically ill.

Also, my father was notoriously unfaithful, and indeed, some of his mistresses were better known than his wife, the queen.

Nonetheless, it was frustrating how she hovered over me. My parents refused to allow me to participate in the campaign in the War of Austrian Succession (I later found out my dear father brought one of his mistresses instead—yes, to a war). What good was being a prince if one could not be a hero? Even when Father became gravely ill and was thought about to die, I was forbidden to visit him, that I should not be endangered. I had to sneak out to see him, and everyone was mad. In all things, I was an heir first, a son second, a man barely at all.

And then there were the servants. We had thousands of them, literally thousands. There was a servant in charge of putting on my right sleeve, and one in charge of my left. There was a whole servant devoted to my gloves. How could I be expected to rule France if I could not even dress myself?

Even in the matter of finding a wife, Mother was at it again.

It was clear that the heir to the throne needed to marry. Indeed, if there were to be the necessary "spare" heir to the throne, he would have to come from my loins, for I had no brothers, only seven surviving sisters.

Also, I quite wished to have a wife. A wife would be someone to talk to, and I preferred conversation to the constant hubbub of balls and hunts. It was amazing how lonely it could be at a ball attended by hundreds, if one had not that special person with whom to share secrets and laugh if someone's wig was askew. I knew the sort of wife I wanted, someone quiet and devout, someone with whom I could play chess and not worry that she would lose on purpose, someone who would love me.

But every time a suitable princess was located, Mother would find something the matter with her. I had long known that, as prince,

I might not marry the woman I chose. It was news to me that I might not marry at all.

First, there was Princess Maria Teresa. She was sweet and shy and also, I must say, quite pretty, with unusual red hair pushing out from beneath her powdered wig and a figure that more than adequately filled out her embroidered bodice. I could not help but imagine our wedding night. Or . . . rather, I felt that she would be a suitable bride who would bear me many sons and heal the rift between our countries, a rift caused by my father. So I thought about our wedding night, and what a joy it would be for all concerned. And for me.

When she came to the palace, we held a small afternoon party in her honor, with entertainment and card games. The princess stood off to the side.

I tried to engage her in conversation.

"Do you play Triomphe?" I asked her. Though I myself did not much care for cards, I wanted the princess to be entertained.

She looked down. "No. I mean, I am sorry. I know what a bore I am, but I never have been very good at cards. I always . . . always . . ." She sighed. "Oh, I talk too much."

This was not going well.

"No, no, that is fine. I just wanted to make certain you were—"

"What is that song?"

I stopped speaking and listened. The singer had started on "Rossignols Amoureux." "It is by Rameau. He is a favorite of my father's, and his music is quite popular here at court."

The princess smiled. "Yes, I thought so. From *Hippolyte et Aricie*?"

"Yes. You know Rameau then?"

"Yes, and Lully too. I have longed to see the whole opera. They have not performed it in Spain. I love France's *tragedie en musique*. In Spain, we have our zarzuela."

She loved music. *I* loved music! I leaned toward her. Here, I could be impressive. "Perhaps you would be interested to know that Father has built an opera house in Versailles. Here, we may have performances whenever we please."

"An opera house too! This chateau is so . . . big. Like a city."

"Confusing, you mean. I don't know every room, and I have lived here all my life. But I like the opera house. Perhaps we can have a performance while you are here." I blushed. That made it sound like I would be sending her back. "I mean . . . sometime . . . soon."

She smiled, and it was as if the sun had come in through the enormous windows of the room. "Yes. Yes, I would like that."

"Then it shall be done." Was I in love? No, merely smitten. But definitely smitten. I wondered how she would look with her red hair undone and falling down her back, as it surely would be on the night of our wedding. The night of our wedding. . . .

But I needed to talk to her, not stand here stupidly, imagining what it would be like to kiss her.

"Do you possess a good ear for music?" I asked.

The princess pondered this, saying finally, "I believe I do. It is hard to say, for though I have often been complimented on it, one never knows whether such compliments are truthful or mere flattery." She bit her lip. "That is what is hard about being a princess. It is part of why I do not care for cards—I always win, and I fear I do not deserve to. Oh, I am talking too much again."

"No, no." I nodded. "I understand. It is one of the things to which I most look forward in marriage, the ability to hear an honest opinion, to have someone to whom I can really talk."

"That is exactly how I feel!" she said.

I felt a sudden wave of great joy wash over me. Finally, someone who truly understood me! Had I not been a prince, and she a princess, I would have taken her hand then, and skipped about the room.

As it was, I smiled, and Maria Teresa smiled back again.

She had a lovely smile.

Oh, I liked her so much.

But, over dinner, Mother began to quiz her on our country's military history.

"What is your opinion of the St. Bartholomew's Day Massacre?" she asked.

"There was a massacre? On St. Bartholomew's Day?" That date, the twenty-third of August, was only about a month past. Princess Maria Teresa looked shocked, and a bit of pheasant fell from her mouth. Although I would ordinarily have found this quite disgusting, so enamored was I of the princess's beauty that I found it rather endearing. "Why ever would you massacre anyone?"

She reached her little hand out in a pleading gesture. Once again, I suppressed the urge to clutch that hand in comfort. Instead, I clenched my own hand so that the fingernails bit into my palm. "Fear not, Your Highness. Mother is merely asking you about an historical event. The massacre in question took place many years ago."

And why was Mother asking Princess Maria Teresa about a massacre that happened well over a hundred years ago? Why because, as you may have ascertained, Mother was a bit difficult and could not confine her conversation to such topics as ballet, gowns, and the weather.

"Yes." Mother nodded, her chin touching her lace collar. "Many years ago. What year, exactly, was that?"

I, of course, knew this subject backwards and forwards, and I began to answer, 1572, but Mother held up her hand.

"I was asking the princess, dear Louis. A future queen of France must have a thorough knowledge of our history." She turned her attention back to Maria Teresa. "Now, what year?"

I, too, turned my attention to Maria Teresa, whose white skin was growing attractively pink. I had heard of those who could communicate without words, so I thought about the number 1572. I thought hard indeed. The princess stared back at me, and I flattered myself that she hoped to impress Mother, hoped to be my wife. I flattered myself, also, that this was not merely because France was a large and powerful country but because she thought me handsome.

It worked! The princess stared back at me and articulated, "I believe it was fifteen . . ."

I held my breath.

"Twenty-seven!" she finished.

"No!" I could not stop the moan from coming from my mouth.

"No!" Mother crowed. "It was fifteen-seventy-two!"

Princess Maria Teresa looked from my crushed face to Mother's triumphant one and said, "Oh, well, that is what I meant. I merely got two numbers mixed."

"Yes, Mother," I said. "She merely got two numbers mixed. She was almost right."

Mother laughed. "A date, dear Louis, cannot be almost right. It is either entirely right or entirely wrong, and in this case . . ." She cast a withering eye upon Maria Teresa. ". . . it was wrong."

Princess Maria Teresa looked from me to Mother, not seeming to understand the import of what had happened. But I understood. There was going to be another angry Spanish princess in France's future. I would not be marrying Maria Teresa.

I should have stopped her from going, but I didn't. I was an obedient son, respectful to my mother. Truth be told, I pitied her. She had enough trouble with my cheating father without more trouble from me.

So instead I dreamed of Maria Teresa every night for the long weeks before the arrival of Princess Eleonora of Savoy.

Eleonora was my father's first cousin, so one would have thought we would be polite to her. One would have thought wrong.

Eleonora was pretty, though not as pretty as Princess Maria Teresa, and nice, though not as nice as Maria Teresa. She did not know the works of Rameau, but her eyes lit up when I mentioned ballet. Still, when I had the princess alone for a moment, I said, "Do you know our history? Can I tell you anything about the St. Bartholomew's Day Massacre?"

The princess laughed. "I heard about the test, and my governess has been quizzing me quite a bit on the subject."

I danced happily. The princess was beautiful and smart and, what was more, prepared to answer questions of French trivia. I did not like her as much as I'd liked Maria Teresa, but I could like her. I was certain of it. We could announce our engagement at a ball in her honor and, finally, my dreadful loneliness would end.

But, over dinner, Mother finished swallowing a bite of squab and said, "If one were shipping our finest French wine to the colony of New York, what would be the best route to take?"

The princess cleared her throat. "Shipping . . . wine?" She swirled her own wine in her glass.

"Mother," I said, trying to help. "Princess Eleonora knows a great deal of French history. Perhaps you should ask her about that."

Mother straightened in her chair. "What sort of test would it be if she knew the subject matter beforehand?"

A fair one!

The princess said, "It is all right, Your Highness." To my mother, she said, "The best route would be the most direct one. Therefore, I would go across the Atlantic Ocean to Newfoundland, then south."

Mother paused for a long moment, and I was certain the princess was right. Right!

But Mother fingered her lace cuff and said, "Newfoundland?"

The princess nodded.

"I see," said Mother. "But what of icebergs?"

"Icebergs?" I could see the princess's lovely throat clench. "What of them?"

"Only that if the ship were to take the very northern route you envision, it would be in danger of encountering an iceberg. This might damage the ship's hull, costing its cargo, not to mention many lives."

"But . . ." The princess gaped at me. "Could not the captain be careful?"

"Careful?" Mother slapped her palm upon the table, causing the crystal goblets to jump. "That goes to show that you know nothing of French wine or French sailors. A sailor who has tasted French wine is in no condition to be careful. No, the best route would be down past Portugal and almost to the Canary Islands, so the ship could cross in warmer waters."

I groaned. She was right.

The princess looked down, then swiped at her eye. Finally, she raised her face to Mother. "I see. You are very wise, Your Majesty."

Mother nodded, but I knew she was not to be flattered.

"But tell me," the princess continued. "Would not those warmer, southern waters be more likely to be infested by pirates?"

"Pirates?" I gasped. So did Mother.

"Yes, pirates. And would not the drunken crew you have described be even more ill-equipped to fight pirates than to avoid icebergs?"

Good point! Oh, a very good point! I felt my heart swell with, if not love, the promise of love. Princess Eleonora was a clever girl, and she could do something even I could not. She could stand up to my mother.

But Mother recovered herself and said, "No. Pirates are, of course, a contingency in any sea voyage. But they are just as likely to be encountered in the north as in the south. Icebergs, however, are a given and are seen only on the northern route."

With that, the door shut on any possibility of marrying Princess Eleonora.

That night, I was angry. After the heartbreak with Princess Maria Teresa, Mother had explained that such tests were necessary so that my bride would be not only beautiful and noble, but also intelligent. But Princess Eleonora was intelligent and had presented a well-thought-out argument which merely differed from Mother's. I began to suspect that Mother simply did not wish me to marry at all.

But did I say any of this to Mother? Indeed, I did not. We put Princess Eleonora in her carriage the next day, and I never saw her again.

"I am sorry, Louis," she said when she left. "You seemed nice."

I nodded. "You did too."

"I have a sister," she said. "Perhaps you could marry her."

"Perhaps." It was seeming unlikely that I'd marry anyone at all.

The next princess failed to remember that *Pantagruel* had been the title of the first book in Rabelais's Gargantua series. "A princess must know our French literature, Louis," Mother said. The mere fact that the princess in question was able to recite, from memory, the inscription on the door of the abbey gate in that book did not impress Mother.

Next came Princesses Frederica, Sophie, and Amelia. They failed Mother's tests on calculus, crop rotation, and astronomy, respectively.

The princess prospects were dwindling, and with them, my hopes. In fact, there was only one eligible princess left, Princess Maria Luisa, sister of the clever Eleonora. She was scheduled to arrive in the coming weeks.

I was bound and determined to have a wife. I sought to do whatever was necessary to secure one.

Perhaps you think I sat down with Mother and had a talk with her about the necessity of my marrying to prevent the cessation of the French line, and that it did not help this cause to have Mother rejecting perfectly good—nay, perfectly perfect princesses for spurious reasons. If you think that, you have not been listening very carefully to my story. Could I have stood up to Mother, this tale would have ended with my marrying Princess Maria Teresa (whom I still liked and thought about every day), and raising red-haired children.

No. More desperate measures were required.

There was a witch who lived in Paris in the shadows of Notre Dame. I know it is customary to say "a woman rumored to be a witch," for most such women hide their powers. But about this witch there could be no doubt.

For one thing, it was said she had lived there for close to a century. For another, she had green hair. I did not know whether, perhaps, people in other parts of the world had green hair, but I doubted it.

For another, it was well known that any youth who crossed her might well find himself turned into a frog.

I only found out about her existence because some of my advisors wished to run her out of Paris at least, or burn her at the stake at most.

But when I was told of the witch, I said, "I would like to meet this woman."

"Meet her?" the Duke of Chatillon asked. "Whatever for?"

"I have my reasons, but it is very important that I see her . . . and that Mother does not know anything about it."

The duke frowned. "I do not know that I can do that, Your Highness." He was afraid of Mother too.

I said, "True, Mother is your queen, but I will be your king someday. Indeed, my father almost died this past summer. Though I am dearly glad he did not, it just shows that circumstances can change in an instant. Surely, it is worthwhile to stand in my good graces if there is no real risk of Mother finding out."

The duke considered. "I suppose if there was no risk."

"I certainly would not tell Mother that I saw a witch. If you do not tell her, how is she to know?"

Finally, the duke agreed, and that night we snuck out the back door of the castle where black horses waited to carry us into Paris under cover of darkness. We wore black cloaks too. It was quite an adventure, much like when I snuck out to visit Father, but I would be in even greater trouble if this escapade were discovered.

It was darker still when we reached the witch's garret. There was no light in the doorway, nor even a candle glowing within. Still the duke knocked on her door.

"Are you certain this is the right place?" I asked. "There is no light." A bird, a crow or perhaps a raven, swooped down from the doorframe, narrowly missing my head.

"The witch is expecting you, Your Highness, and she has been sworn to secrecy."

Indeed, the door opened, and a gnarled hand beckoned me in.

It was with great trepidation that I advanced into the garret. What was I doing? There could be an assassin waiting. It could all be a conspiracy.

But I reminded myself that visiting the witch had been my own idea. Besides, one must take risks in order to secure rewards.

I stepped inside.

The dirt floor felt cold even through my shoes, and the room was darker than anyplace I had ever been. The door slammed behind me. I jumped as if I had heard an assassin's pistol.

But no sooner had the door closed than the room blazed with light, more light than I had ever seen indoors, even at Versailles. Yet there was no flame. I could not see the source of it. The room I occupied seemed spacious and comfortable, unlike the cell I had seen from outside, and the woman who greeted me was beautiful, my own age, and with long black hair. I shielded my eyes and said to the young lady, "I am here to see the witch, Kendra."

"I am she."

She did not hold out her hand. I would not have taken it had she done so. She did not curtsey either.

"But . . ." I remembered the descriptions I had heard, a green-haired crone. Indeed, I recalled the withered claw I had seen only a moment before.

"I can change my shape at will. It comes in handy . . . in spell casting."

And in escaping the blame, I suspected, if something went wrong. But I chose not to say it. I had more pressing business.

I squinted in the bright light. Her eyes were the color of emeralds.

"I require your help."

Those eyes met mine for a moment in what I thought was sympathy.

But then she began to laugh.

"You, the great dauphin of France, need my help?"

"Yes. Yes."

Her laughter halted abruptly. "And you think me—what? A faerie? Or a genii in a bottle, perhaps. Witches do not grant wishes. We do as we please."

I was prepared for this, though not for her disrespectful manner of speech. "I will pay you handsomely for your work." I drew a small sack of coins from my cloak.

"What care I for your money?"

"Most people care quite a bit."

"Then give it to them. You have enough, and many in Paris are going without. I am not most people. I am none but myself."

I stepped back, amazed at the cheek of her. "And I am your prince. I could order you beheaded if I wished, or hanged."

"If you could find me." She waved her arm, and in an instant, she was gone. In her place was only a black crow. It flew at me, and I shielded my face. When I uncovered it, another woman stood before me. She had red hair and was the image of Princess Maria Teresa. I gasped.

But when she spoke, Kendra's voice came out instead. "The ones hanged as witches were not witches. Real witches cannot be caught, and I am a real witch."

Staring into her eyes, especially now that she was disguised as the princess I had most wanted to marry but would now never see again, I felt about to boil over with frustration and rage.

"Please!" I begged. "Please, you must help me! You are my only hope, the only one to whom I can turn!" And then I poured out the whole story of six princesses, mine for the asking, six princesses gone. I will spare you the details of my crying and gnashing of teeth, but suffice it to say that teeth were, indeed, gnashed. "My mother is determined to sabotage every possibility. You must stop her."

Kendra waved her hand and turned into a crone. "You say that by helping you, I would be thwarting your mother's wishes." This seemed to interest her. At least, her toothless mouth formed a slow grin.

"Yes. Yes! She does not wish me to marry. This is clear from her conduct."

Kendra scratched a wart on her long nose, then turned back into a young woman. "I am sorry. 'Tis uncomfortable to be old. I would very much like to upset your mother. She has been no friend to my kind."

It was true. Although the Parlement of Paris had convicted fewer women of witchcraft in recent decades, this was due not at all to my family's influence, and witch hunts still occurred in outlying parts of France.

"I sometimes feel quite burned by her myself." Kendra twisted her long hair, and it seemed to grow longer still. "It would please me to best her. I will do it."

"Good. But how?"

With a wave of her hand, Kendra changed shapes again. I gasped. She was an exact replica of Lady Agnes, one of Mother's ladies-in-waiting. "I will ascertain the sort of test your mother intends to use, and then I will make certain Princess Maria Luisa passes."

"What will you do with Lady Agnes?"

"Something temporary," Kendra replied. "The only payment I ask is that I be invited to your wedding. It would please me to see your mother required to entertain a witch."

I agreed to this, and we arranged that I would contact her through the duke as soon as Princess Maria Luisa arrived.

In those next weeks, I began to hope again. In a month's time, the princess's ship entered our harbor, and the castle's four thousand servants flew to the task of entertaining her.

I watched Lady Agnes, searching for signs that she was not, in fact, Lady Agnes. I found none. I would have, though, had I examined the upstairs scullery closet, for that is where, as I later found out, the real Lady Agnes slept peacefully for a period of four days.

As for Princess Maria Luisa, she seemed a pleasant enough girl, though after what had happened with Princess Maria Teresa (the memory of whom still invaded my dreams), I tried not to fall in love with her. Still, we discussed the usual subjects of young men and women—riding and dance and whether imported goods should be taxed at the same rate as domestic. She was charming and pretty enough that I hoped she would pass.

We continued these subjects over dinner, though it turned out that the princess was a great lover of art.

"I have heard," she said, "that you have in your collection a painting by Leonardo da Vinci, called *La Joconde*, in which the woman's eyes appear to follow one around the room?"

I nodded. "Yes. It hangs in Versailles. It belonged to my great-great-grandfather."

"I would love to see it."

I nodded. I knew the princess was trying to impress my mother with her knowledge of the art that hung in our palace, but I was so busy waiting for the quiz that I could barely hear her. I also knew that if the princess indicated an interest in art, Mother would choose a different subject for her test.

"They say that the woman in the painting is quite plain, but her smile is enigmatic," the princess said.

"Mmm," I replied. Why was Mother so quiet?

"Can you tell me about some of the other art I might see here?" the princess asked.

Had Kendra cast a spell upon Mother so that she would not be mean to the princess? It was too much to hope for. Still, I would not mind.

"Your Highness, I asked—"

"What?" I stared at her. "Oh, yes, of course. I will arrange a tour after dinner. It would be my pleasure." It would. After all, perhaps I was speaking to my future wife.

For the rest of dinner, Mother was the soul of politeness, and as we had dessert in the drawing room (the first time I had done so with any princess—the rest left in tears), I wondered whether we would marry in France or Spain. Even the princess looked relieved. Of course, she had heard of Mother's test from her sister.

But as I dressed for bed (having sent the servants away—and

thank goodness I had) with the extra care taken by a lad who intended to propose marriage the next day, there was a rap at the window.

This would have been less upsetting had my apartment not been on the third floor.

At first, I thought to ignore it, but so persistent did it become that I could not do so. Finally, I opened the casement. No sooner had I done so than a black crow hopped inside.

"Kendra?"

The crow turned into a woman. "Ooh, fancy diggings. Your family had better watch out—this castle's going to get you in trouble someday."

"I really don't—"

"Trust me—*kkkkkkk*." She made a crude gesture, running her finger across her throat as if beheading herself.

"You should not be in my room. It is improper."

Kendra laughed. "What is proper in any of this?"

I nodded. "Of course. I should be grateful to you. Princess Maria Luisa has passed the test. We shall be married."

Kendra stared at me. "Passed? The princess has not passed any test, not yet."

There was ice in her voice, and it invaded my bones. "She has not?"

Kendra shook her head, a gesture very crowlike, which caused the light to reflect off the green and purple highlights in her black hair. Finally, she said, "The test is still to come."

Of course. It was too easy. Mother had something up her long, lacy sleeve to make certain Princess Maria Luisa had to work and work hard for the dubious prize of my hand.

"The test will happen in the night," Kendra said.

"The night? What sort of test—?"

Kendra did not smile. "Do not fear. I will make it impossible for Maria Luisa to fail."

And then, before I could say another word, she turned back into a crow and flew away.

The test will happen in the night. The words haunted me, as words do when one knows one has done wrong. They brought a shadow over the light of happiness I had felt just moments earlier. I entered my bedchamber with great trepidation and did not sleep at all. What sort of test could happen in the night?

Around midnight, I thought I heard a thumping noise. I fumbled for a light, unwilling to rouse the servants, but it stopped before I could rise to investigate.

As the clock struck two, there was a muffled groaning of some sort. But, again, it faded quickly. Or perhaps I was simply too afraid of what I might find. Yes, that was it. I did not sleep more than ten minutes at a time the whole night.

When morning finally dawned, I went to the dining room to find Mother. She looked extremely well rested and embraced me. "Dear son, you are here. Now we will find out together whether Princess Maria Luisa passed my test."

"Test? What test?"

She looked away, adjusting her hood over her lace cap as if nothing of any importance was happening. "A simple test to ascertain whether the princess possesses the delicate nature of a true princess. Lady Agnes helped me dream it up. You see, last night, we placed—"

"Oh, what has become of me?"

It was the princess. Mother held up her hand, and we both turned to look. Then, to gape.

The princess looked nothing like the cheery, normal girl I had met yesterday. Indeed, she resembled someone who had been through some horrible ordeal, a shipwreck perhaps (maybe involving one of Mother's icebergs) or a rock slide. Her wig was off, and her hair stuck out in all directions as if she could not be bothered to brush it or, perhaps, as if she had brushed it only to find it would not obey.

Her clothes—she still wore her dressing gown—were wrinkled, askew, and slightly damp. Her face looked ashen. When she saw me, she fixed me with a pleading look. On whole, she was more like a refugee of war than a princess.

"Did you sleep well, Your Highness?" Mother's voice was made of sugar.

"Sleep well." The princess repeated the words as if Mother had spoken in tongues. "No. No, I did not sleep well."

I remembered the sounds in the night and, looking at the princess's face, I began to imagine what might have happened. But I did not have to imagine long for the princess was more than happy to share her tale of woe.

"I began the night comfortably enough on the twenty mattresses you provided."

"Twenty mattresses?" I stared at Mother who, again, seemed quite interested in her hood.

"It was a bit high," the princess said, "and I am afraid of heights, but Lady Agnes insisted this was the French custom, and I knew the French were prone to excess. I did not wish to offend, even though the featherbeds swayed a bit when I ascended them, and I needed some help reaching the top. But once I turned out the lights, I pretended I was on the ground, and I was comfortable enough."

"Comfortable?" Mother looked surprised, then pleased. "So you felt no discomfort?"

"Mother, how could she be uncomfortable on twenty mattresses?" I asked.

"Well, I wasn't at first," the princess said, "but after a few minutes, it seemed like the mattresses began to move. Indeed, they . . . turned on me."

"Turned on you?" I said.

"They tried to eat me!"

I could only stare. The princess had gone mad. That was the only explanation. Gone mad, and as she was the very last princess of suitable age, I would remain a bachelor forever. Even I could not fault Mother for refusing to allow my union with a princess who was insane.

And yet, Mother seemed unsurprised as the princess described her ordeal.

"Yes, you heard right," the princess said. "The mattresses tried to eat me. At least, one of them did. The ticking opened up and tried to swallow me. I have the feathers to prove it!" She pulled a handful of them from her dressing gown pocket. "I managed to escape with my life and beat it to the ground when a second mattress attacked, then a third. But when I reached for the fourth, it was not in the mood for warfare. Rather, it began to hum."

"Hum?" Mother asked.

"Would you care for some tea, Your Highness?" I tried to change the subject. "You look like you could use some."

"That would be nice," the princess said before turning back to Mother. "Yes, humming. A bourrée, to be precise. Then, three other mattresses rose and sought to persuade me to join them in the dance. They would not stop, even when I told them I would prefer a gavotte. I attempted to settle down on the remaining thirteen mattresses, but they bucked me off like a wild horse. As I lay on the floor with three vanquished mattresses on one side, three dancing ones on the other, it began to rain."

"Rain?" That explained the wetness. Indeed, it explained many things. The princess was not insane. Rather, it was a spell, Kendra's doing. But why did she bewitch the mattresses? And why were there twenty of them in the first place?

"Where is that tea?" Princess Maria Luisa barked at me as if I were a loafing servant boy instead of the heir apparent to the French throne.

"Oh, I am terribly sorry. The servants . . ." Well, the servants were all standing around, listening to her convoluted story. Now one handed her a cup, which she drank down as if it were a glass of sherry. She presented it for a refill.

"That is how it was all night," she continued. "Every hour brought a new horror. At two, the mattresses began playing leapfrog. At three, it was croquet, and at four, they had a fox hunt, using me as the fox. I have never had a worse night's sleep in my entire life."

"You've passed!" Mother crowed.

"What?" The princess drained her tea. "What is she talking about?"

The servant refilled her cup again, and I said, "Mother tests the princesses who wish to marry me. For worthiness. You've heard about that."

"This . . . was . . . a . . . test?" the princess stammered. She was breathing rather shallowly, enough to cause concern.

"And you've passed," Mother said. "You see, I placed a pea, one tiny pea under your mattresses, knowing that a worthy princess would have a sensitive constitution and would not be able to sleep in such a lumpy situation. And you have passed! You are a real princess!"

Princess Maria Luisa stared. Was it sleeplessness that made her gape so, or something else? I gestured to the servant to refill her tea once more, but she waved it away.

"Are you not happy?" Mother asked.

"To be a real princess? Why, I have been a real princess since the day I was born. There was never any question in my mind, or anyone else's."

"No, silly girl." Mother clapped her hands. "To have passed the test, to have bested the others, to be marrying my darling Louis!"

The princess gawked at her, but finally she straightened her dressing gown (several feathers fell out) and said, "No. I would actually rather not."

"What?" Mother screeched.

"Why?" I said, though I knew the answer.

"Why would I wish to marry someone . . ." She glowered at me. ". . . whose mother would subject me to such a torture? What would our marriage be like? What of our children? You are a vicious, cruel woman!"

"B-but . . ." Mother stammered. "I merely placed a pea under the mattresses. I did not make them do any of those other things."

"I would not put it past you," I said.

"And you!" The princess pointed a finger at me. "You are worse than she is! You watched it all happen and did nothing to stop it!"

"But . . . but she is my mother."

"And you are a mama's boy of the worst kind. I would rather marry an undertaker or a street sweeper than someone like you."

She stood and flounced from the room, dripping and trailing feathers as she went. She turned as she reached the door to say, "You will be lucky if you do not go to war with Sardinia over this!"

I followed her, but no form of persuasion would convince her to leave her room. She asked for a servant to see to her packing.

When finally I returned to the dining room, Mother was in tears. "I do not understand. It was merely a pea, a little pea."

I nodded, though I could not help but think she had gotten what she deserved, if not for Princess Maria Luisa, for all the princesses before her, for every time she'd tried to control my life.

Still, I explained what had happened.

And that is how the witch, Kendra, came to be banished from France.

Kendra speaks (briefly)

Yes, banished. Can you believe it? I tried my best to help, and instead, I ended up kicked to the cobblestone curb. France is, as you may have figured out by now, not the only country where I am forbidden entry, maybe not even the nicest. Still, it gnaws on one, particularly because, as you will see from the remainder of this story, no real harm was done. And yet, even when all was well, as Shakespeare said, that ends well, did they say, "Hey, Kendra, we understand that you made a noble effort. Why not come to the palace for some champagne sometime?" Noooooo. They're all, "Get thee from our kingdom, witch, or it's the guillotine." They're lucky I didn't turn them into talking swine.

I only did that some of the time. With Prince Louis, I decided that life with his mother was punishment enough. And I suspected, correctly, it turned out, that the royal family's excesses would someday be their downfall. But that happened with the next generation. And yes, there was a next generation, for Louis did marry, despite his mother's best efforts.

In any case, here is how it turned out.

Back to Louis (the unappreciative boy)

It took several weeks to travel to Madrid by carriage. Yet, I did. For this errand, I had to go myself.

After Princess Maria Luisa left Versailles, the palace grew silent indeed. I took meals in my own apartment and refused to speak to anyone. A palace is a very large place, so if one is determined to avoid someone, it is quite easy, rather like avoiding an enemy in a large city.

And I was determined. There were no princesses left. Mother had chased them all off. Therefore, I would be alone for the rest of my life, and when I died, my cousin would be king.

I was silent for three days. At the end of it, I went to Mother's rooms.

The knock startled us both, coming as it did at the end of several days' silence. But once Mother recovered from the shock, she said, "I see you have come to your senses."

I nodded. "I have. I have realized I cannot listen to you anymore."

"I cannot believe what I am hearing."

Me neither, but I continued. "I know life is hard for you. I try to make you happy, but I am entitled to a measure of happiness of my own."

"I never said—"

"You did not have to. You have thwarted my every effort to find a bride. I will choose a wife. I will choose a wife, and I will marry her."

"We . . . we . . . can throw you out of the palace."

"But you won't. For if you throw me out of the palace, you will be alone in this drafty place, except for the occasional visit from Father's mistresses."

This was a low blow, and I knew it. But I was angry.

Mother sniffed. "Perhaps that would not be so bad. Madame de Mailly is entertaining enough at times."

"And then, there is Ferdie."

My cousin Ferdinand, of Spain, was the closest male heir.

"He would come visit you frequently, no doubt," I said, "in order to appraise the china."

"You are grown very rude, my son."

I knew it, and I felt bad about it, but there was nothing else to be done.

"If, on the other hand, you allow me to marry, I would take care of you for the rest of my life, while you played with your grandchildren."

"Grandchildren?"

I wondered, briefly, if Mother would be similarly controlling of my children. Still, there was time to rectify that. "Yes, grandchildren. If you are nice to my wife, I am certain she could be persuaded to name one or two Marie, after you. But, for that to happen, you must permit me to marry."

She did not answer, and for six hours after, I worried I would have to make good my threat of leaving. As I have said before, it is not easy being a prince. If I left home, my prospects would be few. I had no skills at farming, no aptitude as a blacksmith. I feared I would be all thumbs when it came to carpentry.

But I had an excellent ability to be silent. So I was.

That night, Mother relented. The next day, I sailed to Spain.

One does not generally just show up at a princess's door unannounced. Yet, that is what I did. Or rather, I sent my servant ahead to announce my arrival. He came back, accompanied by one of King Philip's men.

"Her Highness, Princess Maria Teresa, is indisposed," he said.

"I understand." It was as I had feared. She did not wish to speak to me. "Has she married another?"

"Far from it," said the servant. "Since suffering various insults at your mother's hands, she has barely left her room. She will see no one."

Still single.

"Then I must beg you to beg the princess to allow me to see her . . . to apologize."

The servant looked none too happy at this request. In fact, he made a *tsk-tsk*ing noise with his tongue, as if I were an ill-behaved child. Still, he motioned that the duke and I might follow him to the entrance hall of the castle. He bade us take our seats and started upstairs.

"Wait!" I said.

"Yes." The servant turned back as if hoping to hear that I had changed my mind.

"Can you please tell the princess . . ." I stared at my shoes. "Tell her that I wish we had heard *Hippolyte et Aricie* together. Tell her we still can."

I waited. I stared at the duke. The duke stared at me. Half an hour passed. Then forty-five minutes.

"Perhaps she is not coming," the duke said after an hour.

"She has to come. She has to! I will never forgive Mother if she doesn't. I will never forgive myself."

And then, she was there. Princess Maria Teresa. She was thinner than I remembered, but still beautiful, in a gown of light blue brocade that came quite low. She looked like a bride.

"You wished to speak to me, Your Highness?" Her eyes were cold, her expression severe. And yet, there was something of the girl I had admired so much too. I wanted, oh, how I wanted to take her hand. "Have you brought your mother?"

"No. Never. I have come—"

"To apologize. I heard."

"Yes, to apologize, but also to tell you something, something else."

"Tell me what?" Her eyes softened ever so slightly.

It was all I needed. I rushed (or at least walked briskly—I was a prince, after all) to her side. I was about to seize one of her little white hands in my own, but I stopped myself, lest she think me too forward.

"Do you think I would come all the way from Paris merely to apologize? I am apologizing, not only for my mother's rudeness but for my own weakness in not preventing . . . not telling her . . . asking her kindly . . . telling her to take her test and, well, take her own test!"

The princess actually smiled a bit at that. This encouraged me to go on.

"But, more than that, I have come to ask you to return to Paris with me, to go to the opera with me, to give me all your honest opinions, in short . . . will you be my bride?"

"I know nothing of French history. Even being that close on the date of the St. Bartholomew's Day Massacre, it was merely a lucky guess."

"That is what books are for. Princess Maria Teresa, if you will accept me, the only history that will matter will be our own."

I hoped that I had not come all this way only to be refused. At this point, I supposed I could ask any of the other princesses (well, except Princess Maria Luisa) to be my bride, with Mother's blessings, but I did not want any other princess. I wanted this one.

But Maria Teresa looked deep into my eyes and said, "In that case, I will marry you."

Soon after, we were married. Mother, though chagrined that her guidance was thus flouted, chose not to disown me. In fact, once she got to know my bride, they got along famously.

So we were all quite happy.

(Kendra's note: except for the helpful witch, who was still banished.)

KENDRA SPEAKS

So you begin, perhaps, to see a pattern. Kendra sees some poor soul in distress, does her level best to help that person, and ends up being blamed when things don't go exactly according to plan. Is it any wonder I'd rather go shoe shopping?

But I do like Emma. She is innocent and hopeful, seeing only good in people, much like Louis, whom I also liked. As with Louis, I pity Emma too. She's not getting Warner anytime soon. No, no, she's sitting and reading her books while Lisette—wicked Lisette—has all the fun.

It would be easy to turn Lisette into a frog but, of course, there would be . . . ramifications to that. I've done it, turned a human boy into a beast when he made me angry. He got on my bad side one day and . . . I gave him a fur coat. And claws. Put a curse on him and gave him two years to find true love to break it. Fortunately, he was quiet about it, but that can't usually be counted on. No, no, in today's society of litigation and reality television, someone is just as likely to trumpet his misfortune from the rooftops as hide in a basement.

No, if I intend to help, I must be discreet. But how?

Ah, well, I'll think on it while Emma tells some more of her story.

Part Two
Lisette and Emma

1

Two years have passed. A lot has happened. In that time, everything changed, especially my relationship with my father. Basically, I no longer had one. After that October night—and at Lisette's instructions—I became "too busy" to watch *Jeopardy* or go sailing, too busy for everything. I thought Daddy wouldn't really care. After all, he had Lisette now, his real daughter. But, to my surprise, he did. Sometimes, I'd see him looking at me like he wondered what he'd done to push me away, why I hated him. That tore my heart out because my father had been the one I loved most. Now, I had only Mother.

In those two years, I often thought about coming clean with Daddy, telling him the truth about the pumpkin, about Lisette's blackmail, especially after a few months. It just seemed juvenile and lame. So I'd smashed a pumpkin. He probably wouldn't even be mad.

But the thing was, I knew he wouldn't believe me about Lisette, the way he hadn't believed me about the earrings. He thought—everyone did—that she was this sweet little thing who'd never hurt anyone—poor, tragic Lisette. So I kept her secret because I knew if I didn't, I'd be the one who looked bad. Also, I didn't want to hurt Daddy any more than I already had.

The whole thing reminded me of a fairy tale. In stories like *Cinderella* and *Beauty and the Beast*, they always say the heroine is "as good as she is beautiful." I wondered if people just wanted that to be true, wanted the beautiful to be good. I wondered if they wanted the ugly to be bad because then they wouldn't have to feel sorry for them.

I told Mother. Everything. Otherwise, she'd have kept nagging me to spend more time with Daddy. She believed me, of course. She'd seen Lisette's true face from the beginning, the face on the inside of her beautiful outside. Once she found out, she went out of her way to be nice to Lisette too, to make Daddy happy. To keep him. Lisette had been right about that. My mother wouldn't risk his choosing Lisette over us.

So now, Lisette had the bigger room, the nicer computer, and all my former friends.

I just had Kendra. Kendra was my new best friend, and she alone seemed to see Lisette for what she was.

One day, shortly after the pumpkin incident, Lisette had been singing her solo in chorus, and Kendra leaned over to me. "You hate her, don't you?"

"What?" Lisette stood in front, her blond hair flowing around her shoulders, singing like an angel. "I was just thinking about the song."

"Right. If your eyes were lasers, the girl would be dead."

"Who?" But I knew.

"Your . . . sister. You can't stand her. You thought about what I said at the hoedown, and you realized I was right."

Miss Hakes was pointing, gesturing for us to stop talking. Lisette finished her solo. Miss Hakes gave the signal for the chorus to enter.

After we finished, Kendra said, "You didn't answer my question."

"What?" I glanced at Lisette, who actually looked a little bored. "No, of course not. Everyone loves Lisette. She's perfect."

"Exactly. And whenever anyone starts disliking her the teensiest bit—like some people thought she shouldn't have gotten the solo because she was new—she pulls out the dead mother card."

"That's horrible." *True, but horrible.*

Miss Hakes had us start again, from Lisette's solo.

"Don't you wish, for once, she'd fall flat on her face?" Kendra said.

Unconsciously, I nodded.

Suddenly Lisette's throat cracked. Then she started coughing, choking really, and holding her chest.

Miss Hakes ran to her. "Lisette! Lisette, are you okay?"

Lisette couldn't stop coughing. Beside me, I noticed Kendra chuckling.

Miss Hakes yelled for someone to get Lisette some water, and eventually, Lisette stopped hacking. People realized she wasn't actually dying or anything, but she said she didn't feel up to doing the solo that day. Miss Hakes let me do it that once.

It wasn't fun, though. I didn't just want to do the solo. I wanted to be the best, and I wasn't, not at singing, not at anything, not compared to Lisette.

Kendra and I sort of bonded after that. Well, as much as you could bond with Kendra. It was weird. She seemed to have no life outside school, like she didn't exist. At least, she never went to anyone's house or had anyone over to hers. But we sat together at lunch and studied in the library. She was really my only friend at that point. In high school, you need all the friends you can get.

Oh, and Warner? His family moved to Orlando during winter break of eighth grade. I still didn't have a boyfriend. Lisette, of course, had dozens, or at least dozens of guys who were in love with her. But what would you expect? She was beautiful.

2

Creepy things about tenth grade: Mr. Fischer, my chem teacher, had a snake. Some people thought it was cool. I wasn't one of them. I had nothing against snakes per se. The thing that bothered me about it was that I knew Mickey ate mice.

Yes, Mickey. That was the name Mr. Fischer had chosen for the black, scary creature that regularly constricted around real-life Mickeys before swallowing them whole. I'd never actually seen it happen, but one girl had run into Fischer at PetSmart. When she'd complimented him on his cute mouse, he'd told her, "Don't name the food."

Me, I had a soft spot for mice. Once, when I was little, we'd had one in our house. Mother had talked about hiring an exterminator, but before she could, I saw it run across our family room, in front of the TV where I'd been watching (by some great coincidence) *Stuart Little.* "Get him!" I'd screamed, and Daddy had thrown a blanket, immobilizing the tiny, scared creature. It was brownish-gray, with big brown eyes. I'd named it Stuart and wanted to keep it as a pet. We'd compromised on releasing it at a nature preserve near the house.

So, today, I was having a hard time concentrating on our density determination lab because there was a PetSmart bag on Fischer's desk.

The guy in front of me nudged his friend. "Looks like it's feeding time."

"Cool!" his friend said. "Are you going to come after school and watch?"

Ick. Someone should really do background checks on these boys.

Kendra nudged me. "Earth to Emma."

"What?"

"Did you finish measuring?"

"Huh? Oh, I'm sorry." Had that bag moved? No, it must be something else. Who would put a mouse in a closed plastic bag?

"I'll do it now," I told Kendra.

"It's okay." Kendra took the paper from me and wrote down the number. "Now we're supposed to add water."

It did move.

"Water, Emma."

"Oh, sorry." I picked up our container and managed to spill pretty much all of it. I grabbed some paper towels and wiped the filthy linoleum. "Sorry. Sorry."

"Stop apologizing. What's with you today?"

"Sorry." From the floor, I stared up at Mickey. His beady black eyes stared back, and I thought about what it would be like to be a mouse. "It's just . . . the mouse on Fischer's desk."

Kendra followed my eyes. "What makes you think there's a mouse there?"

"The bag." I gestured toward it. It moved. Definitely. "Did you see that?"

"It could be anything in that bag."

"Like what?"

Kendra shrugged and went to get more water. When she came back, she said, "Fang clippers, snake scale medication. I don't know."

"It moved."

"I guarantee there's no mouse in that bag."

"Right. How do you do that?"

Kendra poured the water, then gestured at my purse, which was lying open on the floor. I glanced down. Something small and white was moving inside. "I think he made a break for it."

I shrieked. Kendra's hand landed on mine, too late. Heads turned to stare. Kendra said, "Relax, Emma. Mr. Fischer would never give us flammable liquids." She picked up the container of unknown liquid and measured some into our cylinder. "See?"

"Oh, silly me." I tried not to look down at my purse. "I thought I saw smoke." I laughed. "False alarm."

When people finally looked away, I picked up my purse. "How'd it get there?"

Kendra shrugged. "Guess he ran."

I stuck my finger inside. The mouse nibbled on it. It felt like the teeth of a comb. "What am I supposed to do with it?"

"I don't know. Give it back to Fischer."

"Never." I petted the mouse's soft, bony body with my fingertip. I'd already mentally named him Ralph, for Runaway Ralph from the book. After all, he'd run away. No, this was crazy. How could I steal a mouse?

How could I not?

"Put him in here, quick," Kendra whispered. She reached into her own overstuffed backpack and pulled out a mouse-sized box.

I took it and, with my pen, punched some holes in the top. I didn't ask Kendra how she happened to have the box. She often had strange things in her bag, like foreign coins, antique opera glasses, or once, a preserved butterfly. Careful to keep my eyes forward, I scooped the tiny creature into the box, shut it, then stuffed it into my backpack while Kendra recorded our result.

"Okay," Fisher said. "Everyone done?"

A chorus of yeses and nos. Fischer strode to his desk. "Finish up."

That's when he noticed the flat, empty bag. He patted it. His eyes widened, and he started moving objects on his desk.

"Did you lose something, Mr. Fischer?" someone asked.

He didn't answer. Someone else said, "Did you lose the mouse?"

A girl screamed. Kendra said, "Don't be stupid. He couldn't have lost a mouse. That would be terribly irresponsible, and Mr. Fischer would never be so careless on school property. He always tells us, safety first. Right, Mr. Fischer?"

Fischer stopped patting his desk and said, "That's right. I just misplaced . . . my keys. Oh, here they are." He held them up. "False alarm."

I was practically hyperventilating by then. Kendra rubbed my back. "Calm down. There's only one period left. You saved a life."

At her touch, I felt instantly calmer. My heart, which had been racing like a rabbit's, slowed down. I drew a deep breath. It would be okay.

Next class was journalism, my favorite part of the day. After eighth-grade solo tryouts, Lisette had gone on to become a total star in chorus and drama. She'd even gotten the lead in the eighth-grade play. So I'd switched to newspaper, figuring she'd have no interest. Turned out, it was something I actually rocked at. From the exposé on which world history teacher was the easiest (definitely Mr. Kalevitch, who played Beatles music and ditched textbooks for a PowerPoint presentation) to the political scandal when a student government candidate tore down his opponent's posters, I'd cracked them all. This year, tenth grade, I was creative writing editor for *The Panther*. Next year, I expected to be editor in chief.

On the way to class, I ducked into the girls' bathroom and checked on Ralph. His box was a little crushed, but he was fine. I had a pet!

I got to class late, but Ms. Meinbach, the teacher, liked me, so she said, "Oh, good, you're here. I was hoping you could help our new student." She gestured toward a red-haired boy. "He's interested in creative writing. Emma, I'd like you to meet . . ."

I didn't even hear the next words out of her mouth because he turned. The room froze like a broken DVR. It was Warner.

He started to smile, then stopped. "Hey, I know you. Eighth grade, right?

My face felt hot, then cold. Warner! I tried to say . . . something, to explain what had happened at the hoedown, but it came out as a cough. Then another. I was going to choke to death right in front of him. Or die of embarrassment.

"Are you okay?" He pulled a chair toward me and gestured for me to sit. I nodded, and he saw me. "Hey, you're Emma Bailey, right?"

I breathed in. "Yeah. Warner. I thought you moved."

"I did. We moved back."

"Cool." I nodded a few times too many.

"So what do we do around here? I was on newspaper at my old school, but I did sports."

He didn't say anything about the hoedown. Was it possible he didn't remember, that the experience was so insignificant that he didn't care? Maybe. Still, I wanted to explain.

"That time at the hoedown . . ."

He looked down. "We don't have to talk about that."

"I want to. For two years, I've been wanting to tell you what happened."

"It's okay. Really."

"My friends, they had me arrested."

His left eyebrow kinked up. He had no idea what I was talking about.

"At the hoedown, you could pay a dollar to have someone arrested. Then they'd pay a dollar to get out. Except I didn't have my purse, so I had to stay and stay, and when I finally got out, you were gone."

I sounded crazy. What if, after all this time, he thought I was crazy?

But his expression turned to a smile. "You're talking about when I asked you to go on the hayride. When you blew me off?"

"I didn't blow you off on purpose. I totally wanted to go on the hayride with you. I was so mad. I even broke out of jail, I was so upset about missing it."

He shook his head. "You're kidding."

"I looked for you at school the next day, the next week, even the next month, until I heard you moved, but I never saw you."

He laughed. "Yeah, I was avoiding you. I felt so stupid. I figured you'd been joking when you told me you'd come. You were there with all your cool friends, and I thought you were laughing at this dorky guy who'd invited you on a hayride, like we were in a production of *Oklahoma!* or something. What a nerd."

"No. I love *Oklahoma!* That's exactly the type of thing I like, and I thought it was cute. I really wanted to go. I . . . I liked you. A lot."

Kill me now, I am such a geek.

But Warner said, "I liked you too. You busted out of jail? Is that what you said?"

"Hoedown jail. I ran past all the PTA moms. They were chasing me. It was seriously like a video game."

He laughed.

Ms. Meinbach was walking around the room, checking how

everyone was doing. I pulled some old issues of the paper toward me. "So, we try to have three or four poems in every issue. The staff writes most of them, but if a student submits one, we look at it. We encourage student work."

Ms. Meinbach nodded. "Showing Warner the ropes?"

"Absolutely." *Leave. Please leave. He was going to ask me out.*

Sure enough, the second she left, he said, "I guess it's too late for that hayride, but maybe we could get together, um today after school."

"Y—" The word *yes* was screaming out of my mouth when I remembered Ralph the mouse, trapped in my purse. I shook my head, "God, I can't."

Warner nodded, like he understood. "All righty then. I'll just crawl back into my cave of shame."

"No, it's not like that. I want to go with you. Any other day. It's just . . ." I glanced at my purse. "Can you keep a secret?"

"I guess."

I opened the box, then pointed inside.

Warner drew back, surprised, then leaned forward again. "Is that . . . a mouse?"

"It was about to be fed to a snake," I whispered.

"You stole it?"

"It escaped. But I didn't give it back. I just couldn't." I closed the box. "So, anyway, after school, I have to get my mom to take me to PetSmart. If she doesn't have a heart attack, at least."

"You could release it somewhere."

I shook my head. "I don't like the odds for a white mouse in the wild. No camouflage. Besides, I'm sort of attached to him. I named him Ralph."

"You know what they say—don't name the food." He smiled. "That's pretty typical of you, though."

"What is?"

Ms. Meinbach strolled by again, and Warner said, "So it's typical to have one short story per issue, or more than that?"

I pretended to think. "Sometimes one, sometimes two if they're short. It depends. Oh, and sometimes we put a personal essay."

Warner was writing all this down, like a good student. When Ms. Meinbach left, he turned the paper toward me. It read:

Let me take you to PetSmart.

I wrote:

You have a car?

He must be sixteen. I wasn't yet. I wouldn't be getting a car anyway. Lisette had gotten one for her birthday, a Saab, and Daddy told her to drive me to school and to share it with me once I got my license. What Daddy didn't know was, Lisette dropped me off at the bus stop every morning, then picked up her friends. I knew she wouldn't share either.

Yes, he wrote back.

I thought about it for a second, no more. Mother had told me to ask permission to go in someone's car, but I knew she'd say yes. She was always harping on how I had no social life. She'd probably be happy to see me join a motorcycle gang if it got me out of the house.

So I wrote back, *OK*.

"The student parking lot is like *Animal Planet*," I said to Warner as we walked to his car after school.

Okay, I was trying to be clever. Which is not to say I'd spent the whole rest of the period thinking of something funny (I hoped) to say.

"How so?" he asked. "I mean, not that I think you're wrong."

"It's the whole food chain. At the top are the girls with Audis or boys whose parents buy them a big SUV and don't care how many people they pack into it."

He smirked. "The no-rules kids. My favorites."

It occurred to me that, for all I knew, he could be walking me up to a new SUV, but he said, "And their friends are like the rest of their pride, right?"

"Exactly," I said. "Then, the next step down are kids with their parents' old cars or something. They're like tortoises and skunks, not predators, but at least they have defenses."

"Right," he agreed. "Crawl into their shell."

I nodded. "Then, there are pedestrians, which are the equivalent of bugs. Their only hope is that maybe no one will notice them."

He actually laughed. "And what are you?"

"I take the bus. We're not even part of the animal planet. We're like cattle, bound for the feed lot, heads down, texting each other, trying to pretend it isn't happening as we trudge to our doom." I saw Lisette getting into her—our—white Saab with five friends, one more than the car could hold.

"Lioness at four o'clock," Warner said.

He meant Lisette. "You got that right." I should have told him that she was my stepsister, but then I'd have to introduce them. I did not want to introduce Warner to Lisette. Like, obviously, I'd have to if we got married, but not before then.

I called Mother. Her joy at hearing that I was going out with a boy was so loud I had to pretend to drop the call to keep Warner from hearing. I turned my ringer off. That done, I took shotgun in Warner's not-new-enough-to-be-spoiled-but-not-so-old-it-looks-gangsta Honda Civic.

"Nice car." I tried to check my hair in the side view without being obvious. It actually looked pretty good.

"Spoils of parental guilt. My parents got it for me to make up for moving again." He smiled. "Though, maybe I don't actually mind being back here. Now."

I smiled. "Do you mind if I take out Runaway Ralph? I promise he won't eat your dashboard."

"Go ahead."

I opened the box and petted the mouse's head. He stared up at me with wide, frightened eyes. I'd thought all white mice had red eyes, but his were black. "It's okay, little guy. Really, you're a lot better off in my purse. It may not seem that way, but sometimes, things work out for the best."

"Like me, moving back here." Warner handed me a package of Cheez-Its that were sitting in his cup holder. "See if he wants these."

I took out a cracker. The mouse hesitated, stuck his head into the corner of the box, then turned around and took a few tentative nibbles.

"He'd be dead by now," I said. "Fischer lets students watch him feed the snake right after school."

"Yikes. I'm sure you'll be very happy together."

"Yes." I took the mouse and the cracker out and cupped them both in my hands.

"So, now you can tell me why my mouse-napping was typical. Do you think I'm generally involved in animal trafficking?"

My voice sounded different to me. I actually did sound confident.

Warner laughed. I noticed that when he laughed, he showed both rows of teeth, and they were very straight. I remembered he used to have braces. "You just seem like a really compassionate person."

"Because of the mouse?"

"No. I remember in seventh grade, that kid, Nate, in our civics class."

I nodded. Nate had actually been in my class most years since kindergarten. He had some learning problems, and sometimes he got overwhelmed and cried. Most teachers tried to help him, but our civics teacher, Ms. Hill, seemed to *try* to fluster him, asking questions in a baby voice you'd use for a stupid person or loudly pointing out when he wasn't going fast enough. "Ms. Hill was so mean."

Warner nodded. "I always wanted to do something. It was like one of those nature shows, where the cheetahs are attacking the baby gazelle, and all you can do is watch."

"I hate that."

"But you actually stood up to her."

"Got in big trouble too." I looked out the window, remembering. One day, Nate wasn't copying an assignment off the board. It was a long assignment, guidelines for a project, and Hill was screaming at him for not doing it. People—the usual suspects—were snickering. Finally, I copied it myself and just handed it to him.

"Hill saw me copy the assignment, of course," I said to Warner. "She turned on me, saying, 'He's never going to learn if people do things for him.'"

"You remember what you said to her?" Warner asked.

"Remember? I had to repeat it to the assistant principal. I said, 'Yeah, obviously he learns a lot better when people like you scream at him.'"

"I don't think you said 'people,' though. I almost applauded."

I looked down, embarrassed. "I'm not usually like that, all assertive, I mean. That's practically the only assertive thing I've ever done."

"And freeing a mouse, and breaking out of hoedown jail."

I laughed, flattered he remembered me as some kind of Rebel Girl, even though I wasn't. Usually, I figured no one noticed me at all. "She just made me so mad. I had to say something."

"I know. That's what made it awesome. You were like this perfect student, and there you were, talking back to the teacher. I thought, 'I want to know that girl.'"

"Really?"

"It took me a year to ask you out, and then you blew me off, but I never forgot it."

I gazed out the window because I didn't want him to see my face, see how much I was smiling. We'd finally cleared the parking lot and were on the road. The oaks filtered the sun, making the street glitter like hundreds of diamonds. Was it possible that this was my life, that something was finally going right as it never had since I'd met Lisette?

Possibly.

"What do you think of *Jeopardy*?" It just popped out of my mouth.

"Huh?"

"Never mind. It's stupid."

"The TV show *Jeopardy*?" When I nodded, he said, "It's my favorite. My family watches it every night. We actually schedule dinner around it. I'm taking the online test for the teen tournament next month. Dorky, right?"

I shook my head. "I love *Jeopardy*." I could hear the theme music in my head, feel Daddy's arm on the back of my shoulder. It seemed like I should be able to yank back a curtain and be there again.

"I knew it," Warner said. "The perfect girl."

We spent an hour in PetSmart, choosing a cage, cedar shavings, and a mouse wheel, then another hour at Panera drinking coffee before the manager noticed Ralph and asked us to leave. By the time I got home, I had a new pet and a date for Saturday night—my first ever for both.

I cleared a place for Ralph's cage on my dresser. The mouse was afraid of me and ran whenever I reached into his cage. Still, I was sure he'd get used to me. And, more important, I had a date for Saturday. Saturday!

"Whatcha got there?"

"Oh!" I turned and saw Lisette standing in the doorway of the bathroom that connected our rooms. "What do you want?"

"Now, Emma." Lisette strode into the room. "I don't always want something."

I stared at her.

"Cute guy," she said. "Do I know him?"

I shrugged, trying to look casual, but my hands were shaking. "I have no idea."

"Maybe I should get to know him."

Amazing. No longer content with stealing my jewelry, my books, my friends, and my father, Lisette now wanted to steal Warner. And she could. She was so pretty any guy would go for her. He'd pointed her out: the lioness. Runaway Ralph jogged on his mouse wheel, and I felt like I was on a mouse wheel. I just wanted off.

"Don't you ever get tired of it, Lisette?"

"Tired of what?"

"Tormenting me, taking my stuff. You even take stuff you don't need, like my glasses, or makeup that's the wrong color for you. Doesn't it ever get old?"

"Does it get old living in my house with my father?"

Lisette awaited my answer, even though she was sure she knew it. I surprised her.

"Yeah. Yes, it gets really old. If it was up to me, I'd move out and leave you to him. You don't care about Dad anyway, and we have no relationship left. There's nothing in it for me."

She did look surprised. "Nothing? A big house, nice clothes?"

"Are overrated compared to pride. Maybe I used to be spoiled, but I'm not anymore. It's who you are that's important."

"And who are you, Emma?" Her blue eyes, piercing as the snake's, met mine.

"I'm someone who works hard at school, who's nice to my mother, and who is loyal and has integrity. I'm someone who's going to be fine as soon as I get the hell away from you. Who are you, Lisette?"

She laughed. "God, you're so lame. I'm loyal, blah, blah, blah."

"I have homework, Lisette." Much as I feared turning my back on her, I did. I stuck my finger into Ralph's cage. He cowered in fright.

"I could have him, you know, that guy of yours. I could have him, if I wanted."

I shrugged and didn't look at her. Obviously, she wanted me to beg her to leave Warner alone. "But do you want him, Lisette?

I mean, you've won, haven't you? Do you really need to torture me, like a cat with a mouse?"

Or are you more like a snake who swallows the mouse alive?

"You're right. He's probably not worth my time. I mean, he's a total geek with those freckles." She brushed past me to Ralph's cage. "Isn't that the mouse that disappeared from Fischer's classroom?"

"Yeah. You going to rat me out?" I smirked, realizing the unintentional pun.

"Of course not. I love animals. I'd never want this little guy to be fed to a big, hungry snake."

She reached over and unlatched Ralph's cage, then stuck her hand in. The mouse, who had been hyper and frantic every time I touched him, became still upon seeing Lisette's hand. Then, he hopped into it.

"Aw," she said. "What a cutie."

The mouse nuzzled her finger. Even the mouse loved her.

A minute later, she put Ralph back inside. She shut the cage door and left without saying a word.

My cell phone tone signaled that I had a text. I picked it up.

It was from Warner:

HAD FUN TODAY. LOOKING FORWARD TO SAT NITE.

I texted back:

ME TOO.

3

The search for the missing mouse fizzled pretty quickly. Turned out most people at school liked mice better than snakes, so they weren't too upset about the escape. Ms. Meinbach considered having the paper write an article about the jailbreak, but she decided against it. It wasn't news if no one cared.

Still, I was impressed that Lisette hadn't turned me in. Maybe she really did like animals.

I had other things to worry about, like my date with Warner Saturday.

He was taking me to a party at the home of Brendan Webb, a guy who went to our school but was way too cool to notice me. "We were best friends when we were kids," Warner explained.

"Sounds fun." I tried to pretend that it did, in fact, sound fun. It didn't. I hadn't liked parties since people stopped having skating parties in seventh grade. There were too many people at them, too many opportunities to mess up. I didn't even know what you did at a high school party. If movies were any indication, you got drunk, got molested or arrested, had drugs put into your drink, got pregnant, or jumped off the roof.

But that was stupid. People went to parties, and they (mostly) didn't die.

I told Kendra this. She looked doubtful.

"Have you ever read 'The Masque of the Red Death'?" she asked.

"Edgar Allan Poe, where the guy has a party and someone shows up with the plague or something?" I noticed Kendra visibly shuddered when I said the word *plague*. "What about it?"

"Based on a true story. People don't know that, but it's true. Poe said so himself. Parties can kill. Do you know where Marie Antoinette met Louis XVI? A party. It cost her her life."

"Wait. Are you sure? I thought they were married by proxy. That's what it said in our world history book."

"Yeah, but when she finally got there, you can be sure they had a party. The French royal family were huge partiers, I know. Same with Ann Boleyn. She met Henry VIII at a party. Next thing you know . . ." She drew her finger across her throat. "*Kkkkkkk.*"

"I know that's not true. I read a book that said—"

"Historical fiction? There's a reason they call it fiction—though the history books are sometimes even worse. Trust me, bad things have happened to people at parties. It's a good way to lose your head."

"Yeah, they don't behead people in Miami." Kendra's versions of history were often, um, unique. "So you're saying I shouldn't go out with Warner?"

She seemed to remember that this was a bad idea. "We must not let fear stand in the way of true love."

"Right."

"Just watch your neck."

Subject-change time. "So, what should I wear then?"

Look who I was asking.

"Wear something that looks like you. That's what he likes, right?"

But I had no idea what that was. In the end, I wore a sundress, remembering that he'd liked me in that at the hoedown.

We pulled through the wrought-iron gates of a house on Old Cutler Road. I breathed in, savoring the air inside his car, Warner's car. He'd picked me up at exactly seven, and I'd flattered myself that he was as excited about our date as I was. I'd been ready at six-thirty, but I hadn't let myself sit by the door.

"Here we are." Warner looked at me in the reflected light from the big house. "You look so pretty."

I felt myself blush. "Thanks. You too. I mean, not pretty, but . . . wow, this is some house." Through the car's window, I could hear shrieks of partygoers and the ocean roaring in the background. "And on the water too."

"Brendan's dad does . . . well. We went to a Christmas party here once, and they had women doing water ballet for the entertainment." He took his key from the ignition, and as he did, his arm brushed mine. I felt myself shiver.

"Wow," I said.

I heard a scream coming from above. I looked up to see a figure on the roof, a girl in a skimpy bikini. "Here goes!" she yelled before plunging forward.

She actually was jumping off the roof.

"I hope the pool's down there," Warner said.

"No one's screaming like they saw a dead body."

"They could be too drunk to notice." He led me up the path to the open double doors. "I thought we were early."

Inside was worse than the high school movies I'd seen. It was more like the college movies, the ones where people go on spring break. If the Red Death had been here, they'd never have noticed him through the haze of pot smoke. I had on twice as much clothing as any other girl. They mostly wore butt shorts and camisoles. Many wore less.

This was so not the type of party I went to. If this was the kind of friends Warner had, or wanted, he'd never be into me. On the sofa, a blonde reached her hand down her date's pants. I tried not to stare, tried not to cling to Warner's hand like a scared three-year-old either. I wished I was home, reading *Sense and Sensibility*, or my namesake novel, *Emma*.

"Warner, my man!" Brendan, his Hawaiian shirt unbuttoned and breath smelling of beer, greeted us. "You made it."

"Yeah, when did this party start?" Warner voiced my own question.

Brendan glanced at his wrist, saw that he didn't have on a watch, and shrugged. "Yesterday, I think. That's when my parents left." He noticed me. "Hey, you brought your mom."

Warner frowned. "Funny, Bren. This is Emma. Emma, Brendan."

Brendan had gone back to studying his wrist. He looked back at Warner. "Dude, there's someone who's been waiting to meet you." Finally he spoke to me, but only to say, "Can you excuse us a sec?"

Warner said, "I don't think—"

"It's fine." What else could I say? Brendan was already pulling him out onto the patio.

I walked into the kitchen. Wall to wall people. A couple was making out on the table. I turned to leave.

"Want some punch?" A guy handed me a cup.

I took it. As I did, I got a better look at the girl on the table. Lisette. Yes, this was her type of party. I took one sip of the punch, even though I knew it was probably spiked. It tasted like cough syrup. Maybe it was cough syrup. I shoved through the crowd to the patio and almost got hit by another roof jumper. I escaped, but my dress was swamped by the splash from the pool.

This was all wrong. This was wrong, and I was stupid. I'd put all these hopes onto Warner, and not just for the past few days, but longer, if I was willing to admit it to myself. I'd had this fantasy about this guy who liked me, even though I wasn't that pretty, who somehow didn't think I was all wrong because I liked reading and didn't wear a negative jeans size. Obviously, I was delusional. I stared down at my soaked, ruined dress and felt about to cry. I had to leave. I couldn't find Warner, but I really didn't want to. I'd have to call Mother, get her to pick me up, admit that the night, my first real date, was an epic fail. And I'd have to deal with her disappointment on top of my own. I started back toward the house.

Then suddenly the patio went silent and everything seemed to freeze. Was I hallucinating? Was there acid in that one sip of punch I'd taken? I dumped it out. I surveyed the crowd. They looked turned to stone—Aéropostale-clad versions of the White Witch's victims in Chronicles of Narnia.

Then, a black-clothed figure emerged from the crowd. The first thing I noticed was, she was dressed even wronger than I was, in a black lace dress, purple flowers in her hair. The second thing I noticed was, it was Kendra. Kendra? What was she doing here? She glided through the frozen mob. How did she do that?

"Lose your head yet?" She smiled.

I must be drunk. Yet, other than the small fact that the patio looked like a digital sports photograph, complete with the hanging feet of another roof jumper, I felt fine. What was happening?

"I need to go." I started toward the house again.

"Not that way." Kendra blocked my path. "Go out through the back. The police will be here in a minute."

"How do you know?"

"I know things." She took my arm and led me through the motionless crowd to the coral rock steps that led down to the ocean. It was too dark to see, but her hand steadied me. "Cut through the yard next door, and you'll be in a park, the one by the library. Call your mom from there. I'll tell Warner."

"I don't care about Warner."

"Of course you do."

She was right. I was still hoping the date could be salvaged somehow, but it couldn't.

I looked around. "How is this possible?"

She shrugged. "Lots of things are possible, Emma. We must talk sometime. But now, just go."

She led me to the bottom of the stairs, then released me, pointing down and to the left. "That way."

I obeyed. In the silence, the ocean's roar was louder, harder. The wind whipped my face, and I realized my dress was now completely dry. My high-heeled sandals sunk into the sand. I removed them. I heard a splash in the pool. The jumper. The music started back up, though it was different, something from the Black Crowes' *Croweology* album. Then other noise from the house, and suddenly the wail of sirens. Kendra had been right! I ran in the direction she'd pointed.

Her voice followed me. "Warner likes you too!"

4

I ran until my calves hurt and I wanted to fall down on the damp sand. Suddenly someone else was on the beach. I heard my name.

"Emma! Emma, wait!"

Warner. In spite of myself, I felt a surge of relief, and hope. Still, I said, "I'm leaving. The cops are here. I'm just not cool enough for this party. I'm calling my mother and going home."

"I know. I don't blame you. I'm sorry. You have to believe me, I . . . can I at least walk with you? Please, Emma."

"I can't stop you."

"I'll leave you alone if you want, but I'm really sorry." A siren squealed.

"Do whatever you want. Just be quiet, okay?" I knew I was full of it. I still liked him. You didn't stop liking someone you'd fantasized about for two years. Up on shore, I could see the red and blue lights above the house. The sirens were loud now, and people were screaming, scattering. Thanks to Kendra, we had a good head start. Kendra. I still couldn't wrap my head around what I'd seen back there. It was so weird. It must have been that punch.

I stumbled across the crunchy sand, Warner following. When we reached the fence of the next property, I started to try and climb over it. Warner stopped me with a hand on my shoulder. "Wait! There's a broken piece farther down. I remember from when we were kids."

I followed him. The bougainvillea hedge scraped my bare arms. Warner must have noticed because he stripped off his jacket and held it up to me. "Take it. Please."

"This doesn't make me not mad," I said, taking it, even though it sort of did.

"Understood."

His hands felt warm and competent as he helped me on with the jacket, just like Daddy had when I was little. The fabric felt old and soft, like it had been washed a hundred times. It smelled like Warner. Warner and bleach. We felt along the fence until we found a broken spot, squeezed through, then ran through that yard to the park on the other side. Warner held my hand. I felt a shiver at having him close, having him hold me in the salty night air. It was so exactly how I'd wanted the evening to end.

And so exactly not.

Once we cleared the second fence, we stopped. I couldn't hear the party or the sirens anymore, only the ocean and Warner's breathing, heavy from running.

"They won't follow us this far," he said. "If you want, we could hang out until the cops leave, then I'll drive you home."

"You ditched me." It was appealing, though, not to call my mother.

"I didn't mean to. I'm sorry. Brendan and I were best friends growing up."

"That doesn't fill me with confidence in you."

"I know. He was nicer then. I was shy. Maybe his mom made him be nice to me. Anyway, I guess I thought that connection was worth something, even though he's turned into a complete jerk. I just didn't want to admit we weren't still friends."

I nodded, remembering how I'd clung to Courtney and even Lisette. "I understand."

"And I guess . . ."

"What?" I turned toward him. In the moon's light, I could see his face clearly. His eyelashes were white, which made his eyes look even bluer, bluer than the stars.

"I guess I wanted to impress you too, the big house, my popular friend."

"Wow. That really backfired." But it was sweet.

"I shouldn't have brought you here. This party isn't who I am."

I looked around at the black sky, the deserted park overhung by shadowy palms. The surf pounded against the seawall. I said, "This is nicer, actually."

So much nicer. Here, alone with Warner, I felt safe. No one was watching me. No one judging. The night air enveloped me like a blanket.

"We could still do something," he said. "I could buy you ice cream."

"Next time." I realized I was admitting there would be a next time. I thought of Lisette, at the party with the cops coming. Would she get arrested? Would she be okay? Why did I even care? Lisette certainly wouldn't have cared, if it was me. Besides, nothing bad ever happened to Lisette. The girl led a charmed life. She'd get out of the party, no problem.

I got a jagged rock stuck in my shoe, and I leaned down to pick it up. Then I walked toward the water.

"What are you doing?" Warner said.

"The stars are so pretty. And the water. If you hadn't brought me to that lame party, we wouldn't be here, looking at it."

"That's true." He followed me. The air was silent except for the sound of wind in the palmettos and our feet crunching against the coral rock. Warner's hand brushed mine as we walked. I was still clutching the rock. We reached the seawall, and I raised my hand to hurl it into the water. Warner grabbed my elbow.

"Wait!"

I stopped, surprised. A chill ran up my arm where he'd touched me. "What?"

He pointed out at the still, dark water. "See that?"

At first I didn't see anything. Then I noticed the dark blob in the water. "A manatee. Cool." I dropped the rock and stepped closer.

"Did you know that in West African folklore, manatees are considered sacred?" When I shook my head, Warner said, "It's true. And in days of old, sailors used to mistake them for mermaids."

"Sailors must have been pretty hard up for female companionship, huh? I mean, no offense, but they're a little . . . chunky."

Warner laughed. "I guess maybe you see what you want to see. But I like them." He gazed out at the huge, still creature. The water rippled around it. "When I was a kid, we used to go to my grandma's place in Fort Lauderdale. There were these two manatees in the canal there, and my brother and I would give them lettuce. My mom called them sea cows and said they were ugly, but Grandma said they were angels, docile creatures that would never hurt anyone. That's why we had to watch out for them, she said, as they watched over us. I asked my mom what that meant, and she said that sometimes, older people said things that seemed a little strange. Then my grandmother moved into an assisted living facility, so I didn't see her anymore. When I was ten, she died."

"I'm sorry."

"Yeah, I was really sad. We were close, so I had a hard time getting over it, but the weird thing was, the next year, I went to Vero

Beach with my cousins. We were swimming in the ocean and having a lot of fun bodysurfing when suddenly this huge wave swamped me. I felt my head hit bottom, and my mouth was full of water and sand. I couldn't see anything. I honestly thought I was going to die."

"Wow. That must have been scary."

"Yeah. But then, all of a sudden, there was a manatee. It came out of nowhere. It got under me and nudged me to shore."

"They can do that?" The manatee in front of us moved slightly in the moonlit water.

"I guess. I mean, they're supposed to be really smart, but when I ran up to tell my aunt what had happened, she said she didn't see a manatee. I went back to the water, and I looked and looked, but I couldn't find it either. It was almost like . . ." He shook his head. "It sounds crazy."

"You think it was your grandmother."

"I know it's crazy."

"No, it's not. I absolutely think it's possible. I've had things happen that were unexplainable like that."

And recently too. I thought of Kendra, just showing up at the exact right minute to save me from the party. It was like she could stop time. Like that.

"Really? I never told anyone that before. I figured they'd think I was nuts."

"I wouldn't." I looked at the manatee again. It seemed to have moved closer. "I believe that things happen for a reason. Like that time at the hoedown, when I hit all those targets. Remember?"

Warner nodded.

"Can I tell you, I have never hit a target in my life. I'm completely uncoordinated. But that day, I think it was a sign. I was supposed to talk to you."

A breeze rippled across the water and through the palmettos. I shivered, suddenly cold, and Warner moved closer. He slid his hand down my arm. "So this was supposed to happen? Tonight?"

I looked up at him. "Maybe."

"Just maybe?"

His voice was a whisper. He took my hand. His felt callused on one finger, and I wondered if it was from writing. My hand was the same way. I moved in closer. "Definitely."

I knew he was going to kiss me, and suddenly I didn't want him to, not because I didn't like him. I did. I always had. But because I wanted to preserve this moment, this slice of time when the night was cool and bright with reflected moonlight and the possibility of a kiss hung between us, full of unspent promise. Every event in my life after this would be different because I would have been kissed. Was I ready?

I decided I was.

I leaned toward him, and he said, "I like you so much, Emma." I said nothing, not wanting to hear my voice, because in that moment that our lips met, I wasn't Emma. I wasn't dorky bookworm Emma, Emma who wrote stupid poetry and couldn't hold a candle to her sister. I was some other girl.

I was some girl boys wanted to kiss.

5

When I got home, I was pretty sure I was in love. Pretty sure because it wasn't like I knew Warner really well, and it sounded cheesy to say I loved him. Maybe he was just this character in my fantasies, no more real than Dobbin or Mr. Darcy or Rochester, those guys I loved in my books. No more real than Lisette that first day, when I thought we'd be like sisters.

But Warner was becoming real. At least, I thought so. A real boy with calluses and flaws, a boy who made bad decisions and clung to childhood friends who'd outgrown him, a boy with bony shoulders, who'd kissed me to the music of the pounding surf.

I went into the bathroom between Lisette's bedroom and mine. My side was unlocked, for once, and to my surprise, so was Lisette's. I reached to close the door. I could see her lying on her bed, asleep, so I knew she hadn't been arrested. She slept on her back, which I once read meant you were narcissistic. They got that right. The article said it was the easiest position from which to take a bow. I wondered if she'd really liked that boy she'd been with at the party, liked him the way I liked Warner. Or was he just someone to make her feel wanted, make her feel less lonely with herself. For the first time in my life, I couldn't decide whether to envy or pity her.

I ended up doing neither because, at that moment, the phone vibrated. Kendra never texted. She said that letter writing was a dying art and she wasn't going to hasten its demise by texting. Since it was Saturday, I knew no one would text me about school or the newspaper, and my mother was in bed. Which meant . . .

I dove for the phone. Warner!

I forced myself to click on the text slowly, careful not to delete it. I'd kept the other text he sent me, and I knew I'd keep this one too, on my phone forever, and even transfer it to the SIM card when I got a new phone. Someday, I'd be eighty with some kind of space-age version of a cell phone that read your every thought and answered texts for you, and I'd still have Warner's text.

Assuming it was nice.

Assuming it was even from Warner.

It was. Both things.

SORRY TO TEXT SO LATE BUT I CAN'T STOP THINKING ABOUT YOU. I CAN'T SLEEP.

Definite keeper.

With shaking hands, I composed my response.

ME NEITHER. I'M SO GLAD YOU CAME BACK TO MIAMI. IT'S LIKE DESTINY.

I deleted the last line. Too corny, and he might think I was a stalker. His reply came almost instantly.

IT'S LIKE DESTINY.

OMG!
I texted back.

OMG! I WAS THINKING THAT!

I held on to the phone. I wanted to get dressed for bed, then lie in the darkness with the moonlight streaking through the curtains and read Warner's texts. But it was hard to change clothes if you couldn't, absolutely could not put down the phone. And I couldn't. I didn't want to miss anything. So I tucked the phone between my chin and my neck.

I was rewarded for my vigilance with a text.

OF COURSE YOU WERE. IT'S TRUE.

I texted back.

CAN YOU SEE THE FULL MOON FROM YOUR WINDOW?

I rushed to get undressed, not bothering to hang up my clothes. I only had time to strip and put on my nightgown before he texted back. I chose a long, white old-fashioned one that made me feel like a princess. I glanced in the mirror in the dimly lit bathroom. Then I did a double take. The girl who looked back at me was someone I didn't recognize, not skinny but somehow still beautiful in the half-light, like a Titian Madonna.

When I heard the message tone, I slipped under the covers to read.

YES. I CAN SEE THE MAN IN THE MOON REALLY CLEARLY.

I looked out. I could too. I texted back.

PEOPLE USED TO SAY THAT THE MAN IN THE MOON WAS A THIEF WHO WAS BANISHED FOR HIS CRIME.

Would he think I was dumb? The message tone went again.

I'VE ALSO HEARD CAIN.

Oh, God. He was as big a geek as I was!

I texted back:

IT MUST BE LONELY UP THERE.

Lonely. Sitting in the dark, with his text, I allowed myself to acknowledge how lonely I'd been these past two years, how I'd yearned for someone, not even a boyfriend, but just someone who got me. I tried to think of something else to say, to keep the conversation going. I knew I'd keep answering his texts as long as he kept sending them.

Before I could think of anything, he texted me.

TELL ME 3 THINGS YOU'VE NEVER DONE.

Three things? *Three* things. Try a million. I texted back.

I'VE NEVER HAD A DOG OR CAT, ONLY RALPH.
I'VE NEVER SKYDIVED BECAUSE I'M AFRAID OF HEIGHTS.
UP UNTIL TONIGHT, I'VE NEVER BEEN KISSED.

I hit send, then typed,

YOU?

It took a minute for his replies. I listened to the sounds of the house. The air conditioner turned on and off. The ice-maker downstairs filled with water after spitting out ice.

Finally, the tone sounded.

I'VE NEVER CHEATED IN SCHOOL EVEN WHEN EVERYONE ELSE DOES.
I'M NOT AFRAID OF HEIGHTS, BUT I'VE NEVER WANTED TO GO TO NYC BECAUSE CROWDS FREAK ME OUT.
I'VE NEVER KISSED ANYONE EITHER.

We stayed up texting until the numbers on my digital clock may have said 4:00, but I was too bleary-eyed to be sure. I fell asleep with the phone in my hand.

I was definitely in love.

6

You know how romantic comedies have those montage things, where they show the couple falling in love? Picture one of those if the two people involved were both total nerds. Like, instead of the part where they playfully feed each other ice cream, picture Warner and me making pies for Pi Day (March 14, if you didn't know, for 3.14, the value of pi). Instead of the scene where the cute couple plays touch football and falls, kissing, into a pile of colorful leaves, picture Warner and me taking fencing classes to prepare for next year's Renaissance festival. We watched *Jeopardy* every night, and we both planned to take the online test for the Teen Tournament. For the first time since I'd lost Daddy, I had someone who got me.

And I got Warner. On our second date (taking the train downtown to the big library), Warner told me they'd moved back to Miami because his parents were splitting up. His dad had a girlfriend, and they were getting married as soon as the divorce was final. "So that's why I got the car," Warner said, "as if that somehow makes up for it."

I told Warner my sad story too; well, most of it, about the father I'd never known, the stepfather who only cared about his "real" kid. It felt good, finally saying it all aloud. But I didn't tell him Lisette was my sister, and I kept him away from the house so they wouldn't meet. Lisette had said she wouldn't move in on him, but really, since when could I trust her? Warner probably thought my parents had a meth lab or something, based on how hard I worked to keep him away from my house, my family. Lisette and I had different last names, and the three of us had no classes together. Making sure their paths didn't cross in the halls or the cafeteria was a little like trying to outrun a tornado, but I tried. If Lisette met Warner, I knew she'd ruin it.

But one day in early April I finally invited him over to study. Lisette had gotten a big part in the spring play, and as the date grew closer, they had rehearsals every day. I figured it was safe.

I pointed out my tree house on the way inside. It looked sad now, with falling planks, the once-green paint faded to a mottled gray-brown. Daddy had taken down the ladder the year before because he said it wasn't safe.

"That was my tree house," I told Warner. "I used to study there all the time."

Warner looked up. It was a windy day, and the leaves rustled. "We could fix it."

I felt the callus on his finger again, as it brushed the back of my hand before our fingers intersected. "I don't know anything about construction."

"I do, a little. I made stuff with my dad when I was a kid." He frowned. "How hard could fixing a tree house be, if it's important to you?"

I smelled the orange blossoms in the air, and I pulled him closer. "I love you."

It just popped out. It was bound to, considering I thought it all the time—when we were texting, when he opened the door of his car for me in the student parking lot, when he said he'd actually enjoyed *Wuthering Heights*, unlike every other boy in the tenth grade. But I didn't want to say it first. The girl wasn't supposed to. Besides, what if he didn't say it back?

What if he didn't say it back?

"I love you too, Emma."

I exhaled. "Whew!"

He laughed. "Did you think I wouldn't say it? Of course I love you, Emma."

Of course.

He kissed me, and I felt a warm breeze across my arms and shoulders.

"Maybe we can go to Home Depot after we're done studying," I said a minute later.

"Sure. It will reward you for your good work habits."

I love you. I love you. I love you.

I led him up the steps to the door. Instead of ringing the bell, I used my key to get in, giving myself an extra minute before Mother was there, assessing Warner. Mother and I had become allies in our war with Lisette. Still, I feared her assessments of me and, by extension, Warner. I also worried she'd embarrass me.

When I shook the key out and pushed the door open, Warner breathed a big mock sigh of relief.

"What's that supposed to mean?" I asked.

"We've been together a month, and you haven't had me over

once. I was worried there'd be a dungeon or something."

"Who says there isn't? You haven't seen the whole house yet."

"Then show me."

I closed my eyes, steeling myself by remembering Warner's words. He'd said he loved me. He loved me. I put my hand on Warner's waist and led him into the dragon's lair (by which I meant the kitchen).

But it didn't go badly. Mother didn't seem disapproving, nor was she embarrassingly gushy, like she'd never expected me to bring a boy home. She only used the word "finally" once, and when I said we were going to my room to study, she didn't act like we might possibly be filming a porno in there. She just told me to leave the door open. Lots of moms did that.

Later, in Warner's car on the way to Home Depot, I asked him, "What if there had been something terribly wrong with my house?"

He laughed, then saw I was serious. He took his hand off the wheel and caressed my elbow. "What do you think? I'd love you anyway. I'm just glad you have a happy family."

I didn't correct him, though I wondered, could someone love you if you didn't tell him the whole truth?

"Oh, by the way, Ms. Meinbach asked me if I could cover the school play next Friday for the paper. They're doing *Into the Woods*. It's supposed to be good. Wanna go?"

Lisette's play! *Calm down*. He wouldn't know it was Lisette's play. It was just any old newspaper assignment for him.

"Um, sure. I guess so."

"Well, think about it. It sounds like your kind of thing—a bunch of fairy tales, like a mash-up."

I knew that. Lisette was playing Cinderella.

". . . and she wants me to interview some cast members, like a feature. There's this sophomore girl, Lisa something, who's supposed to be super-talented."

Deep breaths. He doesn't know who she is. He loves you.

"She's playing Cinderella."

Still, the twangy guitars and "Stand by Your Man" rang in my ears, and I said, "Sure, I'll go. Sounds fun."

Warner didn't even seem to notice that my voice was shaking.

7

In the next week, Warner and I said "I love you" a hundred times. It was like some portal or Pandora's box had opened and everything was rushing out. We said it mornings as we parted for class, wrote it on notes left in lockers, texted it to each other, mouthed it across classrooms behind teachers' backs and in crowded hallways. We said it when we made out in Warner's car, and we whispered it into cell phones last thing before bed at night. Yet, every time I heard it, I felt the same, like fireworks were shooting from my head or like Jack, the Pumpkin King, when he discovered Christmas Town in *The Nightmare Before Christmas.* Someone loved me! I felt reborn, like I finally had something of my own after years of nothing. It was nice but scary too. Warner loved me because he thought I was strong and smart, but my terror of losing him told me I was neither. I was weak and needy. At least, that's how I felt a lot of the time.

There was still the matter of Warner meeting Lisette. I tried not to think about it, but one day, I met Kendra at Starbucks, the same Starbucks where I'd gone with Lisette and Courtney two years earlier. I told her everything.

"He's meeting her, Kendra." I took a bite of crumb cake.

"So?"

"So? He'll see her perfection, and that will be it for me."

"Don't be stupid. Perfection is annoying." Kendra took a sip of her caramel macchiato. "What even makes you think she'd want him?"

Now there was a comforting thought—she wouldn't like him. It was true that Lisette had tons of boys around. "She'd steal Warner just to spite me."

Kendra grimaced at her drink. "Cold." She rubbed her hands on the cup, as if that would help. "Warner loves you, Emma. I've seen it on his freckly little face. It's the real thing."

"I guess."

"It's true. Lisette may be witchy, but she has no power over him. He adores you."

I laughed. "Maybe. Why don't you ask them for a new one?"

Kendra ignored me, still rubbing her coffee cup. "And if I'm wrong and he goes with her . . ." She removed her hands from the cup and looked at me.

"What?"

Kendra took a sip of the steaming coffee. ". . . if he does, then we'll fix it. I always help my friends."

Every day after school, while Lisette was at rehearsals, Warner and I worked on my tree house. Warner brought hammer, nails, and a saw, and we sanded, cut, banged, and finally painted until we'd restored it to its former glory. But, even as we did it, the thought dogged me. Warner meeting Lisette. I thought of it as I sanded and almost scraped off a bit of my finger. I thought of it as I hammered, and the thought pounded in my brain. Warner would like Lisette better. Anyone would.

I almost didn't want to go to the play, didn't want to see it happen. Yet I knew I couldn't just surrender. I had to try to keep him.

Two days left. I felt like I was about to be executed. But that was stupid. Warner said he loved me. How could I love him back and yet have so little confidence in him?

Friday afternoon we finished our project. The tree house was once again painted dark green to match the trees. It had a solid fence around it. "For privacy," Warner said. He handed me up the ladder, then stood below, reciting:

"But, soft! what light through yonder window breaks?
It is the east, and Emma is the sun.
Arise, fair sun, and kill the envious moon,
Who is already sick and pale with grief,
That thou, her maid, art far more fair than she."

Romeo and Juliet! We'd read the play in language arts last year. I guess Warner had at his old school too. Warner started to climb the ladder. I giggled. He continued:

"Be not her maid, since she is envious;
Her vestal livery is but sick and green
And none but fools do wear it; cast it off.
It is my lady, O, it is my love!"

He reached the top of the ladder and faced me. "You're so beautiful, Emma."

I laughed. "Beautiful? You think I'm beautiful?"

He gazed into my eyes. "Does that surprise you?"

I nodded like I was agreeing with a child. "You must be blinded by my stunning personality."

"Nope. You're beautiful. Can you honestly not see it?"

I wanted to believe it. "What's so beautiful about me?"

"Why don't you tell me? Tell me something about you that's beautiful."

I tried to laugh it off. I wasn't beautiful; I was smart, but that was never enough, never what I wanted. I was nice, and no one cared. I was a lot of things, but beautiful? Not me. Yet he looked at me so intensely, and in that look, I saw that he believed it. Maybe I really was beautiful and I hadn't noticed it. I tried to picture my face and said, "My eyes?"

He nodded. "A beautiful shade of gray. Keep going."

"I guess my nose isn't bad."

Warner risked falling by taking one hand off the railing and touching my nose. "It's adorable. And your skin, your hair. Can't you see it? You glow from the inside, Emma."

Maybe it was because I was in love. I held out my arms to him, then moved aside to let him up. "I'm so happy." I tried to remember some appropriate line from the play. Finally, I said, "If thou dost love, pronounce it faithfully."

He laughed and kissed me, asking, "What shall I swear by?"

We were interrupted by the sound of Daddy's car pulling into the driveway. He stepped out. "Hey, you fixed it up. It looks great."

He extended his hand upward to Warner. "Tom Cooper, Emma's dad."

"Sir." Warner reached down, saying, "Emma loves this so much."

Daddy smiled at me. "I remember. I built it when you were four or five. Your mother always worried you'd hurt yourself."

"I know. But it was our special thing." I turned away so Warner wouldn't see my eyes, how they filled with tears. Finally, I'd bitten my lip enough times to choke out, "I still love it."

Daddy nodded. "Me too. Sometimes . . ." He stopped.

"What?" A breeze fluttered through the leaves of the old oak, and I shivered.

He shook his head and said, "Sometimes, things change so quickly you don't even know how it happened." He looked at Warner. "Ramblings of an old man."

"I understand." And I did. I understood that he didn't know how our relationship had gone south, had gotten away from him so quickly.

He waved his hand and said, "It's great that you fixed it up." He started for the door.

I wanted to run after him, to chase him and call him Daddy, tell him I was sorry, I loved him. I wanted to be his little girl again. I could have done it. Lisette wasn't there. Even if she had been, what would she have done, told him I smashed a jack-o'-lantern two years earlier? Now I saw so clearly that it had been stupid of me to give in to her blackmail. I had to fix it.

I didn't run after him because of Warner, because I didn't want him to think we were even more messed up than he already knew about. I let him go. Still, I promised myself we'd talk tomorrow.

I glanced at my watch, wishing I could freeze the moment in time, the breeze in my face, the scent of gardenias in the air, and Warner, looking at me, like he thought I was pretty. "Beautiful," he'd said. I inhaled deeply and stared at him, trying to photograph the moment with my mind so that if it all changed, I'd still own it.

Finally, I told him, "I should get ready. Thank you for this."

He hugged me. "I enjoyed it." We separated, and he started down the ladder. "I'll pick you up in an hour."

I nodded. "Sure."

I could have spoken to Daddy then, but Warner was coming back, and I wanted to look pretty, as pretty as I could at least. So, instead of talking to Daddy, I spent that hour showering and choosing an outfit, dressing, and blow-drying my hair, and when Warner came to pick me up he said, again, "You're so beautiful, Emma."

I blushed, hoping it was true.

8

Into the Woods was the type of play I'd have liked, if I hadn't been freaking out about the real-life drama. It was about a baker and his wife, who can't have a baby because of a family curse. The curse could be broken . . . but only if they collected a white cow, a red cape, corn-yellow hair, and a golden slipper from an assortment of fairy tale characters. I loved fairy tales, but I couldn't pay attention to the play or anything except Lisette, looking stunning even in rags as Cinderella, wishing she could go to the king's festival, yet thwarted by her horrible steprelatives. I rooted for her as she prayed to her dead mother. I wished I knew that sweet girl everyone loved.

In the darkness, I swiped at my eyes and hoped I wouldn't look like a raccoon at intermission.

After the play, Warner said, "Wow. You really liked it. We should go backstage and talk to the cast."

"Sure." I realized it was going to look strange to have Lisette recognize me when I hadn't told Warner about her. I looked around, wondering for the first time where Mother and Daddy were. They must have been coming to Lisette's play. I didn't see them.

Backstage was a frenzy of scattered costumes and makeup, Rapunzel hair, wolf ears, and red hoods. First, we interviewed the drama teacher, who gushed about tech stuff we couldn't use. She took us over to the boy who'd played the baker and the girl who'd played the wife. They were both talkative types and, in a minute, Warner had two pages of notes.

"That's great," I said. "You guys were wonderful. I think we have enough for a whole article."

Warner nodded. I glanced around, not seeing Lisette anywhere. I was going to get out without them meeting! Warner took my hand, and we were halfway to the door when I heard her voice.

"Emma!" She'd changed out of her lacy Cinderella gown, but she had on a white dress, and her hair sparkled with some kind of glittery hairspray. She looked, as always, disgustingly perfect, like Cinderella at the ball. "You came to see me!"

"School paper," I said, trying to make it seem like no big deal. I gestured at Warner, who'd gone silent at Lisette's entrance. "Warner, this is Lisette."

Lisette did a mock curtsey. "I'm Emma's stepsister."

"Stepsister?" Warner's eyebrows rose. "You didn't tell me she was your stepsister."

"Emma's a little strange sometimes." Lisette turned to me. "Were you ashamed of me, Em, or of him?"

"What? Neither." The room felt suddenly airless. "Of course not. I just . . . it never came up. You were never around."

Lisette laughed. "Kidding, Emma, kidding." Her tiny white hand brushed Warner's shoulder. "Who could be ashamed of him?"

She said it like she thought I was, and Warner shook his head.

"I'm still working on how she didn't tell me you were her stepsister." He looked at me, questioning.

"Sorry." I knew it was weird.

"Hey." Again, Lisette's hand brushed Warner's arm. "Do you guys want to come to the cast party? I can get you in."

"No, thanks," I said at the same time Warner said, "Sure."

"Great!" Lisette patted Warner's shoulder.

I had been so close to getting out of there. And now, here she was, touching Warner's arm, touching my boyfriend. I wanted to—I don't know—hit her like some girl on a reality show, screaming, "Keep away from my man, skank!" Of course, I couldn't do that, so instead, I was stuck there with Warner and Lisette, my perfect stepsister, making me look petty and plain next to her. I loved him. She didn't. But I knew it wouldn't matter to her. He was mine, so she'd go after him, like she always took everything that was mine. I only hoped that, for once, she wouldn't get what she wanted, that Warner knew me and loved me like he said he did.

Warner wrote down the address of the cast party. "Got it."

"See you there, hottie," Lisette said.

We never made it, though. We were halfway there, Warner casting me hurt looks because, apparently, he actually believed Lisette's b.s. about me being ashamed of him, when I got a text from Mother. I stared at the phone, barely able to read the words because of the shadows of trees through the window, but when I did read it, I had to read it again and again.

Finally, Warner saw me staring at it and said, "What's wrong?"

"Hospital," I choked out. "My father's had a heart attack."

I never got to talk to him. By the time we reached the hospital, he was gone. It was over, and he never knew I still loved him, that I never stopped loving him. I never knew if he still loved me, but I thought he did. I hoped he knew I loved him.

My father was gone. It was over. Any chance was gone.

Of all the things Lisette did to me, that was the one I'd never forgive her for. She'd stolen my father, and I'd let her.

The weeks after his death passed in a blur of flowers and casseroles and friends we didn't even know we had. I saw it as in a PowerPoint—me in a black dress, my eyes red as much from allergies to the flowers as from crying. My father, in his coffin, skin an unrecognizable yellow shade. Lisette, looking beautiful and sad in black lace, weeping, somehow still perfect. Warner's hand closing around my freckled one, his other hand in Lisette's.

The first concrete memory I had was of my mother, the day after the funeral. I was rereading *Vanity Fair*, like comfort food for my mind. I was on my favorite chapter, the part where Amelia's family goes bankrupt and Dobbin buys her piano at the bankruptcy auction. I was crying about that, about the book, about my life, which would have been wretched—wretched—if not for Warner. Thank God for Warner. He called and texted me every day and brought me the work I missed at school, and he loved me. I started to dial his number, even though he was at school, just wanting to hear his voicemail. But then I heard a scream from the next room. Lisette!

I ran out into the hallway. It was my mother. She stood in Lisette's doorway, her arms filled with Lisette's clothes.

"What are you doing?" But I knew. "How can you do this when Daddy's barely gone?"

"It's in the will. Your father and I discussed it. I have to keep her here."

I gestured toward Lisette, who was sobbing on her bed. "Then keep her here."

"I will. But I don't have to pamper her, don't have to treat her like a spoiled pet, like your father did. That's all over now. She's a mean little brat, Emma. You know it. Your father fell for her act, but I didn't."

With that, she started downstairs with Lisette's things. She was moving Lisette back to her old room, where she'd always wanted her. Energized by her hatred, my mother made trip after trip, taking clothes, stuffed animals, books, souvenirs of Lisette's perfect life, with a vigor she'd never possessed before. All the time, Lisette sobbed on the bed, and I knew it was wrong. Lisette had been my father's daughter, and now, both her parents were dead. He'd never have wanted this. I should have said something more to Mother, should have stopped her. I did nothing. I felt mean, mean enough to let this happen, mean enough to let it be payback for all Lisette had done to me.

Still, I shut the door to my room and pretended to read, holding my fist against the hole in my heart, listening to my mother's footsteps, Lisette's sobs, on and on. It was after midnight when it finally went silent. I heard it all.

The next day, I opened the bathroom door into what had been Lisette's room. It was empty. Lisette was gone too. I had done nothing to stop it. Did that make me mean like my mother? Or did it just make me less stupid and naïve than the girl who'd wanted so much to be Lisette's friend?

For my birthday, the next week, Mother gave me Lisette's car. I explained to her that I didn't need it, that I went everywhere with Warner. She said she didn't care. She also said she wasn't paying for any more voice or dance lessons for Lisette, wasn't paying for anything that wasn't legally required. Lisette didn't even have a cell phone anymore. If she wanted those things, Mother said, she'd have to get a job.

"How can I get a job when I don't have a car?" Lisette asked. "Will you drive me?"

Mother shrugged. "Take the bus. That's what poor people do."

It wasn't that I didn't understand why Mother hated Lisette so much. I did, better than anyone. But the idea of acting on my hatred was just foreign to me. I held it in.

She also gave Lisette a ton of chores, cleaning, laundry, straightening up after us. She fired the cleaning lady now that she had Lisette. I felt so bad for her that I started doing extra stuff, my own laundry, and once, I left twenty dollars on her dresser.

She slipped it back under the door. She wanted nothing from me.

Weeks passed. Sometimes, at school or when I was doing my homework, I'd think about Daddy, think maybe I'd talk to him when he got home, try to make things right. Then I'd remember I couldn't, not ever. The feeling made a hollow in my stomach, like a cavity in a tooth. It was over, all over. I could never have it back the way it was.

I couldn't even concentrate in school. All I wanted was to be with Warner. And yet, something was different between us. I felt like I couldn't talk to him either. I felt distant from everyone, like they couldn't hear me, even if I was screaming.

Then, one night, Mother and I were finishing dinner. We'd started eating in the dining room, the better for Lisette to serve us. I hated it. Lisette was clearing our dishes. That was when the phone rang.

"I'll get it!" Lisette said.

I'd walked toward the kitchen to get some water. I heard Lisette whispering into the phone. I stopped. "Have you told her?" she said. "Well, you have to."

A pause. Then she said, "Okay, I'll see you later. But, if you haven't said something by tomorrow, I will." She hung up.

After she left, I checked the caller ID, but I already knew. It had been Warner. When I tried his cell phone, he didn't answer.

I went and sat in my tree house, sinking deep, deep down, remembering how it had been when Daddy first built that house, when I was a little girl. It was May, and the wind whipped around me, turning my hair into hundreds of pins that stung my face.

Soon a car turned the corner, then waited in the street, hidden by tall trees. A slim, white figure emerged from our house and darted toward the car. Before she could get inside, a male figure came around, opened the door for her. It was a silver Civic. The boy and girl embraced. They kissed.

I turned away, pressing my face against the tree house floor, like I had the day Lisette arrived. As then, I thought if I could just stay in the tree house, maybe nothing would change.

I sat there for hours. What else was there for me to do?

10

The next day, Warner came to pick me up for school as usual. Except I knew it wasn't usual at all. It was pouring, the kind of driving Miami rain that hits you like a bus. A wet bus. I ran to Warner's car before he could get out. I started talking.

"Hey, some weather, huh? It was pounding on the roof all night and keeping me awake. There was a lot of lightning too. Finally, I just got up and read." I was babbling, trying to prevent the inevitable. "It even woke Mother up, and usually she sleeps like the dead. She's worried the pool will overflow and the house will get flooded. She doesn't know how to drain it. Daddy always did that."

I stopped, remembering. Then I forced myself to go on.

"But I think it will stop raining before that, don't you?"

Even though I'd asked a question, I didn't stop talking long enough for Warner to answer. I felt like, if I just kept talking until we got to school, he wouldn't tell me about Lisette. He wouldn't break up with me.

"So," I continued. "I really like that book we're reading in language arts, *The Book Thief.* I read ahead, it's so good. I really love how the narrator is Death. It sort of gives a new perspective, I think. I mean . . ."

I was out of breath, and I had to stop talking, just for a second. In that instant that I stopped, Warner said, "Emma, I have to talk to you."

No. No, please. I can't lose this too. "We are talking. We're talking about *The Book Thief.* What do you think about it?"

He shook his head. "I haven't started it, okay?"

"You haven't? But what if there's a quiz? I could tell you—"

"No! Emma, stop. We can't. I need to talk to you about something else. About us. Emma, we need to, it's not working out. We have to break up."

"What?" I tried to look surprised. I was surprised even though I'd known before. It was surprising, wasn't it? Lisette wanted him, but only to spite me. Yet I'd thought Warner was different.

"You're not the person I thought you were, Emma, the sweet girl I thought I was in love with."

"What? I know you've been seeing Lisette behind my back. Now you're making this about me? Like it's something I did?"

"How can it not be about you, Emma, when I know how mean you've been to Lisette?"

"How mean *I've* been?" The rain drummed against the window with the force of a jackhammer, and soon, I'd be out in it, floundering against the tide.

"She told me what you and your mother did, kicking her out of her room, treating her like a servant."

"I didn't do those things." *But I didn't stop them either.*

"Please. You didn't treat Lisette like a sister even before her father died. That's why you never told me about her, didn't introduce us."

"I didn't introduce you because I knew exactly what would happen if I did—and it's happening. She hates me."

"Can you blame her?"

"Yes. I wanted to be friends, to be sisters, but she . . . she . . ." I stared out the mottled windows. It didn't matter what I said or thought. The only truth was Lisette's. "She takes everything that's mine, everything I care about. Now, she's taking you."

"She said you were jealous of her. Lisette said—"

"Lisette said! Lisette said!" I was a different person now. Warner was right. I wasn't the sweet girl he'd fallen in love with. I was a witch. A harpy. A wicked stepsister from the fairy tale. The fairy tales always portrayed the stepsisters as being more pathetic and awkward than actually evil. I was pathetic to have thought I had a chance with Warner, have a chance, even, of anyone believing me. I was awkward. And now, I wanted to be mean.

"Honestly, Warner, do you think she'd be interested in you if it wasn't just to spite me?"

He stared at me as if I'd grown claws and raked them across his face.

I kept scratching. "You think you're her type, Warner? You think she goes for nerdy red-haired newspaper staffers who tell boring stories about their parents' divorce? She's had half the football team. You don't even meet her height requirements. She actually *said* your neck looked like a pencil once."

I could see by his face that I'd hurt him. I was glad. I was so sick of people falling for Lisette's crap. I thought Warner was different, but I guessed when it came down to it, people wanted to believe that Lisette was good. I'd wanted to believe it too.

I was sobbing, but still I screamed. "I know what she's like. You'll find out. I give it a week!"

Through the rain, I could barely make out the school. The car was still moving, but I pushed the door open and jumped out into the rush of rain and darkness, out of the comfort of Warner's car, Warner's love, away from the one place I'd felt warm and wanted, out into the cold wet. I slammed the door, ignoring Warner calling my name. There was no Emma. I wanted to be cold and wet and nameless. The rain pounded me like a hundred fists. I let it. I wished it were a tidal wave, a tsunami, a hurricane that would destroy everything and carry me away, away to a place where Lisette and Warner, Mother and Daddy didn't exist, had never existed. A place where I didn't exist.

Kendra speaks

So now she's done it. Well, really, a lot of its. She's wrecked Emma's relationship with her father, which is now irreparable, a fact which causes my dear girl to cry herself to sleep. Not only that, but she's stolen her boyfriend, a boy who isn't even cool or good-looking enough for someone like Lisette to even want. No, she's done it out of pure spite.

I so do not like this girl.

Emma is miserable, and I want to help her. Still, it's better to be miserable than, well, even more miserable, and that's the kind of thing that can happen when magical experiments backfire. You sometimes reach a point where you wish you'd left well enough alone.

That's what happened in the story of Doria, a little mermaid.

By the twentieth century, there were few countries in which I was welcome. And by "few," I mean none. Oh, I was tolerated in the United States, for they have the greatest patience with freaks and oddities (yes, there were those certain incidents in Salem, 1692, but I was not to be found there). While some Europeans claimed to embrace the spiritualism movement, they were still apt to cry "Witch!" if they could not establish contact with their particular dead relation or, more to the point, find out the location of any buried money. Whatever I am, I am not a huckster. So I stayed in America mostly, and when I grew bored of that, I took to the high seas.

Perhaps you have heard of the ships on which I have sojourned. The *Tayleur* was one of the first. Later came the *Lusitania*, the *Morro Castle*, and the *Andrea Doria*. Yes, I had bad luck in my choice of vessels, but don't suppose for a minute that I was behind these great ships' demise. It was pure coincidence. But the most famous ship on which I stayed was the RMS *Titanic*.

Heard of that one, have you? Then you know there were those who predicted that this "unsinkable" ship would indeed sink. I was one of them, in fact. But people tended to ignore me, and I was rather interested in getting a look at the quarters before they became too waterlogged, and at all the famous passengers before . . . well, ditto. Besides, I had made the mistake of journeying to Ireland for Christmas of 1911, and by April 11, 1912, I was being chased out over the small matter of a Brownie revolt (Brownies, if you don't know, are little Irish fairies, not merely little American Girl Scouts, and they can be quite cantankerous). So the *Titanic*'s docking in Queenstown before making its historic and ill-fated journey across the ocean was fortuitous. I disguised myself as a young stewardess named Bessie Livingston, whom I tricked into debarking in Ireland for a day at the pubs (lucky girl—though she did not consider herself so when she learned that the ship had left without her!) and took her place. Everything was going quite, er, swimmingly until the evening of April 14. But, perhaps I will take you back a bit further and introduce you to my friend Doria (no relation to the aforementioned ship—the name Doria means "from the sea," and you will soon see that this is appropriate here). She can tell the story with greater knowledge.

I'll let you hear it while I think on Emma and Lisette.

The Story of a Mermaid Who Should Have Left Well Enough Alone

There are those who believe there is nothing under the sea but sand and shells and endless darkness. But that is not true. Under the sea, there are flowers in colors seen nowhere else, and what's more, the flowers can speak. We merfolk live in castles with many-hued fish swimming in and out of every window, and the greatest of these castles is that of the Sea King. Its walls are built of coral with a roof formed by shells that open and close to let in the merfolk who are invited.

Surely you have heard of merfolk, mermen and mermaids, people with tails or fish with human torsos, depending on how you look at it. They seemed perfectly normal to me, for I was one. In fact, I was the daughter of the Sea King just mentioned. I lived in that beautiful castle with my father, grandmother, and my sisters.

And yet, it was my fondest wish to swim close to the shore in order to see what there was to see.

Oh, I had seen people before, men mostly. My sisters and I loved to lie on the rocks and icebergs, admire our tails (which were quite beautiful, green and blue and decorated with oyster shells) and sing our songs to the ships going by, that men might appreciate our fine voices. Sometimes, the sailors would look for us and then their ships crashed into the rocks and sank. Usually, the men died. My sister Mariel said it couldn't be helped. Still, I felt terrible and tried not to sing when any human could hear.

But I was a mermaid. Mermaids sang. So I comforted myself that the dead men's bodies would be food for all sea creatures. It was scant consolation, though, for I knew they would have families missing them, families who would wait and wonder, perhaps forever.

Once, I saw a man cast adrift. He was grabbed onto the ship's mast and hung from it for many hours, long after his companions had perished. Then, he slid down to the water and tried to paddle toward shore. I wished I could help him, but I was then only thirteen, and contact between humans and mermaids was strictly forbidden. So I could only watch as he struggled and floundered in the darkening sea. Eventually, he became tired and stopped paddling. All the while, he repeated the same words, "Help me, Lord, help me." But finally, even this became too difficult, and he was silent.

I thought him dead, and I swam closer. Our eyes met. He saw me. I froze and then started to swim away.

His weak voice called me back.

"Wait! Are you an angel?" He asked it in a voice so slight I at first thought it was only the rolling of the waves or the cries of the birds who were already pecking at his shipmates' eyes.

I could not answer.

He said, "Please, angel, take my hand. Pray with me at the hour of my death."

He would die, I knew, so there was no harm in obeying him. No one would know. I swam closer and reached out my hand. I did not know what an angel was, but if it comforted him to believe me one, I saw no harm.

My hands' touch seemed to renew his sapped strength. He started saying words, many words I could not understand. In the end, he said, "Dear Lord, save my soul."

He looked toward the red sky with an expression of great peace upon his face.

And then, he let go of my hand and sank beneath the churning waves.

I felt sad, as I always felt when I saw the sailors die. Yet I was less sad than usual, for this young man seemed ready to go.

The wreck was below me, and I swam around in it, looking at the interesting human objects. Yet I did not pillage from it. We never did. "A mermaid takes nothing without giving something in return," my father had told me, and as I had nothing to give, I took nothing.

During the days the followed, I could not stop thinking about the word: *angel*. I did not know what that meant, but I felt it was good. So I determined to ask my grandmother about it.

I lived with my sisters, my father, and my grandmother. My mother was killed when I was just a child, by a fisherman's net. She managed to escape it, but by the time she did, her heart was too weak. She died and turned to seafoam, as all merfolk do when we die. I saw it happen. First, she was there. Then, only her shape, outlined in rainbow bubbles. Then, the bubbles dissipated, and she was gone. For weeks after, I thought I saw her eye, the color of mother-of-pearl, her ear like an abalone shell. But soon, I had to admit she was no more.

Still, my grandmother was like a mother to me, so that night, over a dinner of lobster, I asked her my question.

"Grandmother, what is an angel?"

Surprise arched one gray eyebrow, and I feared I had said the wrong thing. "Doria, wherever did you hear such a word?"

Now I knew I had said the wrong thing. My sister Marina frowned at me. Clearly, *angel* was a word no thirteen-year-old mermaid should know.

"Answer me," my grandmother said. "You have not been consorting with humans, have you? If the humans find out that we are real, they may steal us, make us a display, or worse—execute us for the crime of singing to the sailors."

"I may have mentioned the word, Grandmother," my sister Sirena said quickly. "I believe I may have heard it when I was ashore."

Clever Sirena! All merfolk were allowed to visit the shore, very discreetly, when they were fifteen. Sirena had just had that birthday.

"But," she continued, "I don't know what it means. Do you know, Grandmother?"

Thus mollified, my grandmother nodded her blue-haired head and said, "Indeed. An angel, or a Daughter of the Air, is the embodiment of a human's immortal soul."

Soul? Now I was more confused than ever.

She must have seen it in my look, for she said, "Humans, when they die, do not turn to foam as we do. While their body turns to dust or fish food, there is a separate part of them called a soul. It contains their heart and their mind, their 'spirit,' they say, and while their body may die, the soul lives forever."

"Forever!" No wonder, then, that the sailor was unafraid of sinking below the sea.

"And angels," my grandmother continued, "are believed by some to be souls that have grown wings, kindhearted souls who watch over the living. They wear beautiful dresses and golden crowns on their heads, and they have long, beautiful golden hair. . . ."

"Like me?" I fingered my own golden locks.

"Indeed," my grandmother said. "And blue eyes like yours too."

"And . . . and would they help the living . . . ?" I remembered the sailor's words: ". . . at the hour of my death."

My grandmother, who was very wise, nodded. "Some believe these Daughters of the Air bring the soul to heaven, a kingdom in the sky."

A kingdom in the sky! From that day on, whenever I saw a shipwreck, I made it my aim to find the dying sailors and act as an angel, holding their hands and comforting them as they died. Even as I watched them thrash and suffer, freeze and drown, even as I imagined the despair of the human women and children who would wait for them on shore, I envied them. These men, the lowliest as well as the highest, had a soul, an "immortal soul," as my grandmother had said, which meant they would live forever, simply because they were human. I imagined the kingdom in the sky as being much like our kingdom beneath the water. But where our kingdom was composed of coral and the shells of dead sea creatures, theirs would be made of clouds. Where ours was all darkness, theirs would be bathed in light.

I wanted to go there. More than that, I wanted to live forever and be an angel, a Daughter of the Air.

When I told my sisters this, they laughed. "That is nonsense," Mariel said. "We mermaids are the most beautiful creatures in the sea, which takes up more than half the earth's surface. Their world is a land of bad smells and rocky places!"

"A place where the sun blazes and the night air freezes the water," agreed Marina. "Far better to be a mermaid, even for our short time."

I pretended to agree with them, but secretly, I longed to see the beauty of the shore.

Finally, finally my fifteenth birthday came. On that day, I swam with my sisters as close to shore as I could. Then they left me to make the rest of the way myself.

"Will you not come with me?" I asked Marina and Sirena, Mariel, Damarion, and Meredith.

"We have seen it once," said Meredith. "That is enough." And they waved their good-byes.

At first, I was scared to proceed without them. But soon, curiosity took hold, and I swam closer.

Nearer the shore, I saw many things, tiny boats with little white sails that that bobbed merrily atop the waves. People waded in, strangely dressed in such billowing clothes that, at first, I believed they were angels. But on closer view, I saw that they had neither crowns nor wings and, in fact, were very much alive. No. This must be how female humans looked. They shrieked in fear when the smallest wave hit them, then collapsed in giggles.

I dared not swim too near, lest they see me. I dove under the water and swam far away, pausing sometimes to glance at the fisherman and the tidy, tiny houses that lined the seaside.

Finally, I found what I sought. It was the building that most resembled our mansions beneath the waves. Like our homes, it was constructed of coral and rock and stood much taller than the other buildings, its spires reaching into the clouds. Unlike our homes, the openings in the side were filled with multicolored jewels, and these jewels formed pictures.

And one of those pictures—I was certain of it—was an angel. She was a beautiful woman clad in white. Her wings of gold were silhouetted against the bright blue sky. The light glinted off her, and she sparkled.

I floated, staring, for the longest time, until a voice interrupted my reverie.

"Hey, would you looka that, Mama?"

"What, dear?" another voice said.

"Over by the rocks. It's a mermaid!"

I dove beneath the waves to hide.

I swam very hard and very far. It was still early. I could have gone to another place, seen something else. It was my birthday after all. But I was too afraid of being found out. Besides, now that I had seen the angel, I wanted nothing more. Her jeweled image was printed upon my brain forever.

So I returned home.

When my sisters saw me, they said, "Ha! You've returned early. Nothing to see, eh?"

"No," I said, "nothing to see." I did not wish to tell them the truth, for if they knew how I longed to return again and again to the shore, they would watch me. If I pretended lack of interest, they would let me alone. I could go as I pleased.

Which is what I did. At first, I waited several days in case the boy had told someone about me.

But I heard nothing about it, so I began to return periodically to shore. My main—indeed, my only—purpose was to search for more angels. I became fascinated, obsessed by them. However, since I could not walk as humans did, I could only find those near the shore. Once, I saw one on the bow of a ship, a winged creature carved in wood. Usually, though, I kept returning to that one glass-jeweled image of the angel. On some days, early in the morning, I heard the most beautiful music emanating from behind the image. Singing. Not singing as merfolk sang, which lured men to their deaths. Instead, the voices I heard sang of worship and rejoicing, and they sang of heaven, the place in the sky where only humans could go.

Still I looked for sailors and the shipwrecks, still held their hands and comforted them, pretending to be an angel. But now that I had seen a real angel, I felt an emptiness at being a false one.

Our castle was located in the cold waters near Newfoundland. It was nearly spring, and we knew that the temperature would soon warm. But, for now, my sisters and I enjoyed playing amongst the icebergs.

But, one night, when the sky was clear and dappled with stars, I saw by their light the strangest thing, an iceberg with a bit of red upon it.

I swam closer to get a look. Was it blood? (I hoped not.) Or a bit of ribbon? (I hoped so.) Upon closer examination, I found that it was what my grandmother called paint, which humans used to color the hulls of their ships.

A ship must have struck an iceberg and left behind some of her lovely red paint.

And then, I heard the screaming!

Not merely one scream or ten, but hundreds; not only men but women's voices too.

I could barely see in the star-spotted darkness but I plunged underwater where my vision was keener, and began to swim in the direction of the voices.

Yet, when I resurfaced closer, the voices were no louder, as if some of them had faded away.

Closer still, I realized why they had faded. The first I saw was a woman, sickly white and so cold, despite the shawl wrapped around her shoulders. The second was the same, and the third, a little girl holding a tiny animal. They were dead, floating, frozen. I closed my eyes. I could not look.

I reminded myself that this was a happy scene. These people, these humans, were gone to live with the angels, to inhabit the starry sky forever.

Then, I heard a voice, so soft I could barely recognize it was real.

"Can you . . . help me?"

I turned and looked across the still, black water. It was a boy, a boy near my own age, or perhaps a bit older. He was more beautiful, though, than any merboy I had ever seen, with light brown hair and eyes black as mussel shells.

I knew he was dying.

I also knew I should comfort him, should give him my hand and assure him he would live forever in the sky. Yet I did not want him to die. He was so beautiful, I wanted him to live. I wanted him to live with me.

Thus, with an instinct sure as the instinct that counseled me to fish or to swim, I plunged through the icy water and swam toward him. Once there, I seized the boy and wrapped my arms around him. He had on some sort of soft, white, cloudlike clothing, and through it, I could feel his heartbeat. So slow! Was it because he was dying?

My first instinct was to pull him beneath the sea, to take him home to our castle. I knew he could not breathe under the water. If I took him with me, I would gain nothing but a beautiful, frozen corpse.

And yet, his ship was gone. I could see it when I looked beneath the water, its golden contents still spiraling toward the ocean floor. The land was so far away that I was sure the boy, with his slow heartbeat, would die before we reached it.

That was when I saw a light.

At first, I thought it was the moon, reflected on the black waves. But then, it hit me in the eyes, and I saw that it was a human light such as I had seen on ships that passed at night. Someone was there!

With not a moment to spare, I grabbed the boy tighter and began to pull him toward the light. He moaned softly at being wrested away. I took this as a sign of life, and I said, "Yes! Yes! Go ahead! Just another minute! Please, don't die."

"What? Who?"

"I am Doria. I will save you."

He went limp in my arms. Still, I felt his heart beating. No time to speak. My arms gripped. My tail churned. I plunged forward through the icy waves.

The light? Where was the light? Was it merely an illusion caused by my own desperate hopes? I turned first one way, then the other, searching for a sign of it. Nothing.

"Who is that?" A voice!

"No one there," another said. "None could live so long in such cold water."

The humans! They were there! I splashed my tail, heedless of the risk of being seen, forgetting everything but the beautiful boy I held in my arms, everything but that he should live on the same earth I inhabited.

"There is someone! He's splashing!"

With the boy, I swam closer to the little white boat. I waved.

"He's there! Get him!"

"No, Mr. Lowe! He'll capsize the boat!"

"We cannot just let him die!"

I swam through the black water, still holding the boy, shoving him ahead of me. They could not leave him. Finally, I reached out, and with one hand, touched the boat's side.

"Hey, there's two of them!"

They couldn't see me, couldn't find me. I tried to push the boy in front of me, concealing myself. As soon as they took him, I would swim away. I had done my part. I had saved him.

And then, I felt something, hands on my shoulders, lifting me, taking not just the boy, but both of us, onto the boat.

I tried to struggle, to keep from being pulled up. They could not see me. Yet refusing to go would give me away just as much. Finally, I let them take me up, and I tucked my tail beneath me, the darkness as my shield. The truth was, I wanted to stay. Most of the small boat's passengers sat, eyes glazed with sleeplessness and maybe fright, staring ahead. A young woman with blond hair much like my own dozed in back. Only two men, the ones who had pulled us in, paid attention.

No. A third passenger, a young woman. Her eyes flicked downward. She had seen my tail. I was certain. I wanted to jump overboard. Yet, when her eyes met mine again, she gave no sign of anything awry. She said, "Oh, you poor dear, let me give you my coat."

Before I could protest, she'd stripped it off and wrapped it around me. It was a long coat, which covered every trace of what I was.

"Poor dear," she cooed again. "You must be half frozen. What is your name?"

I glanced at the boy. He was unconscious, it seemed. Yet I could see he was breathing, for his teeth chattered. "I'm fine. Help him."

"I'll help both of you." She laid her hands on my shoulders, and suddenly, I felt warm, like a summer's day in the Gulf of Mexico. "Better?"

"Yes."

She did the same to the boy. His teeth ceased chattering.

"I am Bessie," the woman said. Her eyes were lovely, green.

"Thank you, Bessie. You saved his—our—lives."

The boy stared at me. To my amazement, he had recovered enough to speak already. "You saved mine. I was . . . thrashing in that water, watching death all around. I had no time. But then, I saw your face, the face of an angel. Where did you come from?"

I was dumbstruck. How could I explain my sudden appearance?

Bessie said, "Silly boy. She was in the water the whole time. Where else would she have been?"

"I don't know." His black eyes shone. All merfolk have eyes the color of the sea. His were so beautiful. "She seemed to come from beneath the water."

Bessie glanced at me from the corner of her eye. "Under this water? She'd be dead, sure as day!"

The boy shook his head. "It just seemed like she came by magic."

Bessie laughed and turned back to me. "Did I clean your cabin, Miss? E deck?"

I recovered enough to say, "Oh, yes. Yes." I had no idea what a cabin was. Or a deck. But I realized she was trying to change the subject. "Yes."

"Not that it matters now, I suppose. Your cabin, everything in it is sunk to the bottom of the ocean. Lost. Lost."

"Lost," I repeated, remembering the great ship I had seen, still sinking, down, down. How many were on board when it sunk? How many went to sleep, never to awaken?

"Two thousand two hundred twenty-three," Bessie said.

"What?" I said.

"How many were on board," Bessie said. "And us few on the boats, seven hundred and six in all, we are the only ones who survived. The rest are sleeping, deep, deep under the waves."

"Their souls gone to heaven!" I could picture them, their souls white as angels, flying up through the air, looking nothing like the bloated, floating cadavers I'd seen around me.

"I would be there, but for you, my angel!" the boy said.

"Oh, no, no," I protested. Mermaids were not supposed to save human lives. We were allowed only to watch, barely even that.

"You did!" he said.

"No!" I wanted to leave, to jump, to leap from the lifeboat and swim away. Yet I didn't want to because I wanted to sit longer with this boy, this boy whose face was more beautiful with every passing moment.

Instead, I did the only other thing I could think to do.

I sang. I sang one of the songs known to the merfolk, my high, clear voice sounding through the cold, starry night.

Under the ocean, seaweed for a bed,
Shells for a pillow, cradle his head.
My lover is resting on the ocean floor.
Soon, he'll turn to seafoam, and I'll see him no more.

Eyes were so lovely; Now, they're fast asleep,
Underneath the ocean, dark and deep.
My lover is resting on the ocean floor.
Soon, he'll turn to seafoam, and I'll see him no more.

The merfolk surround him, sing a lullaby.
Hush, my dearest darling, don't ye cry.
My lover is resting on the ocean floor.
Soon, he'll turn to seafoam, and I'll see him no more.

As I sang the refrain for the third time, Bessie joined in, then the boy, then the others. They joined in too. When I looked around, I saw their eyes were shining, and they wiped away tears born more of weariness from what they had faced than from my song. Soon, only the blond girl in the back remained asleep. I wondered if she was all right.

"That was beautiful," the boy said when I had finished. He reached for my hand and—Poseidon help me—I let him take it, though my mind screamed that it was wrong and wronger.

"Yes, beautiful," Bessie said. "A song like that . . . it is unforgettable."

Something about the way she said "unforgettable" made me glance at her. She smiled.

Slowly, shivering, we all dozed off, first the boy, his hand held in mine, then the other passengers, then Bessie. I knew I should jump overboard then. No one would notice. I extricated my hand from the boy's icy grip. He moaned in protest. I waited, breath held, but he stirred no further. I braced my hands on the edge of the boat. For an instant, I thought I saw Bessie's eye twitch. No. My imagination. With a final glance at the boy's beautiful face, I made to dive.

Just then, a horn blared.

I jumped. We all jumped. It was a ship, large and black, barely visible against the night sky. We were saved! They were saved. I was doomed.

I could dawdle no longer. I plunged into the dark, suddenly cold water. It grabbed me as my mother used to when I swam too close to the surface and pulled me deeper, deeper into its arms, past the doomed ship, her contents now strewn across the ocean floor, past the bodies, half sunk, floating like waving angels. I tried not to look at them, but their dead eyes stared at me.

When I had swum a suitable distance, I reemerged from the water. Now, the air was colder than I remembered. It was still dark, but I could hear sounds, the yells of the rescuers, the shrieks of the rescued. It was too dark to see. Still, I searched for the white shape of the boy's lifeboat, his lifeboat, for one last look. The black ocean tried again to pull me away.

Hours later, when the sun rose, the boy was gone. Still, I watched longer, until the rescue ship was out of sight.

Only after it left did I once again plunge into the inviting water, no longer black but dappled blue by the morning sun. Down, down I plunged, down many fathoms, past the angels until the water was, once again, dark and cold, cold and murky, deeper than I had ever been or wanted to be. But now, I did want to. I wanted to see it once more, his ship. Finally, I found the hull. It was broken in two. I entered the larger part, careful to disturb nothing and to avoid the staring eyes. I knew their souls were in heaven now. Yet, I was still sad.

Down the hallway and grand staircase I flew. My hands found a metal piece covered with the pattern of earth flowers. My tail kicked up sand and other small objects. Around me, sea creatures feasted on bits of what must have been food. Was this where they had dined? I knew that the sharks would come later. Finally, the waves brought me what I sought, something white and small and billowy with a picture of the great ship as it must have looked. I took it, heedless of my father's warnings to take nothing. After all, I had given something. I had saved a boy's life.

Hand on my prize, I swam for home.

I did not tell anyone what I had seen and done and risked. I knew they would be furious. Yet, in the next days, the great ship's sinking was the talk of the merworld. Many went to visit its carcass, which they said was more beautiful than our most glorious castle. I learned that the dead ship's name had been *Titanic*, and that it was thought unsinkable.

"'Tis tempting fate to say a ship is unsinkable," my father said. "And fate did not like it."

The dead, too, filled our conversation, so many dead. I listened to each discussion, rapt with attention, yet pretending to know less than I did. Still, I could think of nothing else. I brought up the subject every day, every hour, asking about the jewels and hangings my sisters had seen, the rumors they had heard. Always, always, I thought of the boy, wondering what had become of him after I had left. Finally, one day, as my sister Marina described the efforts to recover the dead, I asked, "What of the survivors? Were there many?"

"Fewer survived than died," she said. "The humans did not take care."

"Yes, yes," I agreed, remembering the waterlogged, white, waving bodies at the ocean's floor. "But did any survive? Where were they taken?"

Marina said she did not know but could find out. I asked her, you see, because I knew she would.

Still, it could not be quick enough for me. I had to find the boy, had to know he lived still, even though I could not be with him. I had to know he walked the earth yet.

The card I had taken with the picture of the ship and the writing I could not read I placed in a sack that had been Mother's. It was made of the body of a dead octopus. It was there I kept all my treasures. It protected them. But this card I took out so many times it wavered and faded, as I knew his memory of me would fade to nothing also.

The next day, Marina swam to me, tail fairly shaking with excitement. She had information.

"It is the talk of the human world, so I eavesdropped on some who came to salvage. They said the survivors were rescued by a ship called *Carpathia*. They were bound for New York."

New York, I had heard of. Though it was a bit of a journey, I was a strong swimmer. I would visit New York and look for the place where the great ships went. I would wait on the beach there, and surely he would happen by sooner or later. If I could see him safe and sound, I told myself, I would be satisfied.

The next day, while my father and sisters and grandmother still slumbered, I left our castle, taking only the octopus bag and the picture of the *Titanic*. I started in the direction in which I had seen the great ship leave. It was a long journey, and I knew my family would be furious. Yet what harm was there in it? I did not intend to reveal myself, merely to look. Besides, I had been gone so long by that point that I was already in grave trouble. I might as well move forward, for there was no turning back. I rested one night and the next morning swam farther.

Finally, I reached it. I need not have worried about anyone noticing me. The place where the ships went was home not to one or two but to thousands of boats. Each had hundreds of people, embarking or debarking, carrying suitcases or packages.

To one side of the seaport was a statue of a woman. At least, I thought it was a woman, though she was monstrous large and green. To the other side, on the shore, were the castles, taller than any I had seen before, some reaching into the clouds. Could all those castles be full of humans? If so, I would never find the boy. Never.

I sat on a rock that was square, like no real rock I had seen before. I began to cry. My arms and tail and entire body ached. I had swum two days to no avail, and now, I would have to swim two days back and face my father and sisters. A ship's horn blared, mocking me. I slid from the rock, which scraped my body. I hung in the water, weeping. I had no place to go.

The sky darkened, and the air grew cold. Still, I hung near the shore, the dock a barrier I could not breach. Yet I wanted to stay there. I wanted to be near him.

A voice interrupted my churning thoughts.

"Hey, I know you."

My head jerked upward. Of course, the human—a woman—was not speaking to me.

Yet the voice continued. "Yes, you, Mermaid. I remember you. You thought I didn't notice you left the boat last week."

I found my voice. "Boat?"

"Lifeboat fourteen? The *Titanic*? You can't have forgotten. No one could forget that night, even if they'd lived three hundred years. You were the one who brought that boy up out of the water."

I stared at her. It was Bessie, the girl from the lifeboat. She might know where he was!

"You saw the boy? You went to shore with *Carpathia*?"

"And you didn't. Now I know why . . . though I suspected then. I saw your tail in the boat, and I heard your song. It was a mermaid's song."

"You won't . . . tell anyone?"

"Who would believe me?"

I remembered that once my grandmother had said that humans believed themselves to be the only thinking creatures upon the earth.

"The boy lived?" I asked.

"Yes, he was one of the lucky seven hundred and six who lived."

"Seven hundred and six." I remembered her saying the number in the boat. How had she known it, even then? But perhaps she had been making it up, was making it up even now.

"Why are you here?" I asked.

"Rather impertinent question."

"Sorry."

"It's all right. I'll tell you. I am here because I knew you would be back. I saw it by the look in your eyes. You were in love."

In love. I had not used the words until now. But as soon as Bessie said them, I knew it was true. Why else but love would I have journeyed so far, defied my father and grandmother, risked detection? Love! It was the most beautiful word in the world, and the most terrifying. I pressed my tail against the hard, prickly barnacles that coated the rock. I bore down harder, so hard that my tail hurt and there were tears in my eyes.

"What's wrong?" Bessie said.

"I can never see him again."

"Why can't you? You're here."

"Of course. I shall just walk upon my hands until I find him."

"Ah, but I know where he is."

I laughed.

"'Tis true. After all, I knew where you were . . . Doria."

I started when she said my name. I hadn't told it.

"Did you think it mere coincidence, me being here exactly when you were?"

"What else could it be?"

"This world has few coincidences. Usually, what one thinks is coincidence is really magic."

Magic. Many believed that merfolk had magic powers, that magic was why our voices lured sailors to their deaths. But that was not magic, merely bad luck and good singing. Still, there were mermaids who had magical powers. I had been instructed to stay away from them.

This must have shown on my face, for Bessie said, "Are you afraid of me now? Not all witches are wicked, you know."

"Of course not." But I could not keep the quaver from my voice. Still, I said, "How do you know where he is?"

"Ah, would you like to see him?"

With that, I almost lost my grip on the artificial rock. Would I like to see him? I had thought his face was burned upon my memory, and yet, in only one week, it had grown less sharp, like someone seen through murky, churned-up waters.

Bessie did not wait for me to answer but, instead, reached inside the satchel she carried and drew from it a silver object, round with a long handle. I recognized it from the stories of humans my grandmother had told me. A mirror. Humans used it to see themselves, since they could not always look into the water as merfolk did. Bessie held it out to me. "The boy's name is Brewster Davis. Wish aloud to see him, and you shall."

"Wish?" I took the mirror from her. The handle was hard and smooth, warm from Bessie's hand. I saw myself reflected in it. The image was much clearer than in the water, and I saw that I was beautiful, more beautiful than my sisters, so beautiful, indeed, that I almost gasped. Behind me, gray clouds gathered in the once-blue sky.

"Just say, 'I wish to see Brewster Davis,' and you shall."

Brewster Davis. Even his name held beauty and promise. What could be the harm? I took a deep breath of salt air mixed with ships' smoke, then wished.

"I wish I could see Brewster Davis."

Immediately, my own face vanished from the glass, replaced

with a picture I didn't recognize. Then I realized it was a house, one of those too-many castles on New York's shores. I saw the front of it, then went through the window, my first glimpse of a human room.

Two people sat in it. One was a young man with hair the color of sand. His was not the face I sought. He was older than Brewster Davis, my Brewster Davis. But, just as I was about to turn away in protest, I noticed the second. It was him! Though I thought I had forgotten his face, I knew it on sight, the brown hair, curling slightly around his ears, his face open and trustworthy. I leaned closer until I could see his face as close as I had seen my own. I gazed into his eyes and knew they were kind.

Then, he spoke.

"The novels of Charles Dickens are boring, Robert."

"It is because you do not concentrate," said the other man, and the picture widened so I could see him.

"How can I concentrate when you give me such tedious reading material?" He pointed to the object in his lap. "Mr. Dickens was paid by the word. That is why he wrote of such unimportant matters."

"Unimportant?" Robert gestured toward the object. "Dickens wrote of the noblest subjects. *A Tale of Two Cities* is the story of war and love and death."

"Ah, but that is the worst of it. Mr. Dickens may have written of death, but had he seen it firsthand? So much death, Robert, the deaths of a yellow fever epidemic in a single night. And love! I have known that too, though I shall never see her face again."

He sighed and placed the object back in his lap. "Oh, I am sorry, Robert. I am certain it is a wonderful book. It is just too soon. The night I had, I will never forget. The sights I have seen weigh heavy on my mind. I don't expect you to understand. It is one thing to read in a newspaper of fifteen hundred killed. Fifteen hundred is merely a number. But to be there, seeing them choose between those who lived and died, to know that those not chosen were one's dinner companions the night before, and to thrash in frozen water, watching as, one by one, each soul succumbed, and knowing you would be next. That is entirely different. Something like that changes one forever."

Robert nodded. "I understand. Your mother thought reading might ease your mind."

"My mother did not see what I saw. When the ship sank, her only thought was of herself." The boy's dark eyes grew angry.

"Perhaps, instead of reading stories, you should tell me your own, if it is not to painful."

"It is too painful, but that is why I long to tell it, over and over. But you indulge me, Robert. You have already heard it."

"I indulge you because you deserve to be indulged."

The boy needed no further prompting and began his tale.

"I went to bed early that last night. Mother had wanted me to meet a girl, some heiress with bad teeth, no doubt, who had been seasick since we'd left Southampton and hadn't left her cabin."

"Hestia Rivers. And you do not know she has bad teeth."

"All Mother's heiresses have bad teeth. Besides, I am too young to marry. I am only nineteen."

"Almost twenty."

"I am nineteen until I am twenty. In any case, I feigned an illness of my own. Hypochondria has its benefits. I pretended to sleep when Mother came in, but I was wide-awake. I was still wide-awake when the cabin steward pounded upon our door. I answered it.

"Mother began to abuse him for disturbing us for a safety drill, but I could see in his eyes that it was no drill. While Mother cawed about her beauty sleep and the security of her jewels, I grabbed both life belts and led her to the deck."

"Quick thinking, that," Robert said.

"It was freezing cold, giving her something more to moan about.

I wish I lived in her world, where the greatest problem is that it is cold or the toast is singed or what will people think of us if we fail to take our usual box at the Met. While mother performed a monologue about the temperature of her nose, I was assaulted by the worst examples of man's inhumanity to man I have ever seen. Take every pickpocket, wife beater, and murderer in Mr. Dickens' tomes, and it would be nothing to the callous immorality of the *Titanic*'s passengers that night—pushing, shoving, screaming, lying, and the worst of it is, the ones who were behaving are likely at the bottom of the ocean. At one point, gunshots were heard. There were not enough lifeboats. We know that now. The officers said, 'Women and children first.' Mother, secure in her position as a first-class woman (for we know that it was, in reality, first class first, everyone else be damned), screeched when she heard that and tried to persuade the officer that I was thirteen. 'He's merely big for his age.' I nudged her, knowing no one would believe her. I told her that it was not gentlemanly to lie, and do you know what she said?"

Robert nodded.

"She said that the gentlemen would die, and the ruffians would live. The officer was about to let me on a boat, likely just to shut her up. But I could not stand it. I joined the shoving, unruly mob, but I was shoving to get away from her. The officer seated her on a boat. I could hear her screaming all the way down to the ocean."

"That was noble of you," Robert said.

"Yes, it . . . wasn't. It was a fit of pique. Mother always places me in a temper, and this time, I almost died to spite her. I assumed I would get into a later boat, but soon, there were none left. The ship was sinking. We were all doomed, and all the while, the orchestra was playing, as if to give us one more reason to praise the service of the White Star Line."

Robert chuckled. "They won't be doing that."

"No, they won't. But, the grand thing is, they're all too dead to protest. Before I knew it, the boat was wrenched from under me. Hundreds screamed in unison, and then, the shock of icy water against my skin. You know, Robert, how I only wish to swim when the temperature reaches its warmest. And yet, the water, that icy grave to untold hundreds, was not the worst thing about it. Even the screaming wasn't the worst, though the fact that those screams went unheeded by all but two of the lifeboats—including my own mother's—will disgust me until I die. The worst was when I realized that the screaming had nearly stopped. I knew what that meant. It meant that I was the only one left alive in that water, and soon, I would not be there either. It comforted me, in a way, the idea of sinking beneath that deep, peaceful ocean. I began to gaze at the stars. One never sees stars in New York. The light is too bright. But when the screaming stopped and I had resigned myself to meeting my maker, I decided that the stars were the most beautiful I had ever seen."

"It sounds lovely. Ghoulish, but lovely."

"It was. But then, I saw something even more beautiful. It was a girl. I did not know where she came from. I still don't know, but she was swimming toward me, not dead, not cold or screaming. At first, I thought she was an angel, but when I said, 'Can you help me?' she grabbed me around the wrist and pulled me across the water to safety.

"I can barely remember what happened next. I was slipping in and out of consciousness. The only thing I remember for certain was that the girl sat beside me in the lifeboat, and that she sang to me. She had the most beautiful voice I had ever heard, like the sirens in mythology."

"You were delirious," Robert said.

"It was real. I drifted off to sleep with that lovely song in my ears, and had I not awakened, it would have been enough. I would have known complete happiness."

I smiled. I had done my job. I had comforted him.

"And then," he said, "a horn sounded, and I was awake. But the girl, I could see her no more. She was gone. Where I should have felt euphoria, I felt only despair, for it was clear to me that the girl—that girl—was the only one who mattered, no heiress, socialite, or minor royalty, no headstrong beauty would do. The girl was gone, and she was the only one I could ever love."

I sighed. He loved me.

"But then, I felt a hand upon mine, and I heard a voice saying, 'There, there now. It's all right.'"

A voice? What voice?

"She was back in all her glory, the golden-haired angel. She held my hand and stroked my hair and comforted me until we were hoisted onto the *Carpathia*'s deck. Then, she disappeared again."

But I had done none of that. Could the boy have been having visions of me?

"Are you certain she was really there?" Robert echoed my thoughts. "It seems so strange that she would disappear."

"Not strange when you know the whole of it. The moment we reached *Carpathia*'s deck, Mother spotted me. She threw herself at me with all her power, screaming, 'My baby! My poor baby!' The poor girl likely fled at the idea of replacing the terror of a shipwreck with the terror of Mother. I searched all over, but it was too crowded. I did not even know her name."

Slowly, I understood. The blond girl who had slept on the lifeboat. She had hair like mine and was near my age. She was pretty, and she had been there after I had fled. She had comforted him.

I should have been grateful to her for caring for him, so he would not have to be alone. Instead, I felt the tight hand of jealousy closing upon my throat. At his next words, the hand grew claws.

"I love her, Robert. She saved my life. She comforted me, and as long as I live, I will love her and look for her evermore."

The mirror slipped from my grasp. Bessie caught it.

"Are you all right, dear?"

"He loves me. He said so, and I love him more than words can express. But I will never see him again." The truth of those words hit me like a wave. I would go home and be scolded by my father. Then, I would live the rest of my life in loneliness and despair. I let Bessie take the mirror from me. What good was seeing him now?

But Bessie said, "Why will you never see him again?"

Now, even in my despair, I knew that was just stupid. Had she not been listening? Had she no eyes? "I'm a mermaid, and he's a human. We're different species."

Bessie nodded. "That is true, but I am different myself. I'm a witch, so perhaps I can help you."

"Help?"

"Make you human. Give you legs."

"You would help me?" I remembered Father's harsh words against all humans and especially witches. "Why?"

Bessie shrugged. "To be nice, I suppose, to make up for past evils perhaps."

Past evils. I remembered Father's words: "A mermaid takes nothing without giving something in return."

"I could not take that from you, not without . . ."

"Giving something in return?"

"Yes."

Bessie looked at me through narrowed eyes. "But what do you have to give?"

I thought about it. What did I have? Shells? Sand? My hair? The answer was nothing. I had nothing anyone would want. But when I opened my mouth to say it, I instead blurted, "My voice."

"Your voice?"

"Oh . . . no . . . no, I didn't mean to say that. Besides, how could you take that?"

"It can be done, if you are willing. Your voice is beautiful, and really, you have nothing else to give."

"But how can I make him fall in love with me if I cannot speak?"

"You heard him. He loves you already. He will surely recognize you, and with legs, you can stay with him forever."

Forever! But no! No. It was insane. My voice was the only thing about me that mattered. And yet, what was there for me without him, to return to my family and never see him again? I had nothing, nothing.

Just then, there was a commotion, first one voice shouting, "Look! A mermaid!" Then a second, and a third. In an instant, we were surrounded by dozens of feet, dozens of faces, staring at me, separating me from Bessie, hands pulling me from the ocean, voices shrieking of discoveries. I could barely make out Bessie's face. I strained my neck toward her and screamed, "I'll do it!"

A stabbing pain electrified my body. Those who were holding me recoiled, and for an instant, I saw myself above them. Then, everything went black.

Next, I was standing (standing!) on human legs in a place with no water anywhere. I stared down. I wore a dress, a blue one, and in my hand, I held an object, the paper, waterlogged, with a picture of the once-great ship, *Titanic*.

"What have I done?" I tried to say the words aloud, but no sound came out. I had done it. I had lost my voice. I was here, on a street in New York, knowing no one.

What had I done?

Kendra speaks (just for a moment)

Okay, so in retrospect, taking the girl's voice from her was stupid and not cool. I know that now. It was an impulse, and we all know by now that I have some issues with impulse control. Her voice was pretty. I always wanted to be able to sing better (and now I can—really, I could win any one of those TV talent shows, but I feel bad about it, in light of where I got the voice), and it's not like she had anything else to give, just the voice or a soggy transfer from the *Titanic* (which would probably be worth millions now, come to think of it—I should have been diving for the china and silver, instead of leaving it for that Ballard guy). Yes, I should have figured it would be hard for her to get Brewster to fall in love with her with no voice. But you know what they say: Hindsight is 20/20. I never claimed to be perfect, you know. I do my best. Anyway, here's what happened.

The Mermaid's Story Continues to Its End

The sky was dark from the towering castles blocking the sun. Was one of them his? I tried to remember. As I did, an object the size and speed of a shark raced by me. I jumped out of its wake, but it had no wake, for it was no shark. Rather, it was an enormous flying object made by man. Just when I had recovered, another whizzed by. I screamed, but no sound came out. I screamed harder, keeling forward and tried to take a step. But each step on my new legs was like knives, stabbing. Then there were people running toward me, people crowding around as I had never been crowded at home in the wide ocean. The air left my lungs like a fish washed ashore, and I was falling down through the crowds of people and onto the hard earth below.

I felt someone picking me up, and then I was someplace else.

Most of the people were gone, but one, a man, held me in his arms. Could it be the boy? Had he found me? No. It was a different man, a man who had lost most of his hair. A lady was with him. The man lowered me onto something that was softer than the most pliant sand.

"She cannot stay here," another man's voice said. "The mistress will not countenance strangers brought in."

"We understand," said the lady. "But she collapsed in the street. Surely your mistress will not object to her resting a moment. Perhaps she has some paper on her that will help us find her family."

I felt tugging, and then the man seized upon the picture in my hand. "Look at this."

"*Titanic*? Could she have been—"

"Seems like it," said the first man.

"Is this some sort of scam?" asked the second man. "Have you hucksters heard of my mistress and her son being *Titanic* survivors and decided to pull something?"

Titanic survivors? It was him. I grabbed the sleeve of the man who had carried me and pulled hard.

"Do I look like a huckster?" the man who had carried me said. "I am a respectable businessman, and I thank you to remember your station."

"Hey, hey, what is this, Pittman?" A third man's voice interrupted. I opened my eyes. Yes. It was true. It was the voice, the one I'd wanted to hear more than any other. The boy. Brewster. How was I here? And then I realized Bessie with her magic had placed me in his way.

"Mr. Davis," the older man, Pitman, said. "Do not concern yourself. I was merely—"

"Merely throwing a survivor of the great *Titanic* disaster from your house," said the first man.

"*Titanic*? What of it?" said the boy.

"This girl fainted in the street, and we found this in her hand—a transfer from *Titanic* to a ship bound for Florida, in the name of passenger Dorothy Florence Sage."

The boy looked down at me. It was him, definitely him. "Is this you?"

I started to speak, but no sound came out.

"Are you Dorothy?" he asked.

I wasn't, and yet, there was no way of telling him my real name, my true identity. Still, Dorothy sounded a bit like Doria, and at least, if he thought I was Dorothy, he would realize I had been there on the ship. In all likelihood, I realized with a gulp, the real Dorothy Florence Sage was at the bottom of the ocean, one of those waving bodies.

I nodded.

"And you were on *Titanic*, on the lifeboats?"

I nodded again.

"Then we must help her." Brewster reached for my hand, and I felt at his touch a charge of electricity, then warmth. "You will come inside with me."

"But Master Davis," Pitman said. "It could be trickery. Besides, she was a third-class passenger."

The boy grasped my hand. "Enough third-class passengers perished on April fifteenth. I will not add to their number by neglecting this one."

With that, he took my hand and whisked me to another room.

Next, I was sitting on a chair, eating food such as I had never had before, something yellow with soft, white, swirly objects and dots of orange and white. Had I been possessed of a voice, I would have asked what these dainties were called, but that would have been foolish. Indeed, humans probably had such delicacies every day. In any case, one of the ladies who brought it and took it away remarked that it was "nice chicken soup."

But the most wonderful thing about it was that, as I consumed it, the boy, Brewster, once again recounted the story of his dramatic rescue from the ocean. How well I remembered it! I kept waiting for him to recognize me, to remember that it was I who had been his rescuer, but he did not. As he finished his story, he said, "I am being a boor, babbling on and on about what happened to me. It is only that it is such a relief to meet someone who understands what I have been through, what I saw. You do understand, do you not? I am not mistaken?

I nodded.

"And was it the most horrible event you have ever witnessed, one which you will never forget?"

Again, I nodded.

"Something like that changes a person. I feel I will never be the same happy fellow I was before, now that I have witnessed the inhumanity, the selfishness, not to mention the death. Again, I am being rude. Please, Dorothy, do tell your own story. You have not said a word."

I wanted so much to do just that, to open my mouth and tell him that I had been there, that it was I who had rescued him. But, of course, I could not. I opened my lips. No sound issued forth. I pointed to my throat to show that I could not speak. Oh, why had I offered my voice?

"Mute?" he said. "From the trauma, I suppose. Do you know I did not speak for fully a day after reaching shore myself. It is all right, Dorothy. Mr. and Mrs. Wilkins—those are the people who brought you here—they are on their way to the office of the White Star Line to search for information about your family."

My family! This had not occurred to me before. Dorothy Florence Sage might have a family, a family who would know full well that I was not her. I wanted to swim, to run, to fly away from this place before detection. Yet where would I go? Where could I go?

As if reading my thoughts, Brewster said, "Do you have any place to stay, Dorothy, anyone who is looking for you?"

I shook my head.

"Well, then, I will have Mrs. Brimm show you to a guest room. You can stay as long as you need to."

That afternoon, three things happened.

The first was that Mr. Wilkins returned from the White Star office with grim news: The Sage family, eleven in all, were presumed lost at sea. My whole family was gone.

"I was speaking to a man," Mr. Wilkins said, "another survivor who said that the eldest Sage girl, Stella, was actually on his lifeboat. But when she realized that none of her family were with her, she climbed out to her death."

It was so sad even though I had not known the Sage family. Eleven people—parents and nine children—all perished, and the eldest girl giving her life to be with her family in heaven. I felt a strange sensation, one I'd never felt undersea, that of water slipping down my cheeks. Hard as I tried, it would not stop. Tears. That's what they were called, I remembered. Humans shed tears when they were sad.

"What nobility!" Brewster said. "I saw none of that on the decks of *Titanic*. You should be very proud of your sister." He patted my shoulder.

One of the tears slipped into my mouth. It tasted like the ocean. I missed my own family.

The second thing was that Mrs. Davis, Brewster's mother, came home from wherever she had been. She was none too happy to meet me.

"Stay here? Some unknown girl? Impossible, Brewster!"

"Mother, have some compassion."

"I have much compassion. However, it does not extend to

allowing unknown persons, persons who may well be thieves and murderers, to stay in our home."

"She's a little girl, my age if that. She's hardly a thief or a murderer."

"One never knows."

"She has lost everything, everything, her entire family. Imagine it. Imagine how you would have felt, had you lost me."

His mother's face whitened, and though she had lately been trying to have me thrown from the house, I felt for her.

"I almost did lose you, foolish boy," she said.

"I know. I was stupid. I should never have defied you in that way."

This, I knew, was a great effort for him to say.

Next, he said, "I know I would have been devastated had I lost you too. So imagine how it must be for poor Dorothy. She has lost both mother and father."

I had lost both mother and father. I began again to cry.

Mrs. Davis barely glanced at me and said, "Oh, very well. But if she is going to stay, she must earn her keep. We need a serving girl, for Pamela has run off and gotten married without thinking of giving notice." She leveled a hard gaze at me. "Do you know how to work, girl?"

I nodded.

"All right, then. And one more condition. Friday night, you must meet Hestia Rivers for dinner."

That is the third thing that happened. Hestia Rivers.

Brewster sighed. "Very well, but I won't like her. There is only one young woman for me, and I will not rest until I have found her."

I smiled then. He meant me. And yet, why did he not recognize me?

I was next taken to a place called the kitchen where several young women toiled, all to produce food for the Davis family. It struck me as interesting. In the sea, my home, we each of us did for ourselves. If you caught a fish, you ate a fish. If you caught none, you would be hungry. Certainly, those who were more skilled might help others, children, or the elderly, but still, everyone had to do his or her part.

In the human world, people called servants did all the work while others did none.

"I am sorry," Brewster said. "I'm afraid Mother has not a charitable bone in her body."

I shrugged and smiled to show that I did not mind. I didn't. I was near Brewster. Besides, if the human world was divided between those who worked and those who were idle, then I preferred to work.

The household was supervised by a woman in a black dress who showed me my room and gave me some plain clothing to change into. Then, she showed me back to the kitchen, which was supervised by a woman named Cook.

"You've worked in kitchens before?" said Cook.

I nodded. What else could I do?

"That's a good girl. I heard about your family, poor thing. Isn't that always the way—the rich living high while them like us gasp for breath."

I nodded and felt another bit of water come to my eyes, thinking of Dorothy's family. I could almost picture them, a young, handsome father, perhaps with a mustache like my father, round little mother, and nine children, including a younger brother with freckles. Did this water happen to all humans all the time? I did not like it, and what was more, I felt like a liar, pretending to be what I was not.

Cook patted my shoulder. "There, there. Here, help Celia chop the onions. Then no one will notice if ye weep."

Cook pointed to a girl, Celia, who was using a silver object to chop at some beautiful purple things. When I drew closer for a look,

Cook pulled me back. "Careful, dear, the knife is sharp. Can't have you losing your nose!"

The rest of the day went little better. Later, Celia asked me, "Can you turn on the oven for me, love? There are rolls to be made."

I had seen Celia "turn on" the stove earlier, to cook the bright-colored objects she and I had chopped, which she called vegetables. How they had jumped and sizzled on their pan. She had made the stove work by turning a knob. I found a similar knob on the big, square object she called an oven.

I reached out and turned it. Celia nodded, satisfied.

"Now, light it," she said.

At my questioning look, she said, "Silly girl, have you never used an oven before? If you do not light it, the gas leaks out, and you could die from smelling it. Do you not notice the smell?"

I sniffed, and indeed, there was a faint odor, like dead fish left rotting too long. I nodded.

"Well, then, light it." She took from her apron pocket a box of something, removed a long, skinny stick and scraped it against the side of the box. It made a roaring sound, and a bit of orange exploded from it. Celia handed it to me.

It was hot! So hot! I dropped the stick and would have screamed, had I had the voice. Instead, I placed my hurting finger in my mouth and sucked it.

"Stupid girl! Did you really just stick your finger in the flame?" Celia pointed at the stick on the floor. "Pick it up!"

She removed another stick from the box, struck it once again, but this time leaned down and touched it to the part of the stove where the gas made the air wavy. It too turned orange, then blue with a roar.

I watched the beautiful, dangerous thing called a flame, sucked my injured finger, and wondered if I had made a horrible mistake.

Dinner was not much better. Soon, it was discovered that I had no idea how to place the numerous silver and white objects on the table. Celia grabbed them from me, muttering about how stupid I was. I followed, trying to imitate her actions, but my fingers still hurt. Those same fingers impeded me by making it difficult to pass the platters and serve the many dishes. The worst of it was, Brewster didn't even look at me.

But it was all worth it when, as I was dragging my aching legs from the table, I heard a voice.

"Dorothy?"

At first, I forgot that I was Dorothy. Then I felt a hand upon my elbow. I started, almost dropping the heavy plates I was carrying. A firm hand steadied them. I was Dorothy. He was speaking to me.

"I'm sorry." His breath was close to my ear, like a lover's. "I haven't seen you all day. Perhaps—Mother is going out to play bridge soon. When your work is complete, will you join me in the sitting room?"

The heavy dishes made my arms sag under their weight. Still, at his words, they felt lighter. I nodded.

Disregarding my aching human legs, I ran to get more dishes and made such short work of the washing that, finally, Celia stopped scowling at me. "Going to do a decent job after all then? I'm sorry I was so cross before. It must be hard on you."

After dinner, I had only to wait in the tiny room I shared with Celia until Mrs. Davis went out. A bell of some sort rang eight times. Then I snuck into the sitting room.

Brewster was there! He gestured that I should sit on a blue and white seat with him. I wished I could talk to him about the shipwreck and others I had seen, the beautiful ship underneath the ocean, and about this place—New York City, its bright lights and tall castles so far above sea level that their spires seemed to pierce the heavens. So many things had I seen in this one day, seen and touched and felt, more than ever in my life. I wanted to tell him about that life too. Perhaps it was better that I had no voice, for I would surely have told him all about the ocean and its hills and caves, of the castles and of the merfolk concealed in coral reefs. I would have told him that the places where the water grows suddenly colder are where a merperson had been sad or angry, and that the places where the water grew suddenly warmer were like that because they were where a mercouple had fallen in love.

And I would have told him that it was I who had saved him.

Instead, there was silence. I could not speak, and Brewster did not seem to know what to say either.

Finally, I rose and, gesturing for him to follow, I walked toward the glass that showed the outside world. Funny that. I had heard that sometimes humans caught fish and placed them in glass bowls in their homes. It had seemed cruel to me, but now I realized that the humans were in glass bowls themselves. I pulled aside the thing called a curtain and looked out.

It was wondrous! In my world of the sea, the light was the same from day to night. The human world was gray and blue and white by day, but at night, it was inked by octopi. I was used to seeing the inky background broken by hundreds, thousands of tiny stars. But here in New York City, the lights were increased a thousandfold, and they were brighter, many-colored, dancing before us.

I almost stumbled in surprise at the wonder before me. Brewster caught my arm.

"First time in New York City then?"

I nodded.

"Takes a bit of getting used to."

I smiled and gestured broadly with my hand, to show I found it beautiful.

"Like it? Well, people do. But sometimes, it all seems a bit . . . crowded. And crazy. And busy. See that building?" He pointed to the tallest castle, a pointed spire with a glowing circle on its front. "It's the tallest building in the world. When I was younger, there were half as many buildings, and when I'm an old man, there will be twice as many." He paused. "An old man. I always assumed I'd be one someday. But a week ago, it seemed like it wasn't going to happen. Then, someone dragged me out of the water—amazing!"

He was pulling at the curtain himself now, eyes wide, taking in the views. "You know, Dorothy, you're right. It is beautiful. The whole world is."

He stopped, looking at me.

Then he said, "Oh, I am sorry. The world isn't beautiful to you, is it? You've lost your family."

I shook my head slightly to let him know that no apology was necessary.

"You're sweet. But I shouldn't have forgotten."

He was silent again, and we stood staring at the million glowing stars that looked like sunken treasures against the dark wave of the night.

Finally, he said, "Here, I got this today. Maybe you'd like it."

He walked over to a strange object, a box like a pirate's chest with something like a giant conch shell protruding from it. He placed a round, flat object upon it and turned a knob.

There was music! Music, though no one in the room sang or played! How was this possible? I checked Brewster's lips. No, they did not move. Yet it was a man's voice which sang.

Come to me, my melancholy baby . . .

"It's a new song," Brewster said. "I like it because I'm feeling a bit melancholy myself—you know, sad. It was really sad, seeing all those people . . ." He stopped. "Oh, now I've put my foot in it again."

The strange voice sang:

Every cloud must have a silver lining
Wait until the sun shines through
Smile my honey dear, while I kiss away each tear
Or else I shall be melancholy too!

The song ended. I thought it was wonderful that he was so sad for those people, when really, they were happier than ever. They were angels.

I gestured toward the wonderful object.

"Have you seen one before? It's a Victrola."

I gestured toward my ears, that he might know I wished to hear it again.

"Again?" He walked over to it. "Sure. Do you, would you like to dance? I've got two left feet, but I'll try."

I did not know what dancing was, but the truth was, I was happy to do anything he suggested as long as it did not involve talking.

But it was better than I had imagined, for he reached for my arm and drew me toward him. Then we were twirling, turning, stepping around, and each fall of our feet brought me closer, then farther, then closer, then farther, until we moved as one, undulating like the ocean's waves.

We heard the song again, and then others, and finally, the bell rang again, eleven times now, and he said, "She'll be home soon. I should go to bed. You should too. But will you meet me back here tomorrow, same time? And we'll dance some more."

I nodded.

I returned to my room where Celia lay snoring, and I knew that tomorrow, all the knives and stoves and matches in the world could not harm me. He wanted to see me again!

The next day's work was little better, for I was sent to the market to purchase some items. With neither voice nor the ability to read the strange symbols on Cook's paper, I tried to match the symbols on Cook's list to those on the signs at the grocery. It was hard. Finally, I asked one of the clerks for assistance, pointing to the paper.

"Artichokes?" the boy said. "Oh, those is these strange things over here." He led me to something that resembled a green nudibranch, a sort of sea slug.

I pointed to the next. "Cantaloupe? That's this one, always get it mixed up with the honeydew, myself." He pointed to something resembling brain coral, and I placed one in my basket.

But when I pointed to the next, his face darkened. "Aw, now I know you're just fooling with me. Everyone knows what carrots is."

He refused to help me after that, and I had to try to decipher the signs or overhear the conversations of the other customers.

When I finally returned, Cook flicked her dish towel at me. "Four hours, girl. Do that again, and the mistress will fire you for sure, shipwreck victim or no."

"No, she won't," Celia said, "for our little Dorothy was up until all hours with Master Brewster last night."

"With young Brewster? Whatever were they doing?"

"Not talking, that's for sure." Celia winked.

"Funny if he did like her, though," said Celia, "and it would serve the mistress right, her always acting so high and mighty, if her son was to fall for a servant. Is he in love with you, Dorothy?"

She was being friendly again, and I remembered how it felt with Brewster's hands upon my waist, my body pulled in close toward him. Still, all I did was shrug my shoulders, which was something merfolk did to show they had no idea of the answer to a question.

It must have been what humans did too, for Celia laughed. "Oh, she's tricky, but look at her blush."

"Ain't it the truth?" Cook said.

I didn't know what "blush" meant, but I felt my cheeks grow hot as they never had in the water.

Celia said, "You shouldn't go and see him in your uniform. Don't you have anything else to wear?"

I nodded.

"Well, good, and I will fix your hair."

I nodded and smiled.

"But you'll have to stop dropping things and wasting time."

That night at dinner, I was careful with the knives and did not cut myself. I let Celia light the gas oven, and I dropped nothing at dinner, which was difficult, let me tell you, for Brewster was there, and at one moment, he began to hum. I did not have to listen long to know that the song was "My Melancholy Baby," the same song we had heard the night before.

The mistress looked annoyed, but only said, "Don't forget, Hestia comes Friday."

Brewster made a noise rather like the bark of a seal. "Yes, yes, I know. You've told me. I suppose I will have to attend, though it is hard for me to think of romance after what has happened in the past week."

I was then refilling the water glasses as slowly as possible, the better to hear the conversation. I knew Brewster had no desire to meet Hestia Rivers. He loved me, I was certain. Still, I had to hear all, even though the sparkling glass pitcher was heavy in my hands.

"Perhaps it is too soon," Mr. Davis said, his first words in my presence.

"Too soon?" the mistress cried, sounding not unlike a gull. She turned to Brewster. "I am well aware of the tragedy we have faced. Do you think I can forget those terrible hours when I thought you were lost to me?

"Did you not say you had a DAR meeting tonight at seven?" Brewster asked. "Is it not very near that time now?"

Mrs. Davis glanced at her wrist. "Oh, you are quite right. I must be ready and dressed in an hour. Girl! Girl!" She snapped her fingers at me. "Tell Celia we shall have dessert right away."

I nodded.

Brewster met my eyes and mouthed, "An hour."

The dishes done, I dressed in my pretty blue frock. Celia brushed my hair and loaned me her ribbon.

"In this," she said, "he will find you lovelier than any girl he has seen or will, and that will about kill his mother."

When I entered the sitting room, Brewster sat up. "Boy, you look peachy tonight, Dorothy. Forget the skyline—I could look at you all night!"

Again, I felt my cheeks grow warm, but I bowed my head to let him know that I wouldn't mind him looking at me, not at all.

"Gee, you're even prettier when you blush." He patted the cushion beside his own. "Sorry Mother was so rude to you at dinner. She makes me so mad, talking about matchmaking and stuff. Even in Europe, when we were over there, it was supposed to be an educational tour, but I could barely glance at the world-class museums or centuries-old ruins without being interrupted by her blabbing. The only time I had a minute's peace was when we were at sea. Those nights, I used to wait for her to go to sleep, fortified by rich food and too many martinis. Then I would sneak out on deck and stare up at the stars or down at the ocean. It was so peaceful with no one speaking or making a sound that I almost wished I had been born to some other life, to be a sailor or even a merman." He laughed. "You think I'm nuts, right, believing in merfolk?"

I shook my head.

"Oh, don't lie. You think I'm insane. But when I was a little boy, my tutor used to tell me fantastical stories of people living in castles undersea. Mother accused him of filling my head with nonsense, and he stopped. But I don't think it was nonsense, do you?"

When I shook my head, he said, "You know, half the earth's covered with water. To me, it only makes sense that someone would live there, someone besides just fish. There are sailors who say they've seen them, and Barnum, the great showman, had one in his museum. Eliot wrote that poem, 'I have heard the mermaids singing, each to each. I do not think that they will sing to me.' I feel that way sometimes."

I wanted, oh, how I wanted to tell him it was all true, tell him of my life, what I had seen. I searched around for some way of saying, showing, of demonstrating it. My eyes lit upon a pad of paper, a pad much larger than the one upon which Cook had written her grocery list. Beside it, there were many different colored sticks. I wondered if I could use them to write, as Cook had with her stick called a pencil.

"What is it, Dorothy?" Brewster's eyes followed mine, and he spied the pad at which I stared. "Did you wish to write me a note?"

When I nodded, he said, "Well, of course. Stupid of me. Those are Mother's drawing things. She never uses them. She much prefers shopping and meddling in my life. She won't notice. Go ahead."

The pad was mounted on a sort of stand so that it stood up. I seized one of the colored sticks, the one that most resembled the reddish-orange coral we used for our homes. I began to draw our castle. The more I drew, the more memories came back, and I filled in details, the rolling waves, the sea creatures, fish, starfish, octopi, the sandy ocean floor, and finally, my sisters and me. I turned to find Brewster very close, staring over my shoulder.

"Yes," he said, "yes, that is exactly as I'd pictured it, almost as if you read my mind, Dorothy." His hand encircled my waist, and with the other, he pulled me toward him. "You and I are so much alike. If you could only speak . . ."

Then, he kissed me. I knew about kisses, for merfolk kissed too. When a merman kisses a mermaid, it means they will be together forever, and as I kissed Brewster and felt his hands upon my body, I knew that it meant the same in the human world as well.

We kissed and touched and held each other until the click of the key in the lock told us it was time to go to bed.

"Tomorrow?" Brewster asked.

I nodded and was gone, but in my bed that night, I thought of him, his hands on me, lips on mine, and I knew I had done the right thing in coming there, knew I would forever be happy.

The next night, when I entered the sitting room, wearing a pink dress borrowed from Celia, Brewster said, "I got you something."

I looked at him with a question in my eyes, and he took from behind his back a round disc, the kind he had used before on the Victrola.

Music! I loved music more than anything in the world. Well, anything except Brewster. I jumped up and down and clapped my hands.

He laughed. "You don't even know what it is yet."

I gestured that he should put it on the Victrola. He laughed again and did.

A man's voice filled the room. It sang:

You've got me hypnotized.
I'm certainly mesmerized.
I thought I was wise;
Till I gazed in your beautiful eyes.

Brewster drew me to him, and we were dancing again, closer than before, so close I could feel his heartbeat, hear his breath in my ear, and when the song ended, we stood a moment, holding each other, him gazing into my eyes.

I looked away first, nervous. He said, "Do you want to hear it again?"

I nodded. I thought he would go to the Victrola and play the song again. Instead, he gazed deep into my eyes and sang.

You've got me hypnotized . . .

He held me, warm and close, and when he finished, he said, "Your eyes are so beautiful, Dorothy, the color of the ocean."

His lips were on mine, and then we were falling onto the settee. He was crushing against me, touching every inch of me with his strong hands. "Would you . . . can I take you back to my room so we can be alone?" When I nodded, he kissed me so deeply I didn't want it to end. In his room, we were even closer, kissing, caressing, not stopping for anything but the daylight, when I knew I had to leave.

As I stood by the door, ready to go, he called me. "Dorothy?"

I paused, knowing then he would tell me he loved me, ask me to be with him forever.

"I can't see you tonight. My mother has arranged for some horrible heiress to come to dinner."

I nodded. I remembered, Hestia Rivers.

"I don't want to take one day from you, but I have to make the sacrifice. Mother . . ."

I placed my fingers to his lips and nodded to show I understood. Then, I leaned forward and kissed him.

"Saturday," he said. "We'll definitely be together Saturday."

I nodded again. He hadn't said he loved me, but I knew he did.

All day Friday, my feelings played shark and minnow with each other. Washing the dishes, I knew he loved me. Putting them away, I fretted that I would not see him tonight. Washing vegetables, I sang inside, "He kissed me!" Turning on the oven, I knew we had held each other. But as the flaming match drew closer to my fingertips, I knew he would see me only as a serving girl tonight.

Yet, as evening fell and the city lights once again became stars, I knew he loved me. He loved me. He only had to satisfy his mother that Hestia Rivers was not the girl for him. I was. I was, after all, the one who had saved his life.

"Oh, you poor dear," Celia said when Cook told her who was coming. "To have to see him with another girl. Never you worry. I shall do all the serving. You just get things ready in the kitchen."

Again, my emotions scattered like a school of fish, invaded by a predator. Of course I didn't want to see him with another girl. And yet, I wanted desperately to see him.

So, while Celia bustled back and forth, carrying plates and glasses, oysters and soup, I stood by and tried to hear the conversation. Finally, as the dessert was to be brought in, I could stand it no longer. I seized a tray of something called crème brûlée from Celia's hands and practically dove into the dining room with it.

I had hoped to see him perturbed, bored, annoyed. Likewise, I had hoped to see in Hestia Rivers exactly the sort of boorish girl Brewster had described. I was disappointed in both regards. The girl sitting at Brewster's side was lovely, dainty, and delicate with long, blond, curled hair, much like my own. Her blue eyes sparkled as she spoke. There was something strangely familiar about her too.

And Brewster, he was laughing.

"Miss Rivers, that is the cleverest thing I have ever heard," he said.

I, who could say nothing, only stared.

"See," his mother said. "So I was right in making the introduction. You should listen to your mother more often."

"How could I have known?" Brewster said. "I knew I could love only the girl who had rescued me from the ocean, who held my hand as we waited for *Carpathia*." He gazed at the girl, at Hestia, with something approaching adoration.

That was when I recognized her. Of course! Hestia Rivers had been on the lifeboat! She had been the young lady dozing on the other side of it as I pulled Brewster out of the water, as I had saved his life. Then, after I'd left, perhaps she had held his hand, but that was it. I was the one who had saved him. I was the one who loved him, not her. Yet I could say nothing to him, nothing. Brewster thought Hestia had saved him!

I felt the tray of crème brûlée teeter in my frozen hands, and before I could come to my senses enough to stop it, before I could even think to want to, it fell from my fingers and crashed to the floor.

"Clumsy oaf!" his mother shrieked. "You've ruined everything!"

I tried, mutely, to apologize, but I could not even see her through the waves of tears.

"Clean it up!" she screamed as her husband tried to calm her. "Clean it up, and then pack your bags and leave this instant."

"Mother." Brewster came to my rescue. "It was an accident. Surely it is not necessary to throw Dorothy into the streets at night."

I stared up at him with something like gratitude even as my fingers worked among the shattered, sticky dishes. He did love me. It would be all right.

"At least let her stay until morning," he said.

Until morning!

Beside him, Hestia was agreeing. "Yes, Mrs. Davis, it is quite all right. I know a little restaurant on Canal Street that serves dessert. Perhaps Brewster would like to take me there—and then out dancing."

"I'd be glad to," Brewster said, "although I was rather hoping to keep you here. I've purchased some new records for the Victrola. There's a swell one called 'You've Got Me Hypnotized.'"

I felt a sharp pain. A shard of china had jabbed my finger.

"Well, perhaps we can do that tomorrow," Hestia said.

"Yes, tomorrow," Brewster agreed. "Indeed, I wish to see you every night, now that I've found you again."

I sat sucking my bleeding finger; my tears became a tidal wave.

"Oh, for heaven's sakes, okay," said Mrs. Davis. "Stop the blubbering, you little fool, and get Celia to help you with that mess. You can stay until tomorrow, but no longer."

She chased me from the room, so I needed not hear Brewster and Hestia, talking, laughing, making their plans, falling in love.

Eventually, the dishes and every bit of crème brûlée was cleared under Celia's watchful, unsympathetic eye. Eventually, my meager possessions were packed in an old pillowslip, and I went to bed.

But I did not sleep. Instead, I waited, waited for the turn of Brewster's key in the lock, and waited too for some answer to the questions that filled my head. What was I to do? Where was I to go? I had gambled, gambled everything like men on ships did in their card games, and I had lost. I not only had no Brewster, no job, no place to live, I had no family. I had no ocean. I had no voice. I had no tail.

I had nothing.

It was well after the clock had rung twelve times when I finally heard Brewster enter the house. Then, I heard voices.

"How did it go? Tell me everything." That was his mother.

"When you're right, you're right," Brewster said, laughing. "Not only is Hestia Rivers neither fat nor vulgar; she is, in fact, exactly the girl I sought. You shall hear wedding bells within the year, I wager."

Their voices were low, but they filled the silent house, punishing my ears.

"Indeed," his mother said. "I feared you were going to run off with the serving girl."

He laughed. "Oh, that was nothing. Can't expect me to ignore a pretty girl in my own house."

And then the doors closed and the house was silent. It was not in my power to break that silence, and if it had been, I would not have screamed and raged, for it would have defeated my purpose. I knew now what that purpose was.

My purpose was to steal as quietly as possible from my bedroom.

To stop once more to gaze out the window and see the human world with its strings of stars, the world I had so long coveted, the world which had betrayed me.

To walk to the kitchen.

To open the oven door without a squeak.

To turn the knob.

To forget to light a match.

To position myself on the floor beside the oven.

To wait for sleep to come.

Then, I was floating, floating high in the air, above myself, looking down at the kitchen and the oven and, indeed, down upon the golden-haired girl in a borrowed white nightgown. At each side, an arm supported me, and there were voices.

"What shall we do with her?" said the voice to my left.

"I don't know," the voice on my right said. "She is a mermaid. She has no soul."

"A mermaid? Then where is her tail?"

"Still . . ."

I looked from one side to the other. They were women, beautiful women draped in white, their wings flying behind them.

"Are you angels?" I asked, for my voice had returned.

"We are Daughters of the Air. If you are human, we may take you with us, and you'll live in the sky forever."

I stared down at the shell of the girl I used to be. I felt I did not know her, did not understand her stupidity, did not want to know her.

Still, I said, "I was human . . . for a while . . . the last while."

Right looked to Left, then down at my still, silent body. "She has committed a grievous error. Suicide is a mortal sin."

"But perhaps it was not suicide," reasoned Left. "You saw how much trouble she had with the oven. I'm sure it was a tragic accident."

"Do you think so?"

Left nodded. "I do, poor dear."

Right pondered, and I hung, wingless, between them. Finally, Right said, "I think so too."

And, with that, I was one of them, a Daughter of the Air, with wings of white feathers and a dress much more beautiful than the sad nightgown I left on earth. Together, we flew out the window and into the dark, star-spotted city, over the ocean, then up, up into the sky.

Kendra speaks (with great regret)

So you see how that really couldn't have ended any worse, right? When they retell this story, sometimes they change it, so the mermaid gets her man in the end, and together, they defeat the evil Sea Witch, but that's not what happened. This was what happened. The good thing is, no one knew about my involvement. Well, except sea creatures. But still, can you blame me for not wanting to get involved in people's lives?

Emma may be miserable, but she's miserable and alive. She'll have other chances at happiness. Things tend to get a lot easier in college, and after that? Well, have you noticed that a lot of people who were rather nebbishy in high school end up with perfectly nice families and excellent careers? Indeed, seems I've seen a few movie stars who claim they weren't part of the cool crowd. That's because high school is hard.

That's why I'm thinking Emma should just get through this on her own.

Well, maybe with a little help.

Part Three
Lisette and Emma

1

Once, in school, we read a folktale from the Philippines. It was about two sisters, Mangita and Larina. Unlike in Cinderella, both girls were beautiful, but only one was "as good as she was beautiful." The good one, Mangita (a brunette), helps an old woman and becomes sick. The old woman comes back and tells Larina to give Mangita a seed every hour, to make her well. Larina doesn't do this, for she wants her sister to die. Fortunately, the old woman comes back in time. She cures Mangita and makes it so that Larina has to spend the rest of her life combing seeds from her hair. Every time she combs a seed out, a new one appears.

I liked that story. Good was rewarded; Evil was punished.

It didn't work out that way in real life.

So I had to watch Lisette and Warner. Of course, I had been

wrong. It didn't last a week. Her dumping him in a week would have given me what I wanted. Lisette couldn't do that. I wanted him back, so of course she would hold on to him forever. She'd probably marry him and have five kids, just to spite me.

And I missed my father.

Some would say that I shouldn't have wanted Warner back. They'd say he didn't deserve me. They'd be wrong. Warner had fallen under Lisette's spell because he was gullible, like my father. He wanted to believe she wasn't lying. He was sweet like that. He couldn't wrap his brain around the truth about Lisette because it was just too alien. I don't know why he was less willing to believe me, except he was disappointed I'd lied to him. Also, I guess, I really hadn't done anything to stop Mother from being cruel to Lisette. I was guilty of that, of doing nothing. Yes, Lisette had been mean to me first, but I should have been the better person. Now I was paying the price.

So, now, I saw him and Lisette in the hall. They held hands. I saw them in the cafeteria. She fed him grapes. I saw them in the library. She pretended interest in the books he was reading. She rode in his Civic like it was one of her old boyfriends' Mercedes. She was always touching him, holding him, pretending to love him. I knew she didn't, for the best possible reason: Lisette didn't love anyone but Lisette. I actually felt sorry for Warner because, sooner or later, he'd find out. Unfortunately, it would probably be later, too late for me.

I remember Kendra saying that, if Lisette stole Warner, we could fix it. I wished I knew how. On television, the dumped girl gets a new hairstyle and takes back her man. In the movies, she'd put a hit on Lisette. That seemed extreme, but a haircut wouldn't work.

No, it was hopeless.

Yet, sometimes, in journalism class, I'd look over at Warner and find him looking back at me. Was it crazy to think he still loved me, that he didn't believe all her lies?

I threw myself into the one thing that never failed me, school. In language arts, we were doing projects based on *Macbeth*. Even though I loved Shakespeare, I found this particular play difficult. The unfairness of Macbeth killing all those people so he could be king was too much like my own life.

Fortunately, the projects were easy. We could paint a painting, do an interpretive dance, or create a *Macbeth*-themed butterfly garden, stuff you could do without actually reading the play.

My project was a diary in the voice of Lady Macbeth. I chose that because it required no in-class presentation. I laid it on Ms. Delgado's desk when I came in.

Today, Kendra was dressed in a kilt, tunic, and crown. Her long hair was gathered in a ponytail. "Nice costume," I said. "It's really authentic."

Courtney, sitting two seats away, nudged Midori. "Someone's craving attention." She nodded at Kendra's Macbeth costume.

Yes, Courtney, Tayloe, and Midori were still in classes with me. High school is like a hamster wheel that never stops.

"God, doesn't she have parents?" Midori agreed.

Kendra ignored them. I admired her for that, for never caring what people thought.

"What's your project?" I asked.

Before she could answer, Ms. Delgado asked if there were any volunteers to go first. Of course not.

"Well, then, I'll volunteer someone. Tim Minor?"

A tall, skinny boy from the basketball team shuffled to the front of the room. He took up his book, opened it, and started reading Lady Macbeth's "Screw your courage to the sticking place" speech.

A couple of people, including Tim, laughed when he said "nipple," then "screw." No one minded that he couldn't pronounce most of the words. The cool people could actually bludgeon someone to death (and certainly bludgeon the English language) and no one would care.

"That was very nice," Ms. Delgado said when he finished.

I shook my head. Bet he got an A.

Next, Kendra raised her hand.

"I'll be performing a twelve-tone aria based on Macbeth's 'Out, out, brief candle' speech. Twelve-tone music was invented by Arnold Schoenberg in the 1920s. In it, the composer uses all twelve tones of the chromatic scale in a prescribed order called a tone row. He must use them in primary, retrograde, inverted, and inverted retrograde orders."

"Whatever she just said," Courtney whispered.

"My reason for choosing twelve-tone music," Kendra continued, "was that I thought its dissonance best evoked Shakespeare's sentence about 'a tale told by an idiot.'" Did she glance at Courtney when she said "idiot"? She did. "Full of sound and fury, signifying nothing."

"Is that supposed to be a costume?" Midori asked. "Or is it time to do laundry?"

Kendra cleared her throat. "Ms. Delgado, I've incorporated some performance art into my presentation. Would it be possible to turn out the lights?"

A few people whooped, and Courtney said, "Oh, yeah, then we wouldn't have to look at her."

Ms. Delgado said, "I think we have to leave the lights on, Kendra."

Kendra shrugged. "Okay." She pulled a candle from her bag.

"I think there's probably a rule against fires too," Ms. Delgado added.

"Oh, it's not a real candle." Kendra flicked it, and even though it looked exactly like a real candle, it lit with no match or lighter. "See?"

"All right, Kendra. Can we get going?"

"Certainly." Kendra stood up front, holding her candle, which flickered just like a real one. She looked at me. "Would you mind turning the music on after I say 'Out, out, brief candle'?"

Her iPod sat in a portable speaker. It had a cover with a picture of the rock group Counting Crows. I nodded.

Kendra stared up at the fluorescent light. In its glow, her skin seemed almost green. Someone giggled, then someone else. But then the lights began to flicker, then dimmed, until the room seemed bathed in a dull gray glow.

In the dim half-twilight, Kendra said Macbeth's line, "Out, out, brief candle."

My cue. I pressed the play button. The strangest music came out—someone playing notes on a piano in an order that seemed random, yet not, tuneless, yet planned. The music was like breaking glass.

Kendra began to sing.

"*Life's but a walking shadow.*"

Her voice was high and light, like you'd imagine a mermaid would sing. Funny how I never heard her in chorus.

"*A poor player that struts and frets his hour upon the stage and is heard no more. No more.*"

The piano grew louder. It had nothing to do with what Kendra was singing, and yet, she seemed in a trance, in the zone.

"*A tale told by an idiot!*" she sang louder. "*Full of sound and fury! Fury!*"

Her voice and the piano both reached a crescendo, the notes crowding on top of one another.

"*Fury!*" she shrieked.

More notes, growing softer again.

"*Signifying. Nothing.*"

Silence. Kendra blew out the candle, and the room was suddenly dark.

From out of it came a voice. Courtney.

"All right, who killed the cat?"

The room went crazy. The lights came up. Ms. Delgado clapped her hands. "Quiet!

To Courtney, she said, "You're next."

Courtney signaled to her posse, Tayloe and Midori, plus her boyfriend, Eric Rodriguez. "We're doing the witch scene." She glanced at Kendra. "Even though others might be better for the part."

She picked up a plastic Halloween kettle I'd noticed sitting empty beside her desk. As she brushed past Kendra, Kendra stuck her foot out. Courtney stomped on it.

"Clown!" Courtney whispered.

"Clone!" Kendra shot back.

So they started on one of the witch scenes. None of them could act, and I saw Courtney check her hand for her lines. I wondered if they'd practiced even once. They were having trouble with easy words like *entrails*. I glanced at Kendra, looking for someone to snicker with.

But she was watching them like it was great theater.

When they got to the part where all three chanted:

"Double, double, toil and trouble
Fire burn and cauldron bubble!"

I could have sworn I saw the cauldron move.

Probably someone had kicked it.

"Fillet of a fenny snake." Courtney pronounced it *fill-ett* with a hard *T.*

"In the cauldron, boil and bake."

Again the cauldron moved. This time, I was sure no one had touched it.

"Eye of newt and toe of frog, wool of bat and tongue of dog," Courtney chanted.

The kettle was shaking back and forth. I glanced to my side, at Kendra. She was staring forward, not smiling, not even noticing.

I was nuts.

The three girls chanted:

"Double, double, toil and trouble
Fire burn and cauldron bubble!"

There was a pop, like something was actually burning. They must have gotten some kind of trick cauldron. Courtney's family always had big Halloween displays.

But, just as I had this thought, Tayloe screamed. Something thick and red was boiling up, splashing out of the pot, bubbling over the sides. The pot was melting, and its disgusting contents were spilling over the brown linoleum classroom floor. There was all sorts of other stuff in it too, lumps.

Midori, who was apparently even more clueless than I'd thought, read her lines.

"Nose of Turk and Tartar's lips, finger of a birth-strangled babe."

I noticed one of the lumps. It was a tongue. *Tongue of dog.*

It was sliding toward us. Someone screamed. It was me.

"Stop!" Courtney yelled.

The cauldron boiled harder, its contents spilling down the sides. People jumped on chairs, screaming. Now all the stuff they'd mentioned was coming out, fake eyes and fingers (I hoped they were fake), snakes and a frog, and stuff that looked like the slime Mother took out of the turkey at Thanksgiving. Midori finally stopped talking and ran from the shaking, melting cauldron. Ms. Delgado yelled, "Stop it! Make it stop!" Everyone was screaming, grossed out, all but one person, Kendra, who watched it like it was a normal thing to happen.

The cauldron stopped shaking. A teacher from another class poked her head in to see what the problem was. Ms. Delgado, realizing she'd lost all control over her class, resorted to the weapon of choice of every teacher in the face of anarchy.

She flicked the lights on and off.

Courtney stepped on the liquid, which was expanding like Gorilla Glue.

She stuck to the floor. She tried to unstick herself by removing her shoe. Instead, she fell on her butt.

It took the ringing bell to restore order. Courtney was still glued to the floor. Eric, who'd been playing Macbeth, had slipped out, but when Tayloe and Midori tried to make their escape, Ms. Delgado blocked their way.

"Office," she said.

"But . . . but . . . ," Midori stammered. "We didn't do it."

"Who did it then?"

Midori looked back. I slipped past her. There was no one else there.

"You have to believe us," Tayloe said. "The cauldron was empty when we brought it. It's like it was . . . magic."

From the floor, Courtney said, "I think I need an ambulance."

I knew who'd done it. Tayloe was right. It *was* magic. Actual magic.

Suddenly I knew how I was going to get Warner back.

KENDRA SPEAKS

Heh. That was fun, right? Yeah, it was me. Okay, so I probably shouldn't be doing that kind of thing, but I just hate bratty mean girls like Courtney. And besides, sometimes, when you give people their comeuppance, they actually learn something.

I heard from an old friend today. His name's Kyle and he lives in New York City. He was as mean as Courtney, almost as mean as Lisette. He's the one I turned into a beast.

And it worked out! He's a better person, and he actually texted to thank me, if you can believe it. I got thanked for turning someone into a beast.

So there's at least one person out there I actually helped.

Maybe I can help Emma too.

2

Back to Lisette and Emma

After sixth period, I found Kendra in the hall. I tapped her shoulder.

She whirled to face me, and I thought I saw her eyes almost flash green. Then she smiled. “Emma, how’s it going?”

“Great. Hey, I loved your project in Delgado today.”

“Thanks. I’m a great admirer of Schoenberg’s work. Sad man. Did you know he had triskaidekaphobia, fear of the number thirteen? And he was born on the thirteenth and died on the thirteenth too.”

“Interesting.” This type of thing should have been a clue about her, long ago. “Did he live around here?”

“He was born in Austria, but he moved to the United States. California.”

“Hmm. Hey, can I drive you home? You can tell me more about Schoenberg, and there’s something else I want to discuss too.”

Her glance darted downward. “Um, I may be a little busy.”

"I'll drive you wherever you need to go."

"I guess."

We headed toward my newly appropriated Saab. I didn't know how I was going to ask Kendra this, and yet I was sure I was right. In the rear-view, I saw Warner walking Lisette to his car. She turned and brushed a stray hair from his face. He smiled like he used to smile at me.

I had to do this.

I started the motor, shifted into drive. Lisette walked in front of me. She waved.

I could kill her and make it look like an accident.

Okay, we'll call that Plan B.

I said to Kendra, "Interesting what happened with Courtney's project today."

"Wasn't it? You'd think she'd know better than to bring all those animals to school."

"You'd think. Thing is, Courtney doesn't usually do stuff that's unusual."

"That *is* weird." She was playing with something from her purse, a pair of dice.

"And a lot of weird stuff seems to happen . . . when you're around, Kendra." I paused, unsure how to continue.

"Like what?"

"Oh, I don't know. A mouse getting into my purse when it was on a teacher's desk."

"Wasn't that lucky?"

"Me hitting three targets when MVP Courtney couldn't."

"Everyone has good days and bad days."

"You showing up to that party just in time to get me out."

"Serendipity. I think—"

"And now, Courtney's kettle."

"What's your point, Emma?"

Her voice was different, and I turned to face her. I gasped. The outfit she'd been wearing had disappeared. Instead, she had on a blue gown with a square neckline that looked like it was from another era. Long blond braids hung down the bodice. She looked younger.

"My point . . ." I stared at her, and my voice came out a whisper. "My point is that you're a witch."

It sounded crazy.

She raised her hand like she was swearing an oath. "Guilty as charged."

I gasped. I hadn't expected her to admit it. Even in the face of all that evidence, I really hadn't believed it was true. I mean, could there really be magic in the world?

"Trust your instincts, Emma. This is the dress I was wearing when my family died in the plague. The year was 1666." She waved her hand, and her outfit changed to a form-fitting wine-colored dress, her hair a perky bob. "And this is what I wore when I met Herr Schoenberg in 1934." She stared at me, at my open mouth. "Now, what are you going to do about it, Emma? Burn me at the stake? Organize a boycott of all the Harry Potter books because they gave me ideas?"

A witch. She was really a witch. What did that mean, exactly? Why was she here? *Calm down.* I wanted something from the girl. "Of course not, Kendra. You're my best friend."

"Aw, that's so sweet. What is it you want, Emma?"

"Help getting my boyfriend back."

She smiled indulgently, like I was a four-year-old asking for a toy. "Faced with my tremendous powers of bewitchment, she asks not for world peace but, rather, wants her boyfriend back."

"Can you do world peace?" If she could, I should probably go for that.

"Not really."

"I just want Warner to love me again."

"Do you want me to do something to Lisette?"

"No, I . . ." Did I? Of course not. I just wanted her to leave Warner alone.

"Because I can't kill her off. I mean, I *can,* but I won't."

"Of course not!"

"Good. It wouldn't help anyway. He'd be all upset about her dying, and he might even blame you."

"That's fine." I didn't want to harm Lisette. In some secret, shameful, weak place, I still loved Lisette, still wanted to be her sister.

"The thing about help is, it doesn't always work."

I shrugged. "I'll take my chances."

"Sometimes it backfires."

"Backfires how?"

"Oh, don't get me wrong. I've had my successes. Only recently, I turned a selfish pretty boy into a beast . . . and helped him find true love. But there have been other cases where it hasn't worked as well." She got a faraway look on her face, and I waved my hand to rouse her.

"Like what?"

"Sometimes, I help people, and they get ridiculed or baked or turned into seafoam."

"Seafoam?" She wasn't making sense.

She saw my confusion. "I'm just saying it's not without risks."

"But sometimes your magic works, right? I mean, other than humiliating Courtney."

She thought about it a second and smiled.

"It does!" I said. "It works. Can you do a love potion?"

She shook her head. "You have to keep taking anti-rejection drugs forever, like a kidney transplant." She thought about it. "I could make you really beautiful."

"Could you?"

"Sure." She turned and stared a long time, then said, "Check your rearview."

I glanced at it and almost crashed my car. Kendra grabbed the wheel. "Whoa!"

"I'm sorry." The girl who stared back at me wasn't me. I mean, she looked a lot like me, but . . . heightened. She had a thin face, straight chestnut hair, higher cheekbones, green eyes instead of my usual greenish-hazel. "How could you . . . ?"

"Magic."

"Wow." The other stuff, like with Courtney, never seemed as big as this. I glanced at the mirror and almost swerved again. "I can't believe it. It's really real."

"Want me to make it permanent?"

My heart was doing backflips, and I didn't dare look again because I'd probably end up wrapping the car around a telephone pole, but finally, I said, "No, no. Warner . . . I liked that he loved me for *me*. He said he thought I was beautiful anyway. I sort of . . ." I stared at the road, remembering how it had felt when he'd said it.

"What?"

"I sort of believed him. I thought he meant it."

"He did." Her voice was unexpectedly kind.

"How do you know?"

"I just do. Boys are like that sometimes. He loved you."

"He just didn't trust me."

"Maybe he didn't trust himself."

I thought about that, and it made sense. Warner had dealt with his dad's lies, and then what he thought were mine. If he only knew what Lisette was really like, he'd forgive me.

I glanced in the mirror. Kendra's makeover would be just another lie.

I sighed. "I'll have to take a rain check."

"You sure?"

I took one last look at my pretty, straight hair.

"Just the hair?" Kendra offered. "You could tell people you got a keratin treatment."

"It wouldn't help."

"Okay." She flicked her fingers, and I watched myself come back, cheekbones droop, eyes darken.

"Heavy sigh," I said, as my hair poufed up.

"Maybe when you go away to college. It could be a graduation gift."

"I just want Warner back. You have to help me."

She patted my hand, which was weird for her. She wasn't a huggy-kissy girl, um, witch. "Just come up with a risk-free plan, and I will."

But what plan was risk-free?

"Where am I taking you, anyway?" I asked her. "Do I have to go to an enchanted train platform to get there?"

She shook her head. "Now that you know, I guess I don't have to pretend anymore."

"Pretend what?"

She reached over and put down the car window. Then, she disappeared.

I heard a noise, a sort of squawk. I glanced down at the seat where she'd been sitting. A huge black bird, bright-eyed and bigger than a grackle, sat there. A crow?

Did she just turn into a crow?

"Kendra?" I said.

The bird blinked one beady black eye. Then, it flew out the window.

3

Well, that was weird. Somehow, it just never *occurs* to you that the girl at the next desk could be an actual witch, even in the face of really obvious signs. It's sort of like, when there's a big shooting or bombing, and they interview the killer's neighbors on TV. They always say they never thought the guy would do something like that. Well, of course they didn't. It's unthinkable. So is being a witch.

And yet, for the first time, I had hope. If there was magic in the world, anything could happen.

And that night, it did.

We were sitting in the dining room, eating chicken. Lisette had already finished hers and was standing in the kitchen, waiting to clear our dishes, when Mother said, "I have big news."

"What's that?" I picked at my broccoli. Since Daddy had been gone, dinners were awkward. Mother would ask about school, and I'd tell her, filling the silence created by his absence. Food would be choked down, and after the shortest allowable time, I'd make my break.

But now, Mother actually seemed excited, looking over her shoulder to make sure Lisette was listening, and nervously shaking one foot over another before announcing, "One of Daddy's clients had a connection. We've been invited to a party . . ." She paused for dramatic effect. ". . . for Travis Beecher!"

"Travis Beecher?" I said.

"Travis Beecher!" Lisette burst from the kitchen, where she'd been listening.

Let me explain Travis Beecher, in case you've been living in outer space for the past few years. Travis was a teen star so famous even I knew about him. He got his start when he was a kid. His father, Riley Beecher, was the front man for the rock band Barrel of Toads, and Travis had gotten his own cable TV show, *Trav and Me*, coincidentally about a rock star, played by Riley, with a young son, played by Travis when he was eight or nine. Now, at sixteen, he was a rock star too and had made several direct-to-video movies (maybe you've seen *Trav in New York*, *Trav Takes Europe*—my personal favorite, in which Travis thwarts an international spy ring with only his trusty guitar—and *Trav and the Chimp*, which was about Trav and, well, a chimp), and they said he was making a feature film, his first, in Italy over the summer. He also toured. I'd seen him at the American Airlines Arena. He was actually completely awesome, and not just because he was hot. He had real musical talent and even wrote some of his songs!

Mother handed me something about the size of a coffee-table book that turned out to be an invitation. My hand sunk under the weight of it. After paging through the cover and several layers of tulle and feathers, I got to the writing part. It read:

Yo! If you're getting this, and you're a (hot) girl between the ages of 15 and 17, we know you want to come and meet our good friend, Trav. Yes, that's THE Trav. He's in Miami a few weeks, and he wants to meet girls to hang with and whatever, maybe even offer a part in Trav's new feature film, Got No Valentine *(in theaters next Valentine's Day).*

Be at Riley Beecher's house on Star Island (ask at the gate—they'll tell you where), Saturday, May 12, 7:00 until whenever.

Bring your parents if you have to, a date if you must. Really, though, it's all about Trav.

I put it down. "Daddy's . . . business associate wrote that?"

A shriek ripped my eardrums. "Oh! This is so exciting!"

Mother and I both turned and stared at Lisette.

"What is?" Mother asked.

Between shrieks, Lisette spit out, "Travis Beecher! Are you kidding? We're going to meet Travis! Beecher! Travis Beecher! Travis Beecher! This is sooooo exciting!"

And then, I swear, she hugged me. She tried to hug Mother, but Mother isn't huggable.

When the screaming finally stopped, Mother said, "And what, may I ask, would make you think you're going to this party?"

Lisette pointed to the envelope on the table. Mother glanced at it. It said, "To Andrea Bailey and daughters."

"Daughters," Lisette said. "That means we're all invited."

Mother laughed. "A mistake. Clearly, I don't have daughters. I only have Emma."

"But they invited three. You could bring me."

"I could, couldn't I? But I won't. Besides, what would you wear to a party like this?"

I knew that would be no problem for Lisette. She'd find

something even if she had to borrow from Courtney.

"And how would you get there?" Mother continued.

"You witch!" Lisette screamed. "I'd have clothes and a car if you hadn't stolen them."

"Your name isn't on the guest list, only mine. You don't go unless I say so."

Lisette lunged for the envelope in Mother's hand, the proof of her invitation. I wanted to run from the room, but my feet felt rooted to the floor. Mother turned away and ripped the envelope into two, four, eight pieces.

Lisette wailed. "Please, Andrea, please let me go. Please!" She was on the floor now, sobbing like a child. "You have to take me. This is my big chance, my only chance!"

Mother laughed. "There's no possibility that you're going."

Then, she walked out.

"Witch!" Lisette screamed. "Heartless witch!" Her face was red with disappointment, grief, and anger. For the first time, she didn't look pretty. I felt sorry for her.

But I stopped with her next words. She stood and pointed at me.

"You. You're the one who shouldn't be going, Emma. It clearly says the girls should be hot. They'll turn you away at the door."

I smiled. "At least I'll get to the door."

I took the invitation I was still holding and started to walk out, but her voice stopped me.

"Warner told me he was never attracted to you. He dated you because he thought you were nice, even if you were ugly."

I didn't, couldn't turn around. I felt tears bubbling up in my eyes. Had he said that?

"He said you weren't actually *that* fat, but your body was so pasty and flabby, he didn't know why you never worked out. You grossed him out so much."

It wasn't true. It couldn't be. He had loved me. I knew it wasn't a lie. She was just saying that to hurt me. And yet, I believed her. I wanted to run, but I stood there, frozen. My throat hurt. I couldn't have said anything even if I'd had anything to say.

"He says he can't believe someone as beautiful as I am would like him. We sit around and talk about you all the time. He said he couldn't stand the thought of touching you."

Finally, I was able to lift my foot. I made myself slow down. I couldn't let her see how she'd hurt me. Still, it was too much to have all my secret hopes and fears laid bare by my enemy. Had Warner really said that? Had he never loved me?

I wished I was dead. I wished I was dead.

I just kept putting one foot in front of the other. Lisette's voice followed me, making fun of every body part of mine that wasn't as perfect as hers (which was all of them), my hair, my nose, everything. Finally, I reached the stairs. I took off my shoes, so she wouldn't hear me run.

When I reached my room, I held my cell phone in my hand. I wanted to call Warner, to ask him if it was really true, had he really said those things?

I stared at the invitation in my hand. At least I had something Lisette wanted too.

Finally, I hit *67 and called Warner, just to hear his voice saying, "Hello? Hello?" Pathetic. He'd know it was me.

But he didn't even pick up, just his voice mail. I listened to that before hanging up.

I missed him.

So I spent the next week reliving every kiss, every touch Warner and I had shared, second-guessing whether he'd been hating me all along. Now, even my memories of him were ruined. And no, it didn't really help to know that Lisette was suffering too. I wondered if my suffering made her feel better about her life. Probably not.

I thought he'd loved me and dumped me based on a misunderstanding. If he just dumped me because he met someone prettier, he wasn't who I thought he was. It was all a lie.

I didn't want to go to school and face Warner. But I didn't want to stay home with Mother either.

Mother was ridiculously happy. This party put her into overdrive, and she spent hours poring over fashion magazines, showing me pictures of anorexic models wearing clothes on Nordstrom's website or in the pages of *Vogue*. She bought me outfits to try on, dozens of them, all for skinny boobless girls. I'd have the perfect one, even if it cost a thousand dollars.

"Couldn't we give the money to Haitian orphans instead?" I asked when she shoved yet another photo under my nose.

"You were always such a downer, Emma. Can't you see what an opportunity this party is? If Travis Beecher likes you, he might—"

"Might what? Marry me? I'm sixteen. Besides, he's a movie star. There will be hundreds of flashier-looking girls there. He'll pick one of them."

"But you have things they don't have. Intelligence. A quick wit."

Wit? Still, it was interesting to know she even noticed something like that, considering she spent her days griping about my looks. Nice to know she appreciated my brain.

"I'm just asking you to try. Do you think it's been easy for me, seeing you being passed over for things, being dumped on by those mean girls who don't understand how special you are? This would show them all."

Unbelievable. My mother actually sort of understood.

And then, she wrecked our little moment.

Wait for it.

"If you went on Slim-Fast, I could buy this in a size three."

Doubtful, considering I wore a seven, but I said, "I should probably try it on first."

"Terrific. Let's go to the mall."

I actually didn't mind. At least shopping took my thoughts off Warner for an hour or two. Every day at school, I had to watch them, strolling hand and hand in the halls. I used to try to decide if he seemed happy. Now, after what Lisette had said, I couldn't even look at him.

One day, at lunch, I asked Kendra, "Can you tell what people are thinking?"

"Like read minds like Professor Snape in Harry Potter? No one can do that."

"Oh." I couldn't believe my best—and only—friend was a witch and there wasn't a single thing she could do to help me get my boyfriend back.

But she said, "Oh!" and pulled something from her backpack. "There is one thing I can do." She held up an object.

It was a silver mirror, old-fashioned and ornate with a border of silver roses. "I just got this back from a friend in New York. Look at it."

I did. I was shocked at how bad my complexion looked. It had been my greatest asset, but now I had three big zits already out and two more breaking below the surface. Mother had made appointments for facials, hairstylists, and makeup artists before the party. They'd probably charge extra when they saw me. "Blech. What is this, a mirror that makes you look worse?"

"No, unfortunately, that's your skin. I can fix it, but you really need to get a good night's sleep and lay off the Doritos."

She laid her hand on my cheek. When she removed it, my complexion was clear again.

Amazing. "Thanks. Now, what's the deal with the mirror?"

"With it, you can see anyone, anywhere."

"Right."

"No, it's true. Pick someone."

I thought a second, trying to come up with a name other than Warner's. "Tayloe."

In an instant, the image in the mirror changed from my own face to a girl who may have been Tayloe. Except I couldn't see her face because she was crouched over a toilet in the girls' room. She stuck her finger down her throat.

"Ick. Is that really her?" Tayloe had been the only one who was sort of nice. Ish.

Kendra nodded. "Someone should tell her mother. Maybe an anonymous note." She stared into the distance a moment. "Done! Want to choose someone else? The president, maybe?"

"Oh, I don't . . ." But curiosity got the better of me. "Sure. Why not?"

I asked, and the picture switched to the president. He was somewhere, behind a stage, like he was waiting to give a speech. Surrounded by advisors, he riffled through papers. He actually looked nervous.

"So . . ." I said, putting it all together. "I could watch Lisette and Warner together when they don't know I'm watching, see if they're really happy, really in love."

"You could. But, remember, it might hurt you, seeing them together."

I looked in the mirror at the now-smiling president. "It couldn't hurt more than now."

"Don't be too sure. Magic isn't always a good idea. Plenty have seen what they wish they hadn't in this mirror, found out that their friends didn't really care about them, for example."

"Has it worked out for anyone?"

She smiled, and I knew the answer.

I said, "I need to know. They have a date tomorrow night."

Kendra nodded. "If you're sure."

"I'm sure. I'm not really expecting anything. I just want to know the truth."

She put the mirror in her bag. "You will."

5

Friday night, Kendra came over at six. I'd heard Lisette tell Warner on the phone (loudly, for my benefit) to pick her up at six-thirty for a seven-thirty movie.

In my room, Kendra showed me how the mirror worked. "It's like watching TV. You see everything that happens. If you want to see closeups of Warner, ask to watch him. If you want to see Lisette, watch her."

"Got it." It was six-twenty, and I said, "Show me Warner."

The mirror zeroed in on him like it was Google Earth. He was in his car, driving. It was the closest I'd seen him since we broke up, and I was surprised how tired he looked. He flipped through the selections on his iPod. He stopped on "Don't Blame the Moonlight" by Kim Mortal. It had been one of our favorite songs, and we'd planned on going to the concert. He switched with a grimace.

"Terrific," I said to Kendra. "He hates me so much, he's taking it out on Kim Mortal?"

"If you're going to be that sensitive, you shouldn't watch."

"It's okay."

He pulled in front of our house, checking his watch. It was right before six-thirty. Warner was always on time. We agreed that punctuality was important. It showed respect for the other person. Downstairs, I heard the shower running. It must have been Lisette. Warner stepped out of the car, checking his watch again, then walked to the door. Before he got there, he stopped. Something had caught his eye. My tree house. He glanced up at it. I wondered if he was sorry he'd rebuilt it for me. I hadn't been up in it since our breakup. It was too painful, remembering how that was where he'd first said he loved me. He stood, staring at it, then ran his hand against the ladder, admiring his handiwork. He checked his watch again. Six-thirty.

The shower was still running. Warner walked to the door and rang the doorbell. I jumped a little at hearing it ring in person and in the mirror too, sort of like that horror story about the old lady who realizes the puzzle she's putting together is of her own room. I jumped.

A minute passed. Then two. No one answered the door. The water finally stopped, but the hair dryer was running. Was Lisette just going to make Warner stand there? Did she expect me to get it?

Warner glanced at his watch again, then rang the bell a second time.

"Should I get it?" I asked Kendra.

"Do you want to?"

Yes! Yes! I wanted to see him again, be alone with him for just one minute. But maybe I didn't. What if he recoiled at seeing me? What if he told me again how much he hated me? What if he was mean?

"Let him think you're out too," Kendra said. "At least, that's what

I'd do. Of course, what do I know?"

"No, you're right." I watched as Warner picked up his phone and dialed a number.

Our phone rang.

I thrilled—briefly—at the idea that he was calling me. He wanted to talk to me. No. He was calling Lisette to find out where she was. Had he been calling me, he'd have called my cell. I let it ring, even though I really wanted to answer it. I wouldn't have kept him waiting like this.

Downstairs, the hair dryer finally stopped. Warner glanced at his watch. Six-forty. He looked at the tree house again. He turned, as if to leave, then rang the doorbell once more.

This time, Lisette heard. She yelled, "Just a sec!"

Warner checked his watch again. I could see the annoyance on his face. At least, I hoped I could. I wanted him to hate her, regret that he was with her, despite her beauty.

But in another ten minutes when she finally opened the door, I could see him appreciating her. He'd never looked at me like that. People would forgive a lot if you looked like Lisette.

Only when he got in the car did he say, "I hope we can still get tickets."

Lisette shrugged. "You should have bought them online."

"I didn't know we'd be this late."

"Hey, you don't get to look this good by rushing. Maybe *Emma* would have been ready on time, but I'm not a slob."

"Let's leave Emma out of this."

"Gladly." She reached over and started massaging his neck. "I'm sure we'll get in. I usually get what I want."

"I don't think that works on ticket machines."

Sure enough, when they got to the Falls, the movie Lisette wanted, a romantic comedy I'd seen the week before with Mother, was sold out. "Guess we'll have to see something else," Warner said.

"Okay." Lisette studied the timetable. "*I'll Kill You Later* starts at seven-thirty."

Warner bought the tickets, and they walked through the crowds to the ticket taker. "Theater four," the guy said, "first door on the left."

Lisette thanked him, then strolled right past theater four to theater seven.

"Hey, Lisette!" Warner yelled. "Lisette, it's here!"

"No, it's not." Lisette breezed through the crowd. I saw what she was doing, going into the theater with the movie she wanted to see, even though they didn't have tickets.

Warner caught up with her. "If we go here, there won't be seats for someone who actually bought tickets for that movie."

"So?"

"So, it's not fair."

She gestured at him to be quiet. "Life's not fair. It's not fair that my parents are both dead, and I have to live with your ex-girlfriend and her mother either. Now, are you with me or not?"

Warner sighed. "I guess."

"Actually, I'll go find seats. You buy popcorn, okay?"

"Fine."

So I got to watch Warner stand in the popcorn line for twenty minutes.

The movie, which I'd seen before, was super-dumb. It was about a pretty blond actress who, for reasons that weren't explained, was kidnapped by a fan. Because this was fantasyland, they fell in love, even though the guy had already tied her up and put her in the trunk of his car.

Because women are just *that* stupid.

"I can probably fix it so you can see the screen," Kendra said.

"It's okay. The movie was completely degrading."

Had I seen the movie with Warner, we'd have made fun of it the whole time. Lisette and Warner held hands and kissed. I tried not to cry.

After the obligatory chase scene (where the heroine realizes she loves the kidnapping dirtbag and has to stop the police from taking him away), the movie ended.

"Thanks for taking me," Lisette said. "You'll be rewarded."

I turned the mirror away so as not to see Warner's reaction.

Next, they waited an hour to get into P.F. Chang's.

"Maybe we should go someplace else," Warner suggested.

"I like to be where the action is," Lisette said. "Don't you want to be seen with me?"

"Of course."

They ran into Tayloe, who was eating a huge plate of noodles. Lisette hung on their table, saying, "Don't know where you put it, girl." Then she backed up and practically crashed into the waitress. "Oops."

"Maybe we shouldn't stand here, honey," Warner said.

"If they'd seat us, we wouldn't be here," Lisette replied.

Over dinner, they chatted awkwardly. "So, you liked that movie?" Warner said.

"Sure. Loved it. It was very romantic."

"You didn't think it was a little, um, formulaic? I mean, was there any doubt they were going to end up together?"

Lisette shrugged. "Jennifer Conroy's so pretty. I loved her outfit."

"But it kept getting ripped. The movie was sort of degrading to women, don't you think?"

Yes! Exactly!

"Why do you care? You're not a woman." Lisette fed Warner a bite of her brown rice. "You overanalyze things. You're just trying to show everyone how smart you are all the time. If it were up to you, we'd only see movies with subtitles."

Warner and I had loved movies with subtitles.

"What are we doing tomorrow?" Lisette asked.

"I don't know. This is sort of an expensive night. Maybe we could just hang out at my house tomorrow." Warner shook soy sauce onto his food.

"Oh, sorry, I hadn't realized you minded taking me out."

"I love taking you out. But between the tickets and the popcorn, and this . . ." He gestured around the table. "I'm going to drop a hundred dollars tonight."

"Your dad will give it to you."

Warner pursed his lips. "But I don't want to take it from him. He'll feel like he's making up for things."

"That's stupid. I know what it's like to have mean relatives. If I could get anything out of Andrea and Emma, I'd take it."

She had.

"I guess."

"I'm so glad we're together. I saved you from her."

"Can we please not talk about Emma?"

"Okay, you saved me too." Lisette stroked his hair. "Saved me from my life of misery."

Warner tried to make eye contact with the waitress, to get the check.

How could he stand her? On a date with him, she was just as conniving and mean as she was with me. Yet, he took it, even enjoyed it. I watched Lisette move to the seat by his and kiss him. "So, what are we doing tomorrow?" she cooed.

"What do you want to do?" he asked.

Was being pretty that important? After a while, wouldn't you stop noticing the person's looks?

But maybe he liked being seen with her, instead of being seen with me.

That and the fact that Lisette had convinced him I was Satan.

On the way home, she said, "Actually, I'll probably be doing chores most of the day. That's what I do Saturdays. Oh, and Emma makes me do her homework."

"What?" I said it out loud. I turned to Kendra. "Oh no she didn't! As if I'd want her doing my homework."

Warner wasn't buying it either. "You're saying Emma doesn't do her own homework?" Even he had to know I was way smarter than Lisette and wouldn't let her near my homework.

Lisette realized her mistake and backed off. "Oh, just the busywork stuff, like when she has to copy definitions from the book."

"Oh."

They reached the door of our house, and Lisette said, "Want to come in?"

"Can I . . . isn't your stepmom?"

"She's out . . . meeting with her coven." Lisette laughed.

"What about Emma?"

A look of annoyance crossed Lisette's face. "What about her? She's out too, I think."

Warner nodded. "So she's dating someone else?"

Lisette laughed. "Doubtful. No one but you would be that charitable. I think she's with her weirdo friend, Kendra."

"I could make all her hair fall out right now," Kendra said.

I cackled. "No, don't." But it was tempting, because the next thing Lisette did was, she reached for Warner's face and kissed him. "I think we'll be all alone."

Finally, he agreed and followed her to her bedroom.

"Are you sure you want to keep watching?" Kendra asked.

I didn't, not really, but I was glued to it now, like one of those bad reality shows, which is what my life had become. I nodded. "Yeah."

The bedroom was mercifully dark, and they didn't turn on the lights. Still, I could hear them making out, hear them kissing and then more, and I knew it was true what she'd said, that he'd never been attracted to me, as he was to her. We'd never gone this far. I thought it was because he respected me, but I guess I was deluding myself about that too.

Which was why I was pretty shocked when I heard his voice saying, "God, Emma, I love you so much."

Silence. Had I heard him right? Was there a rewind button on this thing?

Then Lisette's voice in the darkness. "What did you just call me?"

I'd heard him right.

"What did you just call me?" She was shouting now.

"Lisette. Sorry. Oh, God, Lisette, it was a slip, just a slip."

"You still love that . . . that . . . her? Knowing how they treated me, and you still—"

"No, Lisette, no. I'm sorry. I'm so sorry."

She snapped on the light. She had on panties and a lacy tank top, which she was pulling back on. She arched her back, showing off her body. "Do I look like Emma?"

Warner blinked against the bright light.

"Look at me, you bastard. Do I look like Emma?"

"Of course not. I told you, I wasn't—"

"How do you think it makes me feel, knowing you told that fat cow you loved her when you've never said it to me?"

"Emma's not . . ." Warner looked down. "Of course I love you, Lisette."

"No, you don't. You love her. You respect her because she's so smart, and I'm just some dumb slut. That's what she's always telling me too."

"No, Lisette."

"She's smart. I'm stupid. Even my own father said he wished I was more like her."

I gasped. He had?

"I didn't mean it, Lisette. Let me make it up to you." He caressed her shoulder.

She moved away. "How?"

"I don't know. However you want, whatever you want."

Lisette considered. "I'll think about it. But you'd better get that money from your dad."

Warner nodded. "Whatever you want. I love you."

He pulled her toward him and they kissed, but this time, I didn't cringe.

I knew he'd told her the truth the first time. He loved me, not her. If he only knew the truth about me and Lisette, I could get him back. I just had to find a way for him to know it.

I handed the mirror back to Kendra. "Thank you. I found out what I needed to know."

She smiled. "That seldom happens."

6

Warner loved me. Me, not Lisette. And, what's more, Lisette was jealous of me for being smart. She didn't just loathe me randomly.

The whole thing felt so great I almost wanted to be nice to her. Almost.

But, not-so-almost, I wanted Warner back.

Whenever I can't figure out a solution to a problem, I sleep on it. They say the subconscious can unravel the most complex of spiderwebs. So when I was having trouble with a study group member who wasn't pulling her weight or when Courtney had picked on me at school, I just went to sleep and hoped for an answer.

I did that that night, for Lisette.

I awoke to the sound of Ralph on his mouse wheel, spinning. I touched the cage's side with my hand, to try to stop the noise. Ralph kept going.

The whirring sound became a song in my head.

Cinderelly, Cinderelly!

A song from a movie I'd seen as a kid.

And suddenly, I knew what to do.

I called Kendra and arranged to meet her at the park.

She was late, so I sat, waiting, watching the kids playing, the squirrels. The birds.

Suddenly she was there.

I was starting to realize how clueless I'd been not to realize she was a witch.

I said, "You've read *Cinderella*, right?" It was a stupid question, yeah, but with Kendra, you could mention something perfectly normal like *Cinderella* or reality shows, and then find out she thought it promoted arranged marriages or foot fetishism or something. She'd never been to McDonald's, and she called hot dogs "frankfurters." She'd never even watched *Barney*. Part of being a witch, I guessed.

But she said, "Read *Cinderella?* I knew Charles Perrault personally . . . I mean, of course I'm familiar with *Cinderella*. Who isn't, right? They made it into a movie."

"Yeah, and before that, it was a fairy tale, about a girl and her stepmother and stepsisters, and no one likes each other."

"I'm cognizant. Except I thought they were ugly stepsisters and a wicked stepmother."

I shrugged. "Maybe they were, maybe they weren't. Sometimes, people see a story differently." After years with Lisette, I didn't know what to believe anymore, even about fairy tales. Maybe Cinderella was the bad guy in the story, and her stepsisters were just nerdy girls who wanted a boyfriend. How politically correct was it, really, to make the villains ugly? And how realistic? In my experience, it was usually the pretty people who were mean to the ugly ones, not the other way around. Probably, I realized, ugly people needed a group to protect their portrayals in books and movies. Except no one would really admit they were ugly, not even to themselves.

I said, "The point is, no one was happy. Cinderella wanted a chance, and so did the steps. So Cinderella went to the ball, met a prince, and moved out, and everyone lived happily ever after. Apart, where they belonged."

Even though that wasn't exactly what the story said. Some versions said that Cinderella forgave her stepsisters. Some said she had them boiled in a pot. Most of them said that the steps wanted to marry the prince themselves. But I figured, considering there were so many versions of the story, they were probably all a little inaccurate.

"If you say so," Kendra said.

"I do. And that's my point. I don't want Lisette to be unhappy. She's had it rough. But I want her gone."

Kendra nodded. "So how do you plan to accomplish that?"

"Same way it happened in *Cinderella*. Lisette needs to go to the ball."

7

In the next week, I had to argue with my mother just to get her to let me attend school. The rest of the time, I tried to study while she had people plucking me, massaging, waxing, personal shopping, microdermabrasion-ing, and straightening me.

I wanted to ask her why this was so important to her, but I didn't. She'd told me why, because she wanted to show everyone how special I was. Also, I wanted to go now too. Just not for the same reasons she wanted me to go.

Saturday, I had to admit I looked sort of pretty in a flowy top that covered my upper arms and tight jeans that cut off my circulation. I still didn't look half as good as Lisette looked when she rolled out of bed, but nobody did.

The party was at seven. Lisette had spent the whole day in her room, crying about not being allowed to go, but I knew she had a date with Warner. At six-fifteen, I teetered out of the house in my new Prada strappy sandals with a five-inch heel (okay, I loved the shoes, but I couldn't walk in them), but not before opening the French door to the patio and letting in one black bird. I had Kendra's mirror. I brought it with me.

My plan was, of course, that Lisette would go to the party, end up with Travis, and Warner would see what she was really like.

"I want to sit in back," I told Mother. "I need more room to spread out, so I don't get messed up."

Mother beamed. "I knew you were excited about this. You could pretend you weren't but—oh, Emma, you look so pretty!"

"Yes. Thanks." I *was* excited, excited to see how our plan was working.

Kendra had taken some persuading. "I'm a witch," she said, "not a fairy godmother. Have you met some of those fairies? They're vicious."

"You're just pretending to be a fairy."

"You could make things worse."

"I'll take my chances."

"There's a flaw in every plan, something that could go wrong."

"Uh-huh." But secretly, I couldn't imagine what could go wrong with the plan. It was perfect. By the end of tonight, Lisette would have exactly what she wanted . . . and so would I.

In the dim backseat, I peered into the mirror.

"What's that?" Mother said.

"Oh, I brought a hand mirror, to check out my lipstick and hair before we go in."

Mother's face must have hurt from all that smiling. "Don't change anything. I paid big bucks for you to look perfect."

"Yes, Mother. I was just admiring. Why don't you turn on the radio?"

Mercifully, she did, which drowned it out a little when I whispered, "Show me Lisette."

The image immediately switched to our house, Lisette's room. When we'd left, she'd been crying. Now she was stomping around, furious.

"So unfair!" she was saying. "So unfair!" Her face was blotchy, her eyes black with smudged mascara. Her hair was the worst I've ever seen it, which was still beautiful.

"Hello?"

At the voice, Lisette jumped, then turned.

Kendra's costume was her wildest ever, maybe a little too good. She'd channeled Glinda in *The Wizard of Oz*, if Glinda had taken a healthy dose of absinthe—seafoam green tulle antebellum-style gown and a big emerald crown that stood a foot higher than her head. Her hair was green too, that day, with ringlets floating all around her. She floated too, down from the ceiling. I wondered how she'd gotten up there without Lisette seeing.

After her greeting, she began to sing:

Wish for diamonds, wish for pearls
Wishes for deserving girls!

"Who the hell are you, and what are you doing here?" Lisette shrieked. She picked up a shoe and aimed at Kendra.

"Hey, watch it. I'm your fairy godmother." She started to trill in a high soprano voice.

"Right." Lisette drew back her arm, then stopped. "Know what? You can take anything you want, actually. Just stay out of my room. There's nothing but crap here anyway. She's got silver in the dining room."

"Do I look like a cat burglar?"

"You look crazy. Actually, you look familiar. Do I know you from somewhere?"

"I'm your fairy godmother." Kendra began her cadenzas again.

"Right. How'd you get here?"

"I flew." She levitated off the ground a little.

Lisette let fly a few swear words.

"You don't believe in me?"

"Would you?"

Kendra stared across the room a second, then another. Suddenly something white started falling from the ceiling above Lisette.

Lisette swiped at it. "What is that?"

"Snow."

"Why is it—?" She turned to Kendra. "You made it snow?"

"I told you, I'm your fairy godmother." The snow started falling harder, then turned pink.

Lisette waved her arms around to keep it off her. "Can you make it stop?"

"You're kidding." Kendra wiggled her fingers and the pink snow started swirling, like a blizzard. "You're in your room, crying over a party you can't attend—a *party*—and someone dressed like this shows up, says she's your fairy godmother, and makes it stinking *snow*, and all you can say is 'make it stop'? Maybe you don't deserve a fairy godmother."

I could barely see through the storm. There were already drifts on the dresser.

"I'm sorry." Lisette was shivering. "It's just, I didn't believe you at first, and my stepmother will get mad if there's a mess. She's super-mean."

Kendra nodded. "So I've heard." With a wave of her hand, the snow disappeared.

"Better?"

"Yeah. So you were saying you can get me to the party?"

Kendra nodded. "We need to get started. It begins at seven, and you're not looking your best at the moment."

"I'm sorry. It's just, I've been crying."

Kendra nodded. "Self-pity is ugly. I'll clean you up."

With a flick of Kendra's hand, Lisette's blotchy skin cleared up. Her hair fixed itself (I noticed her dark roots disappear too), and her makeup was done with professional precision.

Lisette gaped in the mirror.

"Now, your clothes. What do you think?" Kendra flicked her hand again, and Lisette's jeans and T-shirt changed to couture originals in the same green Kendra was wearing.

"Um . . ." Lisette said. "That color doesn't work on everyone."

"How about this?" The ensemble changed to one in pink, then blue, and finally, a lacy number in white.

"Wow! You should be on *Project Runway*."

"It's nothing. Now you need shoes."

"Great."

"I need an old pair to convert."

Lisette nodded then walked to the closet. "These okay?" She showed Kendra a pair. I did a double take. They were the same blue sandals Daddy had bought her the day we'd met. Had she saved them for sentimental reasons? Mine had worn out years ago.

"Perfect. Put them on."

Lisette did, and the next moment, she was wearing impossibly high-heeled, jeweled, clear plastic sandals. They looked like glass slippers.

From the front seat of the car, Mother said, "Aren't you excited?"

"What?" I started. "Oh, I'm sorry. All the hairspray is giving me a headache, but I don't want to open the windows, so I'm being quiet." I looked back at the mirror.

Now, Kendra flitted around Lisette, adding details, earrings, necklace, glittery spray in her hair until Lisette looked like an otherworldly goddess.

"I'm so excited!" She danced around. "They're going to let me in?"

"You're on the guest list now."

"Oh, thank you! Thank you, fairy godmother. I'm sorry about the shoe thing. Those people are so cruel to me."

"I know, I know. I think you're ready."

"How will I get there? Is there a limo?"

Just then, the doorbell rang.

"Oh, no!" Lisette stomped her foot, practically impaling Kendra on her heel. "That's Warner. I have to get rid of him."

"I wouldn't do that, dear," Kendra said.

"Why not?"

"Because he's your ride."

"My ride? That geek? Can't you make a Porsche out of a pumpkin or something?"

Kendra smirked. "You see any pumpkins here?"

"Emma has a mouse in her room."

Kendra shook her head. "I'm afraid not. Warner will drive you, and he'll be your escort."

In the car, I chuckled. This was, of course, my requirement. I wanted Warner at the party, and I knew Lisette wouldn't like it.

She didn't. "My escort? But I'm going there to meet Travis! What kind of stupid fairy godmother are you?"

"Wishes always have rules. Cinderella herself had a time limit. Now, get the door because if he leaves, you'll have no way to get there."

"Oh, he'll wait forever." Nonetheless, Lisette shoved past Kendra and ran for the door.

Warner, sweet, stupid Warner stood there, smiling.

"Wow, you look more awesome than usual."

Okay, maybe he was more stupid than sweet. Could he honestly not see her sneer at him?

"Um, yeah," Lisette said. "Change of plans. We're going to a party on Star Island."

"Star Island? I'm not dressed for—"

"We're going!" Lisette gestured impatiently as the invitation appeared in her hand. "Here." She shoved him toward the door and they left.

"Emma?" Mother was talking to me again.

"What? Huh?" I unglued my eyes from Lisette and Warner.

"We're almost there. Maybe freshen your lipstick."

"Sure."

"Don't you see, Emma?" she said. "This is a chance for someone, for everyone, to realize how special you are."

I stared at her. Did she really believe that, that I was special? *Was* I special? I didn't ask. There was no time. We were pulling into the valet parking.

I reached for the lipstick and glanced at the clock. It had taken us forty-five minutes to drive to the party. That meant, in another forty-five minutes, Lisette would arrive. And Warner.

Travis Beecher's house looked just like you'd expect some spoiled, rich TV star kid's house to look. Two huge doors led to the marble-tiled entrance from which we could see a grand staircase like the one in the *Titanic* movie. We walked through about eight more rooms with jewel-toned walls until we reached a patio overlooking a sparkling bay. My feet already ached.

Once, when I was a kid, my aunt visited from Chicago, and we'd taken her on a boat tour of Miami Beach. The highlights had been the stars' homes, and this house—though it hadn't belonged to Travis Beecher at the time—had been one of them. I remembered it as big and white with dazzling columns, but I also remembered it as empty and hidden from the world.

It wasn't empty today. Hundreds of people, mostly girls my age, filled the patio, talking and giggling, fixing their hair and looking as self-conscious as I felt. Every one of them was pretty, but none was as beautiful as Lisette. They stood in clumps, some with their mothers, some with friends. I wondered if this was what it was like in *Cinderella*, before she arrived, everyone standing there, not knowing what to do.

"Do you see him?" Mother said.

"I don't. No way we're all going to meet him."

"You will. Maybe just take a stroll around the room. We could get some decorating ideas from a place like this."

Yeah, if we were moving into a mansion. I took a step, and my sandal straps dug into my feet. "We could eat something." There was a table spread with a sumptuous, and almost untouched, buffet, ceviche in little cups, a chef slicing into filet mignon. Also, nearby, there were little tables where you could actually sit down. No one was, though.

"Do you want your mouth to be full when he shows up?" Mother demanded.

I didn't care. I was here for Warner. And besides, I was hungry. I hadn't eaten all day, and Mother had been giving me lettuce and water most of the week. Did I mention that?

But I knew none of that would be the right thing to say, so I said, "I guess not."

So we walked and walked until I couldn't lift my foot again, couldn't move another inch in the tourniquet jeans. But when I suggested we at least sit, Mother said, "I heard someone say they saw him. He's out there somewhere."

I understood then how the girls in the story of "The Twelve Dancing Princesses" had danced themselves to illness. I felt sick just walking. I kept my eye out for Lisette, but she wasn't there.

Finally, though, I saw Travis Beecher's blond hair above the crowd.

"Maybe you should find the ladies' room," I said to Mother.

"What? Why?"

"Because he's here. You don't want me to be the one walking around with my mother when he gets here, do you? Like a baby?"

She smiled. "Good thinking, Emma. I'm glad you're finally showing some spirit for once in your life."

Show some spirit? I did have spirit, just not about this. I had spirit about important things like literature and like love. But I didn't say it to her, just watched as, with a wave of her hand, she walked away.

And then, I did what any girl (at least, any smart girl) who didn't want to be at this party in the first place would do if her mother stopped watching. I found a spot in the corner, behind a wicker trunk of some sort, and I took out my book.

Yup, I'd brought a book. It was the smallest one I could find to stuff in my purse, *Candide* by Voltaire. It was a satire about an optimistic young man who braves war, storms at sea, and the slaughter of his beloved's family—all in the first ten chapters.

I was trying to keep an eye out for Lisette and also for Mother, who would literally kill me right there on the patio with actual blood if she knew I was reading. But it was hard because I was enjoying the book so much. It was funny, despite how tragic it was, because Voltaire wrote about war, death, and cannibalism (an old lady's buttock is fed to a starving man) as if it were nothing much. I needed to develop that attitude.

I was just at the part where Candide flees Buenos Aires, where he's been pursued for murder, when I heard a voice above me.

"Good book?" It was a boy.

Pushing back my annoyance at being discovered, not to mention the irritation I always felt when people asked me what I was reading (did they really care, or were they just pointing out that they thought it was weird to read in public?), I tried to reply politely. "Pretty good."

And then I looked up.

Omigod. It was Travis. Travis. Beecher. Himself. I looked down, then back up again. Yes, that was definitely him. He had on a black guayabera, a sort of fancy Cuban shirt, and white pants. He was about my age, not as tall as I'd guessed, but way better looking, with dark blond hair and brown eyes you could drown in.

He also had a zit on his chin. I could only see it because I was below him, but that one zit made it possible for me to answer him without actually hyperventilating. "Um, yeah, it's pretty good. Really good, actually." I showed him the cover.

"Oh, wow. *Candide.* I've been meaning to read that."

Before I could stop myself, I laughed. "I'll bet."

"It's true," he said. "I love satire, not just parody like on TV, but real satire. My favorite novel of all time is *Vanity Fair.*"

My mouth went dry.

I must have looked weirded out because he leaned down, all concerned, and said, "Are you okay?" I couldn't see the zit anymore, but I saw his beautiful eyes even more clearly, which made it worse. "Can I get you a glass of water?"

I closed my mouth and inhaled deeply. Finally, I said, "You've read *Vanity Fair* by Thackeray?"

"Yeah."

"That's my favorite book. I've read it, like, fifteen times."

"Shut up. You haven't."

"It's true. I had to buy a new copy because mine was falling apart. I can't believe you read it."

"Why not? Because I'm—"

"Because I don't know anyone who's read it." *Not even Warner.* "I'm not even sure my English teacher has." Though, to be truthful, he was right. I didn't think someone like him would read *Vanity Fair* or anything but his lines. I figured he'd be out partying all night and going to the beach all day, like those kid stars you read about who are always in and out of rehab.

"Well, I did. I read a lot. It gets really boring on the set between shots, so I read all the time. I'm Travis, by the way."

I looked down. "Yeah. I know."

"So, I guess you're not that into parties."

"Ever read "Masque of the Red Death"? That was about a party." OMG. I was talking to Travis Beecher, and I was quoting *Kendra*?

But he laughed. "I'm not a big partyer either. This was my agent's idea, sort of a publicity thing. Say, do *you* have a name?"

Maybe it was because I was the only girl at the party who *wasn't* trying to go out with him, but I was pretty calm. I said, "Emma."

"I read that too—but only after I saw the movie. Oh, you were telling me your *name*. Nice to meet you, Emma." He held out his hand.

When I took it, he pulled me to standing. "So, do you always read at parties?"

"No, I usually avoid them. This was my mother's idea. She's a little starstruck."

"And you're not?"

"Sorry." My feet still hurt, but I could walk okay. I decided to take a good, long look at Travis while I could.

Man, he was cute. Just sayin'.

"I'd love to be able to do that," he was saying. "Just curl up with a book. But yeah, you do what your parents tell you—mostly."

"Did your parents tell you to be on that show?"

"That show? I gather you're not a fan?"

"It's pretty good. I used to watch it all the time when I was younger."

"Oh."

Okay, I was insulting him. "No. I liked it. It's just, I don't watch much TV at all. I have too much homework."

He shrugged. "I know it's not Shakespeare, but when I'm older, too old to play a kid, I want to do Shakespeare."

Gradually, I became aware of the rest of the room, the people in it. I saw other girls sneaking sidelong glances at us, and I knew they were wondering the same thing I was: How was he talking to me? Me? Yet they didn't look scornful.

"I didn't expect that, you liking Shakespeare."

"You expected some dumb party boy?"

"No . . . I guess I didn't think about it much, or know what to expect."

"We all stereotype, I guess. I don't usually expect to see pretty girls at a party reading Voltaire."

He thought I was pretty.

I wanted to giggle, but I suppressed the urge. How was this happening? Had Kendra done something? Had she made me prettier so that Travis would like me? Was it some sort of trick to test my will?

I glanced out toward the ocean. There was a fountain over by the wall. If I could get to it, I could see my reflection, learn the truth. "It's so nice out . . . Travis. Why don't we take a walk around?"

He smiled, still looking at my face like I was the prettiest girl he'd seen, the way guys looked at Lisette. "Sure." He took my hand again, and I almost forgot how much my feet hurt as we walked between two tall marble statues.

I tried to lead him around to the fountain, but before I even got there, I saw a table with vegetables on a mirror display. He saw me looking at it. "Would you like something to eat?"

I'd barely been able to zip Mother's size-five pants as it was, but I said, "Maybe just one." I moved closer to the table.

"Most girls I know don't eat," Travis was saying.

The display had been picked over a bit, and I found one of the empty pieces of mirror and looked at myself to see what Kendra had done.

I exhaled. It was my face, my normal face. She'd done nothing. Even the magic worked by Mother's team of stylists had faded. My hair didn't even look that great anymore after being in the humid night air, and my makeup had faded.

And yet, my face didn't look bad. I'd been used to thinking of myself as, if not ugly, at least below average in the eyes of the mean girls at school, or compared to Lisette. The girl who stared back at me wasn't ugly at all. She was pretty, pretty enough at least, with hazel eyes and high, arched brows. No, she wasn't the thinnest girl in the room. She wasn't a model. She didn't look like Lisette, but she wasn't bad at all. She was perfectly fine. Something had changed, maybe; maybe when Warner had loved me or maybe even before that. Or maybe nothing had changed, and I'd always been pretty. The girl Travis was seeing wasn't beautiful, but she was pretty enough to stand next to anyone.

Maybe Mother had been right. Maybe I was special.

He . . . Travis was handing me something, a cracker with cheese on it. I took it. "Oh, thank you. What Shakespeare play would you want to be in, if you were doing that?"

He thought about it. "I like the histories a lot, *Richard III* or *Henry VIII*, but they're not performed much. Plus, I don't think anyone is going to buy a former child star as a hunchback. If I were choosing a popular one, probably *Hamlet.* They do that a lot."

I nodded. "I read once that it's the most-filmed story after *Cinderella*."

Cinderella.

"But I wouldn't want to do it on film. I like the idea of being onstage. I've done concerts and stuff, and I remember when I was a kid, before I was on TV, we did a play in school. I had the lead, of course, probably because of who my dad was. . . ."

"I'm sure you were really talented." I hadn't watched the show in years, but I remembered he was good in it.

"Maybe. But it's different than doing television, having the audience actually there, being able to feel their energy. It was cool."

"I bet."

"We have a studio audience for the show, but they just scream because they think . . . never mind. It's embarrassing."

I nodded. Girls screamed because they thought he was hot.

"What's your favorite Shakespeare play?" he asked me.

My first thought was, not *Macbeth.* But instead I said, "Oh, definitely *The Merchant of Venice.*"

"The strong female heroine, Portia. I approve."

"Yeah, that, and well, my favorite part is how, when Bassanio is trying to gain Portia's hand, he has to choose between the three boxes. He chooses the box that's least showy, and that's the right one, not the silver or gold, but the lead." I liked that because of Lisette.

"'So may the outward shows be least themselves,'" he said.

I laughed. "'The world is still deceived with ornament.' You know it!"

"My tutor and I read it last year."

"But you memorized it. That's awesome."

"I believe it, that sometimes you have to look closer to find what's important. Like, sometimes, the girl you want to meet is hiding behind a wicker basket, reading a book."

I didn't know what to say.

We walked out to the railing, toward the seawall. Over it, I could see the dark, churning water, but also the bright, full moon reflected in it.

"It's beautiful here," I said. "You're so lucky to live here, at least part time."

"But it's isolated. I wish I had more friends. That's part of the reason I agreed to let Dad have this party, to at least meet some people my own age who aren't actually screaming."

And then, from the corner of my eye, I saw her. Lisette. She was here.

Even in that room, she was the most beautiful girl there. The crowds seemed to part for her, and people turned to stare, like she really was Cinderella. Warner was with her, but far behind. She walked fast, to keep him at a distance. He looked pale, stumbling, and more than a little stupid.

Travis didn't seem to notice either of them. "It's hard to talk to people at parties, though. It's so artificial."

Lisette came closer. My feet ached again. This was the moment I'd waited for, the moment when she and Travis would see each other, fall in love, and she'd ditch Warner. Then, I could have him back.

So why wasn't I backing off?

"I'm glad your mother made you come," Travis was saying.

Lisette walked closer. She saw me, and she couldn't hide the look of shock on her face, that I was talking to Travis.

"I guess parents aren't always crazy," I said.

"I wouldn't go that far."

I saw Warner watching me too. Travis still didn't see them, but I knew as soon as he did, he'd love Lisette at first sight. Everyone did.

But maybe not. I stood, literally and figuratively, on the precipice. Should I back off, or should I just see what would happen? It wasn't like this teen idol was actually going to fall in love with me.

I glanced at Warner. He'd finally caught up with Lisette and tried to take her hand. She acted like she didn't see him. I almost felt sorry for him. Almost.

A memory came to me. One time, in middle school, a famous author came to talk to our class and give a writing workshop. One of the things she told us about writing a novel was that the story should be about what the main character *wants.* Dorothy wants to go home to Kansas. George Milton wants a farm of his own. Amelia Sedley wants to marry her darling George and live happily ever after. The end of the story, according to the famous author, is when the character either gets what he wants or realizes he's never going to get it. Or sometimes, she said, like Scarlett O'Hara in *Gone With the Wind,* realizes she doesn't actually want what she thought she wanted all along.

My story began with wanting Warner. I wanted him and wanted

him, then got him for a little while, then lost him, partly because of Lisette. But just partly. The other part was, he was a jerk. I gave him my heart, and he threw it away. He didn't trust me, or himself.

Just then, I realized what could go wrong with Kendra's plan, with *my* plan: I could change my mind.

It wasn't being fickle, not really. Warner may have been the love of my life, but I wasn't the love of his. If I had been, he wouldn't have left me for anything.

I looked over at Lisette. Warner had taken her hand against her will. She shook it off. I smiled.

She could have him.

I turned back to Travis. "So you were saying you never met a girl you liked at a party?"

He shrugged. "First time for everything, right? Look, my dad's going to kill me if I don't dance with someone—hopefully you, if you're willing. But maybe tomorrow, you could come over when it's not so crowded, and we could just talk?"

"Tomorrow?"

"If you want, I mean. You could wear something more comfortable." He glanced down at my shoes. "Like flip-flops. We could take a walk on the beach."

I smiled ruefully. "I wish I had some flip-flops right now. I'd love to dance with you, but my feet hurt."

"There's a solution for that," Travis said.

"Hmm?"

Then, right in front of Lisette and everyone, he knelt on the floor beside me like Cinderella's prince, and he said, "Your slippers, milady?"

I knew what he was asking now, and I pointed my toe. He slipped off first one shoe, then the other. He didn't cringe at my big feet. Maybe they weren't *that* big. At least I'd gotten a pedicure so my nail polish wasn't chipped. "It's ridiculous that women have to wear these things." He walked over to one of the little tables, the type they have around at parties for people to put their used-up drinks on. The table happened to be right near Lisette and Warner, and when Travis came close, Lisette tried to greet him, but he just nodded. He dropped the shoes on the table. I knew Mother wouldn't mind. "Now, are you ready to dance?"

I nodded. He held out his hand and led me to the floor.

"Wear something comfortable tomorrow," he said, "and bring a bathing suit."

There are all these clichés about first dances with that special guy, that you forget yourself and dance as if on a cloud. I never forgot myself, but it was wonderful anyway, especially when Travis said, "I never meet anyone at parties because, usually, the girls who show up are like that one over there. All dolled up and fan-girly, like they think I'm going to make them a star or something." He rolled his eyes. "You're not like that, though."

He was gesturing at Lisette. She'd followed him back into the room. I nodded. I wanted to drop the subject, but I remembered what had happened with Warner, so I said, "Okay, I have a confession to make. That's my stepsister."

"Oh." He looked embarrassed. "Oh, I'm so sorry."

"No, don't be. We're not close or anything. She's sort of . . . like you said. I just thought if you found out later on, it would be weird that I hadn't told you. Not that I expect . . . I mean, you'll probably just fly back to LA, and I'll never see you again."

He frowned. "Is that what you see happening?"

"No. I mean, that's not what I *want* to see happen. I just thought—"

He lifted his fingers and placed them over my lips. I knew he was trying to tell me to stop talking, but the gesture had an intimacy to it that felt warm despite how short a time we'd known each other. "Want to know one of the really cool things about being on television?"

"What?"

"The money. They pay you enough that if you want to fly to Miami for the weekend to see this girl you like, or invite her to visit you on your movie set in Italy over the summer so you'll have someone to talk to about books or Shakespeare or whatever, you can."

"Really?" Was he saying what I thought he was saying? "That *is* a cool thing."

"Yeah." And then, he kissed me, just a bump on the cheek, but enough that I felt the warmth of his lips, smelled his cologne, which was like sand and citrus, got the feeling in the pit of my stomach, like the bottom dropping out of a trapdoor, and for a second, we were shoulder to shoulder, hand in hand. Cameras flashed, and I wondered if it was just a photo op, but he said, "Of course, the sucky thing about being on television is, you can't kiss a girl without there being pictures. Really kills the spontaneity."

"I bet."

"I want to kiss you though, Emma. Not just on the cheek. So will you come over tomorrow?"

"Probably," I whispered, then wondered, why did I say that? Of course I was going.

But it was the right thing to say because he laughed and said, "You're not like anyone I've ever met. Guess I should've known when I saw you and *Candide* here. No one I know would say 'probably.' But seriously, if it's a driving thing, I could have someone pick you up."

"Okay. Around noon?"

Was that too early? Too late?

He nodded. "Noon."

I said, "Are you supposed to . . . I mean, does your dad want you to dance with other girls? I'll understand." *But I didn't want him to leave.*

He shook his head. "I'll only go so far for my dad."

So we danced for another hour, past Mother, who was beaming, Lisette, who was scowling, Warner, who kept shaking his head, and about a hundred other girls, all of whom stared at me, probably wondering what I had that they didn't.

Except one, a girl with stunning long ebony hair and a backless black dress that looked like it was from another century. No one else in the room seemed to see her, but she winked at me as I danced past, and I recognized her. Kendra!

I mouthed, "Did you do this?"

She shook her head, then pointed at me.

Then, she turned into a crow and flew off the balcony.

Which no one noticed but me.

KENDRA SPEAKS (DOESN'T SHE HAVE EVERY RIGHT TO, AFTER SUCH A SPECTACULAR AND COMPLETELY UNEXPECTED RESOLUTION?)

Okay, so I changed my mind about helping Emma. But what did I do, really? Did I make Travis fall for Emma, instead of Lisette? Nope. It was just a lucky coincidence. Once every hundred or so years, you get one of those. And I didn't do anything to make her choose him over stupid Warner either. But I'm glad she did.

I don't like to meddle, you know. No, really.

People always want to know what happens *after* the end of the story. Did they fall in love? Did they live happily ever after? Will they marry and have six kids? Too soon to predict. I come by my wisdom through longevity, but I can't predict the future. If I could, I wouldn't have been all worried about that beast kid in New York. What I do know is that Emma did go to Travis's the next day, and the day after, *and* he came back to Miami every chance he got for the rest of the school year. He even picked her up at school once, as a surprise. So it looks pretty promising.

And Lisette? She spent most of the next week ranting to everyone who would listen about how could Travis possibly be into Emma. Finally, someone (Tayloe, maybe) told her to shut up, that she was getting boring, and everyone else agreed.

Oh, and she broke up with Warner a few days after the party, which came as no big surprise to anyone. Except Warner.

In the Grimm version of *Cinderella,* the stepsisters get their eyes pecked out by birds in the end. In Mr. Perrault's, Cinderella forgives them and finds them rich husbands.

Though I wouldn't advise Emma to go that far, I did agree with her when she said she wanted to try to make peace with Lisette.

Here's what happened, in her own words.

Lisette and Emma: The Finale

Okay, so Travis was pretty incredible. But, unlike in fairy tales and movies, falling in love doesn't solve all your problems—though it helps. I still had to live in that house. With Lisette. And my mother. And I couldn't get Kendra to use her magic every day.

Well, maybe I could, but it didn't seem nice.

So the day after Lisette broke up with Warner, when she was slogging through the rain to the bus stop before school, I pulled up beside her. "Get in."

She hesitated, but I said, "If you'd rather your hair frizz than ride with me, be my guest."

She put her hand up to her hair which was, of course, perfect, but she decided to get in anyway. "Courtney was supposed to pick me up, but she texted and said she couldn't."

"She changes her mind sometimes."

"Yeah. Do you always leave this early? I mean, do you have a study group before school or something geeky like that?"

I chose to ignore the obvious insult. "No. I was looking for you."

"Why?" She stared at me.

"I think maybe we should . . ." It was hard to talk with her eyes piercing me. I looked at the road. "Daddy's gone. There's really nothing else to argue about. Really, you won. If your object was to keep me from having a relationship with him, you won. And Warner? I don't care about Warner anymore."

"Neither do I."

"I know. You did me a favor, actually. You let me know what he was like." I dared to look at her. "So, what's left? We're stuck living together for two more years, and I think we should make the best of it."

She rolled her eyes. "The best of it being, I guess, that I do all the work and you get all the stuff?"

"No. I mean, unless you enjoy that type of thing. I was thinking maybe I could talk to Mother, tell her that I didn't think it was fair to treat you like that. But you have to do something too."

"What? You already have everything you want, a hot boyfriend, nice clothes."

"I want you to stop blaming me. I was three when your dad married my mother. I didn't have a choice in it. I didn't make him do it."

She shrugged. "I guess. It's just so unfair. I have no mother and now, no father, and you—"

"I miss him too. He was the only father I had, and I loved him, and I'll never see him again or be able to tell him. But can we stop playing this game of competing to see who's more pathetic? It makes us both pretty pathetic, if you ask me."

Lisette didn't answer for a long time. We were at school now. It was early, not crowded, so I just pulled into the parking lot, and suddenly I realized I was going to ask Mother to be nicer to Lisette, whether or not Lisette agreed to be nicer to me. It just wasn't in me to be mean to her, or to let Mother do it either. Also, it took energy I didn't have.

Besides, I knew Daddy wouldn't have wanted Lisette to be miserable and poor.

I chose a parking place and turned to Lisette. "Look, I just wanted to tell you I'm done. I'm done. Daddy's gone. Warner's gone, as far as I'm concerned, and I'm done fighting. If we can get along, great, and I'll share the chores with you, but otherwise, I'm still done."

I wanted, needed, the conversation to be over. I'd said what I had to say, and Lisette, as usual, wasn't helping at all. "Anyway, I have to go meet, um, Ms. Meinbach about newspaper."

I got out of the car, slammed the door, and started walking toward the school.

"Wait!" She was running after me.

I stopped. "What is it?"

She caught up with me. "My . . . our father. I should tell you."

"What?"

"He always loved you. I tried . . . I felt like I was his daughter. He should love me best, but even after I chased you away, he talked about you all the time, about how close you'd been, how he missed spending time with you."

I felt tears springing to my eyes. "He said that?"

I didn't know, until then, how much I needed to hear it, and from her, because she was the only person who would never lie, never try to be nice.

"Yeah," she said. "Pissed me off, and in the end, I was thinking maybe I was stupid, trying to compete. Maybe I should just back off, try to get along. Then, he died, and it was too late, and your mother was so mean."

I nodded. "I know."

"He loved both of us."

"Thank you for telling me that," I said.

An awkward pause. We both stood there, like you do when you think you're supposed to hug someone, but you really, really don't want to. I didn't love Lisette. I never would. I no longer wanted to be sisters, or even friends. I just wanted to get along, for my father's sake and for my own.

Finally, I started to walk away.

"Meet me here after school. I'll drive you home, and I'll talk to my mom."

Her voice stopped me. "Emma!"

I turned. "What?"

"I'll see you then."

It wasn't the apology it should have been, but I thought it was an agreement. I said, "Okay."

Kendra (again)

Lisette and Emma didn't become bestest friends. They weren't sisters. They became the most they could ever become—two girls, stuck together, who no longer hated each other.

"Do you consider that a success story?" Emma asks me over coffee.

I haven't been to school in a while, but I still drop in on Emma sometimes. When she asks where I've been, I always say, "You don't want to know."

But the truth is, I've been watching a lot of daytime TV, searching the morning talk shows for the next poor soul who needs my help, perhaps. Thought it's hard to admit, I really like helping people find love. It makes the time pass faster.

The problem with spending a hundred or so years in high school is, after a while, it's all review. Even the social parts seem like they've happened before. So sometimes, I take a few months off. I'll start again in the fall. Someplace new.

"A success," I say to Emma. "I'd consider it a rousing one. You're still alive, and I'm not getting toasty at the stake. Some of my fails have been pretty epic."

"I see."

I don't tell her about Doria. There was no need for her to know. But I can't take credit for my successes, like Operation Beastly or Emma's finding love, without also acknowledging my failures.

"How's it going with Travis?" I ask her. "Are you in love?"

Emma tries to act all casual, but I can see her smile.

"You are then?" I say.

"I think so. He invited me to Italy over the summer, to stay in his villa while they're filming his movie."

"Italy?" This sets the wheels in my head to turning. It's been a long while since I've been abroad, nigh upon a hundred years, and longer still since I've seen *Italia.* The people I knew there would be long dead, a good thing in this case.

"And when is that?" I ask.

"June. As soon as school's out. Mother's coming along as a chaperone."

"I see. And Lisette?"

Ah, how I remember Italy in summer. There had been a charming gondolier named Giacomo. He'd admired my blond hair (I was always a blonde when I went to Italy—I like to stand out) and sang me romantic songs. Of course, he was no more, but there would be others, I suspected. And I could make new friends. They say Italian witches always know where to buy the best shoes.

"No, Lisette's not going," Emma says. "I mean, we're getting along better now, sort of, but I just don't think it would be fun."

"Good call."

And, of course, Italian cooking is sublime.

"I thought so," Emma says. "I talked Mother into sending Lisette to theater camp in New York. She's really excited about it."

I'm excited too. Emma's mention of theater camp reminds me how I've always enjoyed the opera. Perhaps I might learn the role of Tosca or Medea and make my debut at La Scala one day, using poor Doria's voice. The world should hear it, and after all, I have nothing but time on my hands.

"I'm happy for you, Emma," I say. "Maybe I'll see you there."

"I was hoping you'd say that. Travis will be working a lot. It would be cool to have a friend there, to sightsee."

A friend. I grin. I've made a friend, a real one, first in a hundred years.

"I'll be there," I say.

Yes, I have nothing but time.

For the moment, that strikes me as a good thing.

Historical Notes

Kendra and Emma aren't real, but some of the stuff in this book is. Specifically:

The Great Plague of 1665 killed about 100,000 people in London and spread to other areas of England. Most notable of these was the village of Eyam in Derbyshire, England. The villagers quarantined themselves, and seventy-five percent of their population died. Many of the descendants of those who survived have been found to have a genetic mutation called Delta 32, which may have protected against the plague and other diseases, possibly including AIDS. You can learn more about Eyam at www.eyamplaguevillage.co.uk.

I have taken some (many) liberties with the story of Louis, Dauphin of France. Louis was a real person who lived from 1729 to 1765. He was the son of Louis XV and the father of Louis XVI, who was the king married to Marie Antoinette. Louis married Maria Teresa Rafaela of Spain. No peas or princess quest was actually involved. However, the two were said to have been very well matched and in love. Sadly, Maria Teresa died a little more than a year after their marriage. Louis, faced with providing an heir, remarried shortly thereafter to Maria Josepha of Saxony. However, when he died almost twenty years later, his heart was buried with Maria Teresa.

On April 15, 1912, the "unsinkable" ship, *Titanic*, sunk on her maiden voyage. One thousand five hundred seventeen people were lost while 706 survived. The ship did not have enough lifeboats, and those they had were released half full. Had the lifeboats been full, another four hundred people could have survived. Only two lifeboats picked up survivors from the water, and only one actually went back to do so. This was Lifeboat 14, led by Fifth Officer Harold Lowe. Among those who died were the Sage family, who were traveling to America, having purchased a pecan farm in Jacksonville, Florida. Mother, father, and nine children all died. It is said that one of the daughters, Stella, was on a lifeboat but got off because her family could not go. Learn more about the people of *Titanic* at www.encyclopedia-titanica.org.

To read some of the "real" stories upon which the stories in this book are based, visit www.surlalunefairytales.com.